STARS FALLEN SERIES

THE DESCENDANTS OF VELTERRA

BOOK THREE

NADINE ABRAHAMS

The Written Word Publishing
Australia
Contact: keltoidrui@hotmail.com
https://nadineabrahams.wixsite.com/author

ISBN: 978-0-9756532-6-5 (paperback)
       978-0-9756532-7-2 (ebook)

Cover design by Mibliart: https://miblart.com
Family tree created by Nadine Abrahams and Jenn Zabinskas

CHAPTER ONE

Ake ran a hand through her damp hair, a pleasant reminder of the aftermath of hours filled with passion. She glanced about the room, sunlight filtered in through the large window, reflecting off the floor-length mirror closest to the window. Reaching for the pitcher on the bedside table, she yelped as she was pulled under the blankets, then giggled as her husband ran his hands over her body.

'What changes has time wrought on your delightful figure since we've been apart?' Lan grinned. 'This scar is new.' He dipped his head to kiss the spot.

'It's bound to happen with all the adventures I've had.'

'What is it from?'

'Poisonous dragon.' She smirked at him and peeled back the covers.

'Did you try to heal the dragon? It's something you would do.' His mouth found hers, before trailing down to her abdomen. 'I love these delicious, curvy hips.' He squeezed them, before his hands cradled her derriere. 'This is wonderful too.'

His head rose to meet her heated face. She placed her hands in front of her abdomen. 'I have gained a little weight. And the stretch marks …'

He pushed her hands away. 'Those scars are a testament to the amazing children you gave me. You are still my beautiful wife.' He winked. 'But easier to hold on to.'

'Are you sure?' Ake ran her hands over his shoulders. 'You are broader across the shoulders and in the torso. You at least look great.'

Lan shrugged. 'I filled out. Unlike Relequis elves, I'm not meant to be slender. Upon nearing a hundred years of age we begin to fill out.' He covered her stomach in kisses before he tickled her. 'Yep, still perfect to me.'

She convulsed with laughter. 'Lan, we must get up.'

'I haven't had my fill.' He gave her a sultry smile.

Ake blushed. 'How many times has it been already?'

'I lost count after the fourth.' He dipped his head to her breasts, and she gave a contented sigh.

Ake's eyes closed; her toes curled as she remembered his kisses, demanding and soul-consuming in their intensity, his mouth claiming hers, his tongue invoking her passion as he savaged her mouth and she had come away breathless. His eyes had smouldered with an otherworldly intensity. Never a vocal lover, Lan had cried out her name like a prayer as he worshipped every inch of her body with his mouth and tongue. She opened her eyes and gave him a lazy smile.

He lifted his head and grinned at her. Her cheeks heated with desire as he pulled her against him.

'We can't be caught in bed.'

Lan's brow furrowed. 'Why not? We are married.'

'The world has changed in the centuries we have been separated.'

Ake, an immortal woman, had been separated from her husband for over a thousand years after the defeat of the dark goddess Drianna. She had whiled away the lonely centuries in the company of her elven son Amities, and her fairy daughter Caoimhe. Ake's merciful decision to allow the evil goddess's soul to be reincarnated had lessened the years of separation. The couple had been reunited after the death of the last elf, their son

Amities. There was a knock on the door. Ake pushed Lan off her and rose. Throwing open the wardrobe, she dressed herself in a simple robe. They had pushed the single beds together and Lan smiled with amusement as Ake tried to pull the beds apart. He yawned and stretched.

'Who is it?' he asked.

'Lawmakers.' They knocked again.

'Go away, I am making love to my wife.' He gave Ake a cheeky grin.

Ake felt suddenly faint and her lip trembled.

'Hell, did I just put us in danger?' Lan scrambled out of bed as the unlocked door was thrown open.

Two green-robed people entered the room. Lan covered himself with the blanket and strode towards the intruders, glaring. 'You can't just barge in here.'

The man and woman gave them a disgusted look as their eyes scanned the room. Ake threw Lan a bathrobe. As he put it on, the lawmakers averted their eyes.

The man took a step towards him. 'I have it on good authority that you two are not married. You may have engaged in acts of passion to fulfil your physical urges instead of using it for its purpose of procreation. You can come with us willingly or face harsher consequences.'

Lan went to push the man away from him when Ake gave him a pleading look and he sighed. 'I assure you we are married.'

The man took out some rope. 'Did you make your vows under Cirichad law?'

Lan glanced towards Ake; his brow furrowed with concern.

'I'll explain later,' she said hastily.

The female lawmaker walked over to Ake. 'Did you engage in acts of passion for the purpose of satisfying your attraction for one another?'

Ake blushed and looked away.

'No.' Lan step towards the other man. 'You see I wanted to, but she denied me. I was the one who was naked.'

'I highly doubt that,' said the male lawmaker.

'Why is it a sin, and what is the punishment for acting on it?' asked Lan.

'It is for procreation only. Cirichad encourages romantic love between brides and grooms, this includes companionship and acts of kindness. That is the essence of wedded bliss, not passionate sins of the flesh,' the other woman sighed.

'Are you citizens of Velterra?' The man glared at them.

Ake played with her robe nervously. 'Refugees of Velterra.'

The female lawmaker relaxed her shoulders and gave them a sympathetic smile.

'That explains it. I am sorry, we still have to take you in. A concerned citizen informed us of your sinful displays, and no one is entitled to break the law,' said the man.

Lan held out his wrists. Ake tried to speak, but her mouth felt suddenly dry as her husband gave her a gentle smile while his wrists were tied together.

'Can we not lodge this paperwork together?' Lan's eyes pleaded with the man as he was turned to face his captor.

'No.' The man tested the knots.

'We can lodge your paperwork, miss, and he will be returned to you.' The other woman stepped towards Ake.

Lan was escorted from the room.

Not again. Ake's heart raced and she struggled to catch her breath. *I am separated from him again.*

The other woman gave her a reassuring smile. 'I know it's distressing to see your companion arrested. I can't imagine the horrors you experienced in Velterra at the hands of wicked magic users and monsters. You are safe.'

Ake and Lan's world had changed much in the centuries they had been separated. After the fall of the Regian empire, war had broken out and countless lives were lost. The countries of Eriu and Breteyne had been absorbed. Two civilisations emerged: Velterra, a lawless country full of mercenaries, monsters and corrupt magic users; and Cirichad, a benevolent society with strict moral laws that followed a monotheistic religion. Ake was startled from her thoughts.

'Come with me, please.'

Ake nodded, grabbing their belongings as she followed the lawmaker out of the room.

—⁓—

The lawmaker unbound Lan's hands then held the gate open to the small cell. It was clean and furnished with a single bed. Morning sunlight filtered in through a small window. Lan entered the cell and lay down on the bed.

He winked at the lawmaker. 'Fine hospitality you have here.'

The lawmaker closed the gate and locked it, giving Lan a kind smile.

'I will bring you food and appropriate clothing.' The lawmaker turned and walked away.

Lan's confidence began to falter. He got up and began to pace. *What is wrong with this place? I hope Ake is okay.*

The man returned with some bread and apples and handed them to Lan through the bars. Lan took them and placed them on the bed.

'I am Erdan. What is your name?'

'I am Trebrelan, or Lan, for short.'

Erdan handed him some strange clothing. The outfit consisted of black shoes; blue neck-cloth made of cotton; grey tights; black knee-length britches; a long, black waistcoat with black tails and silver buttons; and a white, long-sleeved, frill-necked shirt. Erdan also showed him a collection of hats and wigs. Lan frowned, the hats included a black tricorn, a top hat, white wig with a long, tied ponytail and another in black, a grey bowler hat and a red cloth cap.

'This is different to what you are wearing. I also detest hats.'

'It is common clothing for male citizens. It is unacceptable to have your head uncovered for both men and women. Try to rest, it may be a while.' Erdan strode away.

Lan took a bite of the apple; savouring the crisp, sweet taste he'd long forgotten. He closed his eyes, savouring that first bite. He realised he was ravenous and finished his meal. When he had taken on the position of the God of Death, he had not had any physical urges or needs. Waves of fatigue washed over him and he yawned. *This will take some getting used to again. I wonder what powers and skills I have been left with.*

Lan had once been a mystic; a master of unarmed combat and minor magics. His elven ancestry had given him great agility. He touched his ears. When he had returned to the world of the living, his god Sorendee and his wife, the goddess Dee, had made his elven ears appear human. *I wonder how much my appearance has changed?*

He began to dress himself in the clothing, struggling with the tights as they displayed his toned legs. Hating anything close to his throat, he made a noise of contempt and fiddled with the ruffled neckline on his shirt until he sighed and concentrated on his choice of headwear instead. Stuffing the cloth cap into the pocket of his britches, which were worn over his tights, Lan slumped down onto the mattress, drifting into sleep as exhaustion overcame him.

CHAPTER TWO

Alwin removed the box from under the bed and blew off some of the dust. Sneezing, he placed the box on a nearby table. Tears welled in his eyes as the pain from the recent loss of his grandfather, Amities, settled in his chest, and he stifled a sob. *You are nearly twenty, you have to present yourself as a man of Cirichad and maintain a picture of stoicism.* Alwin glanced at the letter on the table, detailed instructions to deliver this box to Amities's father, Lan.

Alwin opened the box, took out the flintlock pistol and wiped it down with a cloth before placing it back in the box. Besides the pistol, Amities had also left behind a long sword, a hammer, an ornate staff and an emerald bow. Alwin was to inherit the bow, but the other items were destined for different owners. Amities's note had mentioned that the weapons would know their masters.

Alwin heard someone knock on the front door. There was a creak as the door was pulled open and his father began a heated discussion with someone. Alwin left his grandfather's room and entered the living room to see Arlys caught up in a discussion with a local lawmaker.

'A couple has entered an inn, and from the sounds, they may have been engaging in acts of depravity. The woman was said to have run from your household, Mr Smith. You will need to accompany me to the lawmaker's keep to make a statement.'

Arlys began to follow the lawmaker out the door; his eyes darted to Alwin. 'Don't leave the house. I will return soon.'

The door was pulled hastily shut and a fairy came out of hiding and pointed to a silver necklace on the ground. She fluttered her gossamer wings as Alwin handed her the piece of jewellery. The fairy donned the necklace and her wings became invisible.

Amities had spent weeks telling him the story of his great-grandparents Ake and Lan. Upon the story's completion, a woman had appeared in angel form in his father's house, accompanied by the fairy in front of him.

I can't believe a sudden heart attack took Grandfather from me. He always seemed in such good health. Then his own mother fled. Goodness knows where she is.

The fairy whistled at him and used some hand gestures to try and convey her thoughts, but Alwin didn't understand. He realised the creature hadn't eaten anything and felt a pang of guilt. Cirichad hospitality encouraged the giving of food and drink to the less fortunate. He knew the fairy had been drinking water from the pitcher on the table. He went to the fruit bowl and offered her some fruit. The creature didn't seem interested. He tried to tempt her with bread and cereal, but she shook her head. He sighed and saw her staring at a vase of flowers.

'Do you want to eat those flowers?'

The fairy nodded and he handed the roses to her and stared. His brows rose in surprise as she consumed the flower petals.

I know Father was never keen on Grandfather, but we should have at least discussed his funeral. Alwin's father, Arlys Smith, had never liked Amities, and didn't even show any emotion when his son had broken down crying. Arlys had wanted to notify the authorities, but Alwin had stopped him. *Grandfather covered his sins by wearing a magical necklace that disguised his elven heritage. All beings that wield magic are considered deviants and anyone associated with them can be punished. I don't want that.* Alwin sighed and retired to his grandfather's room.

They had laid out the body on a bed and covered it with a sheet. *I hope my great-grandmother returns soon so we can bury her beloved son.* He knelt before his grandfather's body, placed his thumbs together and formed a circle with his index fingers touching, and began to recite a prayer.

CHAPTER THREE

Tears brimmed in her eyes as Ake was ushered across the street. She glanced at a small chapel made of grey stone. A single white wooden circle hung over the wooden door. The woman beside her pushed open the door and gestured for Ake to enter.

They entered a small room with a wooden floor; white pews took up the majority of the space. A small stage had been built in front of the pews and another white circle hung above it from a steel chain attached to the roof. A man stood behind a lectern on the stage turning the pages of a book; he glanced up when they entered and gestured them forward. Ake took in his appearance, he wore white robes, a black stole and a wooden circle on a leather thong hung round his neck.

'This woman is a Velterran refugee. She has a companion we arrested as he was trying to get her to engage in sins of the flesh. Devotee, can you absolve her of her sins and see that they take Cirichad marriage vows?' asked the lawmaker.

The man nodded. 'I can do that. Feel free to leave her in my care.'

The lawmaker left and the pastor turned his kind eyes to Ake. 'I am Devotee Timothy. What is your name?'

'I am Telewanake, but everyone calls me Ake.'

'Do you wish to be a citizen of Cirichad?'

Ake nodded. 'If it means I can see my husband again.'

Timothy grabbed a small book off the lectern and handed it to Ake. 'Take a seat at one of the pews and read the contents of the book. You can keep it.'

Ake took a seat and began to read.

Cirichad is a kingdom ruled by our king, may the lord bless him. Where Velterra favours the vulgarity of excess and pleasures of the flesh, Cirichad is a pure country reflecting the morals of our lord.

We oppose the deviancy of any kind including magic, which is punishable by lengthy jail terms. Our society is built on kindness and compassion, and we believe everyone is entitled to food and shelter.

The foundations of our faith recognise the importance of family. Husbands and wives are at the heart of this family, showering each other with acts of kindness and innocent companionship. They shun physical affection except when needing to add to their family unit. Couples remain abstinent until they are willing to have children …

Ake closed the book. Timothy smiled and gestured her forward. He handed her a piece of paper and a pen. She looked it over and filled out her name and Lan's on the marriage certificate. He handed her another form. She filled out the citizenship papers, altering their birthdates to fit the current timeline.

'I see your companion is Trebrelan and he is forty. You are Telewanake and you are thirty-five. Is that correct?' asked Timothy.

Ake nodded.

'Do you have any children?'

'Yes, a five-year-old daughter.'

Caoimhe won't be pleased. Ake and Lan's daughter was over

a thousand years old and immortal like her parents. Being only three foot tall, from a distance she could easily be mistaken for a child. Ake knew she would have to lie about her age to keep her safe.

'Do you agree to follow Cirichad beliefs, and that this man you recognise as your husband will help you uphold these beliefs?' asked Timothy.

Ake gave him a nervous smile. 'Of course.'

'Well, in that case, welcome to Cirichad. Take these forms and the lawmakers will release your husband. The building is ten minutes east of here. It is a large red keep. Good luck.'

Ake took the papers and dashed towards the door. *I hope he is okay.*

The key turned in the lock and the cell to the door screeched open. Lan opened his eyes and ran a hand through his hair.

Erdan left the door open and walked away. Lan swung himself up into a sitting position and looked around as he heard soft footfalls headed towards the cell. Ake rounded a corner and smiled at him. She was outfitted in a new gown. It suited her fair skin. She had styled her now long, dark blonde hair into a crown braid and pinned a lace veil over the top and back of her head. *Her hair has darkened in the time I have been gone.* She wore a long-sleeved gown; the front part of the dress was white and the sides and sleeves were emerald with green laces to adjust it to fit her bust. She appeared anxious, her grey blue eyes darting towards him and back the way she had come.

Lan strode over to her and gave her a reassuring smile.

'You look great.'

Ake's eyes travelled down the length of his body. 'That outfit accentuates your toned build. White doesn't suit you; it clashes with your fair skin. You look even paler.' Ake fumbled in the pockets of her dress and pushed some paperwork into his hands.

Lan gave it a cursory glance and handed it back. 'So, we are legally married in this country too.' Lan squeezed her hand briefly and she gave him an intoxicating smile he couldn't resist; he leant down to kiss her. His lips brushed hers gently.

She pushed him away. 'Not here. We should head back to check on Caoimhe and Alwin.'

'Who is Alwin?'

'You will find out soon enough.'

Lan smiled at her. 'It will be good to see my child again. Where did you get the dress?'

'Local shop. It was the last of my Cirichad coins. I should have brought more gems and exchanged them. I am sorry, we are broke.'

'I am sure I can find work. We will be okay.' Lan placed his hand on her cheek and she held it to her face.

There was a commotion behind them and they broke apart, turning to face the noise. Arlys rushed towards them, followed by Erdan.

'Wait, Mr Smith, please calm yourself. You know a lack of self-control is frowned upon,' said Erdan.

'That woman is my sister and that man is a Velterran. I don't want him in my house.' Arlys glared at Lan.

Lan stared back; his eyes wide. *Why would he tell an obvious lie?*

'Mr Lan, is that true?' asked Erdan.

Ake gave Arlys a fake smile. 'Arlys, you know I brought my husband home hoping to seek refuge in Cirichad. Family is so important here. We have nowhere else to go. You wouldn't deny your sister and her refugee husband hospitality, would you?'

Arlys frowned and mumbled a reply. 'Of course not, sister.'

'Mr Smith, why was your sister's birth never registered in Cirichad?' asked Erdan.

'My father adopted her from Velterra. He kept her a secret from the lawmakers,' lied Arlys.

'What a deceitful thing to do. He is no longer alive, but you will have to pay reparations for the deceit,' said Erdan.

'Go back to the house, sister, and take that husband of yours with you. We will talk later,' said Arlys.

They hurried down the corridor, grateful to get away from Arlys and the lawmaker. Lan slipped the cap onto his head as they exited the keep and they began the walk back to the Smith household.

'I have to ask you something.' Ake glanced at her husband.

Lan smiled. 'Sure.'

'There was a particular oak tree at Caelestis where we …' Ake blushed. 'Who burned our initials into that tree on our anniversary decades after you crossed over?'

Lan frowned and his eyes narrowed. 'The gods are cruel, Ake. I was at my lowest that day and begged to see you. They allowed me one small romantic gesture, barely noticeable. I stood in front of that tree, reliving our last passionate encounter and had all but a moment to leave a message for you. With the mystic fire that was slowly leaving me, I burned our initials into that trunk, and before the flames cooled, I was sent back without even a glimpse of you.'

'Thank you.'

Lan nodded. 'I hope it gave you some comfort.' He reached out and caressed the back of her hand as they reached the front of the Smith household.

'That day I was so happy.'

'I am glad.'

CHAPTER FOUR

Alwin stared, wide-eyed, at the couple seated opposite him. He had been told of their wondrous powers and great exploits. The fairy whistled, and he blinked in surprise as, with a few hand gestures, Ake and the fairy appeared to hold a conversation.

'Alwin, this is Caoimhe. She thanks you for the meal of flowers.' Ake smiled. 'Caoimhe can't use spoken language as we do. Greater fairies talk in whistles and gestures.'

'Why did your father lie about Ake being his sister?' asked Lan.

Alwin paled. 'You two sinned at that inn, apparently.'

Ake blushed.

'Father made the right decision. The whole household could have lost its reputation and been heavily fined. A Velterran refugee acting that way is less unexpected. It also explains your sudden appearance.' Alwin frowned. *This is so strange. My grandfather looked elderly when he died and here I am, faced with his immortal parents who look no older than late thirties to early forties.* Alwin sighed and began to read aloud from the letter Amities had left him.

'My dear Alwin, if you are reading this I have passed away. I will always be nearby as I have taken up my father's position as the God of Death. I know it must be strange to meet my youthful parents. They are good people and will take wonderful care of you. My mother has the painful trait of empathy,

something you and I inherited from her. She is fun-loving, kind and affectionate, something Arlys failed to show you. My father is very proud, protective, honest and intelligent. He will teach you how to be a good man.'

Alwin wiped a tear from his eye and looked at Lan as he continued.

'To my father, I am so sorry you missed out on centuries with Mother and I. Be prepared to have to support her more as she has become anxious and shy. She is prepared to lose those she loves and will likely flee after I pass away.

I have done my research into the God of Death. You will be born anew, experiencing everything again for the first time. Your powers will be dormant as they will need time to awaken, and some may never resurface. The world has changed greatly, and I suggest you embrace it and don't let your pride get in the way. I leave you a flintlock pistol. Your elven legacy will allow you to wield it with masterful precision.

The pellets I have provided are highly explosive. Use them only as necessary. You will have to learn how to clean and care for the weapon. You can also purchase and use normal rounds. Good luck, Father.'

Alwin pushed the box on the table towards Lan.

Lan smiled sadly at Alwin. 'Thank you.' He took the box and pulled out the pistol. He became absorbed in his task, fascinated with the weapon.

Alwin continued.

'There are other descendants. The other weapons I have left behind will know their masters. To my beloved Alwin, I give

you my emerald bow. I hope it protects you like it did me. It does not need arrows and uses earth magic to produce unlimited arrows. Be careful, as I know Cirichad has a great distrust of magic.'

The sword of my beloved twin Mandami must go to our friend whom I wrote to in advance to attend my wake. The staff must go to Beryl's grandchild. The hammer will seek its master, a Velterran descendant. I am not sure how much truth there is in their ancestry. I know they exist, but I could not find out their name or other details. All I know is, they will find you.'

Alwin turned and looked at Ake and continued reading.

'Dear Mother, Father is back, embrace each other and try to find happiness. You were once a beacon of happiness, which was contagious. Please try to find joy again. Good luck to you all. Please don't grieve for me, I had a wonderful and joyous life. I may not be on this plane anymore, but I will always be with you and love you both dearly.'

Ake put her head in her hands and began to sob. Lan put down his weapon and pulled her into his arms. 'It's okay, let it out.'

Alwin stared at Lan. *Is he not sad at all? His son is dead.*

Lan looked up and smiled sadly at Alwin, almost as if he had read his mind. 'Death is not the end, Alwin. I will miss my son. I missed out on so many years of his life. I made a pact to save my daughter and wife's lives, sealing my fate to become the God of Death. I will always regret the lost years with Ake and my children. Amities is now with his beloved wife and daughter in a place that is beautiful. I cannot feel devastated about that. But grieve as you must, for you and Ake have been with him when I could not.'

Alwin's eyes brimmed with tears, and he looked away and tried to compose himself. He took a shuddering breath and turned back to Ake and Lan. 'We need to discuss what to do with his remains.'

Lan sighed. 'Traditionally, we would build a pyre and cremate the body, offering the body up to our gods, Dee and Sorendee.'

'Those gods are forbidden in Cirichad,' said Alwin.

'Why?' asked Lan.

'We believe in one god. His prophet showed us the way to live until his death. The ways of Dee and Sorendee are hedonistic and therefore frowned upon,' said Alwin.

Lan smirked. 'I don't see how Dee, the mother of earth and nature, who promotes beauty and healing, is hedonistic. How can Sorendee, the God of Life, Protection and Honour, be frowned upon?'

'They promote frivolity and magic. Nature is unpredictable and cruel, and we try to counter that with strict moral codes and benevolent hospitality. Magic is powerful and destructive. Velterrans worship magic and are hedonistic in their lifestyles. Their gods are similar to Dee and Sorendee. This is why your gods are frowned upon,' said Alwin.

Ake looked at Alwin and gave him a kind smile. 'What would Amities have wanted?'

'We can cremate the body using the crematorium. I believe that is an acceptable compromise. A mass must be said in the name of our god. I believe you should help plan a wake though,' said Alwin.

'What is a wake?' asked Ake.

'A vigil we observe before we cremate the body. We make sure the tainted one does not come for his soul. We sometimes observe the body overnight and discuss their good deeds and toast them. Friends and family have one last great meal with the deceased before the cremation,' said Alwin.

Where have I heard that before? Ake reached into her pocket and retrieved the small book Timothy had handed her. She began turning the pages until she came upon the mention of the tainted one. Alwin and Lan began to discuss plans for the wake as she read.

The tainted one was the second to last emperor of the Regian empire. He forced his soldiers to be involved in great acts of genocide against the elven people. On the outside, he was a great warlord, but in the company of those who knew him he was a master of slaves and took women against their will.

He was defeated at the hands of an elven lord whose bride had been kidnapped. Their son became a prophet of our lord. He was just and kind, but died on the circle of thorns at the hands of his adopted daughter.

On the dawn of the new day, the last citizens of Regis went to bury the body; only to find it had disappeared. The prophet Mandami had risen at our lord's behest, his sword at the ready to smite the tainted one.

It is a sin to mention the tainted one's name, except in a prayer to ward against him.

'Our lord may you protect us. Be gone, Cephas, you will not lay your taint on me. You are banished from this house-hold.'

Prayer 21.

Ake whimpered and threw the book. 'No, how could they immortalise him?'

Alwin pushed himself up and retrieved the book and handed it to her. 'Destruction of the holy book displeases our lord.'

Ake turned to Lan; her voice shook with anger. 'Cephas is their tainted one, immortalised in their book. Our Mandami is their prophet. My son, brave and loyal, died on a circle of thorns, in great pain. Amities lied to me; he said the citizens of Regis had buried him. I wept at someone else's grave.'

Lan gave Ake a nervous smile and then his gaze fixed on the floor.

'Tell me.' Ake's eyes narrowed on her husband.

Lan sighed and gave her a sheepish grin, but he refused to meet her eyes with his own. 'When Orilan came to take him to the underworld, he noticed the body being pilfered and mutilated. I made a choice. I retrieved the body, and Orilan and I gave Mandami a service Dee and Sorendee would have rejoiced at.'

Ake's voice rose. 'Why was I never told?'

Lan squeezed her hand. 'How could I contact you? And if I could have, what would I say? Hey honey, our beautiful son was murdered by his newly adopted child and heir. She betrayed him and Regis fell. You have already lost me and all our friends and family. Here, let me add more grief.' His eyes, full of remorse, sought hers.

Ake glared at him and pushed his hands away. 'I should have been told.'

The front door slammed as Arlys entered the house. He strode into the kitchen to see Ake and Lan arguing.

'I did the right thing. I am not ashamed. I am your husband and will always try to spare you from further heartache. You were told he had passed and were able to grieve him. Is that not enough?' Lan wrang his hands in frustration.

Arlys's booming voice made them jump. 'Silence, you two. This is my house and I won't allow any unpleasantness in my home.'

'I am sorry, I have forgotten my manners.' Ake stared at the floor. *If I answer back, someone else may walk out of my life.*

Lan glared at Arlys. 'You will not talk to my wife like that. I think we will find our own household.'

'*Father, I have missed you. Now this conversation is done with I can embrace you,*' Caoimhe signed.

Lan stood as the fairy flew into his arms and covered his cheeks in kisses. 'Caoimhe, I missed you too.' He enveloped her in a hug.

Alwin averted his gaze away from the public display of affection.

Arlys cleared his throat and glared at Lan. 'Velterran, you will need to work off your debt. Six hundred credits I am owed for your passionate romp with that woman.' Arlys pointed at Ake, who blushed and dodged his stern look, her eyes fixated on the vase.

Caoimhe glared at Arlys, and flew over and whistled in annoyance at him.

Alwin smiled. 'So very odd, with her wings hidden she looks like a flying girl and not a fairy.'

Caoimhe began to sign and Lan translated. 'Do not embarrass my mother like that. My mother is a good woman and doesn't do bad things.'

Lan smirked at Arlys. 'Let's mourn Amities properly, and we will get out of your hair. I would never allow my family to live in your household.'

Ake gave Lan a sad smile. 'I am not staying with you. You will likely disappear again. I am over you making decisions for me and keeping stuff from me. I have made my own choices for so long and grieved you. We can't just fall back into it. I need time.'

Caoimhe looked at her mother in shock. '*No, Mother. It's Father, you love him. You told me if he ever returned we could be a family.*'

Lan's eyes bore into Ake's, full of a possessive look she had never encountered before. 'Where has this come from? A few hours ago you were languid in my arms and now you want me to leave. That isn't happening, I assure you.'

'After all these centuries, you still haven't learnt not to make decisions for me. How dare you keep secrets from me. I felt the passing of time, did you?' Ake placed her hands on her hips.

'I am sorry time passed quicker for me. It only felt like a decade for me. I understand time has made you bitter and I am sorry for that. Talk about keeping secrets. You never told me about being pregnant with Caoimhe, and often put yourself in danger. How did you expect a loving husband to react?' Lan smirked.

Arlys walked over to Lan and dragged him away by his ear. 'Keep it down, you immature little man. I'll put you to work so you can't yell in my house and draw attention to it again. I run a smith and have a reputation to keep.'

'Enough.' Alwin's eyes brimmed with angry tears. 'My gentle grandfather would be ashamed of you all.'

Ake hung her head in shame. 'I am sorry, Alwin. This is all too much for me. I am going for a walk.'

Alwin nodded. 'Be back here at dusk, we will hold the wake. A friend of ours will attend too. He knew Amities well.'

'Honey, wait. I am sorry.' Lan grabbed Arlys's arm, and with a flick of his wrist, the large muscular man landed on his rear.

Alwin stared at Lan, his mouth open in astonishment. Ake smirked and opened the front door as Caoimhe giggled. Her laughter was infectious and Alwin couldn't help but laugh.

Arlys rose to his feet, glaring as Ake left, Lan hurrying after her.

'I hate Velterrans,' cried Arlys.

CHAPTER FIVE

Lan's feet pounded on the pavement as he hurried after a fast paced Ake. She wiped her eyes with her hand, brushing hot tears away, refusing to catch his sidelong glance as he sprinted until he caught up with her. *I could have heard her heartbeat from a great distance before. I guess my elven hearing is no more.* Several people frowned at Ake as she wept, she glanced back at Lan and turned down an alleyway before stopping suddenly to glare at him.

'Why are you following me?'

'I am not going anywhere, Ake. You are stuck with me.' He gave her a reassuring smile.

'I got you back and then you were taken again.' She shuddered.

'So, that's what it is then. You want me around, but you are fleeing from me in case I disappear again?'

Ake nodded. 'The centuries without you were unbearable.' Tears streaked down her face.

'There will be times when we are apart for a few moments, that's inevitable. But I promise you, this time round I will find you wherever you are. I will also answer any questions you have about those who have passed.' Lan grabbed her hand and pulled her into his arms. He brushed her lips lightly with his own before remembering Cirichad rules about public affection and released her.

Ake smiled through her tears. 'Okay.'

'You should know something now we are alone. Het has returned to this plain of existence. He said he needed to correct a wrong. I cannot pinpoint the exact time he left as time passed differently for me.'

Ake's face drained of colour.

Het had been Ake's childhood friend and a loyal master of arms and apprentice of Lan's druid father, Dane. Dying young to defend Lan's school, Het had loved Ake, though she had not reciprocated his feelings.

'I wonder why he would leave Flo and come back here,' said Ake.

After Ake had chosen Lan, Het had fallen in love with an elven empress, Elder Flower, affectionately called Flo, who had died when the royal ship *Syl* had sunk. They had been reunited in the beautiful underworld Lan had created from his memories of Ake.

'Why would he choose to come here when he could be with Flo and all our friends and family?' Ake leant her hand against the wall for support. 'It must be an awful thing if he left Flo's embrace.'

Lan frowned. 'I don't think we will recognise him either. While elves can't reincarnate, humans and half-elves can, and when they do, they take on new human bodies.'

'That's a problem then.'

'He wouldn't tell me anything, Ake. You are the Goddess of Life and Mercy. Did you not recognise his soul when he was reborn?' asked Lan.

'No, Lan, I choose not to pry. If I looked at their past, I may be shocked and deny them entry into the world, worried they would retain their wicked ways. I must remain neutral.'

'Are you okay now, or do you still need some space from me?' Lan gave her a kind smile.

'No, I should not have said that.' Ake leant into him and stroked his cheek.

'Cut that out.' Someone blew a whistle.

Lan grabbed Ake's hand and sprinted further into the alley-way. A lawmaker chased after them, his feet pounding on the pavement. They turned the corner sharply and went down the side of a building, watching the lawmaker run past them. Ake and Lan tried to quieten their heavy breathing and stifle their giggles. The lawmaker walked back past their hiding spot and glared at them before he left, muttering to himself about their abhorrent behaviour.

Ake pulled Lan closer to her by grabbing his hips. Lan grinned down at her. He dipped his head and kissed her gently. She sighed against him.

'I missed you so much,' he whispered in her ear.

'I was lost without you.' She choked back a sob. The sky suddenly darkened and Ake shivered as a cool breeze whipped about them. Her gaze met Lan's; his eyes were dark pools of emotion, reflecting the tumultuous sky.

Lan rubbed her shoulders, trying to warm her up. 'It's getting late. We should head back. Are you okay?'

'No, this is our son, Lan.' Ake's eyes brimmed with tears.

'Let's do this together. Remember, our son is okay. You saw him after he passed.' Lan gave her a kind smile.

Ake reluctantly nodded. 'True. Let's go.'

They stood apart and walked slowly back to the Smith household, ready to handle the grief together.

CHAPTER SIX

Ake stood subdued, her head bowed, upper lip quivering as Lan knocked on the door. Alwin answered and held open the door as Arlys rushed through holding the body of Amities. The corpse was bundled into what appeared to be a makeshift shroud of two sheets roughly sewn together. As Alwin exited the house and began to close the door behind him, Caoimhe raced through, whistling excitedly and gesturing to her father.

'She's eager to express her grief.' Lan's eyes settled on the deceased's form. 'Me too.'

'We will meet Amities's dear friend at the crematorium,' said Alwin.

Arlys strode away. Caoimhe grabbed her parents' hands and the three followed Alwin. The group was silent as citizens stopped and bowed their heads respectfully.

The sky was jet black, even the stars did not twinkle to guide them on their away. *It is as if they are aware of our grief and hide themselves in mourning.* Ake pulled back, not at all eager to burn her son's body. Arlys kept a fast pace and was well ahead of them.

They reached the crematorium. It was an intimidating structure; a large, black building with few windows and multiple chimneys. Grey smoke billowed up into the air, and Ake shuddered as she brushed ash off her dress. 'I wonder if we are being baptised in remnants of the dead.'

'That is a sad and undesirable thought.' Lan released her hand and hastily brushed the ash from his clothes.

The huge iron doors were open and Arlys entered the building without slowing. The rest followed. Ake's eyes darted around the open-plan room. Six gurneys stood in front of round metal doors. Large metal vats filled with coal had been placed nearby. Potted plants with white flowers were placed cleverly to lessen the harshness of the space, and many globes lit the room.

Ake's eyes fixated on the buttons on the wall. 'How are these globes lit when magic is despised here?'

'I'm curious too,' said Lan.

Sixteen wooden benches stood in the centre of the room, along with a lectern that held a thick book. Devotee Timothy was positioned in front, thumbing through the pages of the book, dressed in purple robes with a gold stole and collar. He looked up and smiled sadly before he returned to his reading.

A woman came out of a door and approached Arlys. 'Please follow me.' Arlys and the others followed her to a gurney. 'Please place the deceased there.'

Arlys placed the body gently on the gurney and straightened it. The woman placed a purple blanket over Amities and ushered them all over. 'Please bow your heads with respect. In a moment, I will ask you to step forward and say your goodbyes before we head over to Pastor Timothy and take service in the deceased's honour.'

They all bowed their heads for a few moments before the woman spoke again. 'Mr Smith, would you go first. I will go prepare the foods for the wake.'

Arlys nodded and the woman went back through the door she had exited.

Arlys cleared his throat. 'If it wasn't for your Anwyn I wouldn't have Alwin. I owe you for that.'

Ake felt the hairs on the back of her neck prickle and looked around. There was a shimmer and Orilan and Amities appeared next to Arlys.

'*What a pathetic goodbye,*' said Orilan's voice in Ake's mind.

Lan blinked and turned towards the apparitions. 'I hear them too Ake.'

'*It's about what you would expect from Arlys,*' replied Amities.

Alwin blinked in shock and stared at the body on the gurney. Next to Amities stood a terrifying skeleton armed with a serrated and curved scimitar. The boy shivered. 'Have I gone mad with grief?'

Amities smiled and turned to Alwin. '*I am well, Alwin, don't grieve. This is my brother Orilan.*'

Orilan removed his mask and grinned at Alwin, showing sharpened canines. His hair was a mass of red curls and he had bright blue eyes and fair skin. '*Fairly normal under this suit, kid. Got to keep up appearances.*'

There was a rustle behind Alwin and he turned. An apparition of a young woman with golden eyes and hair gave him a loving look.

'Mother,' whispered Alwin.

The spectre nodded.

Lan turned his head to watch. He looked back at Ake with a pained expression.

'*What is it?*' Ake signed.

He signed back. '*I'll tell you after.*'

'Do you have something to say, Mother?' whispered Alwin.

The spectre approached her son and embraced him before disappearing. Alwin cried out and tears ran down his face. Arlys cleared his throat and Alwin composed himself.

Lan glared at Arlys and mumbled. 'Poor kid, not even allowed to cry.'

Orilan shook his head and winked at Alwin. He snuck up behind Arlys and booted him in the rear.

Arlys stumbled and growled. 'What in our lord's name was that?'

Ake smirked, trying desperately to retain her composure.

Alwin smiled and stepped forward. He looked at Amities. 'I will miss you, Grandfather. The wonderful stories you shared and the kindness you offered me when Mother left us.'

Arlys looked puzzled and stared at Alwin, wondering why he was talking to an empty space. 'Boy, the body is over here.'

Amities looked at Alwin. '*I will always be with you.*'

Ake stepped forward and gave her son a sad smile. She walked over to his body, her head bowed. She undid the clasp of the leather cord necklace from around her neck and pulled back the blanket. Ake placed the object where she believed Amities's neck would be. The rare starstone on the cord twinkled in the light. It had a gold base and tiny slivers of silver crystal weaving their way to the heart of the stone. Lan smiled, he had given her that and it was a fitting tribute to their son.

'Bless you, Amities. Goodbye, my beloved son,' Ake whispered.

Lan turned as he heard someone enter through the doors behind them. A large man, appearing to be in his forties, strode towards him. The man was heavily muscled and very tall; he even towered over Arlys. The man beamed at Lan, and his hazel eyes flashed with mirth and familiarity. The man had tied his long, curly brown hair back. He was dressed similarly to Lan, but the tights stretched at the seams, barely containing his large muscles, and his britches were blue as was his waistcoat. The man patted Lan sharply on the back, and Lan had to adjust his stance not to stumble as the man grinned at him.

Ake had her eyes closed and tears rolled down her face.

'You are late, Tylluan,' said Arlys.

Lan's eyes widened, and he smiled at Tylluan as he translated the ancient Eriu name for owl. Ake opened her eyes and turned at the commotion. She stared at Tylluan for a moment before composing herself and wandering over to the new arrival.

'Het?' she whispered.

The man nodded.

'Well, Tylluan? You are here to say goodbye to your friend.' Arlys glared at them, disgusted with their lack of respect for the solemn rituals of Cirichad.

Het walked calmly over to Amities's body, bowed his head and attempted a serious face. 'Goodbye, my dear friend. Thank you for finding me nearly two years ago and filling me in on yours and Ake's adventures. Thank you for reminding me of who I am. You were the greatest storyteller and kindest person I know. I will miss you, my old friend. Tell Flo that I am okay, and I will find him and bring him home.'

Het turned and walked over to the benches and sat down. Arlys strode over and the others followed and took their seats.

'Please take out the book of Cirichad and lift your voices in solemn prayer to honour the dead. Page thirty-three, please,' said Timothy.

Arlys, Ake and Alwin took the books from their pockets and turned to the required reading. Lan leant over and read Ake's as everyone sang the hymn. Lan had always had a beautiful melodic voice. Arlys glared at him. Lan shrugged and his voice rose higher in a fitting tribute to his beloved son, and tears glistened in his eyes.

Our grief is strong now you are gone.
From our lives you were torn.
We shall not dwell in sadness long,
You have returned to where we all belong.

Free to roam,
In our lord's home.
Joy is your reward for a moral life lived.
Free of disease and pain.
Be at peace, we will be united again.

Timothy raised his hand for silence and read several passages from the book. He told them to go in peace, then turned and left. The party turned as the woman from earlier came back and gestured them over. She pulled open the large circular door as they wandered over.

'Alwin and his relative, Lan, have decided to hold the wake after the homecoming ritual. May the strongest of you give the deceased to our lord to be cleansed in fire.'

Arlys went to step forward when Het placed his large hand on Arlys's shoulder.

'Not you.' Het picked up the body gently and placed him in the crematorium vault.

'Each of you should place a scuttle of coal in the vault to send your loved one home,' said the woman.

Everyone stepped forward one by one, and added some coal. The woman closed the large door and pressed a large button. There was a loud click. The smell of gas assaulted their nostrils with a large woosh as the body was set alight. The flames rose higher through the small glass panel set in the door as Ake turned her head. Lan pulled her into his arms, closed his eyes and sighed.

'Goodbye, my sweet son,' whispered Lan.

Ake reached up and traced the tears that seeped from his closed eyes. 'You are grieving too.'

Lan smiled sadly and nestled his head into her shoulder.

Alwin wept silently as Het placed his hand on the lad's shoulder. 'It's okay to grieve, lad.'

Lan opened his eyes and glanced around. 'The spirits of Orilan and Amities have disappeared.'

Ake nodded. 'I noticed that too.'

'If you will all please follow me,' said the woman.

They followed the woman through a different door and entered a sparsely furnished room.

The walls were whitewashed and hung with pictures of yellow flowers. A table took up the centre of the room. A few decanters of a burgundy liquid bubbled away. There were dishes of cream and jam, and plates of scones. Crystal goblets were placed in the middle of the table.

'Feel free to stay as long as necessary.' The woman turned and left.

Alwin poured the sparkling grape juice into the glasses and handed them out. 'To Amities,' he toasted.

Everyone raised their glasses. Tylluan drained his glass, turned and beamed at Ake. He opened his arms wide, and she ran into them, laughing through happy tears. He released her and playfully punched her on the arm.

'Is it really you, Het?' asked Ake.

'Yes, Ake.' Het placed his hand on her shoulder.

'Not a word in two years.' Ake frowned.

'Amities tried to send you multiple messages. You had wandered off the major roads, like you no longer wanted to be found,' said Het.

'I didn't. I had lost the zest for life,' said Ake.

'Amities and I gathered that. If it wasn't for Caoimhe visiting us a week ago we would never have found you,' said Het.

Lan's gaze swept over his friend's face. 'You look similar to your old self, just older.'

'The gods were kind to me in that aspect. You haven't changed much, Lan. You cut off your long hair and changed your ears, and maybe gained ten years, but that is about it.' Het patted Lan on the back. 'So, you finally worked out that you were her intended. Is he a good husband, Ake? Does he make you happy?'

Ake laughed. 'Yes. He is a little vain, proud and broods sometimes. But he is brave, protective, kind and incredibly affectionate. He suits me.'

Lan blushed. 'Ake, is that appropriate to say to someone who kissed you.'

Het jumped as Amities appeared in front of them.

'So, this is a wake. A little subdued, isn't it?' asked Amities. The new necklace of starstone shone around his neck.

Het gave Lan a mischievous smile. 'There's the shy mystic I used to know. Is he a good kisser?'

Ake laughed, joining in the antics. 'A natural, among other things.'

'Elves are great lovers, aren't they? Must run in the family.' Het ruffled Lan's hair.

Lan turned his burning face away. Flo had been Lan's niece, and had been openly affectionate. It was something Lan had slowly learnt to embrace. He was a very passionate individual when it came to Ake, but was often reserved when it came to those he respected. His affection towards Ake in public was sweet and respectful. When they were alone it was a different story.

'Poor Lan, he is jealous that he and I never shared a moment.' Het took a step towards Lan.

'Wha—' Lan's eyes widened in shock as Het grabbed his face and planted a brief peck on his cheek.

Amities smiled and Ake broke out into giggles before clamping her mouth shut.

Lan cleared his throat. 'Well, you always did have a thing for elves.'

Het ran his hands through his hair and gave Lan a sheepish grin. 'I believe you are on to something.'

'*That was hilarious. Farewell, my dear ones. Someone has passed and I must go. Remember, you made my life complete.*' Amities shimmered away.

Lan, Ake and Het waved.

'Show some respect, Tylluan,' growled Arlys.

Het glared at Arlys. 'My name is Het. You know I prefer that. Tylluan was the name I gave myself until I remembered who I was.'

'You were born Tylluan. I don't believe all that rubbish of you being resurrected. It's heresy,' said Arlys.

Alwin sighed and made himself some scones with jam and cream. Caoimhe sat on the table scooping piles of cream and jam into a bowl. The fairy shovelled the treat into her mouth and smiled at Alwin.

He smiled back. 'I thought you only ate flowers.' Caoimhe began signing rapidly and Alwin shrugged. 'Sorry, I don't understand. I will have to learn.'

'Caoimhe, come over here,' said Ake.

She leapt off the table and hurried over to her mother. Ake removed her necklace and the fairy's translucent wings became visible.

Het looked from Ake to Lan. 'Who does she belong to?'

Lan had recovered from his embarrassment and stared at Het proudly. 'She belongs to herself. Caoimhe is our daughter.'

Het whistled threw his teeth. 'A fairy. Where's your empire and vast wealth, Ake?'

'I never sought it. So, Caoimhe never provided it,' said Ake.

Het tilted his head and stared at Lan. 'Everyone knows greater fairies are born from the union of divine entities trying to subdue the other in acts of great passion. When did you become a god?'

'You didn't see him in the underworld?' asked Ake.

Het shook his head. 'We saw a shadow being on a throne.

When I arrived, the place was like a cold void where time passed slowly and we became morose and our hope faded as if being sucked of all joy.' Het shivered. 'That was when Drianna was in charge.'

Ake's face drained of colour. 'You went to Drianna? What kind of afterlife is that?'

Het smiled. 'It's changed now.' Het pointed to Lan. 'Did he become the God of Death?'

Lan shivered. 'Yes,' he whispered.

'That explains how it became less morose. Light instead of perpetual twilight; flowers, sea-scented breezes and grass under my feet. And then I saw her, could hold her.' Het stared off into space. 'You are a good man, Lan. Only a pure soul could produce that kind of afterworld.'

The room was soon shrouded in a tense silence.

Alwin spoke, breaking the tension. 'Greater fairies were said to bless people with joy, power and wealth. It was rumoured the founder of the great Regian empire, Lord Regis had kept the company of a fairy.'

Caoimhe replaced her necklace and her wings became invisible again.

Het laughed. 'That explains the afterworld's change from a dreary, lonely place filled with grim spectres to one where loved ones could embrace, filled with vibrant flowers, noble creatures and so many bloody unicorns and cakes. I won't be too bothered if I never see another one.'

'Another what?' asked Alwin.

'Possibly a horned equine.' Grinning, Het leant over and squeezed Ake's shoulder. 'See, I'm fine.'

Ake turned to smile beguilingly at her husband, whose cheeks reddened as she continued to stare. 'I know who you were thinking of.'

'Forgive a man for missing his wife. What do you do now, Het?' asked Lan, trying to divert the conversation.

'I am a soldier. Kind of like a warrior, but we use more modern weapons. I miss the feel of a sword in my hand though,' said Het, swinging his arms like he was handling a blade.

Alwin wandered over. 'Tylluan, Grandfather left you something. Come by the house tomorrow and I will give it to you.' Alwin faced Ake and Lan. 'You can stay at ours tonight. I think it's best you find somewhere else in the morning. I will arrange something for you. Your passionate displays are unsettling, and my father's trade relies on a good reputation. Don't worry, I believe you are who my grandfather said you are, and will eventually hold a place of fondness in my heart as we learn from each other. I am tired and will make my way home.' Alwin turned and left as the funeral attendant entered the room.

'Are we finished here?' asked the woman.

Arlys strode over. 'Yes. Send the bill to that one.' He pointed at Lan.

'Wow, can't even foot the bill for his poor wife's father. It was disgusting how he treated her in the end,' Het mumbled.

Ake looked at Het, worry etched on her brow. 'I saw Anwyn grow up. When she fell for Arlys I didn't understand it. I never approved of their union; I found him cold and distant. I only visited a few times after Alwin's birth as Arlys always made me feel unwelcome. What happened?'

'He once caught Amities without that necklace in the smithy forging some magical bullets. Arlys despises magic users of any kind and labels them Velterrans. This meant Amities's daughter was now of Velterran stock and soiled. Arlys had once been fond of Anwyn and proceeded to push her away,' said Het.

Lan looked at Ake sadly. 'He pushed her to her limits, often saying harsh things to her. She took her own life and I bore witness to it. I could not dissuade her. As she lay dying, she told me of the horrible things he had said to her.'

Arlys left and the rest followed behind. Ake couldn't stop glaring at him behind his back. They soon reached the Smith household.

'I'll see you lot in the morning; it is late.' Het placed his hand on Ake's shoulder.

'Don't go, Het. We have a lot to catch up on.' She grabbed Het's hand as he removed it.

Het smiled gently. 'We will talk in the morning, when your grief isn't so new. You will see me again.' He gave her a brief hug then turned and walked away.

Ake watched his form disappear and her head drooped wearily.

Arlys opened the front door and rushed inside. 'I never pushed Anwyn away because of her father's sins. I heard what you said. There's a shed out back, animals sleep there. After tonight, don't ever come back here.' He slammed the door shut and locked it.

Lan growled and pounded on the door with his fist. 'Why would we come back to a household where the husband drove his wife to kill herself? Shove that up your behind and I hope it soils your reputation.'

Ake dragged him away. 'Think of Alwin, Lan. Let's find another place.'

Neighbours opened their doors to see what the commotion was as Ake hurried her family down the main street. Lan yawned, suddenly overcome with exhaustion, and looked around, hoping to find an open inn. All the bigger establishments were closed.

They came to a small, rundown inn with a flashing sign in the windows that read "vacancies". The screen door hung on its hinge at an angle, and the curtains in the small, dirty windows were tattered. Ake shrugged and opened the poorly painted wooden door that was beginning to splinter. Together, they entered the inn.

CHAPTER SEVEN

Lan surveyed the room. There was a small desk in the tiny entranceway with a book, ink vials and quills. Seated at the tiny desk was what appeared to be a small child. The individual had eyes the colour of sapphires and they twinkled with merriment; his hair was a mass of brown ringlets and he was dressed in brown pants and a black vest over a brown shirt. The lad was umber-skinned with a generous build, and his unshod feet were large and hairy.

The four foot halfling waved. 'How exciting, my first guests. How can I help you on this bonnie evening?'

Lan glanced at a small staircase before peering behind the desk, a trapdoor was set into the floor. The door had been thrown back and a tiny ladder descended into the darkness. 'We need a room for the night.'

If halflings still exist, I wonder if the dwarves do too? I am happy that not all the ancient beings have been lost, thought Lan.

'I can help you with that. I am the proprietor Hurley.' The halfling puffed his chest out proudly. 'I will see to it that you have the best experience. I will even prepare the perfect breakfast, included in the price, of course.'

Caoimhe whistled excitedly.

Hurley cocked his head and listened as the fairy whistled at him. Hurley smiled and whistled back. Then translated to Ake and Lan. 'I will make sure there is honey, cream and milk on the breakfast tray, my lady fairy.'

Lan and Ake looked at him in astonishment.

Hurley grinned at them. 'All halflings speak fairy. The first fairy was born among halflings.'

He translated Caoimhe's angry whistles. 'I am the last fairy. Fairies are born from two gods, not halflings.'

Hurley shook his head. 'You are a greater fairy and the last; the rest died out over a thousand years ago when Drianna slaughtered them. The gods recreated the smaller fairies we have today and they appeared among halflings about six hundred years ago. There are still very few of them though.'

Caoimhe signed angrily, so Hurley couldn't understand her. '*I am aware. I was there.*'

'Can you see through the glamoire spell on that necklace too?' asked Ake, changing the subject as Caoimhe glared at Hurley.

'We don't have much in the way of magic, we aren't elves. But we can speak to fey and fairies and see through any spell that hides things.' Hurley pointed at Lan's ears. 'I see your ears, elf.'

'I'm not an elf. There's no such thing as elves anymore,' whispered Lan.

'It's hazy and disappears.' Hurley peered at Lan's ears.

'About that room?' said Lan.

'Oh, how rude of me. I always go off on a tangent. What kind of room are you looking for? We have four.'

'One with comfy beds in it.' Ake smiled at him.

'I have one with two beds in it and a cute little fireplace for those cold nights. The window has quite the view,' described Hurley.

'How much?' asked Ake. She took out a small bag and began to pull out a few coins. The circular coin was a combination of tin and gold. There was a large hole in the middle and the outer edges had thorns engraved on them.

'Eight credits for the fairy's family; I normally charge ten,' said Hurley.

Ake looked at the coins in her hand, she only had six, and sighed. She placed the coins on the table. Lan felt around in his pockets and produced another coin. Orilan had scavenged the coins off the ground over the years when bringing in the dead and had given them to him. Lan had used the other twelve to pay for his and Ake's room and their dinner when he had returned.

'We have seven,' said Lan.

Hurley smiled at them expectantly.

Caoimhe signed to her parents. *Halflings expect you to haggle. They love the thrill of a bargain. They care little for the value of the money itself and would likely feed you and have you stay for free.*

Lan grinned at Hurley. 'Three.'

'That's too low, what a blow,' rhymed Hurley.

'Four,' said Ake.

'I need more, to be sure.' Hurley grinned.

I gather halflings enjoy rhyming. Lan smiled. 'Five should make you feel alive.'

Hurley laughed. 'Your rhyme did settle the score, no need to pay any more.'

Ake handed over five credits.

Hurley pulled a chain from around his neck. A dozen keys hung from it. 'Follow me up the stairs.'

The stairwell was tiny. Lan and Ake were not tall, but they had to squeeze themselves into the small space.

A place for smaller people like Caoimhe.

Hurley took them down a tiny hallway. Lan felt he had to duck his head as there was an inch clearance between the top of his head and the ceiling. He wasn't even that tall at five foot eight. Ake didn't feel the need to as she was only five foot six.

They came to the door and Hurley tried many of the keys before finding the right one. He opened the door and flicked a switch. Light flooded the room from two hanging orbs.

Hurley whistled to Caoimhe and they held a brief conversation. 'I have offered Caoimhe a room on the house.' Hurley smiled.

'That is kind of you,' said Ake.

'She has accepted, but will join you for breakfast in the morning. Goodnight.' Hurley turned and left as Caoimhe followed him to another door, her head drooping as she let out a long sigh.

Lan and Ake entered their room and closed the door. There were two small beds and a fireplace. The beds had many cushions on them in an array of cheery colours. Ake ran her hands over the fluffy, pink bedspreads before laying down on one of the beds; her feet reached the end. Lan lay down on the other and kicked off his shoes. The bed was soft, but his feet hung off the edge of the bed. He yawned and closed his eyes.

Ake was fascinated by the orb. She climbed off the bed and flicked the switch many times, watching in fascination as the light disappeared and reappeared.

Lan opened his eyes. 'Ake, that is very annoying.'

'The orbs don't use magic. I wonder how it works.'

'No magic. Impossible.'

Lan leapt out of bed and walked over. He flicked the switch before hurrying over to the orb and tapping it. Lan unscrewed the orb from its base; it was hot to the touch so he used his sleeve to unscrew the rest of it. Looking in the base of the orb, he saw a red and blue cord. He felt inside; the cords felt rubbery and sparked when he ran his fingers over them.

'Look, Ake, they have trapped lightning in here. It runs down these cords into the orb and traps the light. That switch activates it.' Lan stared at it in fascination. 'I reckon this is what they call science.'

'Amities loved science.' She smiled sadly.

Lan replaced the globe. 'I wonder if they have a library where I can research these lightning orbs.'

Ake yawned and returned to her bed. 'We can find out in the morning. I think we will have to get jobs too, Lan.'

'Why can't we run our own business?'

Lan had run his own school from the age of thirteen. He had been the heir to the former principal, a noble named Hanton. Lan once had unlimited access to Hanton's vault and had never had to work for someone else. This would be a new experience for him.

'That is not likely, Lan. We have no money to set one up, and Cirichad is quite foreign to us. We will have to start out working for others.'

'Okay.' Lan hurried back to his bed and lay down.

Ake closed her eyes and joined the dream world.

Chapter Eight

It was a few hours before dawn. The fog rolled in off the ocean and covered the city of Cirichad. It was bitterly cold and the young woman blew on her hands to keep them warm. She stood on the large prow of her ship. A huge, white majestic unicorn reared up; its gold-spiralled horn pierced the misty air as it glowed. Its teeth were bared in anger and its eyes were wild with fear. The figure-head had cost her a significant amount of credits. *It is magnificent, the cost was worth it.*

Her crew had changed their Velterran flag for the neutral flag that allowed trade and kept the peace. The flag ruffled in the chilly breeze; a black background with a single credit coin in the centre. Two of her crew lowered the gangplank. The young woman leapt from the prow to the deck of her ship and waited for the dock-master to approach.

Her ship, the *Carnay*, was tied up at the large docks of Cirichad just outside the red-walled city. The city was surrounded by the sea as it took up the whole island. The city was rumoured to have been built on the ancient island of Man'hannon where once a great mystic school and two villages had resided. There were two entrances. The first was the docks to the rear of the city where a large portcullis remained closed and heavily guarded. Very few were allowed to trade with Cirichad; it was a place rich with fertile lands and forests, and their farmers produced almost everything they needed.

The second entrance was through the large forest of Caley;

a small land bridge allowed access to the mainland when the tide was out. The cobbled road was cracked and often flooded. The journey was dangerous as sometimes the ancient forest was known to spew out the odd random monster, and the closely knitted trees often hid murderous highway men and women.

The dockmaster approached the ship. 'Captain Alena, daughter of Blaze, please approach.'

Alena was dressed in leather breeches, high-heeled black boots and a red, sleeveless corset. Her long black hair whipped in her face and she pushed it out of her green eyes as she shivered in the cold morning air. Goosebumps appeared on her russet skin as she rubbed her arms to keep herself warm. Accompanied by her first mate, she approached the dockmaster.

'Why are you here?'

Alena gave him a disarming smile. 'We are in between journeys. We are low on goods. We will only be here a day or two while we make minor repairs to the ship and buy supplies.'

'Who will be entering the city?'

'My first mate and myself. The rest of the crew will stay behind.'

'All weapons must be handed over before you proceed. You will also need to cover yourself more modestly.' He stared at her bare arms, before frowning.

Alena sighed and removed the staff that was strapped across her back. Her first mate handed over several throwing daggers and a large rifle.

'I need a show of coins to prove that you are indeed here to trade with the city.' The dockmaster held out his hand.

Alena handed over the heavy pouch and the dockmaster counted the coins and wrote down the amount in the ledger.

'I need you to sign this waiver stating that if you cause any harm you will forfeit your ship and goods, and you and your crew will be detained.'

Alena took the quill that was offered and made her mark. The dockmaster ushered them forward. Two guards approached and escorted them to the portcullis. Her first mate took off her cloak and put it over Alena's shoulders. Alena gave her a grateful smile. The guards ushered them forward as the portcullis rose.

CHAPTER NINE

There was a gentle knock at the door and it slowly opened. Hurley brought in a large tray and placed it on the fireplace mantel. Lan was already up as he was an early riser.

'Good morning, Hurley.'

Hurley bowed and exited. Ake whimpered in her sleep and thrashed about restlessly. Lan wandered over to her as she began to murmur.

'No, it can't be ... killed by his own child. I never knew. Mandami ... I am sorry. I would have found her for you if I knew.'

Lan lay down on the bed with her and drew her into his arms. Ake sniffled and she began to relax against him. She mumbled a few more incoherent words before her eyes fluttered open.

Lan whispered in her ear. 'What did you dream about that was so distressing?'

Ake turned in his arms; her eyes were haunted. 'Mandami had a short romance with Beryl. The child he adopted was theirs and he didn't know. His child hated him and plotted his murder. She in turn was murdered too by the last citizens of Regis. Mandami's daughter had a baby with one of the last forest elves. Their long-lived child had a child later in her long life and that girl is here, Lan, this very morning.' Ake sobbed.

'Ake, can I ask you something?'

Ake nodded.

'Have any of these vivid dreams ever come true?' asked Lan.

Ake told Lan some of her visions, including one where he was attacked and his eyes had rolled back in his head and he'd had several bouts of fits.

Lan stared at her, his eyes wide with surprise. 'And you never told anyone, including me?'

'I told Flo, but we couldn't be sure any had actually happened.'

'Ake, that did happen. The scars on my face are a gift from when Orilan attacked me with his horned guards.'

Ake stroked the four horizontal, thin white scars on the right side of his face, cheek to chin. They were four centimetres long and a centimetre apart. She shivered.

'I wish you had told me, Ake. I am so sorry you have had to endure these visions alone. If this vision you had is true, we will look for Mandami's great-grandchild together.' Lan brushed her lips with his own.

There was an excited whistling, and Lan and Ake drew apart. Caoimhe entered the room without waiting. She fluttered over to the tray and took a jar of honey, a cup of milk and a bowl of cream and sat on the floor. She opened the jar of honey and used the spoon to ladle it into her mouth.

Lan shook his head, smiling. 'Still our Caoimhe.'

Caoimhe stuck out her tongue and signed rapidly. '*While fairies get most of their nutrients from flowers, we enjoy sweets and honey. I will never pass up a cup of milk or a bowl of cream, our favourite foods. Other foods taste bitter.*'

Ake and Lan laughed and sat up. Lan got out of bed and brought the breakfast tray over to Ake. He handed her a cup of tea. Like her daughter, Ake had a sweet tooth. She spooned four generous teaspoons of sugar into the tea and poured in some milk. Lan grinned at her and poured himself a black cup of coffee from a pot. There were some pretty little cakes on the tray and he pushed them towards Ake.

Lan reached over and grabbed a slice of buttered toast and some fruit. Like most hill elves, he favoured berries and root vegetable dishes, commonly foraged for in the bogs and hills of Eriu. Lan didn't mind some meat, but he ate it sparingly, having been raised in a vegetarian household. Ake pushed the scrambled eggs towards him, she had finished the cakes. She picked at the breakfast sausages, but devoured the bacon.

Caoimhe finished her breakfast. '*I am going to thank Hurley for breakfast.*' She rushed from the room, closing the door behind her.

Ake finished her tea. Lan took the tray and placed it on his bed.

'My typical little sweet tooth. You are so cute and predictable.' He lay down next to her and drew her into his arms. Lan leant in to kiss her and she responded with equal passion. 'Mmm, sweet and bacony. A unique flavour. Can I sample you now?' He pulled up her dress and used his free hand to unfasten his britches.

'Yes, but we will have to be quick, Lan. You know that act is illegal here when done for passion.' Ake looked at the door.

Lan grinned at her and cast a simple spell; the lock slid into place. He had felt the magic surge through him with the sunrise.

'Lan, please don't use magic. It is a jail sentence.' Ake's eyes filled with wariness.

'Okay. But what do you mean by that act? Do you want me to make love to you?' He gave her a charming smile before he kissed the tip of her slightly pointed ear and whispered crude sentiments to her.

'You know exactly what I mean. I am not going to say any of them.' Ake gave him a coy glance. 'But yes. I will always want you.'

Ake lay back and closed her eyes as his hands trailed lower. He grabbed her hands and held them in his against the bed head, not wanting to let them go. He took her passionately and smiled down at her. Her eyes fluttered open, full of desire.

'You are breathtaking. I should keep you in this position permanently.' Lan crushed her into the bed.

Ake squeezed his hands and cried out.

Lan gave her a proud grin. 'That's my woman.'

Ake blushed and he leant down and kissed her before setting a vigorous pace to fulfil his own needs.

He rolled off her and lay next to her, breathing heavily, adjusting his clothes as Ake snuggled into him. He turned and encircled her with his arms.

He took a deep breath. 'You smell like home. By the gods, I have yearned for you. I was lonely too.'

Ake gasped as he squeezed the breath out of her. 'You are hurting me.'

He relaxed and lifted his head so that their eyes met. 'Sorry.'

'What was it like?'

'I could manipulate the underworld for others, making it a paradise. The dead could all intermingle, but I sat upon my throne unable to leave, trapped in a perpetual twilight, and judged the souls that came before me.' Lan shivered. 'The depravity I heard; the innocents ripped from life too soon. I had to judge the worst sorts. My only company was Orilan, when he wasn't gathering souls. The highlights were your messages. They became my only hope. Thoughts of you were the light in the darkness.' His hands trembled as he released her to clutch at the blanket.

Ake caressed his face. 'I thought *I* judged the dead and decided whether they would return to the world of the living or the dead.'

Lan sighed. 'The ones that failed when you gave them a second chance came to me after they died again.'

'So, you were more alone than I.' Ake blinked back tears and kissed him. 'I am so sorry.'

Lan sighed and lay back in the bed. 'It is done now.'

Ake gave him a comforting smile as she ran her hand down his body in a delicate caress. 'So, you are okay?'

Lan nodded as her brows furrowed with concern.

'I know what you are thinking. Amities will not be trapped as I was. I still retain the title of Lord of the Dead so that he will forego that ordeal. He can wander the heaven I made for them, touch grass and feel sunlight on his cheeks as he is reunited with loved ones.'

'You are incredible,' Ake whispered; her smile faltered as she began to shake. 'Does that mean you can be summoned back?'

Lan grabbed her by the shoulders and stared intently into her eyes. 'No. I am yours.'

Ake smiled with relief and clung to him for a little longer before she climbed out of bed, trotted over to the window and drew back the tattered curtain. Their room overlooked a bustling marketplace. Vendors were busy setting up their stalls in the morning light.

'Maybe I can try and get some work there,' Ake muttered.

Someone fiddled with the door handle and whistled in annoyance. Lan scrambled out of bed, slid the bolt back and cautiously opened the door.

Caoimhe tapped her foot at him in annoyance. '*Why did you lock me out?*'

'You should knock, Caoimhe,' said Lan.

'*Why?*'

'I'll let your mother explain that one.'

Ake turned and looked at her husband and daughter. 'Caoimhe, are you okay to stay here with Hurley while your father and I go and try to find work? If we don't, we won't be able to buy more honey.'

Caoimhe fidgeted in distress. '*We can't have that. I will stay here. Hurley is my friend now. He can understand me.*'

'That's great.' Ake walked over and hugged her daughter before leaving the room.

Lan kissed his child on the top of the head and followed Ake.

CHAPTER TEN

Alena wandered through the marketplace making a few more purchases. Her first mate stumbled under the packages of tobacco, jars of fermented cabbage and sacks of flour. Alena took some of the parcels from her and piled them on top of the overloaded handcart she had purchased and gave her companion a heartfelt smile. 'Sorry.'

Vendors barked at her, trying to sell their wares as they resumed their journey. 'I don't need a sacred psalm book or a circle of thorns pendant to protect me from the tainted one.' She glared at the last vendor who tried to sell her that detestable symbol.

Her father Blaze denounced the city of Cirichad and tried to raise her in hate, a tool for revenge against her ancestor's demise.

Alena had bordered a ship at twelve and learnt the ways of the sea. At twenty-one, she had saved enough money and bought an old ship to fix up. Members from the crew of the last ship she had been on had revolted against how cruel the Veltarren citizens treated Cirichad prisoners and had followed her onto her rundown ship. Over time, they had saved enough to fix it up by fulfilling bounties and delivering goods back and forth for small businesses.

She hated her father as he was cruel, bitter and angry. He often killed Cirichad slaves that Veltarren pirates captured. The Cirichad prisoners didn't seem evil, but her father assured her they would kill her if they knew who she was descended from, labelling her an abomination.

Alena had done her research. *Mandami had been a good man. I don't understand why his daughter Jasper hated him.* She sighed and rolled her eyes as several Cirites knelt nearby in prayer. *I can't wait to leave Cirichad. I don't know why they blindly follow a religion that killed their founder. At least they are hospitable despite being a little dull and predictable.*

While Cirichad allowed tobacco, alcohol was frowned upon. She knew her rum stores were low and hoped the tobacco would appease her crew's need for something to break up the monotony of a long voyage.

Her father had sent her a telepathic dream. He was dying and needed her to return so he could settle his affairs. The journey would take two weeks and would be dangerous, crossing seas filled with ancient ocean monsters. Bigger ships could take the journey in ten days or less. She had assured her crew that her father was wealthy and the treasure would be theirs if they agreed to accompany her. After her father's death, she could cut all ties and be free of him.

Alena hurried over to the employment stand. Their last laundress had quit. She had suffered terrible bouts of sea sickness and they needed a new one to keep up with her crew's malodorous piles of hose and shirts. They would also need a few more marksman to help against the devastating monsters.

⸻⁓⸻

Ake and Lan had approached multiple stallholders, asking for work and had been turned away. They had been shown to the employment stall and waited at the back of the line. Lan glanced at a board with scraps of paper on it. He began reading the contents.

Wanted. 'Job board, it seems.' As the line dwindled, the scraps of paper were filed away.

A young woman jostled him as she pushed a handcart past him and his wife. The young woman's companion stumbled under several large parcels. The woman pinned a piece of paper on the noticeboard and turned to survey the people in the line.

His flintlock pistol now hung off his new belt. The young woman's companion pointed at the gun and whispered in the young woman's ear.

There was a commotion behind Lan and he turned to see Het striding towards them, Mandami's famous sword strapped across his back. Alwin was with him and the boy's shoulders drooped as people pointed or glared, discussing the sword.

'How dare he carry a replica of Lord Mandami's sword.'

'Blasphemy.'

Alwin was carrying a backpack and his eyes locked on Lan's. 'Father kicked me out after I confronted him over the way he treated you last night. He said I was like my mother. I have nowhere to go.'

Ake hugged the boy and he sobbed in her arms.

'We know of a place, but we need money to pay for it,' said Lan.

'I can see that. Why else would Lord Trebrelan of Caelestis be in the employment line?' Het laughed.

Alena exchanged surprised glances with her companion before wandering over to the group. 'Excuse me. I believe I heard an unlikely name mentioned.'

The woman released the sobbing boy and stared at Alena in shock. Alena stumbled back as the beautiful woman embraced her, sobbing.

'It's true, he did have a child,' cried Ake.

Alena patted her on the back before gently pushing her away. 'Sorry, do I know you?'

'No, but I know of you. I am Telewanake and that is my husband Trebrelan.'

People glared at them and some lawmakers headed towards them. Alena turned and walked away. If she got fined she could lose her trading licence.

There was a disturbance behind her and one of the male lawmakers grabbed the woman who had hugged her. 'Embracing other adults in public is frowned upon.'

Trebrelan, the man the woman had introduced as her husband, was yelling at the lawmaker. 'Let my wife go. This society is a dictatorship.'

The large man with the sword strapped across his back tried to intervene and pushed the lawmaker off the woman, his eyes flashed fiercely. 'Unhand her.'

The blond boy, who had an emerald bow in one hand and an ornate staff in the other, looked unsure of what to do. Alena sighed and walked back over to them.

She took out her last few coins and handed them out to the lawmakers. 'Here, I will pay their fine.'

'This is acceptable.' The lawmaker shoved his captive towards Trebrelan who grabbed his wife's hand as she stumbled.

Alena observed the small group as Trebrelan stood in front of Telewanake and glared at the lawmakers as they left. The boy with the bow wandered over to the job board and took the last piece of paper, read it and handed it to the taller man with the sword who read the paper before he held a whispered conversation with the woman at the employment stall and filled out a piece of paper.

Trebrelan smiled at Alena. 'Thank you. I will pay you back as soon as I am able.'

'It is fine, Trebrelan. Now, I am a busy person, I will take my leave.'

'Wait, please call me Lan and my wife Ake. I insist on paying you back. It is a matter of ho—'

'Captain Alena, please come here.' The employment officer ushered her over.

Het strode over to Ake and Lan and spoke to them. 'I found us a job. I need to get to Velterra and you need to come with me. I have signed us up as crew on a ship headed there.'

Lan gave him a brooding look. 'Why would you do that without asking us?'

'I'll tell you when we board the ship. It's a binding contract.' Het shrugged.

Alwin fumbled in his pocket and handed Lan a bag. 'Inside is some gunpowder and a smaller container full of shot pellets.'

'Thank you, Alwin,' said Lan.

There was a tug on Alwin's pants and he turned to see Caoimhe holding hands with what appeared to be a young boy. Unlike adults, children holding hands in public was not frowned upon. From a distance, their looks were deceiving. Upon closer inspection, Hurley and Caoimhe looked like permanent young adults.

Caoimhe chirped in the halfling's ear and he translated. 'She asked what is going on.'

Alwin briefly filled them in.

'Well, it's a good thing I locked up the place,' said Hurley.

Hurley ran up to the employment stall and added his name to Alena's contract while the employment officer was caught up in a conversation with the captain.

Alena turned and looked at her strange new crew. If those names were correct, Telewanake and Trebrelan were possibly Mandami's parents, and therefore her grandparents three times removed. She stood looking at her ancestors in disbelief. Trebrelan had defied an empire to fight for his bride's honour, and the woman Telewanake and her son Mandami had defeated the evil goddess Drianna. *Well, according to the legends I have read. Trebrelan doesn't look like an elf, so it's not likely. They might just be named after the divine couple.*

Alena took the parcels from her first mate and wandered over to the large man with the sword. 'What is your name, big fellow?'

'I am Heta Falcon, but everyone calls me Het.'

'Okay, Mr Falcon, you and the others are new members of my crew. You can push that handcart over there,' said Alena.

'Wait. I didn't agree to that,' grumbled Lan.

'It is a legally binding contract. You wanted a job and now you have one.' Alena turned and looked at Ake. 'Okay, affectionate woman, you can carry one of these parcels, as can your husband.' Alena handed them the parcels. 'Follow me.' She turned and set a fast pace.

Everyone followed.

CHAPTER ELEVEN

It was nearly midday as the crew pulled up the gangplank. Alena stood staring at her new crewmembers on the deck of *Carnay*. The sun was high in the sky and the fog had disappeared, leaving the sky blue and clear. She had learnt their names and asked them what they could do. The sailors untied the mooring rope and unfurled the sails. Nuo was at the helm, and the ship caught a large draft as she guided it out of the dock.

Lan was assigned to the marksmen, who would teach him to use the valuable gun he owned. His wife would take on the mountainous loads of washing along with her small daughter. Everyone had to earn their way on a ship as soon as they were able. It was the code of the sea and even children were not spared.

Het would become a gunner. His large size would be valuable on the cannons, including loading the fifteen kilo cannonballs into the weapon. And the halfling would assist the elderly chef.

Alena stared at Alwin, unsure where to place the boy. He had explained he was good at archery. After some consideration, Alena arrived upon a novel idea, she would assign him to the cabin boys below deck to shoot the rats that deteriorated their stores. The boy looked squeamish at her suggestion, but composed himself and nodded.

'On this ship, the men sleep on the cannon decks.' Alena glanced to Ake. 'The women will share the cabin with myself.'

The men nodded and left to complete their chores.

As much as she trusted her crew, the voyages were long. Some of her male crewmembers were already in relationships with each other, but some of the other men might feel tempted to seduce the women on board.

The cabin wasn't large, but there would only be herself, Ake, Caoimhe and two other women including her companion and lover Nuo.

—–∿∿–—

Alena's gaze softened as it alighted on Nuo who was explaining to Ake how to use the washing apparatus below deck. Another crewmember had taken over at the helm and they had been sailing for a few hours.

The first mate was a small woman with fawn-coloured skin and large brown eyes. Her hair was a very dark brown and she wore it in a bun with several ornate dragon hair pins. She was dressed in a long-sleeved, full-length, flowing golden robe, belted at the waist. Nuo's small feet were shrouded in tiny green slippers.

The washing appliance consisted of a large barrel on a wooden stand. When full, a wooden lid with a large wooden paddle attached in the centre of the underside was secured on top. A metal handle on the top of the lid was then turned to agitate the paddle, allowing the clothes to become cleaner than by hand-washing alone. Set on the side of the apparatus was a mangle. Washing was fed through two rollers as another handle was turned, squeezing excess water out of the clothing.

'I have shown you how to use the devices. Now you should be ready to start. Remember, clean water should be added from the water barrels nearby and dirty water will be thrown overboard. You can fill an empty barrel and I will get one of the men to empty it as necessary.' Nuo pointed to the washing line. 'Caoimhe, do you remember how I showed you to peg up the washing?'

Caoimhe nodded and grabbed a handful of the pegs.

'How will she reach?' asked Alena.

'Won't be a problem,' mumbled Ake.

Fresh air filtered down from the metal grates set in the deck-head. The booted feet of crewmembers disturbed the grates as they passed overhead, bringing with them the scent of unwashed bodies and the tangy sea air.

'If you need anything, please feel free to ask Nuo. She is my first mate and you can trust her with anything, as I do.'

Satisfied, Alena and Nuo left Ake and Caoimhe to start their monstrous task.

'Use your bow to protect them. Large rats like to hide among the piles of dirty clothes, their bites carry nasty diseases that could threaten their lives,' Nuo instructed Alwin who had been waiting at the top of the steps.

Alwin nodded. 'Yes, Mistress Nuo.'

Alwin made his way down the stairs and waved at Ake before taking position nearby, his eyes alert for any movement. Ake looked at the mountains of washing and sighed. The work would take her days. Piles of stained hose and shirts sat reeking in large mounds that towered over Caoimhe. Ake tried not to gag and reached for a bar of soap and a scrubbing board. As Ake grated the soap into the washing machine, Caoimhe slowly added buckets of water from the barrels nearby. When the contraption was full, Ake added five shirts and applied the lid. She turned the handle and set the machine to work. Caoimhe turned an hourglass and the sand dripped down into the small chamber. After ten minutes, the sand had ended its journey.

Ake removed the lid and put each shirt through the mangle. She then rinsed them in a small bucket of water before putting them through the mangle again. Caoimhe grabbed the clean shirts and flew up to the line, pegging them in place.

After a few hours, Ake saw Alwin yawn as he leant against the wall of the ship, his bow in his hand. She rolled her eyes. *I can handle a few rats.*

Caoimhe squealed and ran towards her mother as a large rat scrambled from among a pile of dirty washing. The rats were around three feet in length from head to tail. One hissed at them and bared its yellow teeth. Its wiry whiskers twitched as it looked at them, its beady black eyes filled with hunger. Its fur was wiry and coarse, and pus-filled sores ruptured on its body, the yellow liquid dripping onto the floor.

'Alwin, shoot it,' yelled Ake.

Alwin braced himself and drew his bow. It hummed and a vibrant green arrow made of light appeared in the drawn string. Alwin's arms trembled as the rat raced towards him. He checked his aim and fired. The rat squealed and writhed in pain as the magic arrow pierced its disease-ridden body. The dying rat released a cacophony of squeals and more sets of beady black eyes appeared from under the piles of clothes. The nest mates scrambled out from the piles of laundry and surrounded Ake and Caoimhe. There were twenty in total. Some turned and charged Alwin as he fired at them.

Caoimhe escaped by flying and landing on the washing line. She sat there, shivering with fear. Ake hurled handfuls of *Mystic Fire* at the rats and they squealed in pain as they burned alive. The conjured flames spread to several of the clothing piles.

Ake, knowing the fire could spread rapidly, cried, '*Waterius manus.*' Jets of water formed in her hands and doused the flames.

Alwin took down more rats as another dived for Ake. It grazed her boot as she kicked it in the face. Another scrambled up a pile of clothes and leapt onto her shoulder, its teeth centimetres from her neck. Startled, Ake fell back against the side of the ship as more jumped on her. Her eyes turned golden and golden-feathered wings sprouted from her back. She'd had the dress altered for such a situation, retaining her modesty.

A flash of blinding light flung the rats against the opposite wall. Ake had taken her fire angel form, her Anwyn, harnessing her great divine power, a gift from her divine father Gepatok. As quickly as she had called upon the power, she recalled it, worried she could get them into trouble for using magic.

The last of the rats huddled in the corner, afraid of her, and Alwin took them down with his bow. Alwin offered her a hand up and she accepted it gratefully.

'You did well, Alwin.'

Alwin nodded. He slung the bow across his shoulder and whistled. Two young lads, who were killing rats up the other end of the tween deck, rushed over. They sighed and began helping him to carry the bodies of the rats upstairs to throw overboard. Alwin's face looked green as he picked up one of the revolting creatures by its long, scaly tail.

Ake shuddered. *I don't like rats or mice.* She began to prod each pile of washing with a broom before she took any more of the clothes to be washed. Satisfied, she continued her work.

Chapter Twelve

Lan tilted his weapon and used a powder horn to pour a small amount of gunpowder into the muzzle of the pistol. He took one of lead balls, wrapped it in a small scrap of fabric and placed it in next. The cloth was known as a wad and was used to create an airtight seal between the lead ball and the barrel so the ball would not come tumbling out.

Lan withdrew the extendable ramrod from underneath the barrel of the gun and tamped down the lead ball far into the barrel. He made sure it was packed snuggly, hoping it would be compacted enough to reach the breech where the gunpowder now lay. He cocked the hammer and pushed the frizzen—a little lever on the top of the gun—forward and placed a small amount of powder in the pan underneath. Satisfied, he admired the weapon before turning to look at his new teacher.

The middle-aged man, known as Gideon Gunnar, was of a large build and stood at six foot two. He had short-cropped blond hair and green eyes. His bronzed face was pockmarked from childhood diseases and rough from working in the harsh weather that often accompanied sailing. He often trained new marksman, but his main job was gun captain. He was in charge of the crews that fired the cannons on the ship.

'You are a natural. You followed my instructions perfectly,' said Gideon. He gestured to the side of the ship where he had thrown three marked barrels into the water tied with rope and filled with thick, red dye. Lan wandered over and gazed over the edge of the ship.

Lan took the weapon and aimed at one of the barrels. He held the weapon in one hand, his fingers primed on the trigger, the other hand supporting the trigger hand. He was nervous and his hands trembled.

Another man fired a large rifle nearby. There was a puff of smoke and a quick flame as the powder ignited. Sulphuric fumes floated in the air. The man hit one of the targets and the barrel bled its thick dye into the sea.

His teacher cleared his throat and Lan steadied his hands and fired, the weapon stayed silent. *I definitely pulled the trigger.* One of the barrels exploded and the liquid splattered, marking the side of the ship. The teacher and other marksman ran to the side, staring at the barrel, before rushing over to Lan.

'Hand over the gun, lad,' said Gideon.

'No.' Lan pulled the gun away.

'At least take another shot.' The rifleman's eyes flitted to the ancient weapon.

Lan reloaded the gun and fired. Another barrel exploded; the gun remained silent. Amities had designed a remarkable pistol over a thousand years ahead of its time.

'Let me see the weapon, lad. I won't take it from you.'

Lan reluctantly handed it over. Gideon gasped as he ran his hands over the symbol. He handed the precious weapon back to Lan, who put it back on his belt.

'That weapon is ancient. It was crafted by the hands of the last great elven engineer Amities of Eriu. While there were various prototypes, the flintlock pistol known as Hushin was said to be silent, and tapping the barrel while the gun is held downwards is said to be enough to clean it without having to take it apart. Where did you find such an artefact?' asked Gideon.

Lan shrugged. 'Heirloom.'

'Well, be careful not to lose it. That's enough for today,' said Gideon.

There was a flash below as a bright light shone through a grate in the deck nearby. Lan knelt and peered into the gaps, where he was met with the sight of Ake and Alwin fighting off some nasty looking rodents.

Lan rose and turned to Gideon. 'Thank you.'

Lan sprinted to a nearby stairwell and rushed below deck. He stepped against the wall as Alwin and a few boys walked up the stairwell carrying some deceased rats. Alwin looked like he was trying not to vomit. Lan let them pass before he hurried down the last few steps.

He entered the dark tween deck. His nose was assaulted with the stench of unwashed piles of clothes and the rancid bodies of giant rats. Caoimhe was sitting on a washing line while Ake turned the handle on a strange contraption. Caoimhe saw him and fluttered down into his arms. He gave her a hug before placing her on the ground. 'Are you alright?'

Caoimhe nodded.

He rushed over to Ake and was about to embrace her when she stayed him with a hand.

'Not now, we are okay.' She sighed. 'Do you see the ridiculous amount of washing Caoimhe and I must get through?'

'What can I do to help?'

Ake gave him a grateful smile and showed him how to operate the mangle. The three of them worked long into the night and were able to get the washing down to a more manageable level.

Nuo came down and tried to escort Caoimhe and Ake to the cabin a few hours before dawn. Ake shook her head and said she would stay with her husband.

'Orders are orders, please follow me,' said Nuo.

'No, I will not be apart from my husband.' She gave Nuo a stern look.

'Alena will not be pleased if you dismiss her orders.'

Ake shook her head; her hands placed defiantly on her hips.

'Please yourself. But it will be on both your heads.'

Nuo turned and climbed the stairs behind them. Caoimhe was too tired to care and followed Nuo, refusing to stay where evil creatures lurked. The idea of a stretcher bed was more appealing than a bedroll on the deck.

'Caoimhe, will you be okay?' Ake reached for her daughter's hand

'*I will be fine. I am grown, you belong with Father*,' signed Caoimhe.

Ake looked a little sad as Caoimhe followed Nuo up the stairs.

Lan smiled. 'Looks like our last baby is finally asserting her independence.'

'But she is so small and frail.'

'Embrace it, Ake, we are empty nesters.'

Ake rolled her eyes. 'I highly doubt it; we must look out for Alwin. Caoimhe will come back as soon as she is frightened or hungry.'

Lan gave her a secret smile.

'What is it?'

'I believe that little halfling will keep her fed.' Lan smiled.

'You think something is going on there?'

Lan shrugged and took her hand. 'Let's go to bed, I'm tired.'

They exited the stairwell onto the upper deck. Lan led her past crewmembers asleep in hammocks swaying gently in the breeze, to a bed he had made from some commandeered blankets. They glanced at Het on the opposite side of the deck staring out to sea. He had been put on watch. Lan pulled back the blankets and they both clambered in, it was a tight fit and Lan had to spoon Ake to cover them both.

Lan's stomach rumbled and Ake giggled as they both realised they hadn't eaten since breakfast. Lan sighed and closed his eyes, too exhausted to worry about eating. Ake relaxed against him, calmed by his quiet, rhythmic breaths, and drifted into a dreamless sleep.

CHAPTER THIRTEEN

It was an hour after dawn; the couple snuggled under their blankets, avoiding the frigid sea air. Ake giggled as Lan tried to steal a few quick kisses. He grunted as someone booted him in the back and threw back the covers; a scowl fixed on his face to see Alena and some of the crew staring down at them. The captain's mouth was set in a grim line and a few crewmembers glared at the couple.

Nuo hurled Ake up. 'Stay quiet.'

Alena allowed Lan to get to his feet before she dragged him towards her by the collar of his shirt. Her jaw ticked and her gaze narrowed on his. He pushed her hands away and a crewman grabbed him and pinned his hands behind his back.

Alena pointed at him. 'You both disobeyed my orders. You are no better than the rest of the crew. It is life and death at sea, and we have strict orders in place to maintain an organised ship that is fair to all. There is no dallying with other members of the crew when out at sea. If I allow it for one crewmember I allow it for all. Could you imagine the chaos that kind of revelry could cause? I am giving you extra chores.'

The crew grumbled and began to argue among themselves.

'I'm not allowed to share the covers with my partner.'

'Why do these two get special treatment?'

'I thought what was good for one was good for the others. That punishment isn't fitting.'

'They are new to the ship. This punishment is a warning.'

Lan smirked. 'We didn't agree to your rules. We have done nothing wrong. Now let go off my wife.'

Ake shrugged Nuo off. 'Please, there is no need for any of this. We will do the chores.'

'No, we won't.' Lan scowled.

Gideon frowned. 'You've put yourself in it, lad. No need to be disrespectful to the captain who let you off with little more than a warning.'

'Give him a birching, twelve strokes.' Alena's nostrils flared.

'You will not lay a hand on my husband.' Ake stood in front of him and stared at Alena.

'That's a weak punishment usually reserved for a boy,' cried a sailor.

'But the lad isn't very strong looking,' said another crewmember.

'That's more than acceptable for a new crewmember.' Gideon glared at the other sailors and their conversation grew silent.

'Nuo, make sure she completes a mastheading of two days for her outspokenness and disregard for my rules.' Alena sighed. 'Could have been avoided.'

Nuo nodded and Ake struggled as she was dragged over to a mast. Lan resisted his captor, his pride getting the better of him. He slipped his arms out and used a grapple to throw the man onto his back. Lan strode over to Nuo and Ake.

'What an undisciplined brute. Get him and make it the standard twenty strokes. They signed a contract and will abide by it. I am their captain.' Alena crossed her arms, her voice commanding in the silence as the waves gently slapped the boat and a bird called in the distance.

Het sighed and got up from where he was resting. He grabbed Lan and hauled him away from Ake. 'Settle down, Lan. If you push Alena she will be forced to pursue harsher penalties. What will that mean for all of us? Will she throw us overboard? A captain maintains a precarious peace. Ake is a woman; she will not receive a harsh punishment. You will bear the brunt of that. Why is it so hard for you to follow orders?'

'Ake was brutalised at the hands of others. I will not see her beaten or manhandled.'

'I didn't know that, but it matters little to the crew on a lone ship in the middle of the ocean. You are not a powerful mystic anymore, Lan. I know you have always been your own master, but you will have to learn to rely on others. Our time of great magic has passed.' Het gave Lan a kind smile.

Lan sighed and turned to face the angry captain and crew. They took him over and tied him to the mast. His back faced the crew and he leant his head against the timber and ground his teeth in frustration.

'He defied me twice, make his wife watch and use a knotted whip instead. You know what, give the whip to their friend,' said Alena.

The crew made sounds of approval. A crewman handed Het a whip. The handle was made of wood and it had three cords that were knotted and braided.

'No, Het. How can you?' Ake sobbed.

'Do it already, Het. I can handle whatever these scoundrels dish out.' Lan stared the crew down.

'Better I do it, Ake, than someone who is filled with rage.' Het looked briefly at the crew then turned and gave Ake a meaningful look. 'If you act out, Ake, he will get it worse. Then we will be on a ship in the middle of the ocean with a crew that hates us.'

'Do it, but I won't watch,' said Ake.

Alena strode over to Ake. 'You both need to learn to follow rules, woman. If you disobey my instructions the number of lashings will increase. You will watch and learn from it.'

Ake nodded, resigned.

Het trudged over to Lan. 'Brace yourself, old friend.'

'Begin,' said Alena.

Het raised the whip and struck Lan. It made a cracking sound and each cord struck Lan individually, causing his shirt to tear. Three welts appeared on his back at different angles. The marks looked angry and cruel. Blood seeped out from the broken skin. 'I'm fine, Ake.'

'Again,' said Alena.

The whip cracked again and Lan didn't make a sound. Ake began to weep but kept her eyes fixated on her husband's back, her upper lip trembled and tears swam in her eyes.

'I am going to be sick.' Het wiped his mouth as the bile rose in his throat. 'How can you make her watch?' He pointed to Ake.

'Continue.' Alena sighed. 'Ma'am, you can look away now.'

Ake's eyes filled with determination and she locked gazes with the captain. 'No.'

The whip continued to crack as Het delivered the flogging. Lan's shoulders slumped; his back burned and his knees almost buckled as Het delivered blow after blow. Het was a powerful man yet the flogging Lan was receiving could have been much more brutal delivered by someone else. *I know he is holding back.* Lan began to lose sensation in his back and he sagged against the timbers in relief.

The whip cracked once more then Lan felt his bonds loosen and turned to face the crew as Nuo stepped aside. Het's gaze was fastened on the whip. The cords were drenched in Lan's blood and bits of his skin were caught in the knots. Het took a shuddering breath. Lan placed a hand to his back. The skin felt like a jellied mass of crisscrossing welts; when he took his hand away it was covered in skin and blood.

Alena took the weapon from Het. 'It's okay, big fellow. Resume your chores. You were kind to your friend. A lesser person filled with pride would have delivered a harsher blow for that insolence.'

Lan grinned and took an unsteady bow; the crowd cheered.

'The punishment is delivered. Obey the rules next time. Let his wife tend him until evening. After that she will receive her punishment,' said Alena.

Nuo pushed Ake towards Lan. Alena strode towards the helm. The first mate gestured for them to follow her. Lan stumbled. Ake put Lan's arm across her shoulder and he leant heavily on her. They followed Nuo to the ship's infirmary situated below deck.

They entered the small infirmary; shelves were lined with vials and bottles of ointments, shredded cloths for bandages, hooks for suturing, tweezers, and bottles of clear liquid Ake assumed were rubbing alcohol. There were a variety of other tools; some looked terrifying including a bone saw and large metal syringes.

Lan stumbled over to a metal table fixed to the floor. He clambered on to it and lay on his stomach, wincing and grunting with the effort.

'The doctor will be in soon.' Nuo turned and left.

Lan turned his head away from Ake and took heaving breaths. She heard him sob. Ake took his hand and he squeezed it as he let his anguish out. Ake had once been able to call on the gods to help her heal others. In the past, her blood had the potential to cure devastating injuries and she had helped Lan before.

She let go of his hand and placed hers above his wounds. She closed her eyes and began to pray. 'Grandfather Sorendee and Grandmother Dee, I beg of you, please grant me the power to heal him.'

When nothing happened she tried praying harder.

'They won't hear you, Ake. No one calls upon them anymore. They have retired; their last great act was to send me home to you.' Lan wiped his eyes with his hand and swore from the pain.

Ake took a scalpel and cut her hand. She held her hand over Lan's back and let the blood drip on the wound. A green light appeared from her hand and disappeared as quickly as it came. The wound looked a little better and some of the welts had disappeared.

'That should have healed this wound completely.' Ake took a cloth and wrapped her hand.

'Your powers are lessening too. Without the gods, the extraordinary skills we used to have cannot draw enough power from this now low-magic world. You will retain some magic, but it won't be as powerful. I am grateful to our son for the weapons he produced. They will not be affected.' Lan turned his head to look at her and winced, his eyes filled with pain.

There was a knock on the door and a middle-aged woman entered and gave them a kind smile. 'I see you defied our captain's orders.'

The doctor took down some bandages, suture hooks, rubbing alcohol and a jar of white ointment. She opened a drawer and withdrew a small container of rotting meat. Ake could see a mass of white, wriggling maggots consuming the decaying food. The doctor opened the jar and Ake saw Lan's face turn green at the gills.

'You aren't going to use a herbal cleanser instead?' asked Lan.

'These little friends of ours will clean the wound better than herbs.' The doctor took a handful and placed the critters in the wounds.

Ake turned away and waited. After an hour, the woman used some tweezers to pick out each maggot and return it to the jar. Ake inspected the wound; it did appear cleaner.

'Grab that small stick off the shelf will you?' The doctor pointed.

Ake retrieved the item and handed it to her.

'It's for him to bite down on. This next part will hurt.'

'Lan, place this between your teeth.'

'No.'

Ake sighed. 'Please.'

Lan relented and bit down on the stick. Ake watched as the doctor took strands of horsehair and dipped them in some rubbing alcohol along with the suture hooks. Lan grunted as the woman began to suture the largest wounds closed using the hooks and horsehair. Ake took his hand; his grip was intense.

'It could have been worse. You took your punishment valiantly so your wife will not be punished too harshly. So, try not to dwell on it and relax. You are very tense and that makes this process hurt more as I battle against tight muscles.'

'I am sorry, Lan.' Ake's eyes filled with anguish and she looked away from him.

'You didn't order me beaten. Het is right, we will have to obey the rules until we get to wherever we are going. I am angry he signed us up for this voyage though. I will confront him about that.' Lan's eyes flashed with anger.

'Sit up, lad.' The doctor eased Lan up and wrapped a large bandage around his middle. 'We are done here. You can go.'

Lan slid off the table and headed towards the open door. Ake followed. She could see he was in an awful amount of pain and he walked much slower than he usually did.

Nuo met them on deck. 'Mr Marcóir, you will go keep watch with the other marksman as per your contract. Mrs Marcóir, you will come with me.'

'They are not our names,' said Ake.

'When you left Cirichad we had to document your absence. All Cirites must have a surname for their families. It apparently allows for better record keeping, especially if a lot of citizens share the same name. It also cuts out listing the parental lineage that Velterrans do. We assigned you a surname based on your husband's job, as is the norm. The name means marksman,' said Nuo.

Lan leant against the mast briefly. He gave Ake a courteous nod before he walked slowly over to his fellow marksman. They had stopped for lunch and Lan was handed a bowl. Nuo cleared her throat and Ake looked at her.

'You are to endure two days mastheading. You will climb the rigging to the top of the mast. You will stay there two days without food and you will do so in your shift. It will be cold and you will go hungry, but after what your husband endured I believe this should be easy enough,' said Nuo.

Nuo ordered her to strip down to her shift and some of the crew whistled at her. Ake's eyes filled with fear as several men leered at her. She shivered, remembering a pair of eyes she had learnt to fear. Nuo, noticing Ake's distress, pointed at the men. 'Your rations are halved for two days.'

'We meant no harm.'

'Can't have any fun.'

The crewmen grumbled and turned back to their tasks.

Lan glanced at Nuo. 'That is a fair punishment. How dare they leer at my wife.'

Ake was handed a waterskin and started to climb the rigging. She stopped to stare at Lan, who peered down at his lunch. The boiled salted pork sat congealing in a watery broth. A hunk of black bread placed in the bowl began to draw up some of the liquid. He ate some of the meal and she saw him wince and gag before he placed the bowl down next to him and leant over an empty barrel, taking heaving breaths. Alena approached and gestured to the top of the rigging as she handed Lan a waterskin.

'There is some rum in there. It will relieve some of the pain,' said Alena kindly.

'Thanks.'

Alena nodded and walked away as Ake began to climb.

CHAPTER FOURTEEN

Het glanced up. Ake's lids drooped as she sighed wearily, one hand still clinging to the mast. Two days had passed since he had flogged Lan. The night had turned bitterly cold and a light rain had begun to fall as he had started his watch. Ake sneezed thrice and he sighed. *At least her ordeal will be over at dawn. Finally, Lan is keeping to himself and is doing as he is ordered.* They would be arriving at a small port tomorrow to refill their stores of rum. The crew had gotten excited until the captain had told them there would be no shore leave.

A man came over to relieve him. Het yawned. *I should go check on Lan.* He saw his friend sitting on his bedroll reading his book on gun care. Lan looked up at his approach.

'I am annoyed with you.'

Het sat down next to him. 'Is this about the flogging or the fact I signed you up to this voyage?'

Lan gave him a stern look. 'Why would you do that? I just got back here to be with her and now I am on a damn ship sleeping alone.'

'Hau isn't dead.'

'I know he never made it to my underworld. But I assumed the god Bel collected him and took him to the afterlife as he had never met his beloved and would never retire to the stone circles.' Lan glanced at Het before his eyes returned back to the page he was reading.

'Such a horrid rule.' Het shuddered.

Lan glanced up. 'I changed that rule. All those who are good, whether human, elf, halfling or dwarf and so on, will be reunited in the underworld. Unfortunately, that wasn't in place when you and Flo died. I am so sorry.'

Het smiled. 'Thanks to you, I eventually could be with Flo. But I swear to you, Hau is not with Bel. I had stopped watching the world pass by. The night I made the choice to leave the under-world was the night Flo saw snippets of what Hau has become.'

The dinner bell rang and Hurley rushed over with a tray and started handing out bowls of steaming soup to everyone. The lit-tle halfling smiled at them.

Het grinned. 'How can a person who consumes so many sweet foods have such great teeth?'

'Halfling digestive system.' He handed Het their meals and ran off.

Het passed Lan the meaty stew and a hunk of bread.

Lan looked at it in disdain. 'Every meal has meat and bread.'

'It will put some muscle on you.' Het winked. 'But not very palatable for a former elf.'

Lan sighed and put the steaming bowl aside. 'So, if Hau isn't dead, what happened?'

'All I know is he founded Velterra. I need to get there, and I need yours and Ake's help.'

Lan's eyes met his. 'So, all our children have gone on to alter our world.'

'It would seem so. Flo said Hau became a very bitter and cruel man.' Het's eyes welled with tears. 'I have to help him.'

'Just like I intervened and prevented the destruction of Mandami's body. I understand that's what parents do.'

Het looked up at Ake, who was holding onto the rope with one hand; she took a swig from the waterskin. 'What happened to her to make her cling to you? She was always independent and bold.'

'She was kidnapped, beaten and assaulted by an emperor known as Cephas. I was injured and could do nothing to rescue her; she saved herself. I was a lousy husband and couldn't defend her. She doesn't understand why I need to protect her and control the situations we are in. It took her years to overcome her ordeal, and when I was healed and we were finally enjoying family life, I was ripped away from her again. It felt like a decade for me and centuries for her. It was cruel. No man or god will ever take her from me again.' Lan dug his fingers into his palms.

Het's countenance changed to one of anger and he punched the nearest object. The barrel began to pour sand on to the deck as a large crack opened it up. 'I will always have a soft spot for her, Lan. She's like a little sister to me now. Did you kill the fiend?'

'I did and enjoyed it.'

'Good.' Het turned to face him. 'You were never a lousy husband according to Ake; take some comfort in that.'

Alwin wandered over. 'Great-grandfather, it is your turn for the watch. They want you available when she climbs down from there.'

'That's a mouthful, Alwin. Just call me Lan.'

Alwin gave him a reproachful glance. 'That would be disrespectful. What about one of the ancient Elvish words for grandfather and grandmother, *Lufar* and *Luma*?'

Het broke out in boisterous laughter. 'Lan and Ake, great-grandparents. Where's your cane, old man?'

Alwin stared at him. 'What is so funny about something that is true?'

Het ruffled Alwin's hair. 'These kids from Cirichad have no sense of humour.'

'That will do, Alwin.' Lan stood up and walked over to the opposite bulwark to take his watch. His back had stopped hurting hours ago. *Maybe my rapid healing is slowly returning.* He raised his gaze and caught sight of Ake as he heard her cough.

'Not long now,' he yelled.

He saw her shiver and her teeth chattered, but she smiled at him.

—⁓—

Dawn broke and Lan climbed up the rigging to meet Ake at Alena's permission. She was shivering and he put his hand to her head.

'You are burning up.'

She sneezed suddenly and didn't turn her head in time.

'I'm sorry,' said Ake, her voice filled with congestion.

Lan wiped his face, removed his waistcoat and put it on her.

'Don't worry about it.'

Het wolf whistled at him and some of the crewmembers laughed. Ake joined in until she was wracked with a barking cough. Her hands were tinged with blue and he took them in his, trying to warm them.

'Let's get down from here.'

Ake turned and slowly made her way down. Lan's elven agility allowed him to turn and walk down the rigging as easily as if he was walking down a flight of steps. He kept glancing at her until she reached the bottom and Het wrapped her in a blanket.

'The husband can accompany her to the galley for a few moments to see if she is alright.' Alena turned and strode away.

Lan took her hand and led her to the galley. The galley was situated to the bow of the ship near the forecastle, a raised deck at the front of the ship. They passed the main mast with lateen-rigged sails; the large mast loomed up into the early morning sky and stood near the bow.

Ake and Lan climbed a small set of stairs and reached the deck that housed the galley. The wooden structure had double doors and Lan pushed them open, trying to get Ake out of the cold. She stumbled and closed her eyes wearily. He dragged her through the doors and into the humid galley. An elderly chef was stirring a large cauldron on a potbelly stove. A large butcher's block separated him from the rest of the galley. Bunches of dried herbs hung from the ceiling, as did a motley collection of pots from hooks. Shelves took up the rear of the galley and were filled with sacks of flour and jars of pickled vegetables. Lan made Ake sit in one of the few chairs and went to speak to the chef.

Ake shivered and coughed. Hurley refilled a circular iron container with three prongs for legs with a pitcher of water. It was set atop a meat-safe that had been placed on one of the shelves. Hurley opened the door and pulled out a jug of milk.

Lan came over with a pot of tea and a small bowl of sugar. Hurley handed him the milk pitcher and Lan made her a cup of strong, sweet tea. He placed it in her hands and she began to sip it. Lan sat down in the chair next to her and felt her head again.

'You are still hot to the touch.' He looked up at the celling and saw the herbs and his eyes lit up. 'Can I take some of those to ease her cough?'

'Sure, young man. I doubt it will help; her eyes are glazed with fever.' The chef pointed to Ake.

Lan gathered leaves, flowers and bark from a few of the bunches of herbs. 'Can I have a cup of hot water, please?'

The chef gave it to him and Lan broke up the herbs and threw them in, allowing the brew to steep. The tea consisted of elder flowers, white willow bark and yarrow. The herbs would help to relieve her fever and congestion. He took out the herbs as best he could with a spoon and handed Ake the drink to sip.

The ship jolted and there was a thud. Someone rang a bell, followed by the sound of running footsteps. Lan ducked his head outside for a brief moment. 'We have docked and Alena and some of the crew are leaving the ship.'

Hurley brought Ake a bowl of broth, she refused it and set down both the empty drink cups. Lan took the bowl and spoon from Hurley and pulled his chair in front of hers. She gave him a defiant stare and he smirked at her.

'Ake, you haven't eaten in days. I won't leave until you have finished this broth. Please don't be childish.'

Ake scowled at him. 'It's not a matter of being childish. I just want to sleep.'

'You can do so after.' He took the spoon and attempted to feed her. She was too weak to resist and opened her mouth. She swallowed the hot, meaty liquid and felt it warm her innards. Realising she was hungry, she let him feed her the rest.

'You are one of the most attentive and loving people I know. Thank you.'

Lan broke eye contact, spots of red on his cheeks showed his embarrassment. 'That's what a husband is supposed to do.'

Nuo entered the galley to check on them. Her gaze met Ake's. 'If you follow me, I will take you to the cabin and you can rest.'

Ake rose and Lan steadied her.

'You can go back to work, Mr Marcóir,' said Nuo.

Lan squeezed Ake's hand and left.

Ake followed Nuo out of the galley, her head bowed wearily. As they approached the stern, they passed the foremast and took the stairs to the stern castle where Alena's cabin was situated.

Nuo took out a key and unlocked an ornately decorated door. It was carved with angry unicorns rearing, their hooves lashing out at their opponents, their coats an array of colours. Dwarves were painted on the door and she recognised a faded likeness to Mandami holding hands with a dwarven woman that looked similar to Beryl.

Ake smiled. *Alena knows her birthright.* Nuo pushed open the door and flicked a switch. Light flooded the room. There were several stretcher beds with some pillows and coarse blankets.

'That one is unoccupied.' Nuo pointed to one in the corner.

'Do you know if my daughter is okay?' asked Ake.

'Yes, she and Alwin have been completing your tasks. Hurley has been feeding her. She sleeps here every night. Can I ask you an odd question?'

Ake nodded.

'Telewanake, is that a name given to you in honour of the mercy goddess that was instrumental in the battle against Drianna? Or ... forget it, that would be ridiculous.'

'It is my name. Anyone else named that would be so in my honour.'

Nuo stared at her, bewildered, before she turned and hurried through the door. Ake heard her turn the key in the lock. She lay down on the stretcher too tired to care that she was locked in.

Chapter Fifteen

Alena entered the bustling port town. The cobblestone streets were covered in filth from passing horses and drunks vomiting in the streets. The main road consisted of multiple establishments dedicated to drinking and other vices. The air was thick with the voices of merrymakers. Laughter broke her from her observations, and women of dubious occupations showed their ankles, hoping to ply their trade. A man was pushed through a set of saloon doors and stumbled; the bottle he was carrying shattered on the ground. It was early morning, but never too early to drink in Merdref.

She continued down the main street until her eyes alighted on a faded red, wooden-panelled building. A wooden sign swung above the doors that read *The Wharf*.

The building was three storeys high with grimy windows and wide, saloon style doors. Alena pushed open the doors and entered the warehouse. Clerks sat at desks nestled closely together to one side of the parlour, their quills a blur as they noted down trade goods, recorded wages paid and updated stock numbers. A black marble firepit took up the centre of the parlour and several comfortable chairs were placed in front of it. The floor was made of polished granite. The outside was deceiving and devoid of luxury, but the inside displayed it in abundance. A wooden spiral staircase towards the back of the room allowed access to the second floor.

Alena lined up to talk with one of the scribes. The man in front of her was handed a bag of coins and a sheet of paper. He turned and strode towards the entrance, a scowl on his face.

'Next.'

Alena shuffled forward and handed over some forms. The little clerk pushed his half-moon spectacles further up his nose and read the documents.

'So, you wish to buy thirty-four kegs of rum, trading half your tobacco?' asked the scribe.

'Yes, and I will pay the difference,' said Alena.

The man handed her a quill. 'Sign here and it will be delivered to your ship by dusk. Your total is one bar of gold.'

While Cirichad used coins known as credit, Velterrans traded goods and used bars of gold as currency. Alena signed the form and handed over the small gold bar. Thirty-four kegs would give her crew of twenty-five a generous stipend.

Alena thanked the scribe. She turned and ascended the wooden staircase. The second floor was a large wooden platform that overlooked the ground floor. A large bar took up most of it and was lined with stools. Small tables made from barrels graced the rest of the floor; patrons stood at them talking and enjoying some drinks. Alena approached the bar and handed a purple flower to the barkeep. He pocketed the item and nodded to one of the tables to the back. Alena turned to see a hooded figure smoking a pipe seated on one of the few chairs. She ordered a few whiskeys and walked over to the individual, a neutral look on her face. A dainty hand pointed to a seat and Alena sat, handing over the drink.

'Well met, Alena, what have you got for me today?'

'I'm here for information.'

'It will cost you in advance.' The stranger drew her hood further down over her violet eyes and held out her hand as Alena crossed it with gold. Alena took a sip of her drink and placed the glass on the coffee table in front of her. 'Well, ask away.'

'Do you know what happened to a goddess named Telewanake after the fall of Drianna?'

Alena's contact puffed on her pipe; the smoke wafted towards her patron who brushed it away.

'After the battle, Telewanake returned to her husband's school of Caelestis. For one hundred years the school thrived, until the lonely woman left, followed by her fairy child. Her husband Trebrelan had become the God of Death. The woman often adventured with her elven son Amities; they discovered hidden secrets and tried to rid the world of demonic entities and evil monsters. She preferred the name Ake and could take angel form to use divine magic.' The woman stopped and took another sip of her drink before continuing. 'I have heard of angel sightings over the last twenty years close to Cirichad. The island city was supposed to be built on the ruins of the mystic school Caelestis.' The woman held out her palm and Alena handed over another gold bar.

'Thank you.' Alena rose, her drink in her hand.

'Wait, why do you want to know all of this?'

'I like folklore.' Alena shrugged. Her eyes widened in shock. 'Why are your eyes glowing?'

'You will forget my face.'

Alena finished her drink and placed it on a table. She nodded at the woman then turned and walked away.

CHAPTER SIXTEEN

Ake heard the key in the lock and yawned. She opened her eyes as Lan entered the cabin bearing a tray. She sat up as he sat on the ground, cross-legged, the tray on his knees.

'How are you feeling?' He placed a hand on her head. She was still warm to the touch but not as bad as before.

'I'm okay.' She turned her head to cough.

Lan handed her a bowl of rice pudding drizzled with honey. She took up the spoon and ate it with gusto. Lan grinned. He broke up some bread and munched on it before handing her the other half.

'Hurley insisted on making you that sweet dessert. He thought it would encourage you to eat. He was right.'

'Am I allowed out of here now?'

Lan nodded. Ake placed the bowl back on the tray.

'Do you know where my dress is?'

'Caoimhe and Alwin washed and dried it for you. I believe one of them will be by shortly with it.'

'Are you on break?'

'No. I was allowed a few moments to check on you. I have to go now.' Lan placed the tray on the ground and stood. 'There's more of that herbal tea; I'd be happy if you drank it.' Lan smiled.

'Is your back okay?'

'It will be. I am not in any pain.' He reached down and caressed her cheek. 'Ake, there is something you should know. Het came back for Hau, apparently he never died. He has turned into some-thing cruel.'

Ake looked at him in shock and shivered. 'So, that explains Het's return.'

'Hau founded Velterra, the place we are headed to. Het needs our help.'

'I wonder what drove Hau to that path?'

'I guess we will find out.'

There was a whistling from behind them. Caoimhe entered the cabin holding Ake's dress. She handed it to her mother.

'Please leave, Father. Give Mother her privacy,' signed Caoimhe.

Lan waved goodbye and left. Ake stood up, put on her dress and sighed with relief. She had felt naked in just her shift.

'Thank you, Caoimhe.'

'I was worried about you, Mother. Hurley said you would be okay and I trust him.' Caoimhe blushed and looked away.

'Caoimhe, do you have feelings for Hurley?'

Caoimhe nodded. *'Yes, I love him. I want to hold his hand all the time.'*

'Do you know much about him?'

Caoimhe puffed out her chest with pride. *'Hurley, one hundred and fifteen, a small person like Caoimhe. He likes to cook, especially baking, and loves to rhyme. He is kind and funny. He doesn't like seafood despite the rumours that all halflings love it. I know plenty about my Hurley.'*

'Your father may have to have a chat with your Hurley then, Caoimhe. I should also get to know him more.' Ake embraced her daughter. 'I hope you are happy with him.'

Someone knocked on the door and Alena entered. She smiled at them and gestured to Caoimhe to take a seat on one of the beds. The fairy obliged. Alena knelt next to Caoimhe and handed her a bowl of cream. Caoimhe whistled with excitement and forgot herself; she fluttered into the air. Alena stood and stared into her ancestor's face; Ake stared back, wondering what Alena was thinking about Caoimhe's actions.

'I am guessing she is a fairy.'

Ake's brow furrowed. 'I hope this remains between us.'

'For now.' Alena smiled at Ake. 'So, I believe you and your husband may be my grandparents three times removed.'

'Yes, as you are a descendant of Beryl and Mandami.'

'I am their only descendant. That must remain between us also. The boy Alwin, is he a relative of mine?'

Ake nodded. 'He is the grandson of Amities, Mandami's twin. He is a cousin of yours.'

'So, the great elven explorer and engineer produced an heir. That means that boy will inherit some serious power, best we keep an eye on him,' said Alena.

'I arrived in Cirichad to train him. Evil is deepening in the world and I intend to destroy it.' Ake gave Alena a determined look.

'I don't want to ask, but I must have proof.'

Ake sighed. 'What kind of proof?'

'Show me your Anwyn form. And why does your husband have human ears?'

'The god's hated the genocide of the elves. When Amities died, he was the last elf and the gods refused new elven souls' entry into this world. When Lan returned, they made him appear almost human. Amities once told me if Lan returned, the gods would enact a pact to eventually remove all magic from the world, sick of its misuse. My powers are dwindling and Lan's may never fully return. If you intend to use our powers for evil you best look elsewhere.' Ake stared Alena down.

Alena glowered. 'I left Velterra, sick of the way people were mistreated. I give you my word, I will not betray you.'

Ake took in a sharp breath of air. She recognised that look. Alena was very much like Mandami. Alena was charismatic, just, disciplined and commanding. 'Do your actions portray that, Alena?'

'I believe they do.' Alena frowned.

'Why did Beryl never tell Mandami about his daughter Jasper?' asked Ake.

'Borrush was afraid Drianna would come after the child if you and Mandami failed to defeat her. Borrush wanted Beryl to marry a powerful dwarven noble so she would be protected. But Beryl refused. Borrush believed the romance had only just begun, but unbeknown to him, Beryl was eight months pregnant, not just a few.'

'They fled Rock Fell determined to keep the baby safe from Drianna's minions. Borrush asked his king to keep his where-abouts from you. He hoped the baby would be safe, and after Drianna's defeat he would reach out to Mandami. Beryl gave birth in Regis and they raised the child there for a few years.

'They appeared to be safe, so Borrush reached out to Orilan with information on Drianna's whereabouts. For their efforts, father and daughter were murdered by Drianna's minions' days before the evil goddess was defeated. The child fled to an orphan-age in the city where Mandami eventually adopted her as his heir. Beryl never got to tell him about their child,' explained Alena.

Ake began to weep. 'Poor Borrush and Beryl. My gallant Mandami, why didn't you fight for Beryl?'

Alena gave Ake a sad smile. 'In all my reading and talking to storytellers, it was revealed Borrush blackmailed Mandami for Beryl's safety. Borrush would refuse to help you and Lan if Mandami ever tried to contact Beryl.'

Oh Borrush, you were a good man but it seems, like most druids, you manipulated others when you saw fit.

'Who are your parents?' asked Ake.

Alena smiled. 'As you probably know, Mandami created a religion in your honour and denounced his former stepfather. Some of the Regians revolted and had him tied on a wooden circle covered in thorns and slaughtered him.'

Ake sighed. 'I barely visited Regis. I heard talk of a religion Mandami started, but had little interest in religion after my own damned prophecy took my husband.' She scowled. 'I didn't know how my child really died. Amities lied to me, telling me he passed away peacefully. I visited his grave once.'

Alena patted her great-grandmother's shoulder. 'His daughter ruled for a few decades until her anger and resentment lead to a war against Eriu and Breteyne. The war left mass casualties on either side. Several Regians loyal to Mandami murdered Jasper in revenge and the city of Regis fell and along with it the Regian empire.

'After the death of Jasper, her elven lover fled with their baby, Devala, to the newly created country of Velterra. The child grew slowly due to her elven blood and had a child late in life to a human mage named Blaze, my father. My mother died in childbirth and I grew up on the fringes of Velterran society.'

Ake glanced around; piles of books were placed sporadically.

'I see you love to read like me. You are like Mandami, you know.'

Alena smiled. 'I hope they are good traits.'

'The very best.'

Ake closed her eyes and there was a gentle breeze as her golden wings formed. She opened her eyes and they blazed with golden light. Alena stared at Ake; her mouth hung in surprise. Ake retracted the power and returned to her normal form.

'I hope that removes any doubt.'

Alena composed herself and cleared her throat. 'Well, yes. I suppose I best call you Luma. You won't be allowed to do the laundry anymore. Can't have a goddess and my ancestor reduced to that level.'

'I am no better than anyone on this ship. I will continue my errands, but I request hampers for the clothes as it is deplorable below. I need some of your crew to scrub the floors and we need better lighting.'

Alena smiled. 'I can do that for my Luma. Any other requests?'

'Yes, Lan requires fresh fruit and vegetables. Elves can't exist on meat and bread. He may not have all the trappings of an elf anymore, but his ways are theirs. He will also get frustrated if he is at sea for too long, his feet need to touch the earth.'

'Well, we can't have my Lufar withering away. I will see what I can do. I can't give him shore leave this time though; it will upset the others. What other skills do you two have?' asked Alena.

'Lan is an unarmed combat master and healer. I have some mage spells left, and my Anwyn allows me to draw on divine energies, but it isn't as strong as before.'

'Well, I am honoured to meet you, Luma. The battle against Drianna must have been remarkable. You are a very strong woman to overcome Cephas's evil treatment. I have always admired the stories. It was romantic how Lufar defeated Cephas in your honour.' Alena gave her a fleeting smile.

Ake blushed. 'Yes, Lan is a good man. I will have to get used to being called grandmother. How will you explain Lan's and my youthful looks?' asked Ake.

'Velterrans live one hundred and fifty years and maintain their youth into their late seventies. They are longer-lived than Cirites and humans.'

'I know that but we are much older.'

'Everyday people don't though.'

'So, I'm assuming the Velterrans' slower ageing has something to do with Hau.'

'It's kind of unnerving to explain, considering your fidelity to your husband over the centuries. Lord Hau is the opposite.'

Ake shrugged. 'Tell me.'

'It is said Lord Hau believed you and Lan never mourned him or came back for his body. Drianna fuelled that hate. He grew strong in the magical arts and found an island inhabited by monsters. Using human slaves, he built a large keep. After the fall of Relequis and Caley, he put out a call to the last remaining elves and half-elves. They came and he chose the most powerful and intelligent females and filled the palace with his harem. The city of Velterra grew up around him, kept in check by his children and grandchildren, indoctrinated in his hate. As his hate grew, it overwhelmed him and he became an abomination and retired from public view, ruling behind the scenes,' explained Alena.

'That is so sad. Hau was always a timid and kind boy.' Ake's eyes brimmed with tears. 'I wish I had looked in on the emerging civilisation, but in the early days heralds proclaimed its benevolence.'

Alena awkwardly embraced her then released her. 'In the early days Hau *was* benevolent.'

'I think fresh air will do you some good. Take a walk on deck.'

Ake smiled and left the cabin.

CHAPTER SEVENTEEN

Het grinned as he hoisted four barrels across his shoulders. A crewman mumbled, 'Bloody large man, maybe he should do it on his own.'

'Stop complaining, Argarrio, and get on with it. Captain wants these kegs put in the cargo hold.'

Het began to whistle as he pondered Ake's recent conversation with him and Lan, relaying all Alena had said. *So, Hau had tried to rebuild his elven kingdom and turned into an abomination in the process.*

The great city of the mage elves had been ruled by an empress and supported by a druid council. While mage elves married, monogamy was of little importance to most of them as the use of high magic often left them struggling to conceive. Elder Flower, the last empress, had sought a lover outside of Relequis, and Het had sired their sons.

When Cephas had killed his people, Hau was the last heir. *Hau would have had fond memories of his people. I understand Hau's need to recreate the legendary city. What I don't comprehend is Hau's hatred of Ake and Lan, it is misplaced. I hope I can reach my son.*

Het placed the last barrel in the hold when Alwin descended the stairs and hurried over to him.

'Het, we are to go ashore with the first mate and collect some last-minute items.'

Het wiped the sweat from his brow. 'Okay, Alwin.'

The men turned and left the hold. They reached the main deck where Nuo awaited them.

'Come with me.' Nuo strode towards the gangplank. Alwin and Het rushed after her.

The woman trailed them, hidden in the shadows. The crescent moon peeked out from behind grey clouds. She wrapped her cloak tighter and scurried after her quarry. Her violet eyes darted back and forth, watching their every move. The boy didn't look like much of a threat, but the large man with the long sword strapped across his back could be a formidable foe.

Her master had sent her instructions. Lord Hau wanted the crew dead and the Lord of Caelestis and his bride recovered. Her eyes filled with hate. *I can't wait to see them sacrificed in public to appease my lord.*

Hartur watched them, hidden amongst the shadow as her marks entered a fresh produce shop that sold herbs, fish and an array of fruit and vegetables. She waited for a few minutes before entering the building and pretending to peruse the goods. The woman in the golden robe paid for some purchases and handed the packages to her two companions. The big man purchased some wood, a carving tool and a good length of leather cord. A blond-headed youth tilted his head and stared at her. She averted her eyes and walked down another aisle. The boy had pointed ears, something she hadn't seen in years. Curious, she snuck closer to him.

I could kill him right now, but that might cause a scene. She reached out and brushed the tip of his ear. The boy jumped and looked around. Hartur receded into the shadows.

The Velterran came from a long line of assassins in service to Lord Hau. She was descended from the lord's favourite bride Atius, a half-elven woman who had survived the attack on the forest elves of Caley. Ten generations had passed since then, but her hate for the lord and lady of Caelestis was strong.

Her targets exited the shop and headed back towards their ship. The boy with elvish ancestry whispered to the big man who turned and stared behind them. Hartur ducked into an alleyway. The woman in the golden robes stopped at a florist and ordered the boy to keep watch. The big man followed the woman inside.

The boy looked around nervously. An elvish bow was strapped across his back and she scowled. *What right does a human of Cirichad have to wield a Velterran bow?* All things elvish belong to those of elvish blood and that meant the Velterrans, the last stronghold of elven legacy. As she slid out of the shadows she snuck up behind him and felt for a string and found none. *How peculiar.* She lifted the bow and slunk back into the shadows.

—◦◦◦—

Alwin shivered, there was a rush of cold air and he suddenly felt defenceless. His hand reached for his bow, but he couldn't feel it, his breath quickened, panic setting in as his ears filled with a low-pitched humming. He tilted his head, following the noise down an alleyway. He knew he shouldn't leave his post, but he needed his bow back. It was an extraordinary weapon, but it also held great sentimental value.

His ears picked up footsteps and a regular heartbeat. He had never told anyone, but he could hear extraordinarily well, from the soft beat of a swallow's wing to the thunder in the sky before anyone else heard it. Tears brimmed in his eyes and trailed down his long eyelashes. *I am sorry, Grandfather. I will be brave and get it back.* He couldn't see the thief, but he heard her feet move.

The bow hummed loudly and sparked a bright emerald green. Alwin took a chance and jumped on to the figure, causing them both to crash to the ground. He hit the thief in the arm and she released his weapon. She turned her violet eyes towards him; they glowed with anger. Alwin stared at her, lost in the bewitching pools. He didn't see her withdraw a dagger from her boot.

The woman yelped and dropped the knife. Alwin turned to see Nuo glaring at them, another hairpin in her hand ready to throw at the violet-eyed thief. Nuo's hair cascaded down behind her back as it fell from its fastenings. Alwin turned to talk to the thief, but she had disappeared.

'Get up, Mr Smith, we must leave. This does not bode well,' said Nuo.

Alwin picked up his bow and followed Nuo out of the alley-way. They met up with Het and headed back to the ship.

CHAPTER EIGHTEEN

I must have them. The abomination sat upon a wooden throne in his cavernous den. The throne was decorated with graphic scenes of elves slaughtering humans, while other humans knelt at their feet begging for their lives. He stood up and began to pace, finishing at a large porcelain stand with a silver bowl set into it.

'Bring me a slave,' he yelled.

A servant scrambled up from the ground where he had been kneeling with his forehead to the floor, and scurried away. The abomination felt his pointed ears twitch and pulled a large white worm from inside his ear and squeezed it. The worm popped and its innards oozed down his hands. *The deterioration is happening more frequently.* He knew his hazel eyes were void of emotion. When he bathed, his skin cracked and peeled, showing the necrotic tissue underneath. His once luscious chestnut hair was bedraggled and falling out in clumps when he tidied it with a comb. He ran his serpent tongue over his serrated teeth and attempted to smile; a servant nearby covered their mouth, their eyes wide with fear.

'Do you not like my smiles?'

The servant supplicated. 'They are beautiful, my Lord Hau.'

'Liar.' He kicked the servant away from him and continued on his stroll.

Her divine blood will renew the magic of Velterra. Hopefully, my cousin will understand why I did what I needed to and will choose to help me rule. We will create an empire and extinguish the humans, a blight on this world. In the days of Relequis, the elves often married their cousins to continue the royal bloodline. He had no such intentions, but having Ake rule by his side would show his people he upheld the ancient ways, and with a goddess supporting him he couldn't lose.

The only problem is that despicable husband of hers. He has abandoned her on many occasions, citing it was for her own protection or against his will. He intended to devour Lan's elvish soul, making his own half-elven soul complete.

—⁓—

Ake cried out in her sleep and began to sob and thrash about. The vision that had haunted her since her childhood began to take control of her mind and she was powerless to do anything except relive it.

As the sun rose, the north wind caressed a great oak tree's leaves and water shimmered on a lake in a forbidden valley. An old man put flint to stone and prepared his morning meal of tubers and summer berries. His grandchildren splashed in the lake, absorbed in their youthful innocence.

Tears streamed down the elderly man's wizened face as he listened for the screams bound to come. He whiffed the air for the taint of blood and body excretions where the slaves were being beaten into submission. His eyes had been blinded and were little more than white pupils marked with small scars.

'Get up, old man,' someone hollered and pulled him to his feet. 'It is your time.'

The man was dragged before a large porcelain stand with a silver bowl set into it. A man in blood red robes lifted a serrated dagger; he turned his soulless eyes to Ake.

'Come home, cousin. Let's honour our fallen family and rebuild their legacy.'

The abomination brought the dagger down upon the man's ...

Ake screamed and the fever raged through her body. When Nuo had returned she had spoken to Alena and they had ordered the ship's departure. It was the middle of the night and Lan had been called to tend his wife. The doctor had wanted to apply leeches or bleed her, but he had asked her to leave. Nuo had handed him a mortar and pestle and a selection of fresh herbs. Caoimhe had been bringing him buckets of hot and cold water. He applied another compress to her head and had removed her clothes. He had forced her to drink his herbal brews, but she couldn't keep anything down.

She cried out again. 'How could you kill him?'

Lan was horrified as her voice changed. She hissed and spoke in a crackly man's voice. 'I need his blood to be able to contact you.'

'Ake, you need to fight it.' Lan spoke in her mind.

'So, you have returned. Took you long enough, great uncle,' hissed the abomination.

While Ake and Lan were not directly related by blood the manipulation by the elven royal family and their druids had resulted in Lan and Ake sharing some relatives. The elves had hoped to produce a legacy of power to aid the couple. This practice had revolted Ake and Lan, and they had refused to be manipulated by the elves and druids.

Ake arched her back and her eyes opened and rolled back in her head.

Lan lost his composure and yelled, 'What good will killing her do?'

'I don't intend to kill her. You will see,' said the abomination.

Ake cried out and began to shiver. He felt her head; it was ice cold. He grabbed some blankets before stripping off and laying down with her. He drew her into his arms and threw the blankets on them. Ake's teeth chattered and she shook as the chills overtook her body.

'Come on, my darling, please fight it,' he whispered in her ear.

She snarled and bit his hand. He stared at it in shock. She turned, wrapping her hands around his neck. He grabbed her hands in his and she tried to kick him.

'All men take what they want and then leave,' she screamed.

Ake opened her eyes, one pupil was gold, the other red. The abomination continued to talk through her. 'I will take from her what makes her special. She will be lost until she seeks me out.'

Ake howled and the awful sound made Lan flinch. Alena and Nuo charged into the room. They took in the scene. Ake turned her strange eyes to them and hissed with a serpent like tongue. Alena and Nuo recoiled. Ake closed her eyes and relaxed. Lan released her and felt her skin; her temperature was normal.

'What was that?' asked Alena.

'I'll explain later,' said Nuo.

Alena turned and stared at her lover. 'What is it, Nuo?'

Lan sighed. 'I'm sorry, Captain, I don't mean to be disrespectful, but I think we need to concentrate on Ake.'

'Of course, I am sorry, Lufar,' said Alena.

'So, you know,' said Lan.

'Luma just proved what I already suspected.'

Lan nodded. 'That title will take some getting used to. Is it alright if we have some space?'

'We will sleep on deck tonight. Rest well, Lufar.' Alena smiled and gestured to Nuo and they left the room.

Lan rose and covered Ake in the blankets. She whimpered and turned her eyes to him. They were still the same odd colour. She glared at him and he backed off.

'Where's Het? Why are you here, shouldn't you be searching for Orilan?' she whispered.

He has taken her memories of us. Lan's eyes filled with tears. *I have lost her again.*

Ake stared at him confused. 'Why are you naked in my room, Lan?' Ake looked beneath the covers and he saw fear gather in her eyes.

'Ake, it's okay.' *I need to think fast.* 'You were sick and cold and I needed to warm you.'

Ake stared at him. 'Then why do I have a memory of something more?' She glared at him. 'You kissed me, jealous that Het had done so.' Ake began to sob and her anguish chilled Lan to the bone. 'Are we supposed to be in love? No, that can't be it. You are too old for me, Lan. I know I have to marry soon, maybe you can find me a lowly lord. But for now, please leave.' Ake turned her tear-stained eyes away from him. 'I hope I haven't been soiled.'

Lan turned away and clenched his fists. 'No, nothing like that. I will leave now.'

Lan left the cabin as he heard Ake sob. The cold air hit him like a slap in the face and he turned to see Het and Caoimhe keeping watch nearby.

Het rushed over and embraced him, and Lan's desperate cries could be heard all over the ship.

CHAPTER NINETEEN

I wonder why Het and Lan decided to take me on a ship. Are they taking me to be married? It was morning and Ake stood on the stern castle looking out over the edge. *I will have to ask them.* She had insisted on wearing a simple robe and refused to wear the fancy dress they said she owned. The small girl, Caoimhe, had brought it to her after they had found one in the infirmary used for patients. The child had looked at her sadly before running from the room.

Het climbed the stairs to the stern castle. She grinned at him. He had told her a druid spell had gone awry, making him appear older, and would eventually resolve itself.

She giggled. 'Old man Het. You don't look so bad for an ancient guy.'

Het gave her a sad smile. 'Good morning, Ake. What do you remember of last night?'

'I had that horrid dream again. I've told Flo about it before, but she assured me they are just nightmares. Where is she by the way?' Ake turned and saw Lan pacing at the bottom of the stairs. He looked up at her, his eyes filled with anger. Ake turned her eyes back to Het. 'Am I being married off because I did something with him? He has a reputation to keep, I suppose.'

'No, Ake. We decided to do a bit of travelling, that is all.' Het grinned and glanced at Lan. 'You got eels in your pants, mate?'

Lan smirked. 'There's nothing wrong with the eel in my pants.'

Ake bit back her smile. 'I couldn't be with him, you know. He's too moody and really not in touch with his emotions.'

Lan looked up her comment and his eyes filled with despair.

'Let's change the subject, Ake.'

'What should we do today, Het? I bet we can prank some of these sailors. That could be fun.' She hugged him.

Ake saw the captain approach Lan.

'You should get some rest,' said Alena.

Lan's shoulders slumped dejectedly and he turned and walked away. Ake blew a raspberry to his retreating back.

'Ake, that's not very nice,' reprimanded Het.

'You are acting like an old man, Het.'

'Let's go get some breakfast.'

'Okay.' She grabbed his hand.

Het released her hand. 'No, Ake, we cannot do that.'

'Why?'

'Ship rules.'

Ake followed Het to the galley and they sat down and ate some stodgy porridge.

'I have to go now, Ake, I have some work to do. Lan will come by later and check on you. You know he is a healer and you have been sick.' Het stood up.

'What am I supposed to do? I'll get bored,' said Ake.

Hurley rushed over. 'Miss Ake, you can help me if you like. I'm Hurley.' The halfling extended his hand to Ake and she shook it.

Het gave him a grateful smile and left the galley.

Ake spent the rest of the morning washing dishes, chopping vegetables and delivering meals. It kept her busy and she had little time to worry about what had happened the night before.

It was noon when Lan was supposed to meet her. She waited at the bow of the ship with Hurley. As Lan approached, Hurley smiled kindly at her and took off.

'How was your day?'

'Hurley is nice. I nicked myself chopping vegetables. I'm not very good in the kitchen.'

'True.'

Ake's brows knitted in puzzlement. 'How would you know? You have been gone for years.'

'Correct,' Lan replied, his face was devoid of emotion.

'Did you find Orilan?'

'Sort of.'

'This is typical of you, Lan. Always ignoring me or offering little information. Why have you taken me on holiday the day after I graduated? Is it because I suggested you find me someone to marry?' asked Ake.

Lan sighed. *So, she has reverted back to the age of nineteen. The night I returned to Caelestis after years away. I must assume she has forgotten I professed my love to her that evening as well.* Lan gave her a reassuring smile. 'No, it kind of just happened.'

'Where is Dane and Flo?' Ake hugged herself, her eyes darting around.

I can't stand this. I don't know what to do. Lan sighed. 'Dane had druid matters to attend to and Flo had elven matters to see to.'

'You're lying to me.'

'Do you want to take a walk with me, Ake?' Lan gave her a charming smile.

'No, Lan. I think Het would get jealous, he loves me, you know.' Ake blushed.

I will try to use some honesty. 'No, I don't think so, Ake. Het likes Flo. It's more realistic that we love each other after I kissed you and you responded with equal ardour. You are my wife, Ake.' Lan gave her a gentle smile.

Ake stared at him. 'I don't love you, Lan. That was a mistake, this ends now.'

'Sorry. It's true.'

'Did I lay with you?' Ake looked revolted.

Lan grinned 'Wow, am I really that awful?'

'Ship sighted off the starboard,' cried out someone from the crow's nest.

Ake and Lan watched as the crew scrambled to their positions. Lan grabbed Ake's hand and led her over to a man with a strange weapon. Ake's gaze fell to the unusual weapon on Lan's belt. It appeared she had no memory of pistols and rifles.

'Unfriendly,' said the person in the crow's nest.

'Ready the starboard cannons. Marksmen, take your positions,' cried Alena.

Lan loaded his weapon along with the rifleman. There was a loud explosion as a cannon was fired on them. Saltwater splashed them as the projectile landed in the water a short distance from the *Carnay*.

Members of the crew began preparing the two starboard cannons to fire. The cabin boys also acted as powder monkeys, delivering canisters of premeasured gunpowder from below deck to the gunners. The demi-cannons had a barrel length of three point four metres. They weren't the heaviest cannons recommended for their ship size, but it was all Alena could afford.

Het and another gunner took the eighteen pound flannel canisters and pushed them into the barrel of each cannon. Gideon opened a small vent on the back of each cannon and pierced each cartridge with a thin piece of wire.

'Home,' he yelled. Gideon looked at his men. 'Shot your guns.'

Het and another large man hauled each cannon up against the bulwark, grunting with the effort. Another set of men turned each cannon towards the enemy ship using the guide ropes.

Gideon took sight and raised his hand taking the trigger line in one hand as Het did for the cannon he had helped load.

'Fire,' yelled Gideon.

There was a huge puff of sulphurous smoke and several flames flared. Ake covered her ears as a large explosion followed simultaneously by another.

'Missed,' yelled the lad in the crow's nest.

'Reload,' said Gideon.

Het and the other gunners began to repeat the process.

Explosions flared as the other ship fired. A projectile hit the sail on the mizzen-mast. It snapped one of the ropes supporting the mast and the heavy rope swung towards Alena who was at the helm. Alena rolled out of the way. The projectile landed on the bow of the ship and broke a chunk of the ship before it plummeted into the sea.

The cannons of the *Carnay* fired again and the crew cheered as the projectile hit the upper deck of the large enemy ship. It crashed into the decking and lifted some of the planks. Several of the enemy leapt out of the way, but some were crushed under the planks as they were cast into the air and landed on the enemy crew.

The enemy ship turned portside and a sudden wind increased its speed. Its figurehead was a large shaft of bolstered metal designed to ram a ship and splinter it, leaving it to sink.

'Brace for impact,' yelled Alena.

'Lie down, Ake.' Lan pulled her down on the timbers; she struggled.

'This is life and death, sweetheart.'

'I'm not your sweetheart.' Ake glared at him defiantly.

There was a huge crash as the enemy ship collided with the *Carnay*. Lan pushed Ake down onto her stomach and lay on top of her. Debris went flying past. A large piece of wood hit Lan in the back and he grunted. *Great, another injury there.*

'Prepare to be boarded,' yelled Alena.

The enemy crewmen used grappling hooks to clamber from their ship on to the *Carnay*. Lan stood up and offered Ake a hand up; she refused to take it and got to her feet.

'I am fine,' she muttered.

Alwin began to fire his bow as waves of the enemy ran towards them; they were armed with cutlasses and pistols. Alwin's bow hummed with power. And he took down enemies as they neared Het. Het grinned and unstrapped his sword. The sword glowed and burst into flame. Het swung the sword and it arced down, slicing through several enemies and setting more on fire. Men screamed in pain.

Alena left the helm and took off the staff she wore braced on her back. Enemies charged her. She was highly skilled with the staff, and it became a blur as she countered blows and delivered hits using a combination of jabs, blocks, sweeps and strikes.

Lan aimed his gun and fired. The man in front of him stumbled back, looking at him in shock, his hands moved to his abdomen as a huge hole appeared in it. The man stared at his hand covered in blood and fell.

Ake turned and ran towards Het; she shivered, her eyes wide with fear. Lan swore and quickly reloaded his gun. He fired as a man grabbed Ake and tried to slash her with his sword. The man fell forward at Ake's feet, a large whole began to appear on his back, blood poured out. Ake whimpered and clung to Het's back.

'Go back to Lan. He will protect you,' said Het.

Het pushed her away gently and took down three more enemies. Ake looked up at Het, her expression was one of utter betrayal. Het gave her a look of reproach and she turned and ran from him.

Lan caught her in his arms and Ake struggled briefly before giving in. As quickly as the battle had begun it ended. The enemy crew retreated to their ship. The *Carnay* shuddered as the other ship unfurled all their sails and drew apart. The enemy ship's sails billowed as they caught favourable winds and fled. Everyone took a moment to breathe and then began to survey the damage.

Alena glanced at the prow. 'That will cost a lot to fix. The sails on the mizzen-mast can easily be replaced with the spare in the hold.' She sighed. 'We have lost the good doctor and chef.' Her gaze snapped to Lan's. 'You will take over the doctor duties for now.' She strolled over to Hurley. 'And you, young man, are promoted to cook.'

'Yes, Captain.' Hurley smiled.

'Nuo, get the ship up to full pace in an alternate direction. Let's put some distance between us and the enemy ship.'

Ake pushed Lan away and he took a step back.

'You heard the captain. Go find Hurley,' ordered Lan.

Ake nodded wearily and turned and headed to the galley. Ake stuck her tongue out at Het as she walked past, and he patted her on the head. Ake slapped his hand away, stuck her nose in the air and rushed past him.

Alena hoisted up a body as she and the crew tossed the enemy corpses to the deep. She removed the personal belongings of the crewmembers who had died. 'We honour the fallen and we will return their belongings to their loved ones.' Alena stared out to sea as her crew that was left bowed their heads in respect.

CHAPTER TWENTY

Caoimhe sat weeping in the hold. *My dear mother doesn't know me.* Several crewmen descended the stairs with Nuo and grabbed the spare sail. Nuo turned and saw the despondent fairy. She began to sign to Caoimhe. The fairy grinned at her through her tears.

'All will be well, Caoimhe, when we reach Velterra. Until then you cannot call Ake Mother, it will distress her,' said Nuo.

Caoimhe nodded and signed back. *'Where did you learn hand talking?'*

'It is of no consequence. You have done a great job. I am proud of you.'

Nuo looked around the hold; all the washing had been finished and stood in folded piles ready to be collected. Nuo knew Alwin had helped a little, but the little fairy had done a lot of it on her own. Nuo whistled and two cabin boys approached.

'Take the washing up and hand it out to the crew. They are labelled,' she ordered.

The cabin boys began scurrying about.

Nuo turned and patted Caoimhe on the hand. *'Will you be okay down here?'*

'I will stay here a bit. All those explosions were scary. But Hurley has promised me honey cakes for dinner so I will go up then.'

Nuo removed a small knife from beneath her robes and handed it to Caoimhe, handle first. *'For the rats.'*

'I can just fly away.'

'They can climb and you may need it at other times.'

Nuo picked up some tools and strode up the stairwell. Caoimhe sat admiring the blade. It had a wooden handle and the blade was made of sharpened crystal. *She knows iron hurts fairies.* The fairy shivered and looked around. She had felt a warm breeze brush past her ear as if someone had breathed in it.

———

Hartur was pleased. The pirate ship she had hired to attack the *Carnay* had been a great distraction and had allowed her to slip aboard. She watched as the golden-robed woman handed a small girl a knife. As the woman left, Hartur slipped past the child. Concealed in the shadows, she reached the other section of the hold. She would slowly pick off the crewmembers. She had no need to kill a child. When everyone else was dead, and the lord and lady of Caelestis were captured, the child would perish, left aboard the ship as it drifted on the open sea.

Hartur heard footsteps on the stairwell and a small boy with a mass of brown ringlets and hairy feet skipped down the steps. He whistled at the girl and she whistled back; they seemed to be having some kind of conversation. *Interesting.*

The boy hugged the girl and she looked up at him with total adoration.

———

Hurley saw a movement out the corner of his eye. He stared at the spot for a few moments. *I wonder if someone is there.* He shrugged and turned back to Caoimhe. She looked up at him, her eyes filled with devotion.

Hurley's heart beat faster and he smiled. He dipped his head and kissed her gently. Caoimhe blushed. Hurley released her and turned sharply; he saw a large pair of violet eyes. He stared into their deep hypnotic pools. The expression held him and he closed his eyes. Caoimhe squeezed his hand. Hurley opened his eyes and he tried to remember something he had just seen, something he should tell the captain. He shivered and turned back to Caoimhe. The fairy released his hand, smiled and ran up the stairs.

—∾—

Ake poked Het in the back as he sat talking with Lan. Het rolled his eyes, grinned and playfully shoved Ake away with one of his large hands. Lan watched Ake yawn with boredom and wander over to the bulwark, staring off into the distance. He saw Caoimhe run towards her and smile and put a hand to her mouth.

In her excitement, Caoimhe hugged Ake from behind. Ake turned and gave her an amused smile.

'Mother, I had my first kiss, are you happy for me?' signed Caoimhe.

Ake stared at Caoimhe's hand gestures in confusion. 'I am sorry, little girl, I don't understand.'

Caoimhe began to sob and she turned and stared at her father, her eyes full of grief. Hurley followed and translated as Caoimhe whistled her despair. 'I want Mother back.'

Ake looked at Lan in astonishment and she stumbled back against the bulwark. Lan swore and stood, approaching her cautiously. Hurley realised what was happening and dragged Caoimhe away. Het rose and waited, ready to intervene if necessary.

'It's okay, Ake,' said Lan.

'How old is that girl, Lan?' Ake's eyes filled with anger.

'How old do you think she is?' He reached out and grabbed her hand.

'If I went by her height, under five. But I can't be sure, her face is young, yet at the same time it is misleading. Am I her mother?' Ake lay a hand across her abdomen and felt the scar.

'How long have we been married and what did you do to me?' Ake continued to back away from him.

'Long enough, sweetheart. You seem to have forgotten some things.'

Ake stared at him and shivered.

'You are not nineteen and our children were born much later.' He kissed her hand.

'Children, we have more than one? Get your disgusting hands off me.'

His eyes filled with tears and he let go of her hand. 'So be it.' Lan turned away from her and walked to the other side of the deck. *I will have to leave her alone until I figure out how to help her. I seem to be making it worse.*

Ake turned and glared at Het. 'Have I borne his children? If not, who is the father of that girl?'

Het smiled. 'You have always felt bad for the stragglers. But it didn't come about the way you think it did.'

'Did I adopt her?'

'It is whatever you understand it to be for now.'

The dinner bell rang and Ake fled. She had to deliver the evening meals. She gave Lan a look of pure hatred as she ran towards the galley.

Het turned to look at Lan. 'You can't push this, Lan. I am at a loss too. I think you should avoid her for now.'

'Perfect. Separated again. Well, at least this time she isn't bothered by it.' Lan's shoulders drooped and he sighed. 'Okay, I will avoid her and keep my mouth shut.'

Het patted Lan on the back. 'I am sure it will be okay.'

'You don't know that.'

CHAPTER TWENTY-ONE

Nuo blew on the tea, the mug cupped between her hands, and smiled at Alena, who turned to stare at Alwin as he entered the galley and placed a bowl on the butcher's block. The boy approached them with a staff and in one hand, bowed and held the weapon out to the captain.

'This sacred weapon, forged by Amities of Eriu, will help you when you need it most. May his wisdom guide you.'

Alena's eyes widened; she reached out and touched the weapon which sparked blue.

'It is done.' Alwin turned and left the galley.

Alena stroked the gnarled surface of the staff. *It is calling to me.* The staff whispered ancient words, but she could not make them out. Pain filled her body. Starting from where her fingers connected with the timber, a burning sensation surged down her arm. The staff was carved from a single golden branch of elven oak. Various ancient knots were engraved along its surface, representing protection and honour. The pain became intense and she dropped the weapon. It clattered to the floor and she suddenly felt the overwhelming need to pick it up and never take her eyes off it again.

Standing, she retrieved the weapon and replaced her old staff, which was strapped to her back, with the new one; pain was now absent when she handled the weapon.

Nuo smiled at her. 'So, it begins; the heirs of Caelestis are awakening.'

Alena gave her a quizzical look. 'What do you mean by that?'

Nuo was about to answer when Ake entered the galley. She didn't seem to notice the pair as she placed the dirty bowls down on the butcher's block. They watched as she took out a large wooden basin and slammed it down on the bench. Ake scowled at it and turned a small brass tap on the side of the pot belly stove and filled up a bucket with boiling water. She dumped it into the basin and added cold water from a barrel nearby. Then she grabbed a canister from a shelf and poured in some soap flakes. Taking up a scrubbing brush, she began to scrub the bowls with intensity, mumbling to herself all the while.

'How dare he marry me without my knowledge. And we have a child.' Ake counted on her hands briefly. 'Nineteen plus four and add nine months is nearly twenty-four. He is right, I can't be nineteen. I am not stupid, that wound on my stomach is right where a baby grows; I have read many books on it.'

Alena approached her. 'Hello, Miss Ake. Did someone upset you?'

Ake looked up and frowned. 'I'm sorry you had to hear that. I just found out I am a mother.' She began to sob. 'And I don't remember her conception.'

'Nuo, go get Mr Falcon.' Alena leant forward and rubbed Ake's back.

Nuo came back with Het, then left.

'Mr Falcon, you are relieved of your duties for now. You need to stay with her. Her husband is not allowed near her for the time being,' said Alena.

'Captain, don't you think that is a little cruel on him?' asked Het.

Ake shuddered. 'So, he is my husband.'

'I will alter our course and we will make land in two days. There is a Cirite monastery on an island, dedicated to spiritual healing. Maybe they can help her,' said Alena.

Ake refilled the bucket of hot water. She yelped as the water scolded her hand. She turned the tap off and plunged her hand into the cold water barrel. Het took a seat and watched her.

Ake scowled at him. 'You have changed, Het. You used to be so attentive towards me.'

Het gave her a sad smile. 'Those days are gone, Ake.'

'But I have overwhelming feelings for someone. It has to be you,' said Ake.

Het laughed. 'I never thought I would see the day where you professed feelings for me. I had dreamt of it in the past, but now it just seems so odd.'

Ake came over and pulled a face at him. He pulled one back. Alena smiled; as she left the galley she heard them chatting.

'Let's pull a prank for old times' sake,' said Het.

'Okay.' Ake giggled.

Chapter Twenty-Two

Lan lay on his bedroll looking up at the starry night sky. Several men were drinking their stipends of rum and gambling. Some rolled dice and others played cards. A man took out a tin whistle and began to play a folk song. Everyone except Lan joined in. He turned his head as he heard Alwin join the song, his usual monotonous tone had disappeared and his voice was clear and expressive. *Must be a tune from Cirichad.*

I see that look,
That secret smile.
Stay with me a while.

The ancient rhythm sets the scene.
I hope you know what you mean to me.
I take your hand and turn away,
I hear you follow as I lead the way.

I lift you up and you
Express your joy.
My heart melts at the sound.

We were alone in the crowded room,
A contented bride and groom.
The years did flee

And you stood alone
and lamented me.

The song finished and a few men sniffled and drowned their sorrows, remembering lost lovers, spouses and children left at home. Lan saw Caoimhe giggling with Hurley. The halfling had one arm around her shoulder. Lan stood up and strolled over to them.

'Hello you two. Would you take a walk with me, Hurley?'

Hurley shyly removed his arm from around Caoimhe as she gave her father a worried look.

'It's okay, Caoimhe,' said Lan.

Caoimhe nodded. Hurley gave her a reassuring smile and trailed after Lan. When they had put some distance between themselves and Caoimhe, Lan turned to Hurley.

'What are your intentions for my daughter?'

Hurley grinned. 'Marriage.'

'Do you love her?'

'Keenly.'

'Then that is acceptable. May your marriage be blessed like mine was.'

Lan sighed and walked away. Preoccupied by his thoughts, he didn't see the pile of grease someone had applied to the deck. He lost his footing and stumbled, colliding with the man behind him. Lan managed to keep his footing, but his fellow crewman did not. Looking around at the sound of sniggering, his eyes found Het and Ake crouched down behind the mast. The crewman grumbled as he got up and steadied himself, and shook his fist at the pranksters.

'Children.' Lan stuck his tongue out at them. Something he would never normally do.

Ake giggled and threw her shoe at him. Lan caught it and his eyes filled with mischief. He ran off to the side of Het.

'Hey, give it back,' yelled Ake. She gave chase. 'Come on, Het!'

'I'll let you deal with this one, Ake,' said Het. 'Can't let Alena see this.' Het began to clean up the grease with the rags he had borrowed. He ran out and looked around for another. He glanced up, Alena winked and handed him another rag before striding away.

'Didn't expect that.' Het smiled.

Lan laughed and ran past Alena on his way to the galley as Ake grumbled and chased him. He reached the galley first and pushed open the doors, scrambling behind the butcher's block, looking for anything to fill the shoe with. His hands found the scrap bucket and he searched for an implement. The sound of footsteps approached the door and he shrugged.

He took a handful of the stodgy porridge and crammed it into the shoe. Lan grabbed a tray and placed the shoe on it with a single flower. *This is so ridiculous, but enjoyable.*

Ake entered the darkened galley and tried to conjure a flame but failed. While she was concentrating on her task, Lan snuck past and placed the tray on a chair.

He stood in the doorway and grinned at her. 'Dinner is served.'

Lan used his telekinesis to float the tray towards her. She turned to look at him. The full moon dissolved the shadows and he was bathed in its glorious, ethereal glow.

'The moon is reflected in your eyes. I could get lost in them.' Ake sighed.

'Trust me when I say you have.' Lan smiled.

Ake's forehead wrinkled in concentration. Her eyes widened in shock and Lan saw the embers of a memory take root before it fled just out of reach.

Ake glanced at the tray and her shoe filled with gelatinous fare and pretended to gag before snatching her shoe. She scooped the porridge and hurled it at him. It made a soft thud as it landed in his hair. The impact broke his concentration and the tray clattered to the floor. Ake walked past him with her shoe and brushed the porridge from his hair. He grabbed her hand and put it to his cheek.

'Please remember me.'

'I am lost.' She pulled her hand back gently, and, for the briefest of moments, he saw recognition flicker in grey-blue eyes before they reverted to their bespelled colour.

'You are here with me. That is enough.' Lan turned and moved out of the doorway. 'It's late, you should rest.'

'You were fun today, Lan. You always seemed so reserved.'

'I never learnt to play until you came along.'

Ake gave him a little wave as she left, her mouth dimpling as she smiled.

Chapter Twenty-Three

Thwack; the staff cracked against a training sword, blocking a blow as its skilled wielder wrested away their weapon to turn and try and deliver a diagonal blow to their opponent's right knee. It was midday and the sun bore down on them. Beads of sweat formed on the foreheads of the combatants.

'Alwin, you need to steady your hand and strike faster.' Lan took a training sword from a crate nearby and showed the youth several different techniques that could be applied against a reaching weapon like a staff, spear or great sword.

Alena had agreed to be Alwin's training partner for an hour each day. Her experience with a weapon that has reach would be an invaluable asset in Alwin's training. This allowed Lan to assess Alwin's form and correct him as needed. Sweat beaded down Alwin's face as he faltered, his unskilled stance allowing the captain to force him backwards against the bulwark.

'Take a break, Alwin,' said Lan.

Alena smiled at her opponent; he was bent double, taking healing breaths. 'You are very unfit.'

Alwin nodded and stood to his full height. 'I have never trained before. What does one expect?'

'Now, big fellow, your part of the bargain.' Alena took the training sword from Alwin and tossed it to Het. 'You promised to spar with me in exchange for sparring with the boy an hour a day. We need to test the capabilities of the weapons Amities forged.'

Het stepped forward, threw the training sword aside and grinned. 'Little wooden swords are for trainees.'

Ake grumbled as Lan handed her a wooden training sword. 'Why do I have to attend?'

'Being trained by Het and the elves of Relequis may help you remember bits of your past.' Lan turned to Alwin. 'Go do some cooldown exercises.' Alwin strolled a few feet away and began to stretch.

Ake began waving her sword around and went to prod Het in the stomach with it. Het ignored her and unstrapped his long sword. The sword was Amities's most powerful weapon. It had been the sword that had killed Drianna and its only master had been Mandami, until now.

'Cut it out, Ake. That's starting to annoy me,' said Het.

Lan smirked at them. 'I remember two young adults always disturbing others.'

'Now isn't the time, Lan,' said Het.

'I am sure her teachers felt that way too. But you always did take training and fighting seriously. She almost bested me with a sword once,' said Lan.

'Ake using a weapon to take down the great Trebrelan, very different to the innocent and lazy girl I knew,' said Het.

'The Ake I married was never lazy.' Lan's eyes flashed with pride.

'You natter like a bunch of fairies at a high tea. Are we going to spar?' asked Alena.

Alena exchanged her training staff for the one Amities had gifted her. They all heard the familiar humming as Het's sword burst into flame.

Alena's staff fizzled for a few moments and nothing happened. She shook it and it flared blue for a few seconds before the light faded.

'Grandfather always said that one was stubborn and had a

mind of its own. It didn't even tell him its name. Try talking to it,' said Alwin.

Alena gave the staff a sheepish grin. 'Hello, staff. Could you please do whatever it is you do?'

She felt the weapon jolt. Alena nodded at Het and he charged her. He looked like he was about to strike down and she used the staff to block above her head. Het changed his direction and struck upwards. Alena removed a hand from the staff and slid her other hand to the base of the weapon and stepped back. She felt the heat from the flames as it singed the tiny hairs on her arm as she barely avoided the attack.

Alena leapt forward and used the staff to jab Het in the chest. He grunted and grabbed the staff in his free hand. The staff flared blue and zapped his hand and he released it.

'I cannot be taken,' said the staff in Alena's mind. Alena stared at the staff for the briefest of moments. Het's sword flared and came crashing down on the staff and it briefly burst into flames. The sword had the ability to channel any innate magic the user had into the blade, a focal point for their magic. Its last user had favoured solar magic and it still remembered.

Alwin paused, his grip tightening on the wooden sword as a cluster of voices intruded on his thoughts, his gaze snapped to the sword in Hets's hand before drifting to Alena's staff.

'I am Anam Imeall; you will burn with the pure light of the gods,' said the sword.

'It burns. We are not enemies, desist. I do not wish to fight, but I will not let you hurt one of the sacred ones,' yelled the staff.

Lan stared as Alwin covered his ears.

Blue light flared down the shaft of the staff. There was a loud crack that made both Alena and Alwin jump. The light flared brighter until it appeared as a transparent blue wall in front of Alena. Het pulled his sword back.

'That is a useful skill,' said the sword.

The shield glowed and changed to a warm yellow. *'Of course, it is. I am Din, champion of the faith and shield of the descendants of Velterra,'* said Din the staff.

While Alena heard the staff say, "I am Din", Alwin heard the entire unusual conversation. 'Enough,' he muttered.

'We acquiesce, Lord of the Forge,' said the weapons in unison before falling silent.

Het punched the magic shield. He cried out as his fist made contact with the light, he took a sharp breath as his hand felt like it had connected with a brick wall. Het stepped back and the shield slowly disappeared. Ake rushed over, grabbed his hand and examined it. The knuckles were badly grazed and she held the injured hand longer than was necessary. 'You will be okay.' She dropped his hand.

'Ake, you can't act this way towards me.' Het's gaze snapped to Lan's; a flicker of jealousy burned in his eyes before it disappeared.

Ake nodded and looked at Lan who was watching, his expression now impassive.

Het's sword flared and the flames disappeared before he sheathed the weapon and took up a large training sword.

'I am finished for the day.' Alena turned and headed towards the helm.

'Alwin, let a master swordsman put you through your paces.' Het turned and grinned at Lan. 'Long knives aren't swords.'

'More agile than a common sword.' Lan's eyes flashed with mirth.

Alwin carefully approached Het, his training sword raised awkwardly. Het's sword crashed down on the weapon and Alwin dropped it and blew on his stinging hand.

'Pick it up. Feel the strength of the weapon; you must be strong in battle, Alwin. It is an extension of yourself, you must become one with the weapon,' said Het.

Alwin picked up the weapon and they continued their training. The wooden swords thwacked together as the men exerted themselves.

Lan picked up two small training swords and walked over to Ake, she was practicing some of the techniques Alwin had learnt. He saw her make a mistake. *Familiarity seems to be whittling away at the curse she is under.*

'Ake, you need to shift your stance.' He showed her the correct footwork and she adjusted herself.

'This all feels familiar. Spar with me, Lan.'

Lan nodded. 'Elven form twenty-six.'

'I am familiar with that.' She smiled. 'No outbursts, of course.'

Elves are always composed and elegant in front of those who are not family. Even when sparring, manners are necessary and loud exclamations and enthusiasm are restrained. The pair bowed to each other. They heard Alwin cry out as he lost his weapon again.

'Concentrate, Alwin.' Het's boisterous laughter rang out and Ake smiled.

Lan shifted his stance slightly and watched his wife's eyes widen.

'So fast.' Ake hefted her sword as his crashed down on her; she stumbled slightly without reprieve as he swung the other weapon and tapped her gently across the shoulder.

'You know this form.' Lan's eyes darkened. 'And as for unrestrained outbursts, I am a master of getting them out of you.'

Lan drew his blades back before doing a half turn, then stepping just past her and aiming his left weapon at her unprotected side. Ake instinctively countered, preventing the strike, and stared at the sword as her mouth turned up in a smile.

He slid a weapon forward and broke their block. Ake stumbled as both wooden blades, aimed at either side of her waist, nearly made contact and stopped just before they would hit. Ake leapt forward, brushing past her opponent's weapons, and thrust her training blade towards his chest. Lan released his weapons. As they clattered to the floor, he grabbed her wrist and pulled her towards him facing the other way. He moved blindingly fast and captured one of her hands in his and the other held her weapon above her, aimed downwards towards her head.

———⁂———

The silver bowl was slick with blood that roiled and frothed. The abomination peered into its murderous contents and focused on his cousin. *'Remember, he tried to kill you. He would have you dead, cousin.'*

The old man groaned at the feet of the marble stand. Multiple lacerations augmented his dying body.

'Hush, soon I will relieve you of your soul.'

The abomination turned back to his task.

———⁂———

Ake shuddered against Lan and he lowered the raised weapon and turned her towards him. Her eyes flashed grey-blue. 'I know you.'

His heart leapt with joy as she grabbed his face in her hands and crashed her mouth down on his. It took all his will not to respond to her urgent need. She wrapped her legs around him; the swords cluttered to the ground as his hands came up to cup her bottom.

Het laughed. 'Well, well, I'll eat my past words. He really is passionate with her.'

Turning his head, Lan broke the kiss, dropping his arms to the side as Ake slid to her feet. *As much as I want to, I should not kiss her while she is not herself.*

Ake's eyes filled with tears. 'It's me, I'm still here ... It's like a maze and I hear you but can't reach you. I am in a mind battle with Hau. He pushes old painful memories to the surface to block me from coming back.' She shuddered then blinked, when she opened her eyes they were no longer her own, locking on to his in a glare. Thrusting him away, she took heaving breaths.

'I remember. You-you tried ...' she stammered and began to cry. 'To kill me.'

'Yes. I fought it as Drianna tried to steal my soul,' he mumbled.

'Alwin, let's leave them to discuss this,' said Het. Footsteps retreated towards the other end of the ship as the two men left.

The swordplay has brought up that memory. Lan sighed. 'Is that the only memory you have of us?'

'That and your jealous kiss. I can't do this. Stay away from me.' Ake whimpered.

Lan blinked away his tears and pulled her into his arms. He nuzzled her neck. 'Remember me, my darling. What we had was unbelievable.'

She stomped her foot down on his and he released her.

'You are a bad man. You will never compare to Het!'

'I have done things I regret, Ake, and they will always haunt me. But I am not evil.' He clenched his fists, his chest tightened as she smirked at his next words. 'I love you.'

'Touch me again and I will act in self-defence. I can't believe you tried to kill me.'

Ake's eyes glazed over and a horrible voice welled up from within. 'Good, cousin. None of them are good enough. Come home and help me add to my kingdom, and we will destroy the likes of him.'

Lan grabbed her and held her to him. 'Please fight him.'

She loosened a hand and punched him in the nose. He stumbled back as she ran, her feet pounding on the wooden deck as her breath caught in her throat. Tears welled in her eyes and she looked back at him briefly before she fled and cried out, 'I shall.'

CHAPTER TWENTY-FOUR

'Land-ho,' cried the lookout from the crow's nest.

A short while later, the ship glided in to a dock that was in disrepair. It was a few hours before sunset and they had reached The Jagged Isle, an island dedicated to monastic life. All pilgrims were welcome, Velterrans and Cirites alike, as long as they agreed to purge themselves of magic in any form.

Het felt naked without his sword. Alena had confiscated all magic items, locking them in the cabin and setting a watch. The crew were to have shore leave and only Hurley, Nuo, two guards and Caoimhe were to stay behind. He, Alena and Alwin were to escort Ake to the monastery for treatment. He had not seen Lan in two days; Alena had asked him to stay out of sight due to Ake's fear of him. They would leave first, then Lan would go with the crewmen to visit the town. Alena would send a message to him if Ake made progress.

A member of the crew leapt on to the dock and began to tie the mooring rope. Het looked down at his blue robes. He had not worn robes since the night of Ake's graduation. He smiled fondly, remembering that first time in Flo's arms. *I wish she was here. She would know how to help our friend.*

Ake had retreated within herself and her nightmares had gotten worse. Alena had told him Ake spoke in her sleep, calling out to Lord Hau that she would find and serve him.

He was impressed with how Lan was handling the situation. The elf who had once been proud and hard to read was now patient and attentive. Het saw an incredible passion and devotion to Ake in him that was unusual of what he knew of most elves, she just had to remember she felt the same.

He felt a hand slip into his and Ake looked up at him, her expression blank.

'I know you,' she mumbled.

Het squeezed her hand to reassure her and turned to Alwin. 'I will need you to take her hand and guide her, Alwin. I will watch out for any threats.'

Het lifted Ake down on to the dock and Alwin scrambled afterwards. Alena gave Ake a sad smile. Heavy boots thudded on to the dock as Het jumped from the ship to the platform. They all turned to survey the island.

A rocky, mountainous path stretched out before them overgrown with tall grass and patches of brambles. A grey castle stood in the distance.

'Het,' said a familiar voice behind them.

They turned to see Lan gesturing from the ship. Alena walked a distance ahead and Alwin took Ake's hand gently, leading her forward. Lan joined Het on the dock, landing silently.

'I guess no one noticed that Ake isn't wearing decent shoes for that trek. I borrowed a pair from Nuo. They are around the same shoe size,' said Lan.

Het turned and looked at Ake's feet. She was wearing a pair of light slippers.

Het gave Lan an apologetic look. 'I will put them on her myself.' He took the lace up boots and strode over to Ake. 'Sit down on the rocks, Ake.'

Ake sat down and Het bent down, removing her slippers and guiding her feet into the boots before he laced them up. He stood up and took the slippers back to Lan who took them from the outstretched hand.

'I should be going with her.' Lan swallowed hard and he stared wistfully at his wife. 'Should you really be taking the shortcut?'

Alena frowned. 'Ake is becoming weaker. I know the two-hour journey along the path to the town is safer, but I have made the executive decision to take the shortcut through the mountain trail and cut off an hour.'

Lan nodded and glanced up at the sky. 'Aren't you leaving it a bit late? It's nearly sunset.'

'I will bring her back to you, Lan. On my very soul.'

Lan continued to stare at Ake. 'I should be with her.'

Het squeezed Lan's shoulder. 'Have hope.' Then he turned and hurried after the small party.

The sky was streaked with orange, pink and deepening shadows as the sun began to set while they climbed the rough path. Darkened plateaus covered in shrubs and rocks lined the sides of the uneven tracks. Ake trudged along, her expression blank as Alwin guided her. Alena led and Het took up the rear. The hour-long journey would circumvent the small village of Naofa that was dedicated to feeding and clothing the monks cloistered in the monastery who committed their lives to the pursuit of the arts and knowledge, hoping to better the lives of the masses.

Thirty minutes into their trek, the bow on Alwin's shoulder vibrated, setting his skin a-tingle.

'I'm s-orr-y to bother you. So-me-thing is j-ust off the path,' stammered his shy bow.

Alwin stopped. He scanned along the sides of the path, his elvish sight catching movement to the left of them.

Drawing his bow from his shoulder, he pointed to where he had seen the movement. Het's eyes followed the gesture. 'Can't see anything.' He unsheathed his sword. 'I trust you though kid, and your elvish ancestry and its uncanny senses.'

'I am free to defend,' said Imeall.

The sword burst into flame against Het's wishes. A loud squawking erupted from the nearby bushes as the sword alerted the creature to their location.

'Bloody sword! Why do you always do that? I have never channelled fire,' mumbled Het.

'Lo-rd of the F-org-e, I am Dage. He must co-mma-nd the sword to ch-ann-el his power. The s-word must res-pe-ct him,' stammered Alwin's bow.

'Enough, Dage, we must fight,' said Alwin.

Het looked at him as if he was odd. 'You okay, boy?'

Alwin nodded as the creature flew up into the air, squawking at them. Alena grabbed Ake, her staff already in her hand. 'I will protect her.'

The creature was about the size of a large human. It had the head of a vulture, bat wings, human arms and large, clawed toes, and its torso was covered in fur.

'The carnivorous hubature hasn't been seen this close to Cirichad territory in years,' said Alwin.

The monster screeched as Alwin drew the string, invisible to all but him; a magical arrow formed. He sighted the monster and released the string; the arrow shot towards the hideous creature. It pierced the creature's wing and the monster dived towards him. Its claws raked the top of his head, ripping out some of his hair as he ducked. The monster turned and dived at him again.

Het leapt forward, his sword arcing upwards at the hubature. The flames set the creature's torso on fire and it screeched in pain. It flapped its wings, the loud beats caused Ake to cover her ears as it dived towards her and Alena.

Alena put her staff above their heads and held her charge close to her. 'Come on, Luma, shake out of this. We need your unwavering strength.'

'I shall defend,' said Din.

The staff burned a brilliant blue and the shield wall appeared. The hubature raked the shield with its claws and landed on the perch. Its immense weight caused Alena's knees to buckle. The creature shrieked and another hubature flew out of the bushes; attacking Het and Alwin.

The sword blazed and faltered as the creature raked Het across the back and tried to peck out his eyes, diving at him continuously. Het hesitated, allowing the creature to slash at him again. Alwin turned and began firing at the hubature perched on the shield wall.

'*I cannot be hit or taken,*' said Din.

The arrows bounced off the shield wall, missing their target. The hubature attacking Het wheeled around and landed near him. It withdrew a dagger from under its furred torso and threw it at its target. Het dodged it and rushed the creature, his sword no longer a-flame. The monster flew up and Het grabbed its leg, dropping his sword. The monster screeched as he dragged it towards the ground.

Alwin shook himself and closed his mouth as the big man pulled the creature down and grabbed it by the neck. The creature squawked and its eyes bulged with fear. Its mate left its perch and flew towards the warrior. Alwin fired his bow; an arrow pierced the creature and it crashed to the ground.

'*You can win without me. You are a master, I yield,*' cried Imeall.

'The sword respects you now,' cried Alwin.

Imeall began to glow in a hue of interchanging lights.

'The sword can use the spell *Faerie Orb,*' muttered Alwin.

The spell produced a light that would follow the caster and changed to reflect their mood and only offered light to them and their allies. This spell had been Het's favourite and he had the widest range of any druid. While Het had been a master of arms, he had favoured mischievous magic and spells that would protect his friends.

The sword flashed red with Het's anger and he reached for the blade, swiftly dispatching the remaining hubature. The sword flashed a peaceful green as Het's anger quickly ebbed away, reflecting the gentle and affable person he was.

Din's shield faded and Alena stood up and stretched her legs. Ake sat staring into space. Alwin approached her and waved his hands in her face; she didn't blink.

Ake shivered and a terrible voice came out of her mouth. 'Cousin, hurry.'

Ake replied in her own voice. 'I am trying.'

Het stood. Blood ran down his face and streaks of blood began to seep through the back of his robe. 'We must hurry or she will die from this curse.' Ignoring his wounds, Het hefted Ake into his arms and set a fast pace up the path.

CHAPTER TWENTY-FIVE

Lan sat looking down at the cup in his hand. While wine was frowned upon in the capital, the little farming town of Naofa produced some excellent low-alcohol ciders. There was a limit to the amount one could purchase as excess was heavily criticised. He began to relax after the second cup. Before he had become the God of Death, Lan had a great tolerance for alcohol and had sometimes indulged too much. *My current body must react like a new drinker. Ake and I could live here in peace with Caoimhe, Hurley, Het and our descendants.*

Naofa had one main cobblestone street, lined with pastel-coloured, shingle-roofed wooden buildings that catered to the local farming population. Lan had seen orchards on the way in, a few grain and flax farms, and chickens wandered freely. Pigs shuffled in an out of the acorn forest, often blocking the road, and the residents didn't seem bothered. He glanced down at a discarded menu. *So many pork and chicken dishes, maybe they supplement with fresh fish as there are some simple fish dishes on the menu as well.*

There was a commotion in the street and some patrons hurried outside. The hotel owner placed his dish of fish and chips down in front of him, then wandered over to the doors. Lan stuffed some chips in his mouth; when the crunch gave way to a fluffy cloud of salty goodness, he crammed in another. *Amazing.* When he had resided in this world over a thousand years ago this kind of food had been foreign to his elven diet.

The doors crashed open and the crowd surrounded the people who entered. The hotel owner cleared a table. There was a great deal of shuffling around before Lan was filled with a blood-curdling dread. He stood, thrusting the chair backwards, hurrying towards the noise. His stomach dropped.

'Ake, wake up, wake up,' cried Het, his voice booming above the crowd.

Lan was jostled about as he pushed people aside in his effort to reach them.

'Jerk,' said someone in the crowd.

'How can we help tend your wife, pilgrim?' the hotel owner asked Het.

'I don't know how to help her. But she isn't my wife,' said Het.

'Move aside,' yelled Lan.

Several people made way. Ake was laid out on the table, her body shaking. Her eyes were fixated in one place as she fought her internal demons.

'Out of my way.' Lan shouldered the last few remaining people aside and stumbled as one man put out his foot. He gave the villager a glare before he saw Alwin and Alena share worried glances.

'What do we do, Lan?' asked Het, looking lost.

'You're injured. Stay here. I will take her to the monastery, as I should have done in the first place, as her husband. No offence, Het.'

'I agree with you,' said Het.

Alena stared at Lan. 'I thought it was for the best.' She sighed. 'We encountered beasts on the way here. Take this knife and hurry.'

Lan slid the knife into one of his boots, picked Ake up and sprinted from the building.

As he vaulted over fences and charged across the fields, the monastery came into view. His elvish sight saw a path that would join up with the main road. When he was about twenty minutes away, bile rose in his throat and his skin crawled. They were now in a field of tall grass. As if out of nowhere, a stone circle materialised.

He gagged, almost swooning from sudden fatigue as he hurried on. Putting space between him and the monolith, his symptoms eased and restlessness set in. He strode up the path to the monastery and rang the large bell that hung outside the huge, stone castle. Footsteps echoed within and the large wooden doors were hauled open. Artwork littered the walls of the grey stone walls and the domed marble ceiling was a perfect contrast to the slate floor.

A man in grey robes turned and lifted his head from a book he was pursuing at a lectern as the one who opened the doors ushered them in and slammed the doors shut behind them. Lan stood, breathing heavily, his stamina waning. *I am usually fitter than this.*

The monk stepped away from the lectern, approaching them, frowning. 'Are her eyes normally this colour?'

Lan shook his head and clutched his wife to him. 'She needs help.'

'What happened to her?'

'She contracted a fever and a powerful wizard known to us speaks through her, confusing her memories.' Lan gritted his teeth and hoisted his wife in his arms. 'Please do something. I have heard this monastery practices healing.'

'I am Abbot Herman. We will try to help her, son,' said Herman.

Lan bowed his head wearily. 'Okay, please keep me informed.'

'We will send word to you, but you need to hand her over. Unfortunately, only the infirm and the monks may stay here. You will have to return to the town and wait. What is her name?'

'No. I will not leave her side.'

A female monk stepped forward and held out her arms for Ake. 'I will take her.'

Lan shook as he handed her to the woman. 'I'll stay here and wait. Her name is Telewanake and she is more precious than life to me.'

'Unfortunately you need to be a patient—'

The Abbot stopped abruptly as Lan removed the dagger from his boot, running the blade across his palm. Blood pooled on the pale flesh. 'There, I'm a patient that needs attending.'

'I see you are dedicated to her. What is your name?' asked Herman.

'Trebrelan. Now can I stay?' asked Lan.

'Take him to the eastern wing and treat his hand. He can stay until dusk,' said Herman.

Lan watched as two monks carried his Ake away and with her, his life.

Chapter Twenty-Six

The two monks placed Ake on a stone table, knelt and began to pray over her. 'This stone will ground you. Magic has a hard time afflicting stone.' Herman smiled down at Ake. 'We will do our best to aid you, sweet Goddess of Mercy.'

Moonlight filtered in from the large paneless windows. The floor of the small room was made up of irregular granite tiles, and large brass brackets for torches were pinioned to the wall.

The abbot chanted a passage over his charge from the Cirite psalm book. 'Hail be, the vigilant Mandami, Lord of Light, blessed of our Lord. Take your sword and rid this woman of the tainted one. Sever the ties that allowed Cephas a home within her.'

'Where am I?' Ake whispered before erupting in chilling laugher. 'So, Mandami has a religion, how quaint. Cephas is long dead. But the trauma he caused lingers at the edges of her mind.'

'Liar. Be gone, tainted one, defiler of women and keeper of slaves,' said Herman with conviction.

Ake groaned. '*Get up, cousin, kill them,*' her lord muttered in her mind.

She sat up and stared at Herman. 'I shall serve my Lord Hau.'

'Mage-invoked memory curse,' muttered Herman. He walked over to a small bookshelf and removed an ancient tome. The cover was faded and the spine was decaying. He gently turned the pages to a long-forgotten elvish passage, and hurried back over to Ake. He gestured to his fellow monks, six of whom took up places evenly spaced around the stone table, and snatched up brass Censers on silver chains which they began to swing— a different hue billowing from each—creating a circle of sweet-smelling smoke. As the strands of smoke mingled, they wove a counter curse, penned by Dane long ago an ancient tome in Herman's hands.

The two praying monks stood up and pinned Ake's arms down as she struggled and tried to bite at them. She kicked out, but they were able to restrain her.

Herman began to recite. '*Altudia re aiseag bodius. Benvelos olc.*'

'How dare you flaunt the elvish words.' A man's voice erupted from Ake and her stomach lurched with his rage.

Herman continued, placing his hand on Ake's forehead. '*Dee re Sorendee gratus ska.*'

Ake flung herself about, trying to flee her captors. 'Enough. Kill them,' yelled her lord through her lips.

Ake struggled and freed her hand. She reached up and cast *Mystic Flame* at one of the monks. His robes caught on fire and he patted it out. She blasted others with jets of water and they stumbled backwards releasing her. Herman scrambled out of the way as she hoisted herself off the table, chasing him around the table as animalistic growls exited her mouth.

The doors crashed open and Lan forced his way into the room. Ake glared at him and rushed towards him. His hand came up and deflected as she sent a wave of fire at him.

'You will die, Lan.' Ake smiled as her lord spoke to Lan, using her body as a vessel.

With a swift move, Lan threw her over his shoulder. She bit his upper back before he placed her on the stone table and pinned her arms down. 'Continue.'

The monks swinging the incense placed their items down and held her legs.

Ake turned her head as a monk stepped forward with a mirror and she saw a serpent like tongue hissing between her emerging fangs. Herman put his hand on her forehead and she tried to bite him. The elderly monk startled. 'Release me.' She batted her eyelids and pouted.

'Why the mirror?' Lan tilted his head in its direction.

'She needs to scare the demon out of her. Hopefully the shock of her altered appearance will do so.' The monk gulped. 'Hopefully.'

'Get on with it.' Lan gritted his teeth.

'*Ibli sion*,' Ake spat.

'Shut up.' Lan balled up his fist. 'How dare you make my wife utter those detestable words, in elvish of all things.'

Mocking laughter issued forth from Ake's mouth. 'It is true nonetheless.'

'*Cuzen Ibli*.' Lan gripped the edge of the stone table.

Ake shrugged, her voice still deep and mocking. 'Mage elf tradition. Anyway, if it wasn't for your blood niece Flo, this sweet half-elf would have been your cousin and lover, albeit a few times removed. And you wouldn't have known.' Ake ran a hand over her breast and began loosening a ribbon on her bodice.

Lan brushed her hand aside and retied her gown, his voice a near growl. 'Touch her body again against her will and when we meet again I will kill you with my bare hands.' He glanced at the monks, his eyes narrowing on one whose eyes were affixed on Ake's chest. 'Back off and afford her some modesty.'

'Do not engage with the creature.' Herman stared at Lan for a brief moment before he rushed the last of the passage. '*Benvelos Telewanake. Alltudio re devala.*'

Ake hissed and fought. She uttered a howl and closed her eyes. When she opened them again they were grey-blue, she turned her head from the mirror and focused on Lan.

'What is going on?'

Lan released her hands and the monks let go of her legs. 'You were ill, possessed by a terrible spirit.'

Ake shivered.

'Can you come with me, Trebrelan?' asked Herman.

Lan nodded and followed Herman just outside the doorway.

'She isn't cured. We have given you some time. It could be days, weeks or months. You will have to destroy the creature that infiltrated her soul.' Herman shuddered. 'Can you tell me how an elf came to live in these times?'

Lan rubbed an ear. 'What elf?'

Herman gave him a sad smile and fondled a gold chain around his neck. 'Imbued with a clarity spell. You have powerful magic on you, binding your bloodline, but it's there.'

'You wouldn't believe my tale.' Lan craned his head to glance down at the familiar scrawl on the tome.

'Do you recognise the writing?'

Lan shrugged and stared at a picture on the opposing wall. It depicted the last battle of Drianna. A half-elven woman summoned meteorites down upon a serpentine beast made of bones while a half-elven warrior with a flaming sword charged at the monstrosity. In the shadows, an elven man summoned lightening, the piece was called, *The Last days of Drianna* by Herman.

He turned back to the abbot. 'You painted that?'

'I am a huge believer in the legend of Telewanake and Trebrelan, and I am convinced the time of their return is nigh.' The abbot handed Lan the book he was holding. 'Do I greet the Lord of Death?'

Lan nodded before he turned the book over and frowned. 'Where did you get this?'

'The books were gifted by Arlys Smith. They were left to someone called Lan, son of Dane.'

'I will confront Arlys about this.' Lan ground his teeth. 'The author is Dane of Anwyl, my father.'

'That is why I am giving it to you, Trebrelan, Lord of Caelestis. I believe your father wrote the book while training as a druid. It was intercepted by one of Drianna's cult members on its way to Caelestis and the druid delivering it was slain. It was retrieved centuries later when a farmer uncovered a crypt. Take it, with my blessings. I believe you know your next task. To defeat Hau.'

'Why do monks have this stuff if they follow Cirichad beliefs? Won't you need it?' asked Lan.

'Benevolent knowledge is for the good of all, regardless of who you believe in. We have scribed a few copies, so it is yours. I have many accounts of your former life.'

Lan turned back towards his wife.

Ake sat up, eased herself down from the stone table and stumbled over to Lan. He reached out and pulled her to his side. 'Please, let's go home,' whispered Ake.

'Is it safe for her to leave?' Lan lifted his eyes from his wife to Herman.

'She not safe anywhere until the mage who cursed her is destroyed, or you find a powerful way to sever the link.'

'Thank you for your aid. What is the tithe I owe?' Lan held out his hand and Herman shook it.

'Whatever you can afford on the way out. I think I have had enough this day so I bid you farewell, children of the gods.'

Ake began to sob with exhaustion. Lan took her hand and they followed a monk out of the room. The hallway wound around and down and several doors lead off to other rooms. They were led back to the main entrance before the monk pointed to a wooden bowl perched on a stone stand. Lan dropped the last of his coins into it. He bowed low to the monk before the huge doors were swung open, then he picked Ake up and carried her through them.

Ake and Lan were now seated at a table in the hotel.

Ake was looking at the dishes on the menu. Apart from a few concerned glances directed her way, their journey back to town had been almost silent, Lan hadn't answered when she had bombarded him with questions, his head beading with sweat as they passed a stone circle. She looked up and caught him watching her, before her gaze dropped to the engagement ring and wedding band on her finger and she smiled. *I think I remember these.* 'Are you sure you are okay?'

Lan raised a brow. 'What do you mean?'

'Well, after you told the others what happened, you mentioned you had strange feelings near a stone circle.'

He smiled. 'I'm fine, and Alena even handed me an advance for dinner.' Lan reached out and squeezed her hand. 'What do you want?'

'The fish and chips look interesting. Never heard of chips.' She looked up and covered her smile with a hand as Lan launched into an animated description.

'The chips are fried potatoes, crunchy yet fluffy on the inside. It's such a simple concept, but with the right seasoning, magnificent.'

'Let's do that then.'

The hotel owner came over and took their orders before leaving Ake and Lan in awkward silence.

'So,' said Ake.

'How are you feeling?'

'I feel unburdened and refreshed.'

'Do you remember anything about what happened? And about us?' Lan's eyes filled with sadness.

Ake blushed and looked away. 'My memories are odd. I know we are married. I remember holding a smiling infant in my arms and you being there. I know there should be more, but it is lost.'

'Are you frightened of me?'

'How could I ever be frightened of you?'

Lan's eyes filled with pain and he cast his gaze down.

'Lan, look at me,' commanded Ake.

Lan ventured a sideways glance and composed himself. The owner came over with their meals and Lan affixed his attention to his meal as he pushed the food around on his plate with the fork. 'Do you remember that I love you?' he asked.

'Did I forget?'

Lan began to eat his meal in silence.

'I have the right to know.'

'You believed you loved Het. The thing that possessed you forced you to be frightened of me.' Lan sighed. 'It matters little.'

Ake couldn't tear her gaze from him as his eyes filled with tears.

'Please tell me I didn't try anything on Het. He was always like a brother to me.' She grabbed his hand and it trembled in hers.

'Nothing happened, he pushed you away, but you were like a giddy schoolgirl for him.'

'And you didn't stop me? Were you not jealous? That isn't like you.'

'I was sad and, I'll admit, a bit jealous, but you were hardly yourself, and Het is a trustworthy guy who loves Flo. I am hardly the over-jealous youth I used to be.' Lan gave her a sad smile. 'That demon made you call me *ibli sion*.'

'Sibling lover.' Hot tears slid down her cheek. 'I am so sorry.'

Lan gave her a radiant smile. 'Don't worry about it; enjoy the meal.'

Ake began to eat; she gripped the fork so hard her knuckles were white. 'You are right, chips are great, and so is this fish. What kind of topping is it encased in?'

'It is battered and it is very good.'

They finished their meal and Lan went and paid. He chatted

to the proprietor for a few moments before he came back over to her.

'In honour of Alena's trading ship they are putting on something called a waltz in the community hall. We can rest or go if you like. The owner said you should change out of robes into more formal wear.'

'I feel energised; we should at least take a look.'

'Let's get you something from the clothing store.'

Lan's hand clutched one of hers as they followed other patrons outside, the balmy breeze rustling their clothes as they ambled down the main street.

~~~

'It's how much?' asked Alena.

'One hundred credits,' said the clerk.

Alena sighed and handed over the last of her coins. *At least the crew are paid and we have enough stores to get to Velterra. If we are damaged again, I don't know how we will fare.*

Alena had gone to the workers union to request the assistance of skilled workers to fix the prow of the *Carnay*. The building was quite small and two clerks sat behind the long, wooden counter that ran the length of one wall with a single entryway. Lattice work ran the top length of the counter with two metal grills set into it spaced a few feet apart. There was a small gap underneath each of the grills for the exchange of documents and currency.

Behind the counter, set into the wall, were shelves containing various items, including vials of ink, ledgers and small, lockable wooden chests. The other wall had a large sledge set in the wall, and piles of papyrus, inks and sharpened quills were placed for patrons to draft and sign documents.

'It will take between three to four days to complete the work.'

'Thank you.'

Alena turned and left the building to return to her crew on the *Carnay*.

I do hope Luma remembers dear Lufar. He seems like a gentle guy who cares for her deeply.

CHAPTER TWENTY-SEVEN

Hartur felt the humming flow through her again. It was now a few hours after the sun had set and a bone-chilling wind made the sails billow. She crept towards the sole cabin; two crewmen armed with cutlasses were on guard duty. *They must be protecting something important.* One guard smoked a pipe; the earthy smell of tobacco wafted towards her.

'I hope we get at least one day's leave before we set sail,' said the first guard.

'Yeah, let's hope so,' said the other, puffing on his pipe.

'Well, back at it then.' The other guard wandered behind the cabin towards the stern.

Hartur crept behind the cabin. When she was inches from him, she stepped out from the shadows and stared into his eyes. *'Kill the other guard.'* Hartur smiled as the guard's eyes glazed over and he walked over to his friend. The sound of clashing swords disrupted the air.

Hartur returned to the shadows, slunk up to the door of the cabin and began to pick the lock. The door creaked open and she snuck inside. She bumped one of the stretcher beds and lit a match. In the centre of the room were a variety of weapons. She felt her body jolt with electricity and reached out for a ruby hammer with a wooden handle.

'I am Nietra, keeper of the shadows, bringer of gloom,' said the hammer. The voice faded from her mind.

'Great, another talking weapon,' muttered someone on a nearby stretcher bed.

Curious, Hartur approached. Light filtered in through a porthole and shimmered off the boy's golden locks. The boy shivered as if he felt her presence and opened his large, emerald eyes, staring into her hypnotic violet ones.

'I see you have returned.'

'I am not here,' said Hartur in his mind.

The boy gave her a wry smile before he reached out and grabbed her arm. 'Feel real enough.'

No one has ever resisted me before. Hartur tried to pull her arm back, without success.

'What a beautiful woman.' Hartur glared at him as she heard his inner desires; an innate skill that allowed her to briefly read the mind of those she enchanted.

'What do we do now? I should probably call the guard,' the boy pulled her closer and whispered in her ear.

Hartur shivered and locked eyes with him. 'You won't do that.'

'What makes you think that?' asked the boy.

Hartur's eyes filled with desire. *He* is *good looking.* She leant down and kissed him. The boy suddenly tensed, clutching at the sheets with a firm grip.

Hartur crept back into the shadows and fled the cabin, grabbing the hammer as she did so. She came face to face with the gold-robed woman.

'Stop,' yelled Nuo.

Hartur turned and ran to the stern, leaping overboard. As she did so, something whistled past her cheek and grazed it. She landed with a splash in the water and swam to shore.

Alwin stood up as Nuo crashed through the cabin doors. The first mate flicked a switch and light flooded the room.

'She got away, Alwin. She nearly caused the guards to kill each other. What happened?' Nuo stared at him, her eyes filled with anger.

Alwin turned to her. 'The last heir has received her inheritance.'

'You stupid boy. You may have killed us all. You will answer to Alena for this.'

Alwin shrugged.

Nuo glared at him. 'You will stay in here until she returns.' She turned and left the cabin.

Alwin heard the click as she locked the door. He smiled to himself and lay back down on the stretcher. *I have fulfilled Grandfather's list of requests, hopefully he will be at peace. And maybe one day I will talk to that beautiful woman again.*

CHAPTER TWENTY-EIGHT

A small, silver bell chimed as Ake and Lan entered the clothing store. Seated behind a counter was a small man with wiry grey hair darning tights. He looked up as they entered, placed his work on the counter and rose. Ake's eyes darted about the store. Wooden training dummies had been used to model fashions. Cheery sunlight filtered in through the large store window near the entrance and settled on the display featuring fake snow manikins outfitted in warm attire of the times such as cloaks, waistcoats, muffs and shawls. Small tables placed around the store held shirts, hose and shoes.

Ake wandered over to a table that held some unusual garments. The table was modestly wedged between wooden partitions. She picked up a white, knee-length undergarment that narrowed at the bottom of each leg hole and was edged with lace, before placing it back down. The sign read: drawers, one coin. Ake glanced at a strange piece of clothing; the tag read: brassiere. It appeared to cover one's cleavage, according to the instructions, and had laces at the back to draw the garment closed.

She slipped out from behind the partition to see Lan looking up at some dresses.

The tailor appeared bemused, a smile tugging at the corners of his mouth. 'Most married men don't go clothes shopping. These are the errands of a married lady.' The tailor gave Ake a charming smile. 'Madam, how can I help you?'

Lan gave him a look of annoyance.

'You can help both of us,' said Ake.

'How rude of me. I assumed your husband was waiting for you to make your purchases.' The tailor bowed.

Ake surveyed the dresses; they were made of heavy fabric with high neck lines, long sleeves and several layers of long, ruffled petticoats hidden under the floor-length gowns. Two gowns were loose-fitting to offer less shape to the body. A yellow dress with lace petticoats had darts added below the bust line and along the waist to give more shape to the wearer.

'What do you think?' asked Lan.

'The yellow one with the white lace petticoats is very pretty,'

Lan looked at the tailor. 'Is it her size?'

'It is very close. Does madam want to try it on?' asked the tailor.

'Yes, please.' Ake smiled at him.

The tailor removed the dress from the dummy and handed it to Ake. 'You can change behind the partitions. May I suggest you check out the women's items while there.'

Ake wandered behind the partition; the petticoats rustled as she changed into the gown.

'How much?' asked Lan.

'Sixteen coins. The drawers and brassieres are one coin each,' said the tailor.

Ake stepped out from behind the partition and watched Lan count out sixteen coins into the tailor's hands. 'She will want the dress.'

Lan then went around the shop and purchased several changes of clothes for himself, spending the rest of his weekly stipend of twenty Cirite coins as a specialist crewman.

Lan turned and beamed at her with pride. 'Suits you.'

The tailor came over and his eyes scanned her form. 'Fits well. But the boots are all wrong.'

'They will do fine, but we have enough for the dress?' asked Ake.

'I have paid for it so it's yours. I agree, you can't wear those shoes. I left your slippers on the ship,' said Lan.

'I have these gorgeous blue-toe mules with a slight heel,' said the tailor.

Ake glanced at the shoes made of hardened blue leather with no ankle support. The heel was small and the front of the shoe curved at the sides and ended in a point.

'How much?' asked Lan.

'A paltry six credits.' The tailor gave him a charming smile.

Lan sighed. 'I am sorry, I don't have that.'

The tailor turned to Ake. 'Can you darn tights?'

'I can,' said Lan.

'You have an hour before the waltz I assume you are attending. If you can get through twenty pairs of hose, the shoes are hers,' said the tailor.

'Make it twenty-two and throw in two pairs of drawers for her,' bartered Lan.

'You have a deal,' said the tailor.

'Ake, can you amuse yourself for a little while?' asked Lan.

'Sure, I will go for a walk.'

'Ah no, you will sit on that seat over there. You have just recovered and I need you safe.' Lan gestured to a chair.

Ake glared at him. 'Seems a bit of an overreaction. We will discuss it later.'

She went and sat on the chair, one leg crossed over the other. Lan sat behind the counter and took up the darning, threading the needle with deft hands, and finished the first pair quickly as the tailor blinked in astonishment.

'I should have made it more pairs,' grumbled the tailor.

Lan glanced up to see Ake pulling faces at him. 'That's adorable.'

Ake grinned back. Within half an hour, Lan had finished the work. He stood up and grabbed the shoes and knelt in front of Ake, slipping one on to her small foot.

'Fit for a princess going to a dinner party.' Lan gave her an enticing smile.

She blushed as he slid the other shoe on, his hand lingered on her ankle before lifting her dress slightly and squeezing her leg. The movement was so quick Ake felt she may have imagined it. Lan stood up and offered her a hand. She took it and he pulled her up. Not used to heels, she stumbled against him as he slipped his hand around her waist to steady her.

'Careful,' he whispered.

The tailor cleared his throat. 'This is still Cirite territory. Please mind our protocols. Public displays of infatuation outside the right scenario are shunned.'

Lan released her and turned to stare at the tailor. 'It's more lecherous to watch.'

Ake giggled and he grabbed her hand as they left the store.

People were lining up outside the community hall. Several men were dressed in rough-spun pants, boots and worn shirts. The women who accompanied them were dressed similar to Ake, but their dresses were made of coarse fabrics. The hotel owner was dressed splendidly in tights, codpiece and fine shoes. He wore an exquisite purple shirt with embroidered golden leaves along the collar. Some women stared at Ake and she heard them talk among themselves.

'What a fine lady.'

'Her companion is dressed less favourably to be attending her.'

Lan looked down at his stained shirt and Ake saw him blush.

She remembered those of elven heritage were aware of the way they looked and aspired to dress well; Lan more than most.

'I'll be back,' said Lan.

Ake watched him turn, sprint towards a building and enter it. Two ladies approached her.

'Dear lady, where do you hail from?' asked one.

'What a beautiful dress,' said another.

I don't remember. Ake dug her nails into her palms. 'I can't answer that,' said Ake. *I really should go find Lan.* She turned to look at the building Lan had entered. She was tempted to leave when a large familiar hand squeezed her shoulder. She turned to see Het dressed similar to the other men.

'Where is your lordly beau?' Het grinned at her.

Ake smiled. 'Hello Het. Hopefully he is back soon.'

The hotel manager took a large, brass key from his pocket and opened the doors to the community centre. He flicked a switch and light pooled just inside the doors, beckoning the attendees to step inside. The hotel manager strode inside. Several young women arrived, escorted by some of Alena's younger crewmen. They were carrying baskets of refreshments; they too entered the building.

Ake turned to see three robed figures descending the path from the monastery. They were carrying instruments including a harp, lute and tambourine. They smiled at her as they crossed the threshold.

Where is he? Ake watched as the rest of the participants entered the building. 'Well, go on, Het.'

'I will wait.' Het ruffled her hair.

Ake ran her fingers through her hair, trying to straighten it. 'Thanks for that.'

'Do you mean for waiting with you or for your stylish new look?' Het grinned and his eyes flashed with mirth.

'Either.'

They both turned as Lan approached.

Het winked at Ake and turned to greet Lan. 'Oh, you look so wonderful, my lord.' Het held out his hand and did his best impression of a dainty lady.

Lan rolled his eyes. 'Thanks for waiting with her.'

'No problem, elven lord.' Het grinned.

Lan stared at him and Ake giggled. Het patted Lan on the back and entered the building.

Ake's eyes trailed over Lan's form. He wore a long-sleeved robe with a high collar. Ake ran her hands over the ornate buttons that fastened the robe and her hand settled on the black leather belt at his waist. The buckle was made of silver and it shone like it had been freshly polished. He wore loosely fitted black trousers under the robes and soft black riding boots. Ake watched him tug at the neckline.

'Why are you tugging at the collar?' She reached up and adjusted it. She swatted his hands away as he tried to loosen it again.

'I don't know if you remember, but I hate things near my neck. I used to avoid formal mystic robes and only wore them when it was deemed necessary. Such as your graduation.'

'The robes are familiar,' Ake whispered.

'Alwin gave them to me a few days ago. He said you had kept them for me.' Lan reached down and kissed the top of her head. 'Is that true?'

Ake looked away. 'I'm not sure. Why would I keep them for you. Were we separated?'

Lan turned her face towards him. 'Don't worry about it.'

The refrains of gentle music captured his attention and Lan stared at the doors. 'So, it's a dance.' He grinned. 'Well, let's go make fools of ourselves.'

He offered Ake his arm and she linked hers with his, smiling up at him as they entered the building.

———

Floor to ceiling mirrors ran the length of two of the walls; a display of luxury donated by the hotel manager who had done well off trading ships entering the island's port. The floor was of polished mahogany floorboards. Electric lights had been fitted into elaborate chandeliers that hung from the ceiling. Set against the back wall was a stage made of a lighter wood. The three monks were seated on the stage playing their instruments and a harpsichord took up the centre of the small stage. A large table sat in one corner, lined with foods and refreshments. Wooden chairs had been placed up against the remaining wall.

Het piled a plate with food and took a seat in the corner, while Ake nibbled on a biscuit and Lan poured himself a glass of lemonade and took a gulp before placing the cup on the food table.

People turned to stare at them as Lan led Ake on to the dance floor. 'Men lead it seems. I put one hand on the waist and hold the other outstretched and there is movement back and forth making sure we don't step on each other's toes. I think I have it.'

The music stopped and some of the couples left the floor to get themselves some refreshments. Het left his seat, piled his plate again and returned to his chair. The monks began another set.

Ake waited patiently and Lan offered her his hand. He grabbed her waist and drew her against him, taking her other hand in his. The vicinity suddenly rippled with noises of astonishment, some dancers even stopping to stare. The other men kept their partners at arm's length Lan adjusted his hands; people smiled and turned back to their partners.

So, this is how they vent their attraction for one another.

Structured dances with minimal contact. And I thought elves were reserved. Lan gave Ake a smug smile.

'What are you thinking?'

'I may tell you later.'

The gentle music began and Lan took the lead. Ake stepped on his toes, void of his natural grace. The heel of her shoe hit another toe and he winced.

'I am sorry.'

'It takes more than that to damage me.'

They finished the set and Lan led Ake from the dance floor. Het wandered over as Lan was filling two plates; Ake had taken a seat.

'I see you favour sweets like Ake.'

Het grinned. 'It's free and delicious.'

'You really could have been her brother.' Lan laughed.

Het and Lan strolled back over to Ake, and Lan handed her the plate. They sat down and ate their food and watched a few more sets. Ake yawned.

'These people need to lighten up.' Het winked at her before he rose and jumped on to the stage to exclamations from the monks. He gave them brief instructions and sat down at the harpsichord. He began to play a rousing tune.

That key sounds like C major and it appears to have several contrasting movements. Lan had always held an interest in music, often writing his own pieces to accompany his harp as he played and sang. *What a fascinating instrument. How amusing to find Het so accomplished at music.*

The monks struggled to match Het's tune and gave up. Het looked embarrassed suddenly and began to falter.

I am going to regret this. Lan began to sing in his rich melodic voice, making up words as he went along. People stared at him; some gave him pitiful smiles. In Cirrichad, singing was reserved for worship. Ake giggled and he grinned. *This is embarrassing and somewhat exciting. To hear her laugh is worth it.*

'We went to a dance… and saw people prance. Lovers were held afar… It was terribly formal and would curl the toes of those who are normal.'

Lan saw one woman blush and avert her eyes. The men glared at him as the piece ended and he added a few last lines. *Well, all in I guess.*

'We tried to play and lead them a stray to angry stances and astonished glances. I guess we should all get out of here.' Lan grinned at Ake and gestured to the doors.

Three men strode over to Lan, their faces blazing with colour, hands balled into fists as they grunted through clenched teeth. 'Blasted Velterrans.'

Ake dropped her plate; Lan grabbed her hand and they ran, laughing, from the premises. The sound of heavy boots followed them and they saw Het shoulder a few of them as he rushed through the door and followed them. They arrived at the boarding house, leaning against the wall laughing and trying to catch their breaths.

'Thanks, old chap, for helping me out,' said Het.

'It was comical,' said Lan.

Ake turned and grabbed Lan's hand. 'When did you learn to be so fun?'

'An exuberant golden-haired woman taught me.'

Ake blushed.

Het laughed. 'Poor thing, you don't give her a break from your charming compliments and veiled passion. Such a cute elf.'

'What of it?' Lan felt his cheeks burn.

'Take the compliment, mate. You're a charming fellow now that you've almost grown up. Ake, can I have a word with you?'

'Lan, I'll meet you inside.'

Lan nodded and strode over to the building doors, storming inside, muttering aloud. 'The gall of calling a grown elf cute.'

Het turned to Ake. 'Lan hasn't celebrated his hundredth birthday.'

Her brow furrowed. 'Isn't he thirty-three?'

'No, Ake. Remember, he mentioned lost memories. You have forgotten some things.'

She smiled sadly. 'I know it's in there somewhere.'

Het patted her on the head. 'Yes and I believe a coming-of-age ceremony will unlock Lan's full potential, and he might be able to help you. But it needs to be a secret. The poor chap missed out on so much with an absent father and confusing heritage. I would love him to be surprised. Would you help me with it?'

Ake nodded. 'I would be honoured to help. I want to remember him and all our experiences. Goodnight.'

'Goodnight.'

Ake turned and hurried towards the boarding house.

⎯⎯⎯

Lan turned as Ake entered. There was a large wooden counter with a guestbook, ink, quill and bell. Holding out his hand, Ake clasped it and they began to ascend the nearby set of stairs to the upper floor and were met with a narrow landing and numbered doors. He took a key out of his pocket and opened door number four, fumbled around for the switch and flicked it. Light flooded the small room. *The process of harnessing electricity is fascinating.* Alwin had given him the basics when he had asked him about the science behind it.

They entered the room and shut the door. Lan had hired the room earlier but hadn't seen it. Two beds took up the room separated by curtains. There were no windows and the only other piece of furniture was a porcelain washing bowl set on a stand. A pitcher of water, bar of soap and a towel were stored in a shelf underneath and a small mirror was mounted to the wall. *I wonder if I still look the same.* He stared into the mirror and his familiar obsidian eyes and short black hair were reflected back at him. He smiled and turned to Ake.

Ake rolled her eyes. 'Vain elf.'

'Not this time.' He grabbed her and tickled her.

She giggled, diving on to one of the beds and pulling the curtains shut. He snuck up on her, slipping behind the drapes. She squealed when he grabbed her and pulled her towards him.

'Get out, I claim this bed. You get the other one.' He grinned.

'We don't share? Is that some elvish custom?' she asked innocently.

'I am tired.' He glanced away.

Ake pulled back the blankets, slipping beneath them.

'We are married. I want you to sleep with me.' Ake reached out and caressed his face.

'In what context, Ake?' Lan grabbed her hand.

Ake's eyes filled with desire. She ran her hands down his body and began to unbuckle his belt. Lan stopped her hand with his.

'I love you, Ake. But we aren't quite there yet.' He gently pushed her hand away and climbed out of the bed.

Her eyes flitted away then brimmed with tears. 'Don't we have a child?'

'Yes, we do.' He leant down and kissed her cheek. 'I don't feel comfortable making love to someone who has no memory of it. That would be wrong.'

She nodded and turned away from him. He went over to the other bed and removed his robes before climbing under the covers. As her soft sobs filled the quiet room, he rolled over and punched the pillow in anger. *I hate this.*

Eventually, Ake fell asleep and he turned to watch her for a few minutes before drifting off.

CHAPTER TWENTY-NINE

Alwin's head nodded with exhaustion. Alena had returned the night before and had ordered him tied to the mast overnight. This was to be the first of several punishments for putting the crew at risk of danger and sabotage. He heard footsteps and saw his great-grandparents on the dock. Lan looked exhausted as he helped Ake aboard and then tried to leap onto the deck. He stumbled on landing. *That isn't like him.*

Ake cocked her head. 'Why are you tied up?'

Lan's eyes narrowed on the young man's bound hands before he strode towards Alwin, his hands reaching to unravel the ropes.

'Stop, Lufar. It is a just punishment.'

'What happened?'

'A young woman broke into the cabin I was protecting and made away with a sacred weapon. The weapon chose its owner. The problem is, apparently she made two guards fight each other with some kind of hypnosis.'

'Why would you let her get away? And why did you call him grandfather?' asked Ake.

'The circumstances call for it,' said Alwin.

Ake turned and stared at Lan; her eyes full of confusion. He reached out his hand to her and she rejected him before striding away to be alone with her thoughts.

Alena approached Lan and Alwin with Nuo in tow.

'Good morning, Lufar, how was last night?' asked Alena.

'It was memorable. I hope his punishments aren't too harsh, Captain,' said Lan.

'He should be hung for his efforts, Lufar. My crew were almost mutinous. If it wasn't for the fact he is a relative, he would have received that punishment.' Alena sighed. 'He will have to endure his retribution.'

Nuo proceeded to untie Alwin and strip his shirt from him.

'It will be hot today. You will swab the deck in the midday sun without water and protection for your back. While at sea it matters who has your back. That happens to be your crewmates and you betrayed them,' said Alena.

Nuo pushed Alwin forward and handed him a mop and bucket. 'Now get to it.'

They will not find me here. If that was me, I would have caught the imposter to save my own hide. She shifted her weight and peered through the crack. The cabin had hollow walls filled with horsehair and plaster to insulate it. Some of the walls were crumbling and she had removed some timbers and slipped inside, replacing the wood behind her.

Hartur saw the boy falter as the day continued. His back was beginning to burn and she saw him wipe his brow.

One of the crewmen prodded him. 'Get on with it, traitor.'

Alwin scowled at the retreating crewman's back.

So, he does show emotions. Hartur slipped her waterskin to her lips. *Damn, it is hot in here.*

The boy proceeded to mop again.

CHAPTER THIRTY

Het wiped his forehead with the back of his hand as the glorious midday sun hammered down on his shirtless back. Lifting the wooden medallion he had carved, he dabbed on the final coat of paint with a thin brush.

So, Lan doesn't wear the elven coming-of-age pendant. I wonder if the poor fellow has even made it to a hundred, the age of majority for elves. Flo wore her pendant close to her heart and refused to be parted from it. My Flo felt the calling early, taking the ceremony in her sixties, the first elf ever to do so. Lan may have missed the most important ceremony of his people.

During the ceremony, elves reached their full potential, often discovering an unknown talent. Physical, mental and emotional skills were fine-tuned and even the clumsiest of elves were gifted with elven grace.

Lan's revulsion to the stone circle would indicate he never completed the ceremony. If an adult elf refused to embrace the calling of the stone circles they became weaker as the years went on. *I wonder if this is why he hasn't retained his powers.*

Alena had given him permission to leave the ship to set up and conduct the ceremony. Being the former apprentice to the head of the elven druids, Het had learnt the ceremonial rites for this ritual.

Ake would encourage Lan to accompany her to the surprise ceremony. *Lan doesn't need any encouragement when it comes to Ake.* He smiled to himself as he pocketed the pendant. The evening dinner bell rang and Hurley and Caoimhe rushed about delivering meals. Hurley handed Het his bowl.

'Hey Hurley, can you ask Caoimhe how old her father was when he left for the underworld?' asked Het.

Hurley grinned and ran off. After a conversation enunciated with whistles in varying tones and pitches, the halfling ran back over to him. Several crew men laughed, believing it to be some kind of children's game and even whistled to the pair.

'Caoimhe said her father was around seventy and his birthday is the first of July. She is guessing based on her knowledge, as her father never told her his age,' said Hurley.

Het rubbed his chin. *It would explain the sudden appearance of the stone circle, often they are disguised by elven runes until an elf in need of the rite appears.*

'Oh, thank you.' Het smiled. *I wanted to thank Hurley but it seems the cheery little fellow has already scrambled away, intent on delivering the evening meals.*

It was now the first of July, two days after Het has asked her to help with Lan's birthday ceremony. Ake wanted to make Lan's birthday special. She believed she had planned something she hoped Lan would find romantic. *I have so many questions. Either we have grown children and grandchildren, or we share a child and Lan has grandchildren. Maybe Orilan had children. I wonder how old he is now.*

Lan's son had been conceived in evil against his will. The baby had been born on the same day Ake turned nine. Orilan's conception still haunted Lan's dreams.

Ake had tried to purchase an alluring dress with little success.

Alena and Nuo had managed to help her put something together from their collective attire. Alena had covered her in a black cloak, telling her to be careful and only remove the cloak when out of the sight of others, as due to the Cirites' conservative nature, they might not react well to her attire.

With Caoimhe and Hurley's help, Ake had cooked Lan a meal from the ship's limited ingredients. She hoped it was elven enough for him on this auspicious occasion. She had packed two blankets in the picnic basket she was carrying. Het had told her Lan needed to be at the stone circle in a few hours.

Alena had convinced Lan that taking Ake for regular walks on the island may improve her health. Lan had looked at Alena in amusement, but had agreed as he preferred his feet on dry land. Ake walked across the deck towards the dock to see Lan standing near the stern.

Ake lifted her eyes to the sky; the moon was full and the stars twinkled merrily. Lan waited for her to reach him before he helped her onto the dock. He joined her and gave her a brief smile.

'Can I carry the basket?'

'No, I can manage.'

They climbed the path in awkward silence. Lan's shoulders slumped with exhaustion; he'd had dark circles under his eyes since his earlier experience with the stone circle. They walked for about twenty minutes until they found a secluded plateau surrounded by shrubs and rocks. Ake placed down the picnic basket and drew out a blanket. She unfolded it, placed it on the ground and drew out some bowls, utensils, candles, matches, a bottle of rum and a tureen. Ake sat on the empty space of the blanket. Lan sat on a nearby rock, his hands gripped the jagged surface, his knuckles draining of colour.

'Are you okay?'

Lan's gaze sought hers. 'No.'

'What is it?'

He sighed and hopped down from the rock, walking over to her. 'I feel restless and incomplete, like something is just out of reach. I am worried about you as well.'

'We both need a break from all this worry, Lan.' She smiled at him and patted a space next to her. 'Come sit with me.'

Ake took out another blanket as Lan shivered; he wasn't dressed for the frigid night air. Winter had begun and he was without waistcoat or cloak and he'd exchanged the tights he hated for rough-spun loose pants and soft riding boots. Ake had spent her weekly stipend on Lan. He sat down next to her and gratefully accepted the blanket she threw at him, wrapping it around his shoulders.

'Are you hungry?'

'Yes, but not for stew or salted meats. That is tedious.' He sighed.

Ake gave him a smile and lit some candles. She removed her cloak and began to pour them some rum. Lan took the drink she handed him and his eyes settled on her accentuated bosom. She laughed. Dressed in black leather breeches and a blue halter top—the bust trimmed with white lace and tightened with silk ribbon stays to appear even more ample—Ake looked especially beautiful with her long hair tied up in a bun, held with pins and decorated with dried flowers.

Lan drained his drink and lowered his eyes to her legs as she reached across him to retrieve the cup.

'I've never seen you in pants.'

Ake opened the tureen and placed some of the baked fish and asparagus in a bowl, spooning over a creamy lemon sauce. She felt his hands trail down her leg and giggled. He let go when she handed him the meal.

'You seem to like the outfit.'

'It's very sensual. The woman encased in it is tempting with or without it,' he said softly. Desire filled his eyes before they narrowed and he frowned.

Ake lowered her lashes and smiled. 'Anyway eat up.'

Lan tried a mouthful. 'It is tangy and creamy at the same time. The fish flaked away from the bone and was tender and seasoned well; it was an excellent dish.' He finished the meal and placed the bowl down.

Ake nodded. 'I have something for you.' She pulled out a medium-sized, beige box and handed it to him.

'Thanks.' Lan opened the box; two long, silver knives shone in the moonlight. They were accompanied by handcrafted leather wristguards engraved with stars and the elvish symbols for scrying. He took the guards out and placed them on his wrists and slid the long knives into the sheath built into each guard. Lan turned and gave her a smile filled with emotion.

'Thank you,' he mumbled.

'The symbols are the translation of your birth name, Star Scryer, appropriate for your birthday.'

'It's a wonderful gift. I never tried to celebrate my birthday before, even when raised among humans.'

'Why not?'

'It seems stupid now, but back then it seemed disrespectful to my elven heritage.'

A cold wind began to blow and Ake reached for her cloak.

'No, I don't think so. It's my birthday.' He pulled her towards him and wrapped the large blanket around them both. 'I really appreciate this.' His mouth brushed her cheek in a delicate kiss. Lan turned and looked up at the sky. '*We* never really celebrated it either. I did accept your occasional gifts because you put in so much effort to make me happy. Just in case you ask.'

'I don't remember that.'

Lan sighed and turned his head to hers; his eyes dark pools of emotion. 'No, you wouldn't.' Tears brimmed in his eyes.

This is so hard on both of us. I want to remember all the things he claims we had. I am sick of him holding back from worry he will hurt me and letting time pass where we could be making new memories before I slip further away. 'I will try to remember tonight, Lan. Can you not remember for me?'

He nodded. Ake took his mouth gently with hers and broke the kiss swiftly so he wouldn't turn away.

'Where will we be if you forget our relationship suddenly while we are caught up in a passionate moment? I will be the one to frighten you again and you will hate me.'

Ake began to rain kisses all over his face. 'I don't care.'

Lan moved away from her, becoming tangled in the blanket. As he was trying to untangle it, she pushed him by the shoulders onto the ground and kissed him. His arms encircled her and drew her down onto him, though he turned his head away from her.

'No more, Ake, holding you is enough.'

She felt his attraction and with her fingers on his chin, turned his head to look at her. She kissed him again. His eyes flashed briefly with emotion: desire, frustration, despair.

'I am sorry. I will stop. May I ask a favour?' asked Ake.

'Okay.'

'Kiss me once, show me the love we had, and I will never bother you with it again.'

He nodded, pulling her against him and kissing her with abandon. She felt his need become greater and his hand slipped to her breasts; he squeezed them gently before his hands slipped to his sides. 'You will forget this.'

'I will try not to.'

'Thank you for tonight. Shall we head back?'

Ake pushed his hands away and leapt up. 'No, there's

somewhere we have to be.' She threw on her cloak and packed up as Lan rose and helped her. She grabbed his hand; his expression was filled with curiosity.

'Follow me.' She turned and led the way.

CHAPTER THIRTY-ONE

They are running behind schedule. Het was dressed in green robes and was barefoot. His long, curly chestnut hair flowed down his back. He had placed large torches on poles around the outside of the stone circle. He turned to look at it in the torchlight; it shone with ethereal beauty. Most circles were made purely of stone, but the elven masons who had built it had done so with care. The ivory stone pillars stood in a circle four feet apart and were topped with horizontal black marble pillars. He ran his hand down one of the pillars; faint elvish runes were embedded in the stone and he felt each of the eighteen pillars, translating the script.

Devoted, honourable, kind, graceful, protective, noble, disciplined, loving, respectful. The first nine pillars are dedicated to virtues. The last nine represent the vices in one's character. Pride, stubbornness, vanity, greed, bloodlust, lechery, jealousy, laziness and gluttony.

Het took out incense from the pockets of his robe and placed them in various cracks in the ancient pillars. There was a commotion behind him; he heard Lan and Ake arguing.

'I won't go near it, I feel awful.'

Het turned towards them. Lan had gone very pale and his hands shook. Beads of sweat had formed on his brow. Ake stared at her husband, her hands on her hips. 'You must complete this, Lan; that is why you are restless and feel incomplete. You will weaken if you resist.'

Het approached them. 'Welcome, young elf, to the trial of majority, do you come willingly?' Het then repeated the words in elven. '*Falite, Daione Sidhe, bairn iudiciis fasta derbyn.*'

Lan looked from Ake to Het and grimaced. 'I should have been prepared for this. If it will stop me feeling awful, I accept.'

'We had little time and a lack of druids,' said Ake.

Het tried to keep a straight face and failed. 'And we still do. I was some years off completing the apprenticeship. But I am all you have.'

'What do I do?' asked Lan.

'Go behind that tree. Hanging from the branches is what you will wear. You will need to change out of your current clothes.' Het pointed to a tree.

Lan sighed and did as he was told. 'I am not wearing this, Het.'

'You have to,' said Het.

They heard a fluttering of cloth and Lan stepped out wearing the garb. Ake giggled and Het grinned.

'Better you than me,' said Het.

Lan was dressed in a skirt of fabric leaves cut from odd pieces of cloth that barely afforded him modesty.

'Where's the top?'

'That's only woven for women,' said Het.

'Should have made it longer.' Ake giggled.

'Be grateful; Ake made it for you. As is customary, a partner or relative makes it.' Het glanced to Ake.

'I know it's supposed to resemble an ornate pleated kilt of leaves, but I struggled as I only know a few stitches.'

'You are enjoying this a little too much,' said Lan.

'Of course,' said Het.

Lan sighed. 'I appreciate the effort, Ake.'

Ake nodded. 'I know you could have done better if you knew, but it was supposed to be a surprise.'

'Ake, I need you to leave now, this is between the initiate and druid,' said Het.

Ake nodded and walked out of sight.

'I don't like that, Het. There are no elves and druids left; their strict protocols don't hold with me. She is not safe on her own, you should know better,' said Lan.

Het grinned at Lan. 'You are right. You get her, elfling. Run.'

Lan glared at him before sprinting after her, the skirt fluttering in the wind. Lan pulled it down before he reached Ake. He grabbed her hand and they sprinted back. 'Sit there and don't move. Promise me you will stay.'

Ake sat down on some sparse grass, her knees to her chin, and proceeded to watch.

Het headed towards the circle and Lan trailed after him.

'Dee and Sorendee, bless this elfling that would become an elf. Do not deny him the trial of majority.' Het turned to Lan. 'That translation was for Ake's benefit. I doubt she remembers much elvish.' Het turned back towards the circle. 'Dee, Sorendee, *gratas bairn Daione Sidhe. Natas competens majorius.'*

The runes engraved in the stone representing virtues began to glow a brilliant green and those of vice burned red.

Het turned and grinned at Lan. 'Well, I must be druid enough for it to have worked.' Het saw Lan's eyes close and he looked like he was about to swoon. Het steadied him with a hand on his shoulder. 'Lan.'

Lan opened his eyes and they glowed green. 'Leave me be, druid.'

Het released him. Lan walked towards the circle, his eyes glazed over, and his muscles appeared rigid, as if he wasn't in control of himself.

'Wait, I need to bless you first.'

There was a huge flash of green light and Lan disappeared.

Lan heard Het curse. He reached up his hand to touch a see-through ceiling. The sound of Ake's gentle footfalls reached him as she ran towards the circle. *So strange.* He could see her legs and heard her begin to sob. *This is for you, Ake.* Lan forced himself to look away and glanced around the room. He was in a passageway conceived of pure light. Pathways in a variety of colours led off in different directions. Lan shrugged and proceeded down a fluorescent green corridor.

As he walked down the path, the walls seemed to shrink. Tendrils of vines grew out of the wall and became thick with thorns. Several of the vines shook and broke away from the wall and snaked towards him. He grabbed the vines and snapped them. It became a game he was fast losing as the mass of vegetation began to entwine itself around his torso. The thorns pricked him and a wave of jealousy burst through his heart. He began to rip at the vines in anger. *How dare Het kiss her first. Bloody druids trying to get what they want. He was Dane's apprentice and knew full well she was mine and he still kissed her.*

The vines began to squeeze the breath out of him and the thorns broke his skin. *'Embrace the pain of jealousy. You cannot fight it.'*

No, Het is a great guy. He kissed her long before I even made my intentions clear. I do not own Ake. The vines squeezed him harder and he gasped. *I own the fact I was jealous of men around Ake in the past. That is my regret to bare.* Lan heard the vines screech and their grip on him lessened. He glanced down at his hands as they began to blaze with magical fire. Lan threw the *Mystic Fire* at the vines and they screamed and retreated. He turned and ran back to the passageway of light, his breathing ragged with exhaustion, blood welled on his chest where the thorns had pierced the skin.

'No, Het, let me go. I am going in there,' he could hear Ake yelling.

'Ake, you can't. Ow, don't kick me.'

'Then stop trying to drag me back,' she cried.

'You need to trust Lan. Do you think he would want you to follow him through an elven challenge?'

'I already did when we got engaged.' Ake squealed with delight. 'I remember!'

'See, Ake, you need to trust him,' said Het.

'Fine,' grumbled Ake.

Lan smiled and looked at the other coloured paths. *So, the trial of majority is facing your vices. Great, I have more than one. But she's worth it.* Lan walked forward and chose a mirrored hall. He saw countless versions of himself preening and watched as countless unknown faces appeared next to the reflections. Their eyes bored into his, filled with disgust. *I know I am vain. So be it.* His reflections began to speak; the tips of their mouths turned up in a smirk, clearly revolted by his vanity.

'You think you are better than us.'

'That is not true,' said Lan.

The reflections' voices rose in unison and Lan covered his ears.

'Thinks he is better than us yet can't decide whether he is elf or human. Dresses well to hide his shame.'

As the voices reached a crescendo, the mirrors merged and became one large single panel and Lan turned to see his past self before Ake had healed him of terrible injuries.

He had one half decent leg with a slight limp and the other was completely twisted, the skin peeling and wrinkled. The left side of his face was fine apart from the scars from the horned guards. *Oh, but the right.* He put his hand up to his face. His eye was closed over and the skin around it was dry, wrinkled, and many scars ran along the surface.

Lan screamed and held his hands up to his face, the reflection did the same. He began to cry and a single tear slid down the cheek from his one good eye.

'So be it. If this is the penalty I must pay for vanity, I accept. Just so you know, a man is allowed to dress nicely without it being a sin.'

'True, but never at the expense of thinking they are better than someone else,' said a wise voice.

Lan turned to see an ancient elf dressed in green robes, his white hair fell across his shoulders and cascaded down his back, a golden circlet adorned his head like strands of vines that ended in an orange gem shaped like the sun. The elf's obsidian eyes looked at him with fondness. Lan reached out and touched a pale hand. 'Father, why are you here?'

'It was always a father's job to be a guiding force like the sun that lights the way. I am proud of you. Be strong. When you complete this trial, as I know you will, don't let vanity stop you from accepting the gift that will restore Ake.' Dane hugged his son and disappeared.

'Goodbye, Father,' Lan whispered and turned back to the mirror. 'Yes, I am not infallible, I have thought I was better than others before.'

Something formed in his hand, which went numb with the cold, and he gripped a large ball of ice. He smiled and threw it at the mirror, covering his ears as the Mirror of Vanity shattered, a waterfall of broken glass falling to the floor. Lan uncovered his ears and headed back to the hall of light. He heard Het mumbling to himself.

'Makes sense. The pillars light up in the colour of the vice he is defeating,' said Het.

'What is grey and fluorescent green for?' asked Ake.

'Vanity and jealousy.'

'He will have a hard time with those two,' said Ake quietly.

'Thanks for the vote of confidence,' yelled Lan.

'I hear you, Lan. Are you okay? Sorry if I offended you,' said Ake.

'It's fine, Ake, if it's true,' said Lan.

Lan turned back to the corridors. *Right, I guess burgundy.* Lan walked down the burgundy corridor.

A mannequin with a large mouth stood in the centre of a room. As he approached, it took the form of his youth. It glared at him coldly and began to repeat things he had regretted saying in his pride.

'What would you know of sadness? I have no need of pity from a woman,' said the mannequin icily.

Lan stared at it as remorse flooded through him. His heart beat faster and he held his breath for a moment.

'You are the daughter of a prophecy; you can't just marry anyone. There's harm in loving you.'

'Oh, how could I have said that to her?' said Lan.

The mannequin grinned at him. 'Like a baby, an elfling. Don't tell me what to do, my little wife!'

Lan covered his ears. 'That's not what I meant.'

The mannequin strode towards him. 'Wrong. A witnessed wedding; by man's law you're mine and besides—'

Lan backed up against a wall. 'I was young and proud.'

The mannequin grinned and split in two; one become Ake aged twenty-nine and the other, himself in his forties.

'And if you did, I could have you tracked down as mutinous, and punished,' said his image.

Lan watched as his doppelganger grabbed Ake's image and hauled her over to a table it proceeded to conjure. He watched himself force Ake down across the table on her stomach and proceed to deliver two hard smacks across her backside. Lan rushed his replica and hauled it up, thrusting it against the wall, it did not struggle.

'I would never willingly lay a hand on her. Not even in my pride. I regretted what I said and made amends,' he yelled.

He glared and his anger was reflected in the mannequin's eyes.

'The basilisk poison in your blood caused you to say awful things when distressed.'

'That is true and something I tried hard to control.'

The mannequin smirked at him. 'You hurt her with your words.'

Lan let go of the representation. 'That is something I will always regret.' Lan shook as the guilt threatened to overwhelm him. 'I won't make excuses. I could have walked away.'

'Remember, pride is a double-edged axe. You can be proud in a positive way or let it reduce you to cruelty.' The mannequin smiled sadly and it disappeared.

The room began to darken and it filled Lan with dread. He turned and ran as he heard his own voice rent the air in maniacal laughter. The darkness was alive, hunting him, trying to consume him. He reached the hall of light and stood panting as the darkness retreated and the burgundy hallway returned to normal.

He heard Ake sobbing. 'I remember those cruel words.'

Pain tore through Lan and tears ran down his cheeks. The air crackled around him and sparked blue.

'Ake, I am sorry. Please also remember that you forgave me. I can't bear the thought of you hating me again,' he said sadly.

'I know I have forgiven you. But we will have a chat when you return,' she said.

'Of course, my darling,' charmed Lan.

Het laughed. 'I hope Flo and I aren't so cheesy.'

'Ori observed otherwise in our time in the underworld. Let's see, what did he relay? "Oh, Flo, your eyes are like amethysts and just as precious",' said Lan.

'Ah … well … he shouldn't have been listening in,' said Het.

Ake giggled. 'Het blushing. Never thought I would see the day.'

'Well, some things should be kept secret between a man and his beau,' said Het.

'Underworld?' asked Ake.

'Let's worry about that later, honey,' said Lan.

'Okay,' said Ake.

Lan looked at the other remaining colours and felt drawn towards brown. He walked cautiously towards the corridor and tried to continue but there appeared to be an invisible blockade. *Strange.* He pushed on the seal with both hands and it budged a little. Changing his stance, Lan shoved with all his strength. He gasped as a rush of air lifted his garment and toyed with his hair as the corridor suddenly felt wider. *Stubborn seal. I guess it's gone.*

Lan cautiously made his way down the hall. He crashed into another seal and winced. Pinned to the invisible seal was a familiar document. Unpinning it, he began to read.

Date: 325 CE   *Location: Caelestis*

Registration of Marriage

Groom: *Trebrelan Lord of Caelestis*

Bride: *Telewanake of tribe Crykenuak*

Registered: *Summer 325CE*

Notes: *Telewanake was beholden to Trebrelan and agreed to become his lover. This is a binding contract for marriage. As head of his household, Trebrelan holds the right to register this marriage.*

Signed by witnesses: *PE Grabbitz, Mayor of Mencrey. Trebrelan, Lord of Caelestis.*

What of it? This was my right. Lan pushed against the seal but it didn't budge.

'Changing the laws to suit yourself, Trebrelan. Is your conscious clear?' That voice, familiar once, whispering kind words when he was a babe in arms, washed over him, drawing from his inner vulnerabilities.

'I knew it was taboo for a Mystic to marry,' Lan muttered. 'I didn't manipulate any law but knew of loopholes in Regian law. Any child raised by a human lord who had no blood sons, could allow his adopted son to take a bride to produce an heir for his adopted father's holdings, circumventing any legal barriers. And I wanted her, needed her.' Lan's shoulders slumped. 'I can pretend I did it to protect her and that was a major factor in my decision, but I mainly did it for myself. She is the reason I want to exist. And I will not back down when something keeps me from her. And embracing my stubbornness allows me to admit that.'

He shifted his weight in agitation and hurled flame and icy projectiles at it. One of the balls of ice bounced off the seal and hit him in the face. He spluttered as he brushed ice out of his eyes.

'I should have asked her first before registering our marriage.'

He thrust a hand against the seal and stumbled as the resistance suddenly disappeared. *When will this end? I know I have faults, but I didn't realise how many.* He walked forward; arms outstretched in case he hit another seal. His arms touched something firm. *Not again.*

His anger became palpable as electricity flared around him and he called lightning down on the barrier. He dived out of the way as it rebounded and flashed towards him. *That was a stupid idea.*

Weariness washed over him and he sat down for a brief respite, his back against the barrier. *When did stubbornness seriously impact us. I always felt it helped.* He smiled and scrambled to his feet as he came to a sudden realisation.

'I was afraid I would hurt her and left for over four years to protect her from the powers of the Lord of Death. I didn't trust in us enough to believe we could get through it. I missed seeing my boys grow in that time as well. After that, Ake kept things from me, afraid I would leave again after I'd made a pact to stay by her side.'

As the moments passed, Lan sighed and leant against the barrier.

It disappeared and he fell on his rear. He got up, rubbing his posterior and winced. *I hope this test is over. I should head back to the hall of light.* The walk seemed to take too long.

'Stubbornness used in the wrong situation makes the journey longer as you impact your destiny,' said a comforting voice.

Lan turned to his mother. Like Dane, she had passed before he became the Lord of Death and never made it to the underworld. *Yet somehow Flo had. Odd.*

'Hello Ma.' Lan gave his mother, Regona, a sad smile.

The woman appeared around fifty with long, silver hair that flowed down her back in thinning strands. She had loving brown eyes. When she smiled the corners of her mouth suggested mischief. She appeared slightly different from what he remembered, dressed in a silver robe as if it was spun from a moonbeam, a silver crown perched on her head adorned with diamonds in the shape of crescent moons.

'Hello, my boy. You have finally come of age,' said Regona.

'How are you and Father together?' asked Lan.

'The sun and the moon are destined to pair, but when they take mortal form, they too must follow the rules. My stubborn boy. You refused to follow the rules of death and changed the afterlife. Elves in stone circles no longer had to wait a thousand years for their soulmates to find them. Those that had already passed could choose to settle in your underworld or watch the living. In death, your father found my place of rest that the Clerics of Dee erected in my honour after I died,' said Regona.

'Are you happy, Ma?'

'Very. Now, son, you will face your last trial. Do not let your stubbornness and vanity cause you to fail. You cannot help Ake if you do.' Regona gave him a sad smile. 'How did she turn out?'

'Beautiful, strong, kind, merciful, adorable, strong-willed and funny. You would be proud of her.'

Regona began to fade. 'I am proud of you too. I love you, my precious boy.'

'No, Ma.' Lan began to sob. 'I never got to say goodbye.'

She shimmered within reach and embraced him, her hand patting his back as she had when he was tiny.

'Goodbye and give my love to Het as well.' Regona's eyes swam with unshed tears.

'Both Het and Ake can hear you.' Lan's brow furrowed. 'Why love to Het?'

'Just that he was a good boy.' She smiled sadly.

'Het, why do you look pale all of a sudden?' Ake called out.

'Bye Ma. I love you,' said Lan as Regona shimmered before fading away.

Lan wiped his eyes with the back of his hand. *At least this time I got to say goodbye.* He turned and realised he had somehow returned to the hall of light. There were no more coloured corridors and he decided to advance forwards. His shoulders slumped, his emotions in turmoil as sadness and weariness vied for prime position. He shivered as he entered a new area; the air was frigid and the space devoid of light. As his eyes adjusted, he rubbed his forearms as his skin began to crawl. The hairs on the back of his neck stood up as something whispered in his ear.

'Not elf, not human. What are you?'

I'm not sure. For starters, I don't have my elven ears anymore or elven hearing.

'So, you prefer to be human?' asked the voice.

Good question. I always resisted my elven heritage as I thought my elven father had abandoned me. Every elf I met seemed void of any emotion. Yet I never felt human enough either. After meeting the Anwyl elves I realised you can be regal and not be devoid of emotion.

'I am Trebrelan, son of Regona and Dane of Anwyl. I am of the Daione Sidhe and former Lord of Caelestis.' Lan bowed to the darkness, hoping to meet the voice.

Lan's ears burned and he cried out in pain, covering them. When the burning stopped he felt the tips of them and grinned. *So, the gods have restored my elven ears.* He covered them again as his exceptional hearing returned with a loud buzzing. He blinked and listened; the sound of branches shifting as something moved.

'I command you, show yourself.'

The entity obeyed. *So, I can use the command spell again.* The darkness dissipated and the rest of the hallway flooded with light. His body felt like it was floating on air. He closed his eyes as he felt himself swept up in a current of gentle air.

CHAPTER THIRTY-TWO

Lan took a deep breath as he collided with solid ground. He rested a moment and ran his hands along soft, warm grass, breathing in both a foreign yet familiar smell. *It is as if I am home. A mixture of grass clippings, the sun-warmed earth, and the scent of flowers wafting on a gentle breeze.* As he was able to focus again, he glanced around, noticing he was in a great hall made of white stone. The floor was carpeted with grass and flowers. He gasped in surprise when he realised the bright blue sky interlaced with clouds and life-giving sunlight was a ceiling made of deep blue sapphires. Various weapons were mounted on one wall and a large table with a feast graced the adjacent wall. Behind the table bubbled a small creek, fed by the large waterfall that spurted over grey rocks jutting out of the stone wall. Deer grazed in the grass and Lan could see a large minotaur pouring wine. He turned his attention to the back wall where two beings of scintillating light sat upon thrones. One throne was made of branches woven into a dainty seat and covered in an array of flowers. The being seated on this throne wore a crown of crystals; she appeared as a fair woman whose shape shifted as she moved. The other throne was made of flame; the being upon it manifested as a tall, dark, muscular man who carried an ornate spear. The handle of the spear was made of gold and decorated with unknown symbols; the tip made of blue light. The male deity wore a crown of gold and a large flame glowed in the centre of it.

Lan fell on his knees and touched his head to the stone floor, arms outstretched in front of him in supplication. 'Hail, Dee and Sorendee.'

'Rise, son of Merkeri and Luneryion. You are expected,' said an intimidating male voice.

Lan glanced up. Sorendee stood over him; the light that made up his form shifted and his form adjusted. Lan shivered and rose.

Dee stood and approached them. Her voice was as strong as the earth and yet as light as birdsong. 'Do not be frightened, Trebrelan, child of the sun and moon.' She reached out and patted his shoulder. Her grey blue eyes held warmth and merriment like Ake's used to.

Of course, these are Ake's grandparents. Lan grinned cautiously.

Sorendee smiled and it came off as more of a grimace. 'You are no longer an elfling, Trebrelan. It is time for you to accept the mantle of adulthood. We have allowed you to become one of the last Sidhe and reap the benefits that come with it as we need you to restore our grandchild to her former powers. Then, maybe you will both help defeat the abomination that Hau Halfey has become.'

'He called himself Hau Halfey?' asked Lan.

Dee nodded. 'Yes, he was proud of his elven heritage and wanted to make it apparent so he used the elven word for half-elf.'

'I will do anything for Ake.' He turned his head and blushed as his feelings for her burned within.

'I know you will.' Dee patted him on the head and returned to her throne.

'Trebrelan, do not be embarrassed to show your emotions. You are unique for an elf. Adaptable and passionate, and you think of everyone's individual needs, not just those of the elven kingdom. You care for the greater good, but not at the expense of the vulnerable,' said Sorendee.

'You see better things in me than I do,' said Lan.

Sorendee's voice boomed with annoyance. 'Rubbish, the gods do not lie.'

Lan bowed his head. 'I am sorry if I offended you.'

'Husband, he is now mortal, mind yourself,' said Dee.

Lan looked up to see Dee leaning into the corner of her throne, her legs outstretched over the armrest.

'Hmm … maybe too harsh.' Sorendee turned and pushed Lan towards Dee. 'Maybe this one is yours to deal with.'

Dee yawned. 'Yes, he may be a warrior of sorts, but he isn't one of your robust and emotionally distant human knights.'

Sorendee gave her a brooding stare. 'They had emotions. The urge to fight, and were brave and stoic.'

Dee smiled at her husband. 'And how did they fair, sweetheart?'

'Yes, well; not in front of the boy. And that wasn't this world anyway,' said Sorendee.

Dee laughed and Lan felt his heart fill with joy.

'Other worlds?'

Dee winked and sat up. 'There isn't just one plane of existence, Trebrelan. Each of those planes have their own universe and worlds. We are their gods, but they know us by other names and forms. Unfortunately, we now put very little effort into your plane. Thirteen times we have pushed life unto this plane and every time humans have destroyed it.'

'Then why did you send Ake?' Lan asked.

'My husband said it was a wasted effort. Ake's memories will prove whether we destroy your plane permanently. As it is, magic is leaving your world. But I could not totally abandon you all.'

'Get on with it. I am sure the boy wants to get out of here,' commanded Sorendee.

'Oh hush, dear.' She turned and glared at her husband.

Wait till Ake hears about this. She is so much like her grand-mother. Lan grinned at the arguing deities.

Dee turned back to him and smiled. 'Sorry you had to see that. Now where was I? That's right. When you became the God of Death, we offered Hau the position of the Lord of Justice after he took the rite of majority. He refused, saying he would become powerful without our help and build an elven legacy that would change the world, bringing justice to elves alone. We need you to become the Lord of Justice and Protection.'

'Why must I become another lord of something? Can I not just be free of such things?' asked Lan.

'I thought you made him smart.' Sorendee smirked at Dee.

She sighed. 'Dear one, you need the powers to defeat Hau and restore Ake, remember.' She patted Lan on the head like he was a tiny child. 'When the sun and moon created your soul, my husband and I had an argument over what you should become. Your soul was powerful, like those of newborn deities. Only one other soul of pure compassion and mercy was as powerful. As I was blessing you with the title of the Lord of Justice and Protection appropriate for your nature, your soul clicked with the other one and it chose you for its future mate. It bequeathed you its counterpart title, the God of Death, activated only by choice. My husband agreed and awarded you the title. Unfortunately, Drianna tricked you into giving up your godhood. My husband was annoyed with you for that, among other reasons, and refused to bring your bride into the world.' Dee winked at him. 'You and I sorted that problem out. With you returning freely of your own choice to defeat Drianna.'

Lan frowned. 'Other reasons—'

Sorendee's voice rose an octave as he interrupted. 'I decided to gift a prophecy of the lovers of life and death to mortals. You and your beloved's soul sat in stasis for thousands of years.'

Dee plucked a flower out of her hair and tossed it to her husband who caught it. 'When you were reborn, the corrupt druids wanted you separated from Ake so they had Dane be involved in a dark ritual to activate the darkness in your blood. You had a less than joyous youth so your Arakaen blood, a joyous thing, lay dormant and the darkness woke and haunted you. The evil ones meant for death to corrupt you, but out of love you chose the mantle of the God of Death. Amities knew all of this and chose an early death. It was the sacrifice needed to barter for the title of the God of Death if you were willing to give it up. And you did so for Ake.'

'Oh, our poor Amities.' Lan's eyes brimmed with tears. 'I thought it was just his time.'

'Your father, Dane in this mortal lifetime, was son of the King of the Arakaen in elvish, or Fiadhri in the Eriu language. That is why you were born Arakaen, prince of Anwyl—a realm of hills, peatlands and unpredictable storms. Dane's mother also was the queen of faeries. Her home and that of her mate's was the last bastion of their people. But they too have perished. At one time, there were many Sidhe ruling over many domains and keeping balance. Now they too are gone.' Sorendee frowned. 'But that heritage must now be awakened in you.'

Lan's eyes narrowed. 'What manner of evil could harm those wise little elves?'

'Humans found the last few and put them to death.' A single tear rolled down Dee's cheek. 'I was fond of them.'

Sorendee sighed. 'Did you not ever wonder how a mystic could command storms and other high magics usually reserved for mage elves? It kind of helps to have the moon and the sun for parents.'

Lan's eyes widened with shock. 'No, I didn't, and my grandmother explains how I sired my fairy child. The God of Death and a mercy goddess should have produced a hybrid of darkness and light, not our wonderful Caoimhe.' Lan sighed. 'How is it Drianna could walk our plane but the greater gods cannot?'

Sorendee frowned and his booming voice caused Lan to cover his ears. 'Not all gods can walk the world as immortals. We are immortal in the realm of gods but mortal on earth. Drianna consumed souls to prolong her life.'

'But Ake—' Lan cringed as Sorendee yelled.

'Silence!' Sorendee's voice dropped a few octaves as Dee glowered at him. 'A great sacrifice born of love and divine magic made her body immortal and we sacrificed our ability to enter your plane ever again to allow you to become immortal on this plane. That is why we could not kill Drianna ourselves and have very little influence in your realm.'

Lan bowed. 'I apologise. But how is it Bel entered our world?'

'Beldivin.' Dee smiled gently. 'The humans always shorten his name and he hates that. It's elvish for divine trickster. Please use his correct name. Beldivin is a trickster and record keeper. He can leave this realm to count the dead on every plane. He is a very busy god.'

Sorendee waved Lan's prostrations away. 'It matters little about which gods can enter the mortal realms longer than others.'

'I have never head the names Merkeri and Luneryion used before.' Lan's brows furrowed.

Dee yawned. 'Hmm, humans are always using the wrong names for the divine. Mercury and Artemis are a version not found in your plane, but sometimes travellers' cross planes and the timelines interconnect and names get muddled.'

Dee's eyes filled with mischief and she smiled at her husband. 'Can I play just a little?'

Sorendee laughed and it echoed off the walls.

'Why not? I may join in.' Sorendee grinned at Lan.

Lan's gaze roamed from one to the other. 'What does this game involve?'

Dee giggled. 'Translucent fairy wings.'

Lan caught sight of his reflection in the ceiling as a large pair of fairy wings sprouted from his back and shimmered in the light.

This must be what Father and Ma meant. I must accept this gift without vanity and stubbornness. Gods help me, I would have preferred something less pretty.

'We are trying to do that,' said Dee.

'Well, Caoimhe would be pleased.' *They can read my mind.*

'Of course we can. Now let me see … dragon wings,' said Sorendee.

Lan watched in fascination as the fairy wings fluttered to the ground and a large pair of red, leathery wings sprouted from his back, the tips covered in claws. Lan stumbled under the weight.

'No, they don't suit him.' Sorendee smiled. 'He's not built for strength. What about these?' Sorendee pointed to Lan and the dragon wings disappeared in a puff of smoke.

Lan watched as dragonfly wings replaced the previous ones.

'Not suitable.' Dee gestured to the mirror and Lan now sported wings made of green leaves.

Sorendee smiled. 'That is hilarious. Let me see; the boy is fairly edgy and prone to weather magic. He needs something dark yet portrays his inner light. I know just the thing.'

Lan closed his eyes as a bright light reflected off the mirror. When he opened them, a smile spread across his face and joy danced in his eyes.

'See, the boy is happy. It is masculine yet suitable for an Arakaen.' Sorendee smiled at his creation.

Lan's wings were made up of stormy clouds that resembled dragon wings. The clouds occasionally sparked and lighting wove its way to the clawed tips.

Now these are perfect. Lan's grin widened.

'Every Arakaen has something unique to their domain. You have command over storms and weather, and favour the skies as well as the land. Wings should have been your birthright as they were our granddaughter's. I also grant you two favours. You can request great healing or treasure. Make sure you word the request clearly. It is your reward for your time apart from your bride. Goodbye, Trebrelan,' said Dee.

Lan bowed. 'You have my gratitude. May I ask a question?'

Dee nodded.

'Why did my father not have a pair of wings? And why did he not have dominion over the elements? Also, I briefly remember Swan Rider mentioning them, but I have forgotten. What is an Arakaen?'

'He lost his wings for a good cause. In regard to giving up his dominion of the elements, I suggest you read that book of his. An Arakaen is a lord of a specific domain, usually one of elements and usually an elf. Hence the elvish words,' said Dee.

That makes sense, ara means domain or element and kaen means ruler or royal. Lan glanced at Sorendee.

'I award you with the ability to fly without the need for practice. I also gift you a riddle, the answer will help your wife.' Sorendee smiled broadly. 'Trust our gift will hold. In her love, her memories will unfold. Anger you will have to face, but behold a lovers' embrace.'

So, trust in my wings and Ake will follow with her memories unlocked. Lan smiled. *I must be prepared to face her anger. She's cute whether she's angry or happy. I can handle that if I get my whole Ake back.*

'I told you he had a sharp mind,' said Dee.

Lan smirked and Sorendee's eyes narrowed on his. 'Out with the joke.'

'No wonder my parents fought bitterly; the sun and the moon are so different.'

Dee gave Lan a gentle smile. 'Fiercely in love but needing their space until the heavens claim them again.'

'So, they will have peace?' Lan smiled.

'Goodbye, young man. You are no longer a boy. And you are not entitled to all our information. There must be some mystery left, even for you.' Sorendee pushed him away.

Lan's wings disappeared and he stumbled and fell on the soft grass. When he looked up, he saw the full moon and stars twinkling in the night sky as if they were wishing him farewell. He heard Ake gasp.

'You have become an adult, what name do you give yourself?' asked Het.

'Still just Trebrelan.'

'Behold, Trebrelan, go with grace,' said Het.

Lan sat up and looked at the pillars of virtue that began to flash in a variety of the colours.

'That is beautiful. What does it mean?' asked Ake.

'Orange for devoted, purple for honourable, pink for kindness, blue for graceful, white for protection, gold for noble, red for loving and silver for respectful. These are his virtues. He only lacks discipline which would have been black,' explained Het.

The colours faded and Lan heard the pillars of vice begin to crack. He ran, grabbing Ake, who had just entered the circle, and threw them both out of the way as the pillars collapsed in on themselves. Lan raised his head and saw Het jump out of the way. Lan stood up and pulled Ake up with him. He turned and surveyed her body for any injury. His eyes met hers and her terrified expression changed to one of love as she reached up to touch his pointed ears.

'Your ears are back to normal. I guess you finally accepted the fact you are an elf,' she whispered and moved her hands to touch the tips of his hair. 'The tips of silver on the ends of your hair are magnificent.'

She doesn't remember; I had accepted I was an elf a long time ago. He nodded. 'I have accepted that, among other things.'

'The ceremony shows a true elf's age, regardless of when they take it. You may have not made it physically to one hundred before, but your soul has passed many a century.' Het walked over to them. 'I believe you have earned this.'

Het placed a pendant around Lan's neck. The painted wooden pendant was in the shape of a rearing black stallion, flames bursting from its snorting nose as it kicked out at an invisible enemy. Mounted on the animal was a golden-winged girl in a diaphanous robe made of stars. Her golden blonde hair cascaded down her back. Her grey-blue eyes were filled with fear as if the stallion strove to protect her.

'This is magnificent, Het.' Lan bowed. 'Thank you for conducting the ceremony and the wonderful pendant. I appreciate it.'

'Think nothing of it,' said Het.

'I am not always the damsel in distress, Het.' Ake glared at him.

Het laughed, ruffling her hair and it fell over her face. Ake spat the hair out of her mouth and turned to Lan.

'Are you okay?' She squeezed his hand.

'I am tired. Let's get back to the ship. I'll explain what happened on the walk back.'

Lan walked behind the tree and recovered his clothing. He threw on his shirt but forgot to take the skirt off. He shivered and Ake took off her cloak and handed it to him. Grateful, he slipped it on.

The three friends turned and made their way back to the *Carnay*. Het and Ake were in awe as Lan explained his journey to adulthood, omitting the part where he met the gods. *I want to tell Ake first.*

Chapter Thirty-Three

As they reached the dock, Lan stopped suddenly and turned to look at Het and Ake.

'I've changed my mind, Het. Tell Alena we will be back soon.' Lan grabbed Ake's hand. 'There's something I have to do. Come with me.'

'Alena won't be pleased, Lan. The ship's repairs will be finished soon and she will order us to leave,' said Het.

'It will be on my head,' said Lan.

Ake turned and gave Het a smile as Lan sprinted away, pulling her in tow. Het turned to see Alena watching him.

'You don't need to tell me, Mr Falcon, I have seen it for myself. I will give them until midday and after that we will depart, with or without them. And what the hell was Lufar wearing?'

'I'm starving. I'll explain on the way to the galley,' said Het.

Alena nodded and Het boarded the ship.

———

They both stood staring up at the imposing monastery. The building appeared to be over six storeys, with open windows appearing at six alternating levels. Lan headed towards the back door and tested the handle. He grinned at Ake expectantly.

'You want me to break in? Why?'

'Let's go to the roof top and catch the dawn.'

Ake took the pins from her hair and her golden locks cascaded down. Lan ran his hands threw the soft strands, but she pushed his hands away, set on her task. Lan kept watch. There was an audible click as the lock was picked. Ake tested the handle and the door swung open.

'It's times like this I am glad Het taught you thieving skills,' whispered Lan.

Ake ignored him and cautiously stepped through the door. She reached a flight of stone steps and proceeded to climb them as Lan followed. They passed six landings; as they reached the top, the hallway narrowed and continued up, eventually coming to a small door. They opened it and saw light filtering in from a small hole in the roof, a rope ladder hung from the entrance. The room had five large brass bells attached to the bell tower, ropes used to ring them trailed to the floor.

Lan turned and smiled at Ake. He threw off his cloak and shirt and cried, 'Catch the elf.'

He bolted, climbed the ladder and disappeared. Ake smiled and ran towards the ladder; as she climbed, the dawn sunlight filtered down, warming her. She reached the top and saw Lan standing on the battlements. Fear flooded through her and she shuddered. Slowly, she approached him.

'Get down from there.'

'Not until you climb up too. You should see the view.' Lan grinned.

'How did you get up there?'

Lan leapt down and walked over to her. He lifted her in his arms and she struggled.

'Put me down,' she yelled.

Lan ignored her and ran and jumped up onto the battlements. She screamed and clung to him. He placed her down gently. 'Take a look.'

Ake opened her eyes and gasped. She could see the forest and the river that wound its way through it to meet the farms; the buildings of the town looked tiny.

'Beautiful,' she whispered.

'It is, but not as much as you.' He squeezed her hand before his eyes glistened with emotion. 'I need you to remember us. I have waited far too long.'

'How long?'

Instead of answering, he hummed a tune before his words followed.

Worlds apart,
separated by the ancient dark
Biding his time
To feel again.

Born from the light,
She feels his plight.
Scattered across aeons
yearning for her mate

The wheels of fate turn,
And while in their hearts true love does burn
Their epic tales are lost to time,
As the weeds devour their shrine.

His cries echo on a divine chord
I am the dark lord,
Wait for me,
I will cross sea and land
Until you cleave only to me.

Death's bell tolls
Eyes as red as burning coal
He begins the chase,
Now swept up in death's embrace.

'I know this song.' Ake brushed his arm with her fingers before whispering the final words to the song.

Her cries echo on a divine chord
I have found my dark lord,
And waited for thee,
I crossed sea and land
Now you cleave only to me.

'I have faith that you will remember us.' Lan turned and walked along the battlement. He swivelled and smiled sweetly at her. 'I love you.'

A scream ripped from her as he stepped off the edge. She ran along the edge and saw him falling; her breath halted momentarily in her lungs as her heart threatened to pound through her chest. Tears ran down her face and she dug her nails into her palms.

'No!' She took a heaving breath. 'What do I do?' *How could he? I had just started to remember.*

A voice whispered in the back of her mind. *'He is dying; don't think, act. You know you can save him.'*

Ake sobbed and jumped. *At least we will die together.* She closed her eyes and something broke in her.

—⁓—

The abomination screamed in pain. He tore at his burning face and peeled away several layers of skin. *So, Lan figured out how to break her curse. Oh well, this means a bigger challenge. They will not defeat me.*

'Bring me another slave,' screamed the abomination.

———~~~———

Ake's shoulders burned and she cried out as her golden wings sprouted from her back. All her memories collided and she gasped as they merged with the current ones. She opened her eyes and saw Lan about to hit the ground. *I have only ever used these wings for gliding.* With immense effort, she fluttered her wings and dived towards him. *I won't make it.* Her body shook, her heart clenching with fear as the ground rose up to meet her, the wind roaring in her ears.

Just before Lan hit the ground, a stunning set of stormy dragon wings sprang from his back. He flapped them to keep his purchase in the air.

How dare he. He omitted the part about gaining wings.

Lan turned and smiled at her. 'I had to do this, Ake.'

Her eyes burned with tears. 'How dare you.' Ake turned and flew off towards a high mountain. Lan began to pursue her.

Ake landed on the mountain peak and stalked towards the cover of the few gargantuan ancient trees. Lan landed and followed. She glanced back and sprinted away from him, but her husband was faster. He snatched her up in his arms and smiled when she aimed a kick at him as he took flight and landed on a branch the breadth of three men.

'Put me down,' she yelled.

He released her and sat leaning his back against the ancient trunk. Ake lowered herself down on the branch and wrapped her wings around herself to hide her sobs.

'I am not sorry. I assume you have your memory back?'

She unfurled her wings and their gazes locked. 'That was cruel.'

'No. It would have been cruel if it was done in jest. I knew it would work.' Lan gave her a gentle smile.

'You wretch.' She stood up and walked over to him. He grabbed her and pushed her down on the branch. She raised a hand and tried to push him away, but he caught it and kissed it.

'You don't mean that.'

He leant down and kissed her forehead, his mouth trailing down her cheek and jaw before his lips brushed hers. With her other hand, she grabbed the back of his head; their mouths collided. His breath was warm and his lips tasted of the spearmint she knew he chewed to freshen his breath. He used his tongue to deepen the kiss before he pulled away.

'You still taste like spearmint.'

Lan laughed. 'And you of the rosewater you rinse your mouth with after meals.'

'How romantic.' Ake giggled.

Lan shrugged and leant down to whisper in her ear. 'I have a surprise for you. I demand you become whole, healing something that was taken from you without the pain and discomfort associated with it.'

Ake screamed as she panicked, her whole body shaking as she was flooded with green light. He released her hands and watched her clutch her middle.

'Was it painful?' he asked gently.

'Very little pain. It was like I wasn't in control of my body and something was being forced to heal deep inside. I was scared.'

He smiled gently. 'Are you very angry with me?'

She nodded and wiped a tear from her eyes.

'I wanted it to be a surprise. I thought the effects would be subtle. I am sorry.'

'What did you do?'

'I have healed that part of you that you lost with Caoimhe's birth. But you will not suffer those ailments once a month, and birth will be easier. Are you still angry with me?' He hugged her.

She smiled and returned the hug. 'Thank you. How can I be angry after that?'

He loosened the hug and looked down at her. 'Be prepared; if there are more children they will be different.'

'How did you do it?'

Lan smiled gently. 'As payment for my time as the Lord of Death the gods granted me two favours. I know not being able to have more children made you sad; it was something I could now fix.' He leant down and nuzzled her neck. 'I want many babies, if you want them too, my darling.'

'I do, but years from now. Let's just enjoy each other for now.' Ake smiled. 'You met my grandparents?'

'Yes, they gifted me these wings. Apparently, I am an Arakaen, also known as Fiadhri. A type of elven royal that rules over areas of nature, and the wings were supposed to be my birthright. I will tell you the rest later. We should really head back.'

Ake nodded and Lan scooped her up in his arms, taking to the air. His powerful wing beats sliced through the air and they landed gracefully and he gently eased her to her feet.

'How come you can fly better than me already?'

'I'll explain that too.' He leant in and kissed her.

CHAPTER THIRTY-FOUR

Ake smiled coyly at Lan who winked and loosed a breathy laugh as they sprinted down the path and on to the dock just as a crewman untied the mooring rope, their wings hidden once more. The cold wind billowed the sails as Lan helped hoist Ake over the bulwark and leapt after her. Caoimhe scowled at them, her eyes puffy from crying, as Hurley patted her hand.

Het paced back and forth, then turned to give Lan a reprimanding stare. 'Why did you leave your daughter and drag Ake into the unknown?'

Ake hurried over to Caoimhe and the little fairy's eyes filled with shock as she was lifted into her mother's arms. 'My darling daughter, I missed you.'

Ake put her down and Caoimhe whistled with delight.

Hurley smiled and translated. 'I missed you too, Mother. Are you back? Do you remember Father?'

Ake laughed. 'I remember it all.'

Het's mouth spread in a wide grin. He clasped Lan in a giant bear hug as the ship began to sail out of the harbour.

'Well done.' Het released Lan and he turned to Ake. 'Amnesia takes a toll. Are you sure you remember everything?'

'It wasn't like amnesia.' Ake's eyes widened in fear and she frowned. Lan squeezed her hand.

'Describe it,' suggested Het.

'I never forgot anything, instead I relived it, trapped in a dark maze as my past chased me. I had to escape each terrible memory. I could smell, taste and feel each encounter, the scenes were more horrific than reality.' Ake gulped back a sob. 'In one instance, I remember an unknown presence hitting me; I felt each strike. As I ran, I became entangled in a mass of brambles; the haggard bodies of those I love writhed among them wailing for my help. Their cries broke me but I knew I had to run. If this entity caught me I knew I would be forever trapped. Blood splattered in my face as the creature tore our loved ones apart; the metallic taste lingered on my lips. After each triumph I could briefly communicate with others on our plane, but the timelines were distorted and I became confused. It wouldn't be too long before I had to deal with a new horrific scenario interlaced with an event from my past to overcome.' Ake shuddered.

'That's why it seemed as if at times you gained your memory but you were a younger version of yourself. You shouldn't have even been able to do that much. But you have always been strong-willed. The real Ake never forgot.' Het winked.

'Memory curse, how cruel. Making her forget would have been kinder. As the mind is tortured one's will is destroyed, the body weakens and succumbs. Hau will pay for this!' Lan pulled Ake into his arms and ground his teeth in anger.

Ake reached up and kissed the tip of Lan's nose. 'I am okay.'

Lan slowly released her; cupping her cheeks in his hand, he leant his forehead against hers. They shared a comforting moment, their breath mingling, mouths almost touching, before he slowly drew away. 'Good to hear.'

Alena left the helm in Nuo's capable hands and descended the steps. 'I will have order on this ship. You all have chores for which you get paid.'

Het nodded and strode over to Gideon who set him to cleaning the cannons.

Alena walked over to Ake and embraced her briefly. 'Welcome back, Luma. Now, I believe you may both want to get changed before you get to work. Enough time has been lost from damage to the ship, and we all need to do our bit.'

'Thanks for the outfit,' said Ake.

'Keep it. It suits you,' said Alena.

'Agreed,' said Lan hastily.

Het laughed as Lan's cheeks turned red.

Ake smiled. 'Laundry or galley?'

'Galley. Alwin is on laundry duty at the moment,' said Alena.

'How is the discipline going?' asked Lan.

'Well, first, let's say congratulations on your coming-of-age and whatever you and Luma did to restore her memories.' Alena smiled.

'Jumped off the top off the monastery. She followed and remembered she had wings. Forced her to break the curse.' Lan shrugged.

Alena stared at him; mouth hanging open in shock. She took a deep breath and composed herself. 'Bit drastic, but it appears to have worked. In answer to your question, Alwin has been tied to the mast overnight, swabbed the deck in the hot sun, washed the dishes from every meal and must now complete the laundry for two days. He has done his tasks without complaint or rebellion. We had a vote this morning and the crew have decided this is the last task.'

'He's very reserved,' said Lan.

'Yes, even for a Cirite.' Alena glanced towards the stairs.

'Well, back to it then, I guess.' Lan looked down at his outfit. 'After I change.'

'You have permission for a few minutes reprieve, then I want you in the crow's nest. With ears like that, I assume you have an elf's sight and hearing. Well, hop to it, Lufar.'

Lan turned and strode away to change.

Ake scrubbed at the vegetables in the bucket. She was in the galley listening to Caoimhe's excited recount of her first kiss. It filled her with happiness as they gossiped and chatted together about relationships and marriage. They had been sailing for two days and everyone seemed to have settled back into their routines.

Hurley was pottering around the stove, filling the bubbling pot with ingredients. The stew smelt wonderful and Ake and Caoimhe breathed in with a smile.

Ake had filled her daughter in on almost everything and blushed at a certain memory.

Caoimhe tilted her head curiously as Ake looked down at her task and smiled. *I wonder if I smile like that when I think of Hurley. Mother has her own smile for Father.*

The ship lurched suddenly as if something had passed under it. Cutlery and bowls crashed to the floor. There was a loud bellowing like an animal in distress and the ship lurched again.

Hurley rushed to Caoimhe and the couple ran and hid under the butchers block that was bolted to the floor.

'I will go check it out,' said Ake.

'Be safe, Mother,' Caoimhe signed.

'I will.' Ake smiled and left the galley.

Lan grabbed onto a nearby rope as the ship lurched. He looked around and saw an enormous shark fin dip under the surface of the water. From his perch in the crow's nest and his elven sight, he could see extremely far. Something broke the water's surface and an immense black tentacle with huge suckers briefly stretched up from the inky depths.

What is that thing? His elven hearing picked up the sound of whale song, something he was familiar with being an elf that had lived most of his life on an island.

He yelled down to the crew. 'Something strange off the prow. Enormous fin and black tentacles. Bellows like a whale.'

'Man the guns. Octoquark spotted off the prow,' yelled Gideon.

Several crewmen shivered; their eyes widened in fear as they hurried to do Gideon's bidding.

Lan turned and watched the creature's grey, shark-like tail rise above the water. As it rolled playfully, he glimpsed its white belly and markings that could be gills. *I count eight tentacles.* The creature rolled back to its front and lifted a purple octopus-like head above the water. Its beak opened wide as it called out, revealing rows of serrated teeth. *What an incredible creature.*

Lan watched as the gunners loaded two cannons under Gideon's command. Alwin was hauled up from below and partnered with Lan. The other rifleman stood near the prow and loaded his weapon.

Lan shouted to Gideon as the creature moved slowly towards the vessel. 'It's headed this way.'

Alwin climbed into the crow's nest and readied his bow. 'You should load that weapon just in case.'—Alwin nodded to the pistol at Lan's hip—'It's a creature that could kill us.'

Lan summoned three balls of solid ice. 'Maybe I can scare it away before it reaches us.'

'Wait,' cried Alwin as Lan hurled them at the creature.

The projectiles made a resounding thud as they struck the monster in the head. It screeched in anger and increased its speed.

'It's attracted to magic.' Alwin sighed.

Lan turned to see Ake grab on to the doorframe as the ship lurched. The Octoquark had reached the side of the *Carnay* and struck the boat. Lan loaded his gun and fired as the creature latched its tentacles around the side of the ship. The silent ammunition struck one of the creature's tentacles and it screeched in an octave only he could hear. Lan covered his ears, they rang and he winced; the world became a blurry mess as a wave of dizziness washed over him.

Ake conjured bursts of *Mystic Fire*; flames streaked towards the monster's open maw. It screeched and thrust a tentacle towards her. She rolled out of its way as one of the cannons exploded and sulphur rent the air, assaulting their noses. The Octoquark bellowed in agony as the explosion destroyed an appendage. It raised its remaining extremities high in the air, lashing out at the second cannon as it fired. The crew cheered after the sulphur had cleared, the blow ripping the monster's dorsal fin in half. It let out an ear-piercing scream and everyone covered their ears as a keening known as the siren's call pierced the air. Before Alwin could grab him, Lan fell, the netting below catching him.

The Octoquark's cry continued to subdue the crew. *Carnay* shuddered as the monster rushed towards the cabin, bent on destruction. Its tentacles slammed down on the roof, shattering it in a deluge of beams and splinters. As the building caved, Hartur crawled out from the rubble and surveyed the creature, shaking with fear. Alwin scrambled down the rigging exceptionally fast and ran towards her. He thrust her away as tentacles lashed out and wrapped around him.

His bow hummed to life. '*We... ll this is a b... it of a tight situation.*'

Alwin wheezed in pain as he tried to catch his breath. Hartur pushed herself to her feet and searched hastily through the rubble and her hand landed on the hammer.

Het pushed the cannon in view of the beast as some of the crew trembled nearby covering their ears. With the aid of Gideon, the cannon fired again and hit the side of the beast. The Octoquark howled, dropping Alwin. He hit the deck and groaned; his breath rasped in his chest.

Hartur dragged him away from the monster. 'Stupid hammer, do something.'

'I am Nietra, I will not obey someone who deems me stupid, even if it has some truth,' came Nietra's gloomy telepathic reply.

Alwin groaned. 'Oh shut up.'

Hartur glared at him. 'I am just trying to save your life.'

'I meant the hammer.' Alwin coughed into his hand; as he drew it away it was covered in pink, frothy blood. He groaned in pain, and fear made his insides clench. *I want to live.*

The cannons fired again and missed. The creature turned its attention to the gunners. Its tentacles dragged one of the cannons forward and flung it into the ocean with little effort.

'Hasten to aid your master,' whispered Alwin.

'I am honoured to answer you, Master of the Forge,' cried Nietra.

Lan uncovered his ears and used the ropes nearby to clamber down from the netting, retrieving his gun that had landed a foot away. The beast's tentacles reached towards Lan cautiously. As if sensing magic, it whined in pain. Ake rushed towards him and gripped his hand, summoning water in her hand to shield her husband if necessary.

Alwin heard the whispers of magic, his innate abilities responding to the magically forged items. *'Power, fire, force.'*

'Run for cover,' cried Alwin.

'I am so sorry.' Lan fumbled with his weapon before aiming it at the beast. 'This is my fault.'

'Wait, Lufar. Don't fire, it will avoid the magic it can sense,' Alwin screamed and coughed again. Blood oozed at the corners of his mouth. 'Woman, take the hammer and strike at the monster's tail.'

'And risk my life?' She stepped away from him.

'Please, I am dying,' begged Alwin.

'Fine, if I get killed, I will haunt you.' She glared at him.

Alwin chuckled softly and coughed again, spitting out blood.

The woman ran towards the monster and swung her hammer at its tail as she reached the bulwark. Nothing happened. Then the hammer glowed scarlet as a smoky mist seeped from the ruby head. The mist grew in mass and entered the wounds of the beast. The creature stopped and blinked, then it began to attack itself.

'Fire, Lufar,' yelled Alwin.

Lan took aim and fired. The creature bellowed and, for a moment, it appeared as if nothing was going to happen. The *Carnay* was lifted up by the force of the silent explosion and landed with a resounding slap in the water. The creature bellowed, catching on fire from within. It rolled over, engaged in death throes as it tried to fight for its life before sinking beneath the waves.

CHAPTER THIRTY-FIVE

'Nuo, take her to the hold,' cried Alena.

The stowaway who had saved Alwin's life, lashed out as Nuo grabbed her and dragged her away.

'Let me go. I want to know he's okay; I have a debt,' screamed the violet-eyed woman.

'Please don't hurt her,' mumbled Alwin as he lay with his back flat against the deck, his hands cradling his stomach as he coughed up blood.

Lan scrambled past the debris from the shattered cabin and lowered himself to rest on his haunches to lay his hands on Alwin's body; the skin was darkening quickly where the tentacles had wrapped around him. As Lan applied pressure, the boy groaned, trying to pull away.

'Please stop.' Alwin swallowed hard as his eyes filled with tears and he clutched his stomach. 'No more.'

'How are you not screaming in agony?'

'The pain is unbearable.' Alwin wheezed the last word as blood pooled at the corner of his mouth.

'You are allowed to show emotion, Alwin, despite what Cirites want you to believe.' Lan smiled gently.

Alwin shook his head, he spat out frothy mucous and his eyes locked on Lan's. 'I've seen how it destroys countries when passion and pride lead to war. No thank you.' Alwin sighed. 'But I would have liked to have lived longer to get to know the girl with the purple eyes.'

'Sailor, grab some first aid supplies, liquor and aid Mr Macóir,' Alena shouted.

A sailor crashed to his knees beside them, unravelling clean bandages and handing Lan some alcohol. 'Sip this, boy.' The sailor held the bottle to Alwin's lips. He took a swig, his face a horrid shade of green as he fought to keep it down. 'This is pretty dire, kid.'

'I think I'm dying.' Alwin's eyes swam with tears. 'Tell my dad I love him.'

Lan's eyes shone with determination. 'You will live!' He moved his hands to Alwin's belly. 'Thanks be to Dee and Sorendee, may you please heal Alwin of his life-threatening wounds?'

The scent of freshly scythed grass whipped around them as the dying boy's body was filled with emerald light, healing Alwin's injury.

'That was my last favour. No more putting yourself at risk like that,' said Lan.

Alwin turned and glared at Lan for the briefest of moments. 'I thank you for extending my current lifespan. You need to learn to listen, or educate yourself on the creatures of this world. That Octoquark was passing by and would have let us be if it wasn't for you conjuring magical hail and throwing it at the beast. This world is dangerous, Lufar, and you should be well prepared for it. Alena will most likely punish you for not waiting for direct orders. She will also demand recompense for the destruction of the cabin.'

Alwin stood and brushed Lan's hand away as he tried to steady him. 'Alena will hang her. I need to prevent it,' said Alwin.

Alena strode towards them, her face a mask of fury. 'Lufar, you have put the lives of my crew at risk again. You do not attack a monster without waiting for my command. You are hereby stripped of your title as a marksman and member of the crew.

You are to be put ashore at the next stop in two days. Your wife, as a member of my crew, is to stay aboard. You should hang for this, but I care for you, so exile is all I can do.'

Lan stared at her. 'You will not separate Ake from me. If you have the power to break my contract then you have the power to do so with her.'

Alena stared him down. 'Alwin needs to be trained. He needs someone who has self-restraint. Not once has your wife put anyone in danger.'

'You will not separate me from her,' yelled Lan.

Lan felt a hand on his shoulder. 'Lan, we will work this out.'

He turned and looked at Ake. 'Are you okay with this?'

Ake's eyes brimmed with tears. 'How could I be? Please, Alena, stop this.'

'I have made up my mind.' Alena turned her attention to Alwin. 'I will hang the stowaway shortly.'

'Wait, please.' Alwin's eyes filled with concern. The expression quickly disappeared and was replaced with indifference. 'I invoke the mariner's right of sanctuary for both Lufar and the girl.'

Alena smirked at him. 'Alwin, that is only for family or spouses.'

Alwin gave her a cunning smile. 'She is my betrothed. You are a captain, marry us and I swear to you she will be no trouble. And Lufar *is* our relative; yours and mine both.'

Alena frowned. 'You don't even know the woman.'

'Cirichad law. I have shared with her affection reserved for procreation. You dishonour my reputation and that of my household if you don't marry us,' said Alwin.

Alena, Ake and Lan stared at him in shock.

'Did you lay with her on my ship?' asked Alena curiously.

Alwin blushed for the briefest of moments. 'I am not inclined to do that sort of thing. I *have* kissed her though.'

Alena began to pace. 'She hasn't killed anyone, but almost

drove two guards to do so. What makes you believe you are immune to her wiles?'

'I am willing to prove it,' said Alwin.

Nuo approached Alena and whispered in her ear. 'She is a Velterran descendant. We have them all.'

Lan tilted his head, his eyes narrowing on the pair. *Something unusual about this whole arrangement. Alena is aware of her background and now has those belonging to her past gathered in one spot. I wonder if she intends to hand us over? She is a bounty hunter after all. I need to stay with my family,* thought Lan. He bowed deeply. 'I am responsible for the damage to the ship and putting everyone's life at risk again. I wish to stay on this ship until we reach Velterra. I will pay the crew's wages for a month and reimburse you for damage to the ship when we reach our destination.'

'You will remain tied in the brig with no meals and only water. If you do not keep your word, you will be handed over to the authorities when we reach Velterra.' Alena gestured to Gideon and he rushed over. 'Gideon, take him away.' Alena turned to Nuo. 'Bring the woman up.'

Ake wept as Lan was taken away; she turned and fled to the galley.

—⁓—

Hartur dug her heels in, making it hard for her captor to drag her up from the hold, but the other woman was determined and pushed the stowaway towards the others.

Hartur tilted her head and stared into her captor's eyes, grinning as they fixated on hers. *'Release me.'*

'She's going to run, Nuo.' The boy bolted towards them, his blond hair waving in a salt-flecked draft.

Nuo released her, her blank eyes out of focus as Hartur sprinted to the bulwark near the mizzen-mast. Glancing over her shoulder, Hartur grinned as Nuo shook herself. The first mate's eyes filled with anger as she sprinted after her. Hartur grunted as her next breath was forced out of her lungs when she collided with a warm male chest.

'It's okay. I've got you.'

Hartur struggled and the boy winced. She stared down at his blood-soaked shirt.

'I can't have you put my family members at risk. I won't allow you to be killed either. I have invoked the mariner's law of sanctuary. You are to be my wife. I would know your name.'

'We have not been intimate so there is no reason for us to wed. I would rather hang.'

'Wrong. You kissed me.' Alwin's lips briefly brushed hers. 'See, we have sinned.'

'*Slap yourself,*' Hartur commanded.

The boy raised his hand in jest as if to strike himself and smiled briefly. 'I don't think I will hit myself.'

Hartur glared at him. 'Never has anyone resisted my abilities.'

Alena approached them and whispered to Nuo. Hartur tried to struggle against the boy, but he was stronger. Being a tiny and dextrous girl, she was suited to an assassin or spy, not against the strength of Alwin.

'How are you so strong?' Hartur asked.

'I am a bowman and former apprentice blacksmith.' The boy squeezed her tighter and winced as she thrashed about in his arms.

Hartur watched Nuo stroll towards the galley. After a few minutes, she came back and handed a small book to the captain who flicked through the book and scanned a page.

'Hold hands you two,' said the captain.

The boy released Hartur and she tried to run, but he grabbed her hand.

'I won't marry anyone,' Hartur yelled.

The captain glared at her. 'Then you will hang immediately. Do it, Nuo.'

Hartur's gaze briefly met the boy's and she saw genuine concern there.

'I am trying to save your life, like you tried to save mine by attacking that monster. That kiss was for show, I do not have any designs on your body,' the boy muttered.

Nuo grabbed her; she lashed out, delivering a kick to the woman's leg.

'Fine, yes, I will do it.' Hartur struggled. 'And you saved mine first, boy; I was trying to repay the favour.'

'My name is Alwin Smith. You should know that much at least.' His face was devoid of any emotion.

The captain struck Hartur across the face. 'That is for trying to have my guards kill each other. Your hands will be bound and you will be blindfolded while on my ship. If you so much as take off the blindfold you will be permanently blinded. Do you understand?'

Hartur glared at the captain. 'I understand.'

The captain began to read from the book. 'We have witnessed their public shame. Their sin is known to all. I wed them under the mariner's act to offer sanctuary to husband and wife. I, Alena, captain of the *Carnay*, hereby declare them wed by the god of Cirichad, and that, while in Cirichad territory, their marriage is binding until death does part them.'

Nuo released her and Hartur rubbed her swelling cheek. She watched Alwin rip an unsoiled piece of cloth from his shirt and stride towards her. Nuo pushed her towards her new husband.

'What a pity.' Alwin wrapped the blindfold around her eyes.

She heard the thud of heavy boots and a large hand grabbed hers as manacles were slipped over her wrists. She heard the key as it turned in the lock. Someone grabbed her hand and led her forward. Tears of frustration welled in her eyes. *I will punish them all.*

Chapter Thirty-Six

Hartur sat on Alwin's bedroll, her knees up to her chin, weeping and cursing. Her new husband had told her it was now dawn and two days since they were wed. The cold air fluttered at the ends of her blindfold and she shivered.

'It's not all bad. I promise you I am not a brute,' Alwin muttered.

'I just fled an awful engagement. Now I'm married to a stranger, and a cold one at that. From one overzealous stalker to an impassive freak. I have quite the luck.' Hartur spat at the ground.

'Very crass.'

Hartur growled. 'Shut up. At least I have emotions.'

'I can see you are a very impassioned girl. This is good; we are getting to know one another. I shall introduce myself. You already know my name. I am nineteen, a former apprentice blacksmith and I excel at archery. I love to read and complete any duties asked of me.'

'Great, I am married to a boring bookworm.' She sighed. 'I am Hartur Halfey, twenty-two. That is all.'

'Your name suits you. You are the epitome of spite.' Alwin sighed. 'You call me boring yet you seem to have no interests.'

'That is all I am willing to share.'

'It's a start. But you made a mistake.'

'No I didn't.'

'It's Hartur Smith now. And I will be a good husband to you.

I will curb my tongue from now on and never raise my hand to you.' Alwin squeezed her hand gently.

'Wow, the bare minimum.' Hartur laughed derisively.

Alwin released her hand. 'It wasn't the bare minimum for my poor mother.'

'So, your father is an ass?'

'He wasn't always. Something changed in him when he caught my grandfather, Amities, forging magical things.'

Bloody hell. This boy is the grandson of Amities. No wonder he can resist my abilities. I didn't know the divine couple had grand-children. I wonder if Lord Hau knows?

The breakfast bell rang. The sound of tiny feet padded nearby.

'Here you go, Alwin and Alwin's wife. I am Hurley.'

'What a sweet gesture,' said Alwin.

'It was mistress Ake's idea. Cake to cheer everyone up and celebrate a wedding,' said Hurley.

'Hartur, hold out your hands, wrists bared,' said Alwin.

Hartur turned her palms face up and Hurley placed some cake on them. 'Thank you.'

As she began to eat, she heard the rattle of chains. Heavy boots approached them; she listened intently, trying to gather information.

'Hello Het,' said Alwin.

'Hello Alwin. Alena has ordered you two chained together,' said Het.

'Why? What did I do?'

Het sighed. 'Alena felt you made a stupid decision to marry a would-be cutthroat. She is not taking any chances with your loyalty.'

'Let her eat first, Het. She must be hungry.'

'Fair enough, Alwin. I will wait. I'll be glad to get off this ship.'

'Alena is a bit harsh,' said Alwin.

'She is nothing compared to a Velterran captain. She is quaint. I would be dead if she were one.' Hartur finished the last of her cake and stood up. 'Okay, let's get on with this childish punishment.'

—✷—

The metal screeched as the door to the small cage swung open. 'I am glad to see you.' Lan smiled as his eyes opened and roamed over Ake in her green and white dress.

'Het and I have done something terrible.'

He raised a brow as she took out the stolen keys and unbolted his arms from the cage. Lan rubbed his wrists as he stood up. 'What happened?'

'We drugged some of the cake. Het will guide the ship into the next harbour and we will all escape then.' Ake shivered. 'I hope the dose was correct from what I remember of my lessons at Caelestis.'

'Hell, Ake. I already had a plan, and you were not always a good student.'

'I was a terrible one, and we have no money to pay for the wages and damage you promised to fix.'

'I wanted to bide my time.'

Ake rolled her eyes. 'While locked up? Sure.'

Lan laughed. 'Het and Ake, espionage extraordinaires. Has a ring to it.'

There was an angry whistling behind them. Caoimhe stood tapping her feet and glaring at her parents. Even Hurley looked annoyed as he began to translate the fairy's angry whistles.

'Mother, what you did was bad. Nuo and Alena are trustworthy; they are kind to me. Stop this escape. Hurley will say the food was rotten and that's why everyone felt awful.'

Ake stared at her defiant daughter. 'No, Caoimhe. I am sure Alena is a good person. But I will not have my husband's life threatened for a mistake. Would you?'

Caoimhe turned to stare at Hurley before glancing back at her mother. '*I suppose not. There were better ways, Mother. Leave, but Caoimhe and Hurley will stay with Alena's ship until we finish our contract. You must go because Alena will have you for this,*' she signed.

'No, Caoimhe, I have never been separated from you.' Ake wept.

Caoimhe ran into her mother's arms. '*I am not angry, just sad. When you forgot me I learnt I was grown. We will see each other again, but I must make my own way.*'

Ake nodded. 'I understand, my beautiful daughter.'

The ship shuddered as it made contact with the dock. Lan hugged his daughter then rushed up on to the deck where Nuo had been reefing the last sail. With the help of Alwin and Hartur, they had rolled up the sails and pinned them in their stays to slow the ship's entrance into the port. Lan looked around; some of the crew were snoring, fast asleep on the deck.

Nuo turned and bowed to him. 'Lord of Caelestis. I am a servant of the cause.' She handed him a small card. 'Look for our agents in Velterra.'

Lan smirked. 'Why would you dishonour your captain?'

'I didn't. This time Alena has gone too far in the name of justice. Flee and be safe. I will placate her. Try and pay her for the damage somehow, Lord Trebrelan. It would be just,' said Nuo.

'I will try,' said Lan.

Het rushed down the set of stairs that led to the helm. One of Hartur's and Alwin's wrists were manacled together, but Alwin had removed Hartur's blindfold.

'Why have you chained them together?' asked Lan.

'Don't trust two kids with magical aptitude who are clearly in love.' Het held up a key, laughing. 'They earn their freedom when they prove themselves.'

Hartur growled. 'I don't love him.'

Alwin stared at her for a moment. 'That's not quite true. I wouldn't call it love, but more of a mutual need to get to know each other.'

'Stop reading my thoughts.'

Alwin didn't budge as her tiny hands shoved him. 'I don't read thoughts. I get images from emotions. When you use that eye ability I can hear your thoughts then. Your emotions give you away as you lack the discipline to control them. Like most Velterrans.'

Hartur appeared to compose herself before twisting a strand of her bright red hair around a finger. She gazed up at Alwin, a coy smile on her lips. Her violet eyes flashed briefly.

Alwin sighed. 'That doesn't work on me. I will also not tell everyone here that I don't like you. I don't lie.'

Ake ran up the stairs from the hold before leaping on to the dock. She turned and smiled as Hurley and Caoimhe exited the hold and joined Nuo on the deck.

As Nuo tied the mooring line, Caoimhe fluttered overboard to settle herself on the dock, her tiny footsteps almost silent. Lan, jumping overboard, swept his daughter up in his arms and embraced her. When he placed her down she didn't giggle like she used to.

'Goodbye, my darling Caoimhe. We will see you again,' said Lan sadly.

Caoimhe bowed and signed the elven for goodbye. *'Faell, leven.'*

'Faell.' Lan bowed back before he turned and sprinted away, brushing away his tears, refusing to look back.

CHAPTER THIRTY-SEVEN

The sun was high in the sky when they saw a small town on the horizon; a cold, driving wind made everyone shiver. Lan closed his eyes; the smell of freshly fallen snow made his nose twitch before the tinkling sound of shattering icicles caused his eyes to snap open. 'It will snow tonight.'

Het, who was leading, turned and frowned. 'Look at how clear the sky is. It's not going to snow.'

'Trust me.' Lan winked.

Hartur smirked derisively at Alwin as she dragged her feet and pulled on the chain.

Alwin stumbled and turned to glare at her. 'Please stop this childish behaviour. You are a woman grown.'

'Finally, a rebuke after an hour of doing so. You are very tolerant.'

'It was a hard lesson learnt at the hands of my father.' Alwin sighed.

'What exactly did he do to you?'

'After my mother's death, anything I did annoyed him. It's not what he did, it is what he didn't. We were like strangers; he ignored me and when we did interact it was for work or meals. There was little conversation and the house was solemn. If it wasn't for my grandfather cooking for me and teaching me, I would have succumbed to neglect. And now he is gone.' Alwin's eyes swam with despair for a few moments before he composed himself.

'How old were you when your mother died?'

'Eight.'

Behind them, Ake kept pausing to look back over her shoulder. Lan hurried up to her. 'What is it?'

'I keep checking to see if Caoimhe followed. We were there for each other all those centuries after all.'

'I miss her too, my *jaen*.'

Ake blushed. 'So, I'm beautiful.'

Lan squeezed her rear. 'You know you are.'

She sighed and looked at Alwin. 'How could Arlys treat his own child like that?'

'I intend to discuss several things with Arlys when we see him again.' said Lan through clenched teeth.

Ake grabbed his hand. 'Don't cause a scene. Talk, yes, but mind yourself; for Alwin's sake.'

Lan nodded.

Alwin's shoulders slumped with fatigue.

'Maybe we should help him.' Ake stared at the back of her great-grandson, breaking her gait as Het kept a strenuous pace and the couple in front of them stopped again to argue.

Alwin rounded on them. His eyes flashed with annoyance as he stared at them. 'I can handle it.'

Hartur shifted from one foot to the other. She jabbed her husband in the back, but he ignored her.

'Playful isn't she.' Lan winked at Ake before he squeezed her rear. 'Two can play at that game.'

Ake swatted at him and bolted, overtaking the newlyweds who hassled each other as they continued along the path.

'End of the path.' Het called out a few moments later and halted as Ake hurtled towards him and crashed into his side.

Lan's shoulders heaved with silent laughter as he pulled Ake into his arms; her cute giggles made the elf's eyes light up.

Het cleared his throat. 'Edge of a cliff right here.'

Lan released his wife and stared over the cliff. The others joined them.

'What do you see with your elven sight?' asked Het.

'The path stops abruptly. I'd say maybe forty or fifty feet below.' Lan scanned the area. 'The path resumes on another plateau, over there.' Lan pointed to a spot in the distance. 'There is a large manor house on a hill surrounded by a forest.'

A familiar voice called out from behind them.

'Halt. Capture them,' yelled Alena.

Lan and the others turned. Alena rushed towards them, her brow furrowed, her staff clutched in her hands as her dark hair swayed in the rapidly cooling air, like a soldier ready for war.

Ake's gaze softened. 'So like Mandami on the eve of war. He looked valiant too.'

Caoimhe fluttered above the crew—armed with guns and carrying ropes and other belongings—whistling urgently as Hurley translated, 'Please don't harm them. They are good.'

Alena turned and smiled sadly up at the fairy. 'They drugged my crew, disobeyed my orders, put our ship in danger from a monster and let a spy get away. They are not good actions and I have a score to settle with them.'

'Alena, let it go. They are to rid us of a great evil; that is more important than your devotion to justice,' said Nuo.

Alena glared at her first mate. 'That is my father's domain over there. They are not welcome there and would just charge in there and get themselves killed. I would rather see them in chains in my hold than dead at the hands of my father. Plus, I seek justice for their actions, as is my right.'

Het unchained Alwin and Hartur. 'I will not let you hang them. Get them out of here, Ake.'

'I will need your help, Lan,' said Ake.

Het unstrapped his sword. There were gasps as Ake's golden wings unfolded from her back, her now golden eyes blazed fiercely as she gave the crew a determined grin.

'By the gods, what the hell?' cried Het as Lan's stormy dragon wings spread from his back; the clouds swirled and lightning streaked across the surface. 'One of the Fiadhri, who would have thought it.'

Hartur tried to make a run for it. Ake grabbed the girl who struggled against the older woman. 'Trust me.' Hartur, caught up in Ake's stride, struggled to keep up and screamed as the pair stepped off the edge of the cliff.

With his keen hearing, Lan heard a rifle click and rolled out of the way as a bullet whizzed past his ear.

'Who told you to fire?' Alena yelled at the man who had fired the gun.

'Okay, let's get this over with, Lufar.' Alwin walked off the edge.

Lan swore and dived over after him, grabbing the boy by his arms. Not used to flying and carrying a load, Lan faltered briefly before reaching the other side. He dropped Alwin, who landed roughly and got to his feet.

'We have to get Het,' said Ake. She took to the sky, her majestic golden wings beating the air and capturing an updraught as she flew towards Het, her husband soon flying after her.

The crash of weapons made Lan cover his ears. Six crewmen surrounded Het, their weapons connecting with his as they desperately tried to disarm the warrior. Het disarmed one man and threw the weapon away from him. A sword struck Het, opening a large gash. The warrior grunted as his sword swung upward to block a cutlass. A man yelled as he was lifted from his feet. The huge warrior's muscles almost rippled, a sheen of sweat covering them, as he tossed the man with his unnatural strength.

Het lunged forward and used his large hand to pull a sword

from another assailant, turning suddenly to deflect a blow from his right side. He ducked under another strike, grabbed the man by the scruff of his neck and shoved him towards his last attacker who sidestepped and drove his sword through Het's powerful flank. The weapon dug into the flesh, blood welling up from the wound. Het sucked in a breath as he withdrew the sword before kicking his assailant in the knee. There was a sharp snap as the man collapsed on the ground cradling his leg and crying out obscenities.

Alena growled and lunged at Het.

'It is best you don't. You need to tend to your crew,' advised Nuo.

Alena let out an angry cry as Het turned and jumped off the edge.

'As swift as night descends.' Het grinned and flapped his arms as he called out his battle cry.

Ake screamed as she dived to rescue her friend; Lan joining her descent. The couple caught Het before he hit the ground, Ake breathing heavily as she clutched at the big warrior's hands. 'You are slipping.'

Het winked at them. 'I finally get to feel like an owl soaring above the ground.'

Lan laughed. 'I wouldn't call this soaring, big fellow. Maybe falling with flair.'

As they landed, Ake glared at Het. 'Why would you jump like that?'

'I trust you, my two best friends in the world.' Het crushed them both in a bear hug.

'Hartur has fled. We better get away from here,' said Alwin, a wistful expression on his face.

Up on the clifftop, Alena peered over the edge as she rummaged in a pocket and withdrew a medallion. '*Resutis bregaris fo.'* A bell chimed on top of a post nearby. There was a screeching noise as a steel bridge slowly began to slide out from the rock face.

The small party turned and ran towards the forest.

'Please stop. Don't go into that forest,' yelled Alena.

The crew of *Carnay* stared in shock as Caoimhe took off her necklace and unfurled her wings. Hurley translated. 'You were unkind, Alena. Your need for justice drove your family away as it did with Mandami.' The wise fairy gave Alena a sad smile.

The little halfling giggled as Caoimhe hoisted him in the air by his arms and gracefully took wing, making her parents look like beginners.

Chapter Thirty-Eight

The small party reached the outskirts of a foreboding forest. It was late afternoon and the sun still shone but didn't seem to penetrate the darkness within. Tall trees with dark leaves and trunks clashed with each other, their branches entwined in an ancient war, blocking out the sun. A frosty breeze tousled the party's clothing. The crunching sound of many booted feet could be heard running towards them. The group turned to see Alena and the crew surging across the steel bridge in pursuit.

'I don't like this forest. It doesn't feel trustworthy,' whistled Caoimhe as Hurley translated.

'We have no choice.' Lan trudged ahead and disappeared into the gloom.

'Lan,' yelled Ake.

Lan poked his head back out. 'I'm fine, hurry. There is little light so I will lead.'

Alwin approached Hartur who was shivering on a rock nearby, her eyes cast down. He reached out and sensed her fear. 'We meet again, Hartur.' He held out his hand to shake hers, she slapped it away. 'We need to hurry.'

'No,' whispered Hartur.

'I command you to stop,' yelled Alena, rapidly approaching as Ake, Het, Caoimhe and Hurley followed Lan into the embrace of the trees.

Alwin picked Hartur up and she clung to him, sobbing, and he ran after the others.

'Light a torch and tie everyone to each other with a length of rope,' yelled Alena behind them.

Lan waited for the others to catch up. They were loud, snapping branches in a rush, and their breathing was deeper due to their exertions. Het swore and stepped out from behind a tree. Lan saw blood flowing freely down the warrior's leg, making a gentle patter as it dripped on the nearby leaves.

Ake jumped when someone brushed her cheek with the gentlest touch.

'It's me, honey,' said Lan.

'That is creepy, Lan. Your eyes are shining; it looks like a pair of eerie grey pupils watching us in the darkness where even shadows cease to exist.' Ake shuddered.

Lan chuckled quietly and the noise sounded deafening in the silent forest. 'They never glowed before. Arakaen must have what is called *tapetum lucidum,* or the shining layer, like a cat. I had to have a little light before, but now, even in full darkness, I can make out the grey shapes of things around me.' Lan studied the party for a moment. 'Where are Alwin and Hartur?'

'I don't know,' said Ake.

'Wait here, I will go check,' said Lan, bolting away. His eyes flashed several times as he flitted through the trees before dissolving into the darkness.

'That is creepy as heck.' Het stared in the direction Lan had taken. 'Arrgh, I think I'm injured.'

'Where?' Ake reached out and touched what she assumed to be his shoulder, her hand came away sticky. 'Eww.'

'That's the injured one.' Het ripped his shirt and handed her the cloth.

Ake set about bandaging Het's leg while they waited. There was a lot of fumbling and giggling as she ended up tripping.

'This darkness is annoying,' muttered Hurley.

Caoimhe whistled and Hurley translated. 'I can see. Mother, you need to move to the left.' The fairy slid past her boyfriend and guided her mother's hands. Het slipped her some fresh cloth and Ake tended the correct wound.

'We dare not move until Lan gets back.' Ake stared into the distance. 'Shh.'

They all quietened as the sound of heavy boots crunched close at hand, several torches passed them and they heard subdued talking.

'I hope Alena knows the way,' mumbled Gideon.

'I grew up in this forest. Wait I hear something.' Alena stepped closer to a tree, peering around the trunk. She shook her head. 'Nothing I guess. Blaze's influence over this forest does something to the mind.'

'That is something I would have rather not known,' mumbled the rifleman.

Nuo began to call out softly. 'Please come out Trebrelan and Telewanake. It is not safe in Blaze's forest.'

'Luma and Lufar, I am sorry, I let my pride best me. I would never turn your husband over to the authorities, Luma,' yelled Alena.

Alena's party trudged on and the torches passed out of sight. Ake jumped as something grabbed her hand. She turned and peered into Lan's eyes. 'Hell, don't do that.'

'I can't find them. I looked near the entrance and even fol-lowed Alena's party for a bit. I hope they are okay,' said Lan.

'Umm Het, why haven't you cast faerie orb yet?' asked Ake.

'Ah yes, that is very dumb of me.' Het laughed.

They heard him fumble with the strap of his sword before a gentle blue light shone from the sword.

'At least this time the sword won't give our location away,' said Het.

'Let's circle back again,' said Ake.

The group followed Lan as he led them back towards the entrance.

'Hold up, Lan. You are going too fast,' yelled Ake.

Lan stopped suddenly. 'I saw them. Let me circle back to make sure.'

The others waited until he returned. After a few moments, Lan ran up to them, panting. 'They went down a path. As I tried to follow, the branches of the trees entwined, cutting off my attempts. We will have to move forward in that direction and hope we find them.'

The others nodded and followed him.

———⚬⚬⚬———

Hartur shivered as Alwin carried her through the ancient forest. He looked down at her; her violet eyes shone in the dark.

'Can you see?' asked Alwin.

'Yes.'

'How?'

'Generations of forest elf blood being mixed with that of forest spirits.'

Alwin placed her on her feet. She clung to his chest, her hands clenched in fists against him.

'If you can see, why are you so frightened?' asked Alwin.

'It doesn't matter.' Hartur pushed him gently away, took a few deep breaths and gave him a half smile. Alwin snatched her hand and hauled her behind a tree as boots crunched amongst the undergrowth as a group passed, lifting their light sources to peer around trees; the light causing shadows to bounce off the foliage and cast a shadow of Alena's face.

Hartur pressed herself against Alwin whose back leant against the tree; his arms tensed as they alighted on her shoulders. Leaves crunched nearby.

'No one here, Captain.'

'Onwards then. My father will kill them, we must find them first,' Alena commanded.

Alwin tapped Hartur on the shoulder. 'It's safe.'

Hartur drew away and peered out from behind the tree. 'Seems so.'

Alwin began hurrying through the trees away from the fading light and Hartur trailed behind him.

'What the hell was that?' Alena yelled in the distance.

Hartur screamed as she saw a pair of grey eyes heading silently towards her. She turned and ran in a random direction, branches cracked as she stumbled onwards. Alwin chased after her blindly.

Alwin heard her sobbing again and followed the noise. He reached out and felt her shoulder as she leant against the rough base of a tree.

'Why are you so frightened? I insist you tell me.' Alwin patted her on the shoulder awkwardly.

'I was once chased in this forest trying to flee the manor house. Giant cats followed me for days until I was captured and dragged back. Those eyes reminded me of that time,' said Hartur.

'You know Alena's father?'

'We have met.'

'Are you well now?'

Hartur ignored him and her eyes skimmed their surroundings. 'I am afraid we are lost. We will likely die in this forest.'

Alwin fumbled in his bag and attempted to light a lantern. Hartur took it from him; a match flared and she lit the wick. The lantern burned, its limited light offering small comfort. Alwin took one of his shirts from his bag and handed it to her.

'To wipe your face.'

She nodded and wiped away her tears.

'We will be okay.' Alwin smiled.

'I doubt it.'

Hartur jumped as she saw the creepy eyes run past them, then circle back.

'Please, let's get away from that.'

Hartur turned and ran down a small pathway. Alwin followed her as she set a tiring pace. He looked back as the branches of the trees began to entwine and close on them, blocking their retreat. Alwin yelped as the pair of gloomy eyes stared at them.

'Wait,' said the familiar voice.

Alwin reached out a hand as the branches sealed the gap. Tendrils of thick vines began to weave around his hand causing him to drop their only source of light. A large branch entangled his backpack and tried to lift him off the ground, another tried to steal his bow. He fought hard and managed to keep the weapon.

'Run, Alwin,' yelled Hartur.

Alwin turned and sprinted down the path as the branches and vines attempted to ensnare and trip them.

———

Alena made it through the forest quickly. Her crew followed, spooked with how easily she navigated the forest. Their suspicious gazes unnerved her and her jaw clenched as she set a tiring pace. It was common knowledge Blaze derived satisfaction from challenging others and his forest was a dangerous maze for those not of his blood. *I am a disappointment to him, but I will never bow down to Hau. Father wallows in the demise of Mother's legacy.* She scoffed, the sound startling in the dense and almost unnaturally silent forest.

Father must die and then I can access his wealth and outfit my crew properly. In time, she wanted to build a fleet and defend the vulnerable against pirates and ancient, vicious monsters. She had hoped her Lufar and Luma would want to follow her cause, but they only seemed interested in each other and not the greater good. *I suppose they have a right to want a normal life swept up in each other. They have fulfilled their duties.*

The hair on Alena's neck stood up as they exited the forest. Her father kept the area around Morteredin Manor in a perpetual twilight so the effects of his fire magic were more noticeable.

'*Safety in the Blood*, what a strange name for a manor. I still can't get used to it after all these years,' whispered Alena.

The eerie, black stone manor appeared to be three storeys tall. The roof was made of grey slate. A large gargoyle made of marble, wings outstretched, raked his claws across a huge scaly dragon made of red stone. Its huge mouth was wide open, showing rows of sharp teeth. Flames exited its mouth at regular intervals, making the statue appear almost alive. Alena strode forward and stopped near a crimson archway covered in red flowers. The vines spelled out the name Blaze.

'Set up camp here, Nuo. Whatever you hear or see, do not cross under the archway, he will kill you.'

Nuo began ordering the crew to make a fire and set up tents. Alena turned and walked up the huge stone steps. The crimson double doors swung outwards. A middle-aged man in crimson robes strode through the door confidently. He had vermillion hair and eyes, and his resplendent salamander red skin glowed like an ember; usually attributed to a descendent of a fire elemental.

Alena's eyes widened. 'You look well for someone who was supposed to be near death's door.'

'Daughter, you have returned. I have heard from Lord Hau that you travel with the Lord and Lady of Caelestis.' Blaze grinned at her and conjured a flame in his hand, only to throw it past her head to light the torches behind her.

'I don't know what you mean.' Alena drew her staff.

'Oh, so we are still at odds,' said Blaze hurrying towards her.

'You kill Cirites for fun,' yelled Alena.

'What else are they good for?' Blaze's evil laughter hung in the air like a warning as Alena rushed towards him, her staff blazing blue. Her gaze narrowed on her father.

'*Magna Din*,' cried Blaze.

A wall of roaring flames appeared in front of Alena and she stumbled back. Blaze walked forward; the wall of fire pushed Alena back, the heat singeing her fine eyelashes. She coughed as the smoke, heat and taste of burnt hair pressed in on her.

'Alena,' yelled Nuo.

'Stay back, beloved,' cried Alena. Smoke from the flames rushed into her lungs and she gasped for air.

The staff flared a bright blue and its protective shield halted the fire wall's advancement. Alena pushed back and Blaze was forced to give way.

'Where are they, Alena?'

'I gave my word I wouldn't betray them.' Alena grinned.

Blaze dropped his fire wall and teleported behind Alena. Nuo pulled a pin from her hair and flung it towards the evil mage. He turned to glare at Nuo; his hand flung up, snatching at the poisonous projectile before it hit his neck. Alena walloped him on the back of his head with her staff and he stumbled down the steps, dazed. 'Surrender, Father. I won't kill you.'

The evil magic user recovered and raised his hand towards the dragon. '*Crono glenda*.'

The crew gasped as the dragon statue lowered its huge head and spat a huge fireball at Alena.

As the dragon lowered its head, her beloved Nuo sprinted

towards Blaze, vaulting over him and shoving her aside. The hiss of sizzling flesh and the smell of burning skin assaulted her nose as Alena stumbled backwards. She screamed as her girlfriend fell to the ground, a satisfied smile on her scorched face, as the heat continued to burn away, erasing that precious face forever. 'My Nuo, my darling Nuo.'

Her beloved's last words came out in a raspy wheeze. 'You should know I was charged to protect you and the other descendants. Your kindness, loyalty and sense of duty caused me to fall for you. I was honoured to love you.' Nuo gave a weak sigh as she drew her last breath.

The rest of the crew turned as Blaze whistled. Three large, orange cats, with bob tails and huge paws, padded silently into the clearing. They hissed and bared large sabre-like teeth as they began rounding the crew up, their manes a mass of writhing flames.

Alena lifted Nuo's face and kissed her gently before she lay her down. The double doors opened again and soldiers in black, spiked armour struck her in the side of the head with the handle of a serrated spear. The remaining soldiers jostled the crew together and bound them with ropes.

Blaze turned to his pets. 'Hunt out all who smell of magic in the forest. Bring them to me alive.'

The cats turned and silently padded into the forest. Alena's lip quivered; her gaze grew blurry as tears swam in her eyes before she drifted into unconsciousness.

— ᔕᑎᔕ —

'We should rest,' said Alwin.

'Not in this hateful forest,' replied Hartur.

Alwin stopped, sat down on the path they had cleared by snapping branches and leant against a tree.

'Get up, Alwin.'

'No, I want to rest. You can do as you wish.'

Hartur made a sound of annoyance and flopped down beside him. 'You are a stubborn ass.'

'And you are so wilful that you would unnecessarily burden yourself.' Alwin smiled.

Hartur poked him in the ribs. 'What do you mean by that?'

'Careful, it still hurts.' Alwin winced. 'You are tired, but you would push yourself past usefulness out of pure stubbornness.'

'What the hell are you talking about?'

'You won't rest out of stubbornness.'

'You are dense.' Hartur moved away from him.

He saw her shiver as a twig snapped and a loud yowling like cats fighting could be heard.

'I am frightened, Alwin, of the things lurking in this forest. I push myself to get out of here.' She began to shake as the yowling came closer. Her eyes glazed over and she moaned as a man's voice came from her mouth.

'Hello Hartur. Run, my feisty little kitten, before I catch you.'

Twigs snapped nearby and Alwin clambered to his feet. He threw Hartur over his shoulder and ran in the opposite direction. The branches tore at his clothes and he floundered several times in the darkness. He stopped as strange large cats with flaming manes began to circle them—magnapardus. He leant his companion against the trunk of a tree and drew his bow. As it hummed to life, two of the beasts pounced. The arrow struck true; with a thud, it drove into the raised paw of one beast. Hissing, the cat backed off. The other leapt on to Alwin's chest and pinned his arms down, the bow dropping to the ground.

'Nietra, answer the Master of the Forge. I bid you protect your master and his wife.'

The magnapardus began to drag him backwards, unpinning

his arms. Alwin scrambled to grab his bow. The ruby head of Nietra glowed where it lay attached to Hartur's hip.

The hammer spoke in its gloomy tone. *'I obey, Master of the Forge.'*

Alwin watched the cats swat at some imaginary thing, caught up in some kind of game.

'I find the weakness within,' said Nietra.

Alwin rushed to his feet, grabbed his bow and shook Hartur. Her eyes cleared and she scrambled up, pushing against the trunk. She turned to stare at the cats and backed away as her eyes widened.

'Let's go.'

As Hartur turned on her heel and ran, Nietra's spell broke and the magnapardus hissed and gave chase. Alwin and Hartur sprinted in the opposite direction. The terrible yowling followed them. They came to a dead end and turned to watch the creatures stalking them. Hartur gasped as Alwin lifted her up onto the nearest branch.

'Climb.' Alwin turned and his bow hummed to life as one of the cats pounced on him. It bit his arm as he tried to fire and he cried out. The creature's hot, sour breath made him hold his own. Warm blood dripped down his arm and spattered onto the leaves in the glow from the light of his emerald bow.

Hartur threw her hammer at another cat.

'How insulting,' whispered Nietra.

The magnapardus hissed as the weapon thumped it on the side of its jaw and it proceeded to screech at the hammer. Its mane flared and it bit the hammer, and flames spewed from its mouth.

Hartur swore and leapt down from her perch as Alwin slammed his free fist into his captor's face. The cat spat a small flame at him. His clothes lit on fire and he tried to pat them out. Hartur hid in the darkness and dived for her hammer. Teeth raked across her hand, almost questing, as if not to harm her but warn her. She snatched up the hammer and ran.

Alwin scrambled into the branches. 'Hartur, how far up are you?'
'I forgot you can barely see.'

'Hartur, where are you?' he asked, panic evident in his voice.

The creatures turned their big feline heads to Hartur and she dived out of the way as two lowered on their haunches and sprang towards her. Hartur belted towards the tree, her breath ragged with exhaustion. Alwin heard her heart beat rapidly from fear. She tried to climb and stumbled, not strong enough to pull herself up as one of the cats tore her pants and swiped her shoes.

Distracted, it began to play with the shoe and the other cat fought its companion over it.

'Stupid cats, get them,' yelled Blaze's voice from out of the familiars' mouths.

Alwin leant down, the muscles in his arms straining as Hartur's hand scrabbled for his strong one. His hand closed over hers and he pulled her up into the branches as the cats leapt and clawed at the base of the tree. His arms encircled her as she cursed; her warm cheek pressed into his bicep.

The cats grew bored, their ears twitched and they turned their gaze to stare off into the distance as if searching for prey, they circled the tree once before padding away silently into the darkness.

Alwin felt her acute fear as she began to sob and shake uncontrollably. Hartur gulped in huge amounts of air, trying to control the rising panic. *I have never been that afraid. Why did Alena's father put Hartur through that ordeal?* He began to see pictures of cats and men stalking Hartur for days in the forest, of Hartur afraid, hungry and alone. Alwin held her to him, unsure of what else to do. Eventually, her sobs faded and her breathing regulated. He turned and shuffled his back against the tree. He had chosen the widest branch to accommodate them. He reached into his pocket and pulled out an apple, the only food he had grabbed in their hurried escape from the ship. Het had packed his bag and he hadn't had a proper chance to scour its contents before it was lost. *At least Het had the sense to pack a lantern and shirt.*

'Hartur.'

She looked up him.

He opened her clenched fist and pushed the apple into her hand. 'Eat it.'

'We can share it.'

'No, Hartur it is too small. Eat it, for my sake.'

He heard several crunches as she ate the apple. He felt something cold and firm pushed up against his mouth and felt the half-eaten apple. He took a bite and she pulled it back.

'Satisfied?'

'Yes,' she whispered.

Something pressed against his mouth and he opened it to bite the apple again but instead he felt her tongue slip into his mouth, her lips pressed against his. *Why would she do that with her tongue?* He felt her climb onto his lap, her legs either side of him, and she kissed him with skill and urgency. He tried to duplicate her and she broke the kiss.

'Easy, Alwin, let me teach you,' she whispered against his lips, starting with a gentle kiss. She gave him some respite and he put his hand to his mouth.

'I didn't think you would let me kiss you, Alwin.'

'A chaste kiss is perfectly acceptable between married couples when out of sight. It is a confession of love and sentiment, and is not usually a passionate thing.' His eyes darted away from hers that glowed in the darkness. 'Why did you put your tongue in my mouth?'

'Let me show you.' Before he could answer, she took his mouth with hers again.

He broke the kiss and pushed himself firmly against the tree. She laughed gently and slipped her hands between his legs. He pulled her off him and she sat next to him.

'That tongue kissing will not happen again.'

'So, you *do* want me.'

'I *can* desire you. There is a difference. I don't usually feel it unless it is initiated by either party. For my people it takes longer for us to feel it. The process is long and drawn out and takes a toll on our need for personal space.'

Hartur laughed. 'Cirites are so cold and efficient.'

'Was I cold just now?'

'We shared a moment that could have been beautiful and you turned into a conversation about a lack of need and desire.'

'Lack of desire. I am inexperienced at kissing and tried my best. Sorry I am lacking.'

'I'm your first?'

'That would be correct.'

'Your hand is bleeding.' Hartur glanced at her damaged pants; with a ripping sound, she tore away the remnants and bandaged his injuries. 'Can I check that stomach wound of yours?'

Alwin nodded, took off his coat and unbuttoned his shirt. She ran her hands across the welt-like bruises streaking across his abdomen. She traced them and leant in to kiss them. Alwin felt her grab his hand and put it to her chest. He felt his cheeks heat but didn't pull the hand away. *Soft and pleasant.*

'So cute and *I* get to teach you,' she whispered in his ear.

He began to button up his shirt. 'I'm catching on to your little game. How many have you taught this way?' He blinked in surprise when he realised it bothered him.

'I had a boyfriend for a few weeks, then a fiancé that I did it with once.'

'One lover and I assume the boyfriend was the one you practiced that tongue kissing with.'

'Yes.'

Alwin turned away from her. 'Get some rest, Hartur.'

'Are you suddenly disgusted with me?'

'Did you love them?'

'I thought I did.'

'I see.'

'What the hell do you mean by that?' She squeezed his arm.

'So, you could easily think yourself in love with me and reciprocate what they taught you. I am sorry, Hartur, I will not be a moment's passion to fulfil your physical desires every time you are emotionally stressed, just because I am here with you. Lovemaking means a lot to Cirites. It's a sacred act, and when it does happen, I want it to be with someone who truly loves me.'

'It's not that simple. Love can be complicated. I opened up to you and you humiliated me.' She rolled away from him and began to sob. 'Callous b——.'

He placed his hand on her back and she swatted it away. 'Go away, and do not touch me again, Alwin. I am not some ruined garment to be tossed out with the trash just because you have never done it.'

He withdrew his hand and turned away from her. 'It is a sin for my people if it is casually given. My people's sins do not make it your sin, Hartur. I was thinking of my own soul and never intended to hurt your feelings. I apologise.'

He heard her breathing slow down and assumed she had fallen asleep. He closed his eyes and drifted in the death-like sleep of the exhausted.

—⁓—

Alena's eyes fluttered awake. She leapt from the bed in the darkened room and tried the door handle again; it was still locked. *Why hasn't my father killed me yet?*

'Get away from the door,' yelled Blaze.

Alena backed up as the key turned in the lock. Blaze entered the room and he summoned flames. The room lit up and Alena blinked in the sudden light.

'Half your crew is dead, Alena.' Blaze's eyes narrowed and his lips turned up in a smirk. 'You have even lost a lover who saved your worthless hide. You will agree to my terms. You will go free and denounce being my heir. What loyalty could you have had to a man and woman who have disobeyed your every order as you tried to protect them? You would sacrifice your loyal crew for the former nobles of Caelestis?'

Alena glared at him. 'You are a cruel man, Father.'

'I am well aware of my flaws, daughter. Do you agree to my terms?'

'If you agree to return our weapons and promise not to harm the fairy or the halfling.' Alena's jaw ticked and her heart fluttered, almost stalling as guilt washed over her.

'So, you agree the Lord and Lady of Caelestis are mine?' Blaze raised a brow.

'Have you captured a blond boy and redheaded woman?'

'No. Who are they?'

'The blond boy is Alwin Smith and the woman is named Hartur.'

'You just gave up their information too easily. Do you still trust your father?' Blaze smiled cruelly. 'My own daughter brings my fiancée to me.'

'She is no longer your fiancée and is therefore of little concern to you. I want their freedom.' Alena stared him down.

'Hartur will be my bride and therefore she is very much my concern.'

'I have to inform you I married the pair. Under the mariner's act, Alwin and his wife have sanctuary while they are a part of my crew.'

'You are on *my* island. My familiars will find the pair. I will give you the boy after I have questioned him. Hartur will be my bride if she is free of his taint or she will die if she has mated him.'

'That sweet, innocent, impassive boy is incapable of that sort of thing.'

'We shall see. Now follow me.' Blaze turned and walked from the room. Alena's shoulders slumped as she stepped in line behind her sire.

Ake's small group entered the clearing; the embers of a dying fire and half erected tents met their gaze while torches burned and lit the clearing. Ake screamed and ran through an archway, collapsing to the earth she held the remnants of charred golden robes to her cheek and sobbed before she reached out and brushed the singed hair out of the badly burnt face. 'Poor Nuo.'

Caoimhe whistled in distress and hid her face in Hurley's shoulder.

Lan wandered over to Ake; tears coursed down his face. 'Poor woman.'

Ake drew a blanket from her bag and placed it over a burnt body. Something glinted on the ground and she leant down and picked it up before running into Lan's outstretched arms. A terrible yowling came from the forest and three large cats slunk towards them.

'They are incredible.' Ake muttered through her tears.

'They look dangerous,' said Lan.

Het withdrew his sword as the creatures hissed and bared their fangs. The halfling and the fairy backed up and ran behind their warrior friend. Lan conjured hail and thew it at each of the cats. The magnapardus howled as each icy projectile belted them in the nose.

Doors screeched open behind them.

'Thank goodness,' said Hurley.

They turned to see a man in crimson robes exit, followed by guards in nightmarish armour.

'Welcome to Morteredin Manor, Lady of Mercy and Lord of Death. I am Blaze,' said the man.

The cats forced them towards him. Then the earth began to rumble; stones fell from the roof as a hideous stone gargoyle reached down and grabbed Lan and Het in its cold, vice like grip. The warrior's sword clattered to the ground as the men struggled in the gargoyle's grip.

Lan cried out. 'There goes a rib.'

'Now, my fair lady, time for you to surrender.' Blaze gestured and Ake was surrounded by a circle of flame. She went to step out of the circle and the flames roared higher. She covered her face as sparks singed her hair.

The cat-like creatures hunched down on powerful paws. They pounced towards Hurley and Caoimhe. The air crackled with electricity as lightening formed above and streaked down towards the beasts. The creatures roared in pain and the smell of burning fur caused Lan to wrinkle his nose.

'Caoimhe, take Hurley and get out of here.' cried Lan. He sighed in relief as the little couple fled into the undergrowth.

Blaze glared at Lan. 'I would kill you, but that pleasure is for Lord Hau.'

In the distraction, Het had used his incredible strength to pry the gargoyle's fingers free, pulling himself up onto the creature's arm before sprinting up it. The statue roared, flailing its fist in a futile attempt to flatten the warrior. With an equally formidable roar, Het leapt on to the gargoyle's head, his large fist driving into its eye. The creature released Lan, who dropped to the ground, landing on his feet with a wince. There was a large crack as stone shattered. Lan dived out of the way as the gargoyle's head and arms tumbled to the ground. A flurry of stone dust caused him to cough.

'Nice face paint.' Het yelped as he landed on his rear. 'That is going to hurt for weeks.'

'*Arguardia duss.*' Bolts of flame appeared in Blaze's hand and he threw them at his opponents. Het and Lan weaved among flame and smoke, grinning at each other as they dodged the arrows with ease.

'Seize the big brute,' Blaze hissed through gritted teeth.

'*Waterius,*' cried Ake. A large bubble of swirling water encircled her and she proceeded to hurry through the wall of flames.

Blaze grinned at her. 'I was always told you were a solar mage.'

He conjured flame in his hands and manipulated it into ropes which he began swirling above his head. The ropes became a raging whirlwind of scorching flame and he sent it spiralling towards Lan, who swore and conjured his wings, flying over the danger and gallantly sweeping his mate up as Blaze sent a fireball towards her. Blaze turned as Het retrieved his sword; it flared with multicolour light as the big man charged several guards. Het's sword was a blur as he began slaughtering the guards, their screams a cacophony in the din that was death, fire and agony.

Fireballs rained down upon the party as Blaze roared in an unfamiliar language. The clearing was a hideous scene of burning tents, freshly slaughtered corpses and mounds of shattered stone. Het bellowed in pain as two guards drove their spears into his thigh and side, and he fell to his knees.

'Do not kill our Lord's father,' said Blaze.

Lan landed and placed Ake down tenderly. He scowled at Blaze as he charged, leaping over a guard, his mystic knives now in his hands. A knife glinted in the torchlight as he delivered an unnaturally fast strike. The man clutched his throat and collapsed, his eyes bulging, realising if his opponent had wanted to kill him he would be dead.

Ake conjured jets of water and threw them at Blaze. He lost his concentration, and the fireballs hissed and began to burn out as steam dispersed into the air.

Blaze grinned. '*Crono glenda.*'

The ground began to shake as the huge dragon statue aimed its head at Ake. Lan dived towards her as the dragon spewed forth a huge wall of flame.

'*Waterius moldis manas,*' Ake screamed.

Lan was enclosed in a bubble of water. He held his breath and sprinted towards the evil mage. The water shield began to hiss and steam and the liquid inside roiled. Lan reached Blaze and yelled in pain as the boiling water began to blister him, but the dragon wouldn't relent as Lan leapt over his opponent and landed behind him.

'Clever.' Blaze laughed. 'Cease.'

The statue closed its mouth; the stifling temperature relented as the fire was snuffed out. Lan coughed as Ake dissolved her water shield.

Blaze winked. '*Flameriaus digitis.*'

Ake screamed as a huge hand made of fire was conjured into existence and snatched her up.

'Oh, we mustn't injure you.' Blaze waved his hand and the flames dulled. 'Hau has uses for a beautiful half-elven woman.'

Ake's eyes turned golden. She unfurled her wings and a barrier of solar light engulfed her and she fell to the ground.

'Sleep, cousin,' a familiar voice commanded.

Ake's eyes were hazy and she muttered to herself, 'Four sacrifices just to make me sleep.' She slumped to the ground and closed her eyes.

Blaze hollered as Lan punched him the face while delivering

a strike to his side with a knife. The mage stumbled back and retreated down the steps.

Lan followed him, scowling. 'No one touches my mate.'

The mage backed away towards his familiars. Lan struck; the mage shook his head and glanced at the blood on his hands. Three guards jumped on Lan and he delivered multiple strikes that took their lives.

The cowardly Blaze turned and ran, his face a mask of fear. Lan pursued him, stumbling over one of the cats. Caught up in his rage, he didn't see the beast rise; it clamped down on his shoulder with its huge teeth. He cried out before striking the creature in a series of deadly blows. The cat released him and collapsed as Blaze conjured a cage of pure fire that encapsulated his target.

Lan reached out his hand, gripping bars of flame and spitting out an array of crude obscenities, his hands blistering under the onslaught until he finally collapsed from pain.

CHAPTER THIRTY-NINE

Alwin's eyes snapped open. He glanced around before he loosed a long, drawn out breath and scrambled down the tree.

He unslung his bow and stared at it. 'Dage, are you able to give off more than dim light.'

'*Yes, Master of the Forge. I can also keep track of the days and sense danger. The former Master of the Forge added these features to protect you and keep you on track. The day is July 5th, midday, the year 1700 CE.*' Dage flared brightly.

Alwin was able to see a few feet in front of him. They were in a tiny clearing and his stomach rumbled. His throat was dry from lack of water. He wandered over to the edge of the tree line as he heard water splashing playfully over rocks, and looked up at a magnificent waterfall. The air was humid. He reached his hand out to grace the rocks. *Hot to the touch. The water is probably heated from the thermal activity below. I wonder if it is okay to drink.* He looked around for any insects that would show that the water was pure and found none. He sighed and cupped his hands, placing them under the flow. The water tasted okay. He drank some more. *I will test it to make sure it's safe for her to drink.*

Alwin placed the bow on a rock nearby and began to strip. *I have never smelt this awful or been this dirty.* He climbed under the waterfall and sighed as the water tumbled over him. He reached down and grabbed some sand and scrubbed himself, wincing as his hands crossed his abdomen. He heard a gentle splash behind him and saw Hartur enter the water relieved of her clothing. She ignored him and began to wash herself.

She opened her mouth to drink the water and he pulled her out of the direct stream of the water. 'Don't, it could be dangerous to drink.'

'I saw you do it.'

'Yes, give it some time and we will see if it impacts my health.'

'So, you are willing to die for me, save my soul, but not willing to join our bodies.' Hartur sighed.

'You make it sound so puritanical.'

Hartur shrugged and grinned at him. 'Maybe you are. I will see.'

Alwin turned his gaze as she grabbed his hand and placed it on her chest.

'Hartur, you are beautiful, but I am not interested in sinning with you.'

'That's fine.' She reached up and kissed him gently; his arms encircled her and he felt her press against him. Her hands trailed down and he felt the gentle stirrings of a subdued passion.

'I see. Cirites really are only attracted to people you are fond of.'

'I already said that.'

'You are married, Alwin. Romance is bound to happen sometime.'

She laughed softly and kissed him. He closed his eyes and his hands trailed down to her derriere. He pulled her against him, and she sighed when his hands moved and began to explore her. He kept his face free of any desire, but smiled when she cried out with pleasure.

'Where did you learn to do that?'

'We are all taught the way a body works. I may not be willing to sin with you, Hartur, but I can offer you some relief of your Velterran desire for me. It's as biological for a Velterran to be passionate in nature as it is for Cirites not to be.' He gave her a chaste kiss.

She broke the kiss and glared at him. 'Willing to allow me to sin and see me vulnerable, but not willing to offer the same. You really are callous. Partners share equally. You profess you want to get to know me, but when I am willing you are not.'

'Your personality, Hartur, show me the real you. I know your body now.' He gave her a warm smile.

Her cheeks burned and she whipped her gaze away from his. 'I bet you are on a spiritual high now. Alwin the great, satisfying a sin-filled, pitiful Velterran while he takes the moral high ground and his soul is free of fault.'

Alwin blinked at her in sudden confusion. 'That's not what I was trying to do. I care for you and want to see you happy. I thought you may be frustrated as you keep pushing your desires on me. I wanted to ease that burden for you.'

She made a sound of frustration. 'I guess you mean well. I am not to be pitied, Alwin. It is humiliating. When someone is fond of another, and are usually attracted to them, it's not some uncontrollable urge that needs to be relieved. It is a mutual joining of bodies to express that feeling.'

'And what of those who do so regularly without fondness?'

Hartur growled. 'So, that's how you see me.'

Alwin smiled. 'No, Hartur. I was just curious about it, that's all. I was trying to understand something I am free of. Most Cirites hate judgement; we aren't all unkind and judgemental lawmakers.'

'Then why not feel some pleasure for yourself if you are giving it freely?'

He took a deep breath. 'I have explained myself. I care for you and wanted to give you a gift to meet your needs. Why is it so hard for you to fathom that one can make another feel happy without the need to fulfil some desire of their own?'

Hartur smirked at him and wandered over to the waterfall.

'That water appears fine.'

Hartur drank her fill before they donned what was left of their tattered clothing.

Alwin glanced at her bare feet. 'I will piggyback you.'

Hartur clambered up his back. 'This is ridiculous.'

'Plain necessity.'

Alwin hoisted his glowing bow and headed in a new direction. They walked for several hours, according to Dage, and exited the forest into another tiny clearing. Blaze turned and smiled at them. Alwin felt Hartur tremble against him as she slid from his back.

'You must be Alwin. I must reward you for bringing my fiancée back to me.' Blaze teleported Hartur into his arms and she struggled as he kissed her. 'Welcome home, Hartur. It is time we were married.'

Alwin strode over to him. 'I believe you are mistaken. I am her husband.'

Blaze's eyes filled with jealousy. He released Hartur and dragged her by her arm.

'Run, Alwin,' yelled Hartur.

Alwin aimed his bow. 'Let her go.'

Blaze glared at him and smiled as flames erupted from his hands. 'D-ive, ma-ster, no-w,' said Dage nervously.

Alwin stumbled out of the way and yelped as his ankle streaked with pain before he limped towards Blaze, wincing.

'You chose a boy for a husband over an experienced lover. You are a passionate woman, Hartur. Release the boy from his marriage vows and I will have him imprisoned rather than slaughtered,' said Blaze.

'Cirite marriage vows can't be broken. Unhand my wife.'

Hartur gave Blaze a flirtatious smile. 'I didn't choose him. It was marriage or death. There is nothing more to it,' said Hartur.

Alwin felt like a dagger had pierced his heart. He reached for Hartur's emotions, trying to ascertain her feelings, but she had guarded her heart against him. 'So, that's how it is.'

Blaze broke out in hysterical laughter. 'My beautiful Hartur, always using others for self-preservation. Could you be anymore Veltarren?' He pulled her face towards him. 'Did the boy try anything on you? You are mine and I will punish you if you have tarnished yourself with others.'

'He is Cirite, Blaze, incapable of desire.' She gave him a disarming smile.

The mage whistled and three familiar big cats surrounded Alwin.

'Those cat things were injured; how come they look unharmed?'

'My magnapardus are also my familiars. Like any familiar, they respawn the next day and can't truly be killed unless I die.'

Alwin dropped his bow. His stomach churned from hunger and bitterness as waves of fatigue washed over him. *This is over, I am a fool for giving my heart to a spy and manipulator.* 'Where is Alena and her crew?'

'The crew are being slaughtered slowly for my entertainment. Alena is in chains. I will put her to death when Hartur here produces me an heir worthy of my legacy. You will also have the honour of seeing your ancestor Trebrelan tortured, Alwin, grandson of Amities.' Blaze laughed as the big cats pounced on Alwin and began tearing at him with their big claws.

Hartur turned her big eyes to Blaze.

The mage was lost in them a few moments before he shook himself. 'You liar, you do care for the boy.'

Blaze pushed her to the ground and teleported Alwin to him.

Alwin's legs gave way. The mage conjured a giant hand to carry Hartur, and Alwin was dragged by the scruff of the neck into the manor.

CHAPTER FORTY

Ake spat Nuo's hairpins from her mouth and on to her palm. She was locked in a cell across from the men. Lan's eyes shone in the dark as he studied her from across the way. Torches burned in the hallway, but the cells were in perpetual darkness. Ake inserted the pins into the lock of the manacles attached to her wrists.

'Bloody creepy eyes, mate. Don't think I will get used to that.' Het laughed then groaned; the pain in his voice accompanied by the sound of dragging chains.

Ignoring the jest, Lan changed the subject, his next words uttered in a near whisper. 'Ake is going to get us out of here with a skill you taught her.'

'What skill?'

'Lock picking.'

'Ah, I never taught her that. That's something she must have taught herself.'

'They really don't take care of this place; the ground is littered with stone from the decaying walls.' Lan's eyes shone, and pebbles clattered outside the cell. 'Ake, you okay?'

'Our host probably doesn't care.' Het laughed. 'Ah, that hurts.'

Lan chuckled. 'Four men it took to hold you down. Yet you still fought when they clapped you in irons and shackled you to the wall.'

'A man's gotta try.'

As the lock clicked, Ake rubbed her wrists, restoring the feeling from the tight restraints. *Yeah, I practiced it in my youth and perfected it while captured by Cephas.* Ake shuddered at the memory. *I could get out of the palace but not past the guards.* Turning her attention to the door, she inserted the pin into the lock. With a click and a scraping of metal, she slowly swung the door open and padded softly over to the opposite cell, picked the lock and opened the door. As she fumbled in the dark, Lan guided her hands to his restraints; within minutes she had released him.

The sound of booted feet drew near, a guard yawned and stared at the open door of Ake's former cell. 'The goddess has escaped.'

A guard rounded the corner and joined his companion in examining the cell Ake had fled.

Lan slipped through the door as a guard tried to slam it shut. With an almost inaudible oof, the guard slumped to the ground as Lan delivered an unarmed strike to the back of his head.

Ake, hands trembling, began to work on Het's leg and wrist shackles.

'Hurry,' whispered Lan urgently.

Ake worked on the last of four restraints, when the pin snapped in her trembling fingers, she picked up a rock and lifted it to strike the manacle.

Het brushed her hand aside. 'I'd rather you didn't break my wrist. Now, get out of here you two.'

'We can't leave you,' said Lan.

'Find the others,' cried Het.

Lan entered the cell, dragging Ake away as she fought him to get back to her dear friend. 'Lan, you know leaving him is wrong.' She dropped the rock.

Shouts from the guards and the stomp of running feet surged towards the cells. Lan dragged his wife down the hallway as she thrashed about. Opening a door to thrust her inside, he entered after her, slowly closing the door with a subtle click. The clanging of metal on stone was accompanied by the frenzy of hollering guards.

'The big guy escaped. After him.'

The sound of frenzied activity faded and Lan opened the door, light flooding the small space. It was a storage cupboard. Ake rummaged around to no avail. 'He got away.'

'Thank the gods.' Lan smiled.

'Let's find the others.'

The couple left the small space, peering around the corner and moving slowly out of the dungeons, as they snuck past the guard, Ake lifted a set of keys from his belt.

Alena's eyes narrowed as she glanced over her shoulder to give her childhood home a final cursory stare. Her back stung as a guard prodded her with the tip of a spear before he took a step back towards the manor behind him. Turning, she hurried towards the forest; her six remaining crewmembers followed silently, including Gideon. As they entered the forest, Hurley and Caoimhe crawled out from the underbrush and scrambled over to her.

Hurley translated the fairy's high-pitched whistles. 'My mother and father. Where are they?'

Alena rubbed her stinging eyes with her sleeve as the bitter tears flowed. 'I couldn't rescue them.'

The halfling puffed out his chest. 'Well, Hurley will save them.'

Alena grabbed the tiny pair and hoisted them under her arms. 'Luma and Lufar would want you out of danger. Let's get out of here.'

She set an easy pace as the fairy whistled franticly. Hurley did not need to translate the stressed whistles.

Alena paused some distance from the manor. 'Hush, we will wait here and watch the guards. Then we will make our move and rescue the others.'

—•∿•—

Het wandered down the halls, peering past a wall as he came to another bend. A guard paced the corridor. There were two doors nearby; stilted conversation drifted from one, the other was silent. As the guard turned to face the opposite direction, Het made a dash to the nearest door and tested the handle. It turned and he slipped inside, his eyes adjusting as moonlight streamed in through an open window. A collection of shelves behind a metal cage contained small chests, gems and other treasures. Their weapons caught his gaze. The door of the cage had a large brass padlock hanging from the latch.

Het scanned the room looking for a key. *Gods, I am naive sometimes. As if they would leave the key lying around.* He jiggled the lock and stifled a yelp as heat surged from the lock and burned his bare hands. He blew on his hands and shook them in attempt to ease the pain. *We need these weapons.* Sliding his long sleeves over his hands, he grabbed the lock and pulled.

The lock heated once more and he gritted his teeth against the pain until his shirt caught alight. He patted it out before glaring at the lock, snapping his mouth shut to avoid unleashing a wave of obscenities. *There could be ladies present.* He grinned and booted the latch. The padlock cracked and fell to the floor in pieces and a bell began to toll. His heart leapt into his mouth as he stomped the lock until the noise fell silent. The shattered pieces seared his leather boots on contact. Smoke rose from his apparel and the smell of burning hair from the hide on his boots caused him to cover his nose.

The door behind him opened. He turned just in time as a guard charged him, spear thrust towards his middle. Bending down, Het scooped up pieces of the lock and threw them at the guard. The objects struck the guard who grabbed his face as his moustache caught alight.

'Truly sorry, old fellow, that was a magnificent crumb-catcher.' He grabbed the man's spear and walloped him on the top of the head. The helmet made a crunching noise as the guard slumped to the ground.

Het opened the door to the cage and grabbed their stolen weapons, slinging them over his shoulders, wincing as pain and heat washed over his injured hands. Leaving the room, he moved almost silently, remembering his hunting trips with Ake in their youth. He slunk towards the other door. A faint conversation drifted towards him as his hand settled on the handle of the door.

—◆◆◆—

The room flooded with light as Blaze threw minute balls of fire towards the torches attached to the walls. Hartur's gaze settled on a large four-poster bed carved from dark wood. The canopy was a blood red, the burgundy silk sheets were a harsh reminder of when she had made-out with her former fiancé, the bright orange coverlet once wrapped around her in the aftermath of inattentive lovemaking. The room was lined with wooden shelves and held many ancient and worn tomes, while the ebony walls and slate floor were a direct contrast to the garish manchester. She blushed as her gaze settled on a red woollen shag on the floor.

Her captor gave her a wicked smile and turned to the guard who had followed them. 'Set two on watch outside. I don't want to be disturbed until dawn.'

The guard dragged Alwin to a corner of the room and deposited him on the floor before exiting through one of the two doors out of Blaze's boudoir.

Hartur landed on the shag with a slight exclamation as Blaze dispelled the giant hand that had hauled her here, before he leant down, hauled her up and shoved her back against a bedpost.

'Where were we? Ah yes, our first time was here, wasn't it?' The mage robe swished as he stepped forward, his bare feet stepping in between her legs.

Hartur's brows rose. 'I know I lost mine. But why no shoes, Blaze?'

The mage scoffed and ran a bare foot up her thigh. 'You have forgotten my bloodline.' With the blood of fire elementals and elves running through his veins, the mage needed to feel the earth beneath his feet to ground his power and remain in control, so he never wore shoes.

Hartur shuffled towards Alwin while Blaze lifted his foot higher, maintaining his balance with the aid of the bedpost. Alwin's eyes locked on hers and shimmered with anger.

'You were going to free the boy and the rest of the crew if I promised to stay with you.'

'Marry me, Hartur. I won't settle for a lover. I have my pick of those. With the capture of the divine couple I want to build on your predecessor's legacy. My regal Hartur, descended from Lord Hau's favourite bride Atius. Our lord will favour me and my descendants. Alena forsook her amazing blood to favour the weak and vulnerable. With your devotion to Lord Hau's cause our children will please our lord.' Blaze reached for her.

Hartur clutched at his sleeve. 'Only if you promise me Ake will come to no harm and Alwin and the others will be freed.'

'I swear to you on our mutual feelings.'

'Yes, do that.'

Blaze reached out and placed his hand on her heart. 'But that is on the condition that you give yourself to me completely, heart and soul.'

'Of course.' Hartur gave him a weak grin and edged sideways.

'I am not stupid, Hartur. I see the direction you are headed.' His hand grabbed her hip.

Alwin's eyes snapped towards an ancient tome as it fell open onto the floor. Its pages turned rapidly until it settled on a page of unfamiliar text and a picture of decaying ropes. He scrambled backwards as the mage uttered the words in the book.

'*Morte Cordes.*'

A rope wound its way up from the pages like a serpent searching for prey. It lunged towards Alwin and entwined itself around his throat and arms. Alwin's eyes bulged and he clutched at his throat as he began to gag.

Hartur grabbed the mage's face. 'Love me, Blaze.'

Blaze turned towards her. Alwin took a gasping breath when the ropes loosened as their captor's lecherous gaze locked on Hartur's.

Hartur shivered as Blaze's hand grabbed a breast and squeezed through the fabric. 'You fled from my advances this year past. Why would I believe you would reciprocate them now?'

'I have grown up this last year. You are the only one to ever show me any tenderness.' Hartur batted her eyelids at him.

'And what of this boy you call husband?'

Alwin winced as Blaze made a circular motion with his left hand; the ropes tightened around his throat.

'He is a Cirite. He doesn't know what to do with a woman.' She smiled. 'I will give myself to you freely. Let him go.'

Blaze gave her a cruel grin. 'Prove it now. In front of this boy.'

Trying not to shudder, Hartur grabbed their captor's face and gave him a chaste kiss. Alwin looked away, his head snapping back towards the pair as Hartur cried out. Blood welled on Hartur's chin as Blaze savaged her mouth, his teeth dragging over her lips. Her fear fluttered around Alwin like an aura ready to manipulate. His innate ability to read emotions made his heart clench as her fear rushed over him, but her expression was a paradox, more of forced merriment. Hartur pushed Blaze towards the bed; the mage let himself fall and laughed as their mouths met.

Maybe I'll gouge my eyes out after this, thought Alwin.

Blaze rolled Hartur onto her back and scowled at her. 'You are trembling like it's your first time with me. This is a façade.'

Hartur winked at her ex. 'Of course I'm trembling. It's just as exciting.'

Alwin began to struggle against the cords as his chest tightened. *She will not indulge in infidelity to free me.*

Hartur stared into Blaze's eyes. 'Let the boy go and ignore his presence.'

The mage's eyes glazed over, his head turning to his other victim. With a gesture the cords receded; Alwin gasped and held his throat as he scrambled to his feet.

Hartur's thoughts flooded into Alwin's mind for a brief moment. *Please flee. He will be annoyed when he finds out how close we became. You are too good, we are incompatible.*

Blaze's hands encircled her throat. 'You like it rough.' He smirked as Hartur choked when he increased the pressure, before he suddenly let go.

Hartur's eyes found Alwin's, pleading with them.

She is right about our differences. She will stop at nothing to seek Hau's favour. But I can't leave her like this. Not when I love her. Alwin glanced to the open door and urged himself towards it, his stubborn body and soul refused. *If I die, so be it,* thought Alwin. He grabbed Blaze's head from behind and twisted it sharply to the left. With a snap, the unprepared mage slumped forward on to Hartur.

'Eww.' Hartur shoved the corpse and, as the body slid to the floor, its eyes bulged.

Alwin glanced down to see his hands trembling, his stomach roiled as he turned to stare at Hartur. 'I murdered someone for you. Can you not see that I care for you?' He pulled the door open and brushed the tears out of his eyes before stepping out into the corridor.

Hartur rose from the bed, her back to the door, and kicked the corpse. 'That first and only time was because I was lonely, and that was before I saw you murder others for fun.' She kicked it again. 'After that, you stalked me relentlessly. No matter where I moved you would find someone to chase me and demand my return even if it meant injury to my person.' She began to weep. 'I even had to kill a few to get away from them. After their deaths something changed in me and I agreed to enter the higher ranks of the guild and become an assassin. To capture the divine couple and kill Alena's crew was my task. I couldn't do it. Not for lack of skill but because I am no cold-blooded killer.' Hartur's voice rose in despair. She slapped the corpse. 'All because of you!' she screamed, flinching at the sound of the door softly closing.

A moment later, Alwin wrapped her in his arms. 'I am sorry I left you.'

She turned towards him and sobbed. 'Did you hear all that?' she asked.

Alwin nodded. 'I would be willing to make this marriage work, and even try to offer some more affection, if you let my Luma and Lufar go.'

'I love you, Alwin. But I cannot do that. Lord Hau wants to return the elven legacy to its former glory. As his direct descendant my destiny is to honour that. He needs Lan's sacrifice to honour the gods and restore Velterra. Your Luma will not be harmed.' She turned her violet eyes towards his and sobbed. 'Believe me when I say I am torn with doubt.'

Alwin tilted his head towards the door. 'Someone is treading softly near the door. We need to go now.'

'Go, Alwin. I can at least give you a head start.' She turned away from him.

Hartur gasped as Alwin pushed her onto the bed, her back pressing into the firm mattress as he leant over her, his face inches from hers.

'Oh god, not near a corpse. I knew Cirites are odd in their affections but not this,' she murmured.

Alwin grabbed either side of the sheet and pulled it over her. She struggled as he tied her up like a parcel, leaving her head free.

'What the hell!' Hartur wriggled, trying to loosen the sheet.

The door swung open and Het ran into the room, staring at them both before closing the door.

'I won't let you do the wrong thing, Hartur. You will regret it and it will stain your soul. Mine is now marked by that man's death. I could have just knocked him out, but I was filled with rage that you might have to sin for my freedom. I won't reach paradise, but you still might.' Alwin hoisted her into his arms and she struggled as he hurried through the doorway.

Het waited outside the door, whistling to himself, before he turned and grinned at them. 'Did I interrupt your kiss after you rescued the damsel in distress?'

'Wouldn't have put you down as a hopeless romantic, Het. Especially a weird one. There was a corpse in that room. I have explained that I have no immediate designs on her body.' Alwin stared at him.

'In our day people got caught up in the moment. The lover is rescued; the couple are so happy that they share a brief romantic moment before fleeing.' Het laughed.

'And did you ever indulge that?' asked Alwin.

'Once, before a battle, with a girl who was destined for someone else. The next time, I died defending that same girl and her beau. My own lover fled after my death. What I wouldn't have given to be able to kiss her afterwards and raise our sons.' Het wiped a tear from his eyes and grinned. 'You waste your youth, Alwin.'

'Incapable of love, like most Cirites,' said Hartur.

Alwin blinked in surprise and glanced down at her. 'Incapable of love? You are surely mistaken. Have I not been attentive enough to you? Have I not shown you enough?'

Hartur glared at him. 'Where are the impassioned kisses, the all-encompassing embraces and the vows of great passion?'

Alwin sighed. 'I am in love with you. Desire is irrelevant at such an early stage. I want to know all about you, make sure you are comfortable and happy. When I am happy about something I want you to be the first to know. When you are injured or hurting I want to fix it. When you are absent I am incomplete. Is that not love?'

Hartur's brows furrowed in confusion. 'And what of passion, jealousy and the overwhelming urge to keep that person all to yourself?'

'I killed willingly for you. I was worried for your safety and that of your eternal soul. Hartur, what you describe is lust and possession, not love. Cirites love deeply. Our love is kind, gentle and respectful.' Alwin's cheeks burned. 'And I am not opposed to your touch; it is not unpleasant. It's just new and confusing, that's all.'

'You are wise for your age, Alwin. My relationship with Flo is similar in many ways to what you have described.' Het winked.

They hurried towards a set of stairs. Het moved slowly and Alwin looked around cautiously as he followed.

'And what of the passion between your Luma and Lufar?' asked Hartur.

'Lufar is Arakaen, notoriously amorous with their soulmate

and no one else. Luma was loyal to him for over a thousand years. She kept herself for him, showing great self-control. They love each other deeply; they are also different people.' Alwin hoisted her up in his arms as the silk sheet slipped.

'I am not a Velterran or a god, Hartur, and my body is of Cirite stock. Cirites descended from a group of people known as the Calirions. I assure you, Cirites can be passionate when the need arises. I also love you enough to make sure you go to paradise at my own expense. Unbridled vice is a one-way passage to a bad afterlife. Blaze didn't love you, Hartur. He wanted to possess you.'

Het piped up. 'Don't Cirites trade in Monks Pepper?'

Alwin smiled. 'Yes, it's our biggest trade commodity.'

'I've seen you snacking on those red berries.' Het made an exaggerated chewing motion. 'Mmm, peppery.'

'So, for generations, when a boy turns eighteen he consumes the berries daily until he wishes to have children.'

'What do the berries do?' Hartur asked.

They hurried down the stairs and continued quietly down the hallway. A door creaked open and Hartur saw Ake peak her head out, she fumbled with the door and withdrew a key attached to a large keyring while her husband peeked over her shoulder.

'They decrease the libido and the ones the mystics grew were often imbued with magic to stop pregnancy just in case one of us broke a vow,' Lan answered for him, rubbing his chin. 'Mystics consumed them in adulthood as we were supposed to be celibate, but Grand Master mystics never took the altered ones as it was believed it could affect their magic long term.'

Ake frowned. 'Did you take them when you married me?'

Spots of colour appeared on Lan's cheeks as he and Ake stepped through the opening. 'I didn't stop taking the non-imbued ones until I died.'

Ake blinked in surprise. 'But our love-life wasn't lacking.'

Lan looked at her through lowered lashes. 'You wouldn't have left my bed and nothing would have been done if I hadn't taken them.'

'Well, someone would have been done.' Hartur giggled.

Ake covered her face as Lan whispered in her ear. 'She was done and often.'

Hartur struggled in Alwin's arms, turning her attention back to him. 'But you don't love me enough to free me and make my own decisions. I also doubt your Luma was loyal to him during those lonely centuries. And why should she be, he was technically dead.'

Ake glared at Hartur. 'I proved my loyalty. I chased death looking for him. Sure I was lonely but—'

'Well, sorry I'm mortal and come with the sins that entails.' Hartur scowled.

Lan smiled kindly. 'Alwin adores you. He's got your "wrapped" attention.'

Het rolled his eyes and groaned. 'The curse of the father jokes has been unleashed.'

'Best to keep your conversation down, I heard you down the corridor.' Said Lan stepping around Ake, who followed him.

Het grinned. 'We were quiet, it's those elvish ears of you that allows you to eavesdrop.'

'In regard to this conversation'—Lan gestured to himself—'as an Arakaen, once I am mated I cannot experience desire for others. If Ake did seek some comfort I wouldn't blame her. Over a thousand years is a long time to wait on a mere possibility.' Lan's brows rose. 'I've read about the Calirions; they're a type of gentle, granite-skinned, long-lived fey who dwelt near granite falls, blending in with their surroundings. My mother often told me tales of them, saying their numbers were low as they rarely produced children due to their biannual reproduction cycle. It's likely a hereditary condition for Cirites as well; I heard that some Calirions bred with mystics. Hmm, I wonder if those berries left a genetic trait on their libido? T—'

'Oh great, Lan is now in teacher mode.' Het paused to stare over his shoulder. 'And here comes act two, waffle on, great elven mystic.'

'I was once driven by jealousy, pride, love and passion and suspect I will be in the future if something threatens my wife. I took on an emperor and a dark goddess used those feelings to almost corrupt me. We aren't all flawless and divine. To be mortal is to never be truly free of sin and emotion. Ake and Het drugged a crew, and my wife is a thief when the need arises. Even a druid and a goddess aren't without sin.' Lan winked at Ake.

Alwin's cheeks reddened. 'They do not need to know about my ancestor's reproductive cycles. We can desire others greatly twice a year as per our ancestors. The berries control that and reduce the risk of overpopulation on our small isle.'

'Ha, so you can be randy too. Oh the sinless Cirites, pretending they don't desire others.' Hartur smirked.

Alwin's gaze dropped to Hartur. 'I never said we couldn't desire others. We choose not to as we see how greed, lust and other such vices lead to poverty. Velterra is proof of that.'

'Shut up. My lord knows what is best.' Hartur began to wriggle and utter curse words, which made Alwin stare into the distance.

'Uncouth.'

'No need for that, you two.' Het clapped the younger man on the shoulder as Alwin caught up to him. 'You alright?'

Ake sighed stepping up next to Alwin. 'I am sorry, Hartur. I am not without flaws.'

'Yeah, sorry, kid. I'm not perfect either.' Het sighed. 'I could tell stories that would make your blood curdle. But that's in the past.'

Alwin glanced down at Hartur. 'Lufar is correct. An ancient

race of fey had children with human survivors, mainly mystics on the former mystic isle of Man'hannon. Eventually, human traits of passion dwindled among their population, surfacing only twice a year, and making Cirites what they are today.' Alwin grimaced. 'That is why we did away with the elven festival of love. It comes around when all the women become extremely romantic. Too many children were being born at the same time and the island couldn't keep up. We take family planning seriously.'

'Do humans still exist?' asked Lan.

'I have heard that many humans fled to unmapped lands and that their technology exceeds that of Cirichad's,' said Het.

Alwin nodded. 'That is the main belief.'

Het gestured to himself. 'Well, one human still exists.'

Alwin smiled. 'True enough.'

They hurried through the door and down a small corridor to a set of tiny stairs. The stairwell was too small for Alwin to carry Hartur down. He placed her on the ground and untied the sheet; it fluttered to the ground as he offered her a hand up, which she accepted.

Alwin turned to the others. 'Give me a moment.'

'Okay, but hurry.' Ake's eyes flitted about before she followed the others hurrying down the stairs.

'Leave, Hartur, and do not follow. I will not allow you to capture and sacrifice my Luma and Lufar. Remember, I truly loved you.' Alwin gave her a sad smile and his eyes were filled with kindness.

Hartur began to weep. She pulled his face towards her and kissed him. He closed his eyes and responded with a gentle tenderness. She thrust her body against him and they slammed into the wall as her hands gripped his rear. Alwin snatched them in his as she tried to unbutton his britches.

'You will never see me again, Alwin. Lay with me in a proper goodbye.' Her heart hammered in her chest; she blinked back her tears as she clung to him. He was her lifeboat in the chaotic sea of her emotions.

'No, Hartur.' Alwin opened his eyes and let go of her hands. 'I would not have you left with even the remote possibility of carrying my child and suffering in poverty because of it. If you find yourself in danger I live in Cirichad in the market district. My father runs a smithy; his name is Arlys Smith. Goodbye, my wife; be happy. There will be no one else for me.'

Alwin slipped past her and rushed down the stairwell. Hartur stared after him for a few minutes before fleeing in the opposite direction, tears of frustration welling in her eyes.

—◦◦◦—

The small group exited through a door in the back of the manor and sprinted to the cover of a wall. They entered a gate and found themselves in a small courtyard. They crossed to the other side where, several hundred metres away, the ancient forest greeted them like a shady friend.

Ake strode ahead of Lan, her hands tensed into fists, her movements rigid as Het and Lan followed her, Alwin trailing at the rear.

Het lay a hand on Lan's shoulder. 'You have either offended her or something is bothering her. We have a few minutes. Talk to her. Alwin and I will walk a little apart from you.'

Ake felt someone grip her hand and tried to pull away. She let out a huge sigh before stopping suddenly to stare at her husband. 'Over the centuries I saw new friends and acquaintances I met die. On occasion I was set up on blind dates. The men were kind, funny and handsome, and any lonely woman would have been honoured to be with them.' Ake began to take deep heaving breaths. 'I was never attracted to them, but envious of what I had lost and could never recreate. One even tried to hold my hand and I had an overwhelming need to flee, coupled with a sudden wave of nausea.' Ake's bottom lip trembled. 'What if one day I had given in?'

Lan gave her an enigmatic smile. 'It wouldn't matter. All that matters is I get to be with you now.'

Ake tried to wrench her hand away and Lan pulled her towards him.

'If *you* had died, would you want me to be lonely or happy?'

Ake pulled her hand away and glared at him; tears of anger welled in her eyes. 'It isn't the same. You are one of the Fiadhri, incapable of laying with anyone else but your mate.'

Het wandered over and cleared his throat. 'If one of the Fiadhri mates with his soulmate it makes that partner incapable of being attracted to others. If you had slept with anyone else, Ake, you would not be his soulmate. It's a curse and a blessing for immortals. Seeking an emotional connection with a human is not the same as an overwhelming romantic connection between Fiadhri and mate.'

Ake blushed and stared at Lan. 'Were you aware that I could not take another lover?'

Lan ran his fingers through his hair and glanced away before Ake cupped his face with her hands. 'It is easy to be magnanimous and lack jealously when you know I can't be tempted to love another. Why would you try to get a reaction like that from me?' Ake dropped her hands to her sides.

'Give us a minute.' Lan tilted his head in the direction of the forest.

'Hurry.' Het and Alwin sprinted towards the cover of the trees.

Lan pulled Ake towards him. 'My darling spirited wife, it is good to see some fire in you again.' He smiled sadly. 'It tortured me knowing you bore this alone, and I would never deny you happiness, especially when I made that pact to give up my life for my womenfolk and could not be by your side.'

Ake glared at him and crossed her arms. 'Are you not angry at me for my feelings of envy and going on those dates?'

He took a step towards her, tilted her chin and kissed her tenderly. As he pulled away his eyes were full of intense sorrow. 'Far from it. I am glad you found joy in those friendships.'

'What if you had returned and I had been living with another?'

'Despite the fact it wouldn't have happened, I would hope that you would choose whoever made you the happiest.'

'Damn you. You know I will always choose you.' She blushed and stared at her feet.

Lan's brows rose in surprise before he laughed. 'I left you reeling with my admission.'

Alwin left the cover of the trees and sprinted towards them. 'Reeling isn't the right word. Swooning would be more accurate, Lufar. Now, we must go.'

Ake raised a brow. 'How do you know that?'

Alwin's eyes didn't meet hers. 'No reason.' The boy turned and retreated to the forest.

Lan grinned, and as the temperature dropped around them, he glanced up as snow began to fall. The moon was hidden behind shadowy clouds. 'I was right.'

Lan grabbed Ake's hand. She followed quietly as he led her towards the forest, safe in his loyalty and love.

CHAPTER FORTY-ONE

Lord Hau Halfey, also known as the abomination, stood on the castle ramparts overlooking the city of Velterra, built from the ruins of the Regian empire. The cold, wintry air whipped his waist-length hair into a frenzy and nipped at his ankle-length purple robes. As a powerful half-elven blood mage, he had sensed the pull of familiar blood.

My cousin and great uncle must have entered my city. He licked his lips and sighed. *When I find Lan I will drain him of his lifeforce. His powerful elven soul will enhance my abilities and rid my body of this abhorrent human blood.* He leapt off the rampart of the ancient palace. His robes billowed out as they caught an updraft and he descended slowly and gracefully, landing on the cobblestone road. He summoned a faerie orb above his head, giving him enough light to see in the darkness. It was a few hours after midnight.

It is high time my citizens saw me.

The large metal gates that were set into the high stone walls of the palace creaked open as if by some magical force; the metal jolted and rang out as it scraped against the cobblestones. The city was separated into quadrants; the palace overlooked an ancient market square which Hau now proceeded towards. Vendors still plied wares here like their ancient counterparts; wares that were popular for evening entertainment. The substances were illegal in Cirichad; herbal remedies that could be smoked to induce visions, alcohol and suggestive artwork to enhance the marriage bed.

Hau had no need of lawmakers. He believed that the strong should prevail. Each quadrant was ruled by a mage whose gangs of underlings dealt swift punishments for debts not paid, settled blood feuds and killed those that became too powerful and upset the precarious balance. Those mages paid a tithe to Hau, and when they became too powerful for his liking, he consumed their souls and replaced them.

Hau entered the former industrial area which was now a collection of alchemical workshops, magical smiths and ancient libraries housing valuable magic books. The white stone buildings were lit up by the magical orbs from the many mages who traversed the dark on their way home.

A mage in orange robes bowed to him. 'My lord.'

Hau tilted his head to him before turning down an alleyway and entering the hospitality district through a large sandstone arch. He was assaulted with the smell of frying food from the street vendors, calls from wenches trying to tempt him to their bed and conmen plying faulty goods.

'Hey, my lord, look at these magnificent orbs awaiting a fine lord's passionate touch.'

'Oil of curez, one gold bar. A paltry sum for a cure that will render the plague futile.'

'Fried unicorn hind. Tasty, magical and will enhance the libido. Two gold bars.'

The hospitality quadrant was a collection of sandstone buildings that housed brothels, bars and hotels. The high end ones could afford guards to protect their assets and patrons, but the poorer establishments were known to harbour cutthroats and despots. He turned and stared at a small building with a small faded wooden sign depicting an ale mug and frowned. A sense of familiarity washed over him, pulling him like an invisible cord was tethered to his entire being. *I sense Ake's blood. Maybe she is hiding out here?*

He entered a small bar. The floor was covered in filthy straw that soaked up blood, vomit and urine. The place smelt of stale beer and body odour. The wooden bar had a large, solemn man drying poorly washed glasses.

Hau felt someone prod him in the back with a sharp object and turned. A small, dirty, malnourished boy stepped back.

'Show us your coin. Don't want no trouble. My da needs paying for any drink.'

Hau glared at the child. 'Do not touch my person, boy.'

The boy prodded him again. Hau growled and rounded on the insolent child. '*Hylt.*'

The child cried out before his body stiffened and collapsed to the ground, paralysed. Hau leant over and lifted the boy's arm. A numeral decorated the boy's wrist.

'Twelve, typical; weak bloodline, notoriously known for ill-breeding and poor manners.' He walked over to the bar.

The bartender glared at him. 'How dare you bespell my child and belittle our bloodlines. We are still descended from Lord Hau.' The man drew a dagger from his pocket and stepped out from behind the bar. Hau threw back his hood. The bartender dropped to the floor in a prone position. 'My Lord Hau, I beg forgiveness. I did not think such a great lord would seek my pitiful bar.'

Hau scowled. *Low rank boys are of no use to me.* 'The boy's life is forfeit.'

'No, my lord. He is my only son,' begged the barkeeper.

'Unless you can offer me better compensation, your child will die.' Hau placed his black leather boot on the man's neck.

'My dau-ghter, twel-fth g-gen-er-at-ion. A fine add-i-tion to your harem,' stammered the man.

Twelfth generation female, that is rare indeed. I haven't heard of any females being born lower than a fourteenth in fifty years.

'Get up, you pitiful wretch, and bring her to me.' Hau removed his boot.

The man rose and scurried through a door behind the bar. With a resounding slap, the door reopened and the man dragged a young woman through it by her hair. The woman was crying from the rough treatment.

'This is Vera.'

Hau's eyes trailed down her form. Long, black, unkempt hair. Her golden eyes were filled with fear and her lips quivered. He drew the hair away from the nape of her fair skin and stared at her slightly pointed ears. Turning her head towards him, he stared into her eyes and smiled as they glazed over. 'Why wasn't she registered as mageborn?'

'Didn't have the money, my lord,' said the barkeep.

'Liar. I see the truth in her eyes. You took the scholarship funds and drank it away.'

Hau grabbed the woman's hand and dragged her towards the door. The straw caught alight as he left the bar, turning as the bar exploded. Flames consumed the building and it collapsed upon itself, taking the life of the occupants. *Detestable scum.*

The woman began to wail and dropped to her knees. 'Father, brother.'

'Quiet. They are not worthy of your grief. Who was your mother?'

Too frightened not to answer, she shivered and replied, 'My father's first wife, Anwyn.'

'And who were her parents?'

'I would rather not say,' whispered Vera.

'Answer me, you idiotic girl,' warned Hau.

'My mother was Anwyn, the daughter of Amities of Eriu and Carolina.'

Hau grabbed her wrist and his eyes blazed with light. The

woman screamed as her wrist burned with a bright red light, the flesh sizzling. He released her arm and she stared down at the golden number four that replaced the eleven.

Vera's eyes bulged. 'Why such a regal number?'

Hau's scowled. 'Do you know nothing of your heritage?

She shook her head. 'No, my lord.'

'All Velterrans are marked at birth with a magical tattoo. We keep stringent records but your beautiful mother was hidden from me.'

Vera's lip trembled. 'That is not of my doing, my lord. When my mother placed me at the orphanage she only gave my father's name. His number is ten so I became an eleven.'

Hau reached out to brush her hair away from her face and she flinched. 'I have never called myself emperor, have I?

'Correct, my lord.'

'There is a reason for this.' Hau sighed.

Vera lowered her eyes. 'Why, my lord?'

'So, it is common knowledge elves follow a matriarchal lineage, is it not?'

Vera nodded. 'Yes. Even I know of this.'

'My mother was the last empress. With no daughter of her own, as most first ladies only ever had sons, the heir was her closest female cousin. In this case, Telewanake, a princess of Relequis and Anwyn's grandmother. Our kings have always sired daughters first, their eldest sons become the next king. The new king then marries his closest female cousin, preferably a third cousin who will rule when the former first lady passes on or abdicates. Being a second cousin, Ake was too close in blood and a substitute mother for me.'

'But what of your heirs, my lord?' Vera's voice wavered. 'Surely I am not needed?

Hau's breath quickened and his eyes narrowed. 'Why do you

force me to remember such an atrocity. My unborn daughter, Musen, died during the war. Caoimhe is my third cousin but is not elf so cannot rule by my side as my queen or become empress. As I did not know of your mother, Velterrans trace their lines through my mother and Eldan, my second and fully elven daughter. When I am free of this illness you will bare me an elven daughter. As Ake is Flo's heir, our child will validate my right to be on the throne.'

Vera shrank back. 'But we are of the same blood.'

'For elves who struggle to bear young it is acceptable to marry a third cousin and so on. You are rather pretty.' He tilted her chin to peer into her eyes. 'How old are you?'

'Fifty-two.'

A fifth cousin and Lan and Ake's great-grandchild, what a delightful and unexpected treat. 'You will enter the harem and learn to read and study magecraft. When you are worthy of me, you will share my bed. You will be treated well, granddaughter of my beloved Amities.' Hau turned and walked back towards the palace. Vera followed behind; her head bowed in obedience.

He heard her sobs and sighed, glancing back at her briefly. 'While I do not share your grief, I am sure it will pass with the passage of time.' He gritted his teeth. 'Trust me, I know.'

—◆—

Alena glanced towards the tolling bells as she exited the forest. Behind her, the remaining crew left deep footprints in the snow that had fallen overnight. The sun's rays streaked across the sky, welcoming the dawn as a variety of people stepped towards her, from horned humanoids to reptilian people to dwarves and halflings and many more. Blaze's former guards had all but scattered.

'What has happened here?' Alena hurried over to a guard who was shedding their armour.

'Lord Blaze is dead, my lady.' The guard tossed her sword aside and knelt before Alena.

Alena gripped the guard's shoulder. 'And his prisoners?'

'Got away, my lady.' The guard trembled. 'They are alive and have escaped.'

Alena loosed a long breath. 'Thank goodness.' She turned to the gathered group. 'The curse of Blaze will be lifted from this forest I will see to it.'

'All hail the blood, the legacy. We bow down to you, Lady of Morteredin Manor. May your lordly father's soul blaze on into eternity, his magnificent light a presence in your life.'

He murdered my Nuo. May he burn forever, his soul in a perpetual state of agony.

The townsfolk bowed their heads and sang the song of mourning; tears streaked down faces and voices wavered with grief as it was sung in the Eriu tongue then followed with the ancient elvish.

The road has opened; the gods await.
Dear one be free.
Your kin mourn you, but you
Have earned your rest.
Reap your reward.

Odet moldis,
Dee and Sorendee hylt.
Leven feyla.
Ea glenda kren eu.
Ea iudiciis plez.
Takus ea gifu.

The kindly townsfolk had built a pyre near the arch and entrance to the manor and placed Blaze's body upon it; the forest was like a guard of honour behind it. Alena reached deep within and summoned the first spell her father had insisted she learn. *How can I despise someone so much, yet feel such a great sense of loss?*

'*Magna.*'

She conjured the tiniest flame in her hand and walked over to the pyre. The guards stepped back and bowed. Placing her hand on the pyre, she waited for the weak flame to take hold. As it fed on her father's body, she turned to the townsfolk.

'Alena is surrounded by the townsfolk who appear to be singing a funeral dirge. They must be holding Nuo's funeral,' said Het.

Ake's lip trembled. 'Tragic. What a waste of life. Nuo was a wonderful person. I wish I could comfort Alena but she would have our lives.'

Lan put his hand on Ake's shoulder. 'Are you okay?'

His wife shook her head. 'Caoimhe is so close.'

Het whistled low and Caoimhe cocked her head in their direction as Alwin popped his head out from behind a tree and gestured to the fairy.

The halfling and fairy turned and ran towards the forest, and Alwin slipped back into the cover of the trees.

Caoimhe wrapped her arms around her mother's legs and looked up; her eyes glowing in the dark.

'They shine in the dark just like your father's.' Ake tucked a loose strand of hair behind the fairy's ear.

'Now would be the time to sneak past Alena.' Het peered past the group. 'But let's avoid this unnerving forest and slip past the town.'

'Right, let's get out of here,' said Ake.

Lan turned as he heard a subtle weeping and glanced at Alwin; the boy was trying to hold back his tears. He walked over to the boy and wrapped him in an embrace. 'The stirrings of first love are often painful.'

Alwin pushed him away. 'You got to keep yours.'

'Not really, Alwin. I got around seventeen years with many gaps in between.' Lan's eyes flitted away and his shoulders slumped.

He patted Lan's shoulder. 'That was cruel of me. Sorry, Lufar, I am hurting.'

'I am here if you want to talk about it. But now we must get out of here.'

Alwin nodded and Lan turned his attention back to Het and Ake, who were discussing which direction to take.

'It's two days north overland,' said Ake.

Het grinned. 'Ever been there?'

'Centuries ago, so a lot has changed. Have you?' Ake placed her hands on her hips.

'No.' Het grinned again. 'Are you making those directions up?'

'Yes,' said Ake.

Alwin groaned. 'Hurley, have you been to Velterra?'

'Several times, but I fled as the city is dangerous for the weak and small,' replied Hurley.

'What is the direction?' asked Lan.

'Two days overland, but south,' said Hurley.

'Right, that is our direction,' said Lan.

They edged out of the forest, their movements swift and silent.

Hurley gave Lan a sad smile and whispered, 'Caoimhe would be captured by evil mages and used for potions. I do not want her to go with you. Please let us stay here. Alena won't harm us.'

Ake turned to Caoimhe. 'Do you want to stay here with Hurley?'

The fairy nodded.

'Then go with our blessing.'

The little couple hugged them briefly before scurrying away. Ake's eyes shone with tears. 'My little girl is a woman now.'

The small party turned their attention back to Alena who was addressing the townspeople.

'My father lied to you. He told you he had no money and needed to win favour from Lord Hau in order for the town to flourish. He took slaves and killed the vulnerable. I will fix up your town and see to your needs. My first order is that my ship be fixed,' commanded Alena.

Whistles and cheers surrounded her as she was hoisted into the air and carried past the manor and down a sloping path towards the township. The smell of cooking fires and cries of folk made the party creeping south halt. As Alena was lowered to her feet in the township, a crowd surrounded her and Ake ducked low, running towards a low wall and into an alley. She stopped and waited as a guard spoke to their former captain. Lan tilted his head in his wife's direction, then one by one, the rest of their group hurried into the alley to join Ake before they skirted to the southern edge of the town and continued towards Velterra.

—⁓—

It was the morning after Blaze's funeral and the oppressive darkness was slowly lifting from the ancient forest. The venerable trees still clustered together and blotted out most of the sun, but small patches of sunlight filtered down through breaks in the canopy. Alena knelt beside a human-sized hole. An unleashed sob caused her to take a deep breath; the earthy smells of decaying leaves and soil seeping into her very being as she stared at her hands, a testament to her heritage. The calloused fingers were caked in dirt; her unnaturally sharp and resilient nails designed for digging through the soil or tearing bark from trees. She hoisted Nuo's body, wrapped in golden silk, and lowered her gently into the earth. Tears spattered on to the ground as she covered her beloved's body with the soil.

My beautiful, sweet Nuo. I will miss you. Go in peace. I will always love you.

The villagers had wanted to give Nuo a great send-off, but Alena had decided to say her farewells in private. Her muscles heaving with effort and her breath ragged, she placed a large piece of granite over the grave, and took out a hammer and chisel from her pocket, engraving sentimental words into the stone.

'This rock is as heavy as the stony grief that clings to my heart, my darling.'

She wiped the sweat from her brow and stood. Her back cracked and the pain made her wince. Alena leant against a tree; she felt the lifeforce hum throughout it, the hidden essence reaching out to her. She drew on its lifeforce and, as the tree sacrificed some of its life for her, tendrils of green vines erupted from the tombstone; buds began to form and open, and golden flowers spawned over the grave, a testament to Nuo's golden character. Alena turned and ran through the forest, Dee's blood apparent in her movement and nature, as if the very forest bent to her will, giving passage as hot tears welled in her eyes.

—✳—

Alena thrashed about, sweat beaded down her face and her legs became tangled in the sheets. She jolted awake suddenly and found herself on the floor of her bedroom. She untangled her legs from the blanket and stood. A whisper tingled on the back of her neck; she shivered and withdrew a dagger, glancing around.

A shadow flickered past. 'Alena,' it whispered.

'Show yourself!'

The sole candle nearby spluttered and went out. She ran for the door, but an ethereal form materialised in front of her and wrapped her arms around her. A scream worked its way up from her lungs and halted in her throat as the spectre drew away.

Tears coursed down Alena's face as she realised the spectre favoured the appearance of Nuo, but more radiant, her face a mask of peace.

'Goodbye, my love. Live, Alena; love and surround yourself with joy.'

The spirit began to melt away into the shadows.

'I loved you, Nuo. I can sacrifice myself to bring you back, like my ancestor did.' Her lip quivered.

'I know, but you are needed here,' whispered Nuo as she faded into the oppressive darkness.

Alena threw herself on to the bed and sobbed. 'Bring her back; she was my soulmate.'

And the gods answered, if only in jest. *Sometimes people come into our lives for a chapter, if only to show us what love is so that when we find the one we do not waste a moment fixating on trivial things and strive forward confidently.*

Vera's hand trembled as she held her palm upright, sweat beading on her brows as her eyes flitted to Hau and back to her palm.

'Concentrate, Vera, you have great potential.' His eyes softened. 'If you get this wrong it could kill you. Now breathe and recite the words I have taught you.'

Vera took a deep breath and squared her shoulders. '*Divinty arescus more.*' A small wisp of air tickled her palm before it began to twirl in the air, gathering power.

'Control it. Watch—' Hau stepped back as papers were caught in the updraft, his voice was lost in the deafening roar of the wind.

She stumbled backwards as a large tome was flung towards her. Her lord stepped in the way. He snapped his fingers and the spell dispersed, and the items in flight crashed to the carpeted floor with a dull thud.

'Are you okay?' He turned slowly. Her hands shook and he snatched one up, his eyes full of concern before he dropped her hand. 'You are unharmed it seems. But congratulations, most do not master that spell in the time you have been under my tutelage.'

Tears welled in her eyes. 'Thank you for your kindness.'

He frowned. 'Done in with a simple compliment. Were they so irregular?'

Her shoulders slumped. 'The first kind one was when I met my mother nearly twenty years ago. I never saw her again.'

Hau's eyes widened and he turned away. 'I know what it is like to lose a mother.'

'But she never abandoned you, my lord.'

Hau rounded on her, his eyes wild. 'She got herself killed for your ancestor Telewanake. The pain never lessens.' He took a step back and composed himself. 'Being mortal again causes my self-control to weaken. You will not be bothered by my outbursts again. Now, where were we?'

Vera sobbed, covering her face with her hands. 'I am sorry, my lord, do not strike me for my ancestor's faults.'

He made a sound of disgust and she stiffened as he pulled her hands away from her face. 'I do not strike women or girls unless in self-defence.'

'But the headmaster at the orphanage and my own father struck me to admonish me. Was it not fitting?'

Hau reached out a hand before he pulled it back suddenly. *She is wary of hands I assume. Ake draws nearer and could contest my throne. Without a female heir my legacy is not established. But never have I been unkind to women in my bed and I cannot rush that on this poor emotionally starved girl.*

He pulled her into a brief embrace but as he tried to draw away she gripped his robes, sobbing on his chest. 'You will be fine, now release me.'

She dropped her hands and backed away and fell to her knees. 'Forgive me, my lord.'

Hau laughed. 'You are brave to touch such a feared mage.'

Her head snapped up her brows furrowed. 'My lord. Are you well?'

He frowned. 'Get up. It is pathetic you cower from me. You are important enough to my legacy that I demand you do not tremble before me like a dying leaf lost in a storm.'

She gave him a quizzical look. 'I am important to you?'

'In a sense.'

He watched fascinated as her soul warred within, she frowned while her eyes filled with hope then fear. Her breath quickened and she stepped towards him, stood up on tippy toes and kissed him on the cheek.

'Brave or stupid.' His breath caught in his throat and he bit his lip as he felt an ancient stirring in his loins. 'Well, how many centuries has it been since that has occurred.'

'What do you mean?'

'Have you ever lain with a man?'

She shook her head.

'Are you opposed to what you see before you?'

'No, my lord.'

'Are you stupid?' He stepped towards her, grabbing the back of her neck and pulling her face up close to his. 'I could destroy you with a click of my fingers. You would dance with death?'

She smiled and her face was striking.

'But you were kind to me, my lord. I would repay that kindness.'

'You would give your body in exchange for a few kind words?' He scowled.

Her lip quivered before she shuddered. 'You have taken me from poverty and taught me as an equal. If you can make use of my body as some small atonement, do so.'

'No.' He released her and she fell on her bottom. 'We will do the deed but not when you are willing to exchange your body for simply providing you with dignity befitting your birthright.'

She stared up at him moon-eyed. 'Thank you, my lord.'

His heart clenched. *What is wrong with her?* He turned and strode from the room.

CHAPTER FORTY-TWO

Lan stretched and threw back the covers. He turned and kissed Ake on the top of her head and climbed out of bed. Walking over to the window, he looked out over the sprawling city. The moon was invisible among the hundreds of magical orbs that fluttered above magic users as they wandered from buildings looking to make merry.

They had arrived in Velterra a week ago after making a two-day trek overland. *I have never been in a city this size. I know the city is dangerous, but the way they embrace magic makes me joyous.* Like most newcomers, he was fascinated by the novelty of high magic use and lack of inhibition, but was unaware of the notorious gangs, rampant slavery and high mortality rates from violence, illness and poverty. He had only witnessed a few bar fights and cutpurses lifting wallets from unwary victims, but had never entered the more notorious areas.

Lan had tried to find employment but failed. In a city of the highly educated, a mystic whose knowledge was outdated was of little use. Alwin had managed to get work in a forge as a bellow boy and Het had gotten money by winning arm wrestling competitions. Several men had accused Het of cheating until the six-foot-eight man had stood up from his chair and they had fled. Lan laughed at the memory.

He glanced around the small, clean room. There was a double bed with thick woollen blankets and firm pillows; the mattress made of linen stuffed with straw. They had a window overlooking the hospitality quarter and the inn was even able to afford to pay two night guards. The rooms were expensive at a medium gold bar a week. Lan walked over to a small table with a metal basin and a pitcher of water on it. He poured some of the water into the basin and it made a splashing sound as it hit the bowl. He lathered up some soap in the water and proceeded to wash himself. The soap frothed up nicely, and he ran his hands over the slight stubble that had appeared on his chin and other parts of his jaw. *I have grown facial hair. Odd, but then again, I never asked how my elven father could grow a beard. I assumed it was magic. It must be something male Anwyl elves can do upon attaining adulthood.* He laughed. *Mage and forest elves could not.* Some bubbles rose from the bowl of water and he popped them. The water had turned a vibrant blue. *Unusual soap.* He scooped some bubbles up in his hands and breathed in the smell of lilac and blueberries. Lan laughed at the beard of bubbles he had given himself. Quiet footsteps pattered behind him and gentle breath tickled his neck as he caught sight of a figure in the mirror.

'How distinguished.'

Lan jumped and turned towards her. 'Hell, Ake.'

She reached out, scooping up more bubbles, and gave him a moustache. She ran her hands over the stubble and raised a brow.

'Do you dislike it?'

'No, but I believe eventually you will want to shave it off.'

'I doubt that.' Lan smiled and grabbed more bubbles, putting them in her hair. 'We really need to make some money.'

She curtseyed. 'I am a lady, look at my bubble crown.'

Lan dipped his head. 'My lady, I have heard of a great race that takes place at sunrise. The prize a purse of coins.'

Ake frowned and shook her head. 'I've heard people chatting in the streets about how dangerous it is.'

'I am a skilled rider and we need the money.'

'What if Hau takes notice?'

'I'll disguise myself.'

Her eyes locked with his and she sighed. 'Promise me you will take care.'

'Off course.' He winked. 'Besides, I can practice riding my own mare.'

'You compare me to a horse.' She ran away laughing until he grabbed her and kissed her. He lifted her up and she wrapped her legs around his waist and leant in to trail kisses up his chest.

'I do not try to offend.' He nickered in a ridiculous attempt to soothe or seduce her. 'I remember centuries ago referring to ourselves as stallion and mare and a certain person getting cozy with me in the stables.'

Ake giggle and leant in, nuzzling his neck. 'Mmm, pine and oakmoss, your usual scent. And now lilac too.'

'New soap.' He kissed her wrist and inhaled sharply. 'Can't get enough of your familiar scent either.'

'What is mine?' Ake giggled.

'Lavender with traces of honey and vanilla.'

'I didn't mean my perfume.'

Lan mouthed her wrist. 'Hmm. Your natural scent is almost indescribable. Like any mated Arakaen, our scents are unique and only discernible by each other. It's like coming home. To me, you smell of fresh air and the tang of the sea.'

'Counters your electric one, like excitement or static before a thunderstorm. So hard to describe.' Ake ran her hand down his chest in a seductive caress.

'How is it I can be perfectly fine then one touch from you and I'm an amorous mess?' he whispered in her ear.

'Because I am irresistible.' She giggled.

'Of course. I am in your power and I cannot resist it.' He carried her over to the bed.

'Well, go on then, prove it.' She gave him a flirtatious smile.

'At least here I don't have to keep myself from indulging in you.'

He tossed her gently on to the pillows before he knelt on the bed, knees slightly apart, drawing her against his chest. As he took her with a ferocious intensity, he bowed his head to nuzzle her neck, his hands trailing in her hair. He glanced up, sweat beading on his brow.

'Why have you gotten so intense of late?'

He slowed his pace. 'Is that okay?'

'I am not complaining. Just surprised,' she panted.

'Was I a bad lover before?' He grinned.

'Far from it. But ever since that circle you have been an expert.' She blushed.

He laughed softly. 'Has nothing to do with that. Seeing the reality of death made me realise that if I ever found you again I would not hold back my feelings for you. First couple of times I wanted it to be comforting and reassuring. Now I want to show you the depths of my need for you more often. You are also not lacking in skill yourself.'

Ake gave him a coy smile.

'And I thought you holding back was from you being frightened you would scare me.'

Lan clucked his tongue. 'Partly that.' His eyes darkened. 'When we were newly married I was still following the tradition of chewing monks pepper berries like all mystics that come of age. I ingested them daily from when I hit puberty in my thirties and throughout our marriage.'

'That's when I couldn't get my mind off you.' She gave a breathless moan.

'I'm well aware.' Lan winked. 'We were linked as mates even back then and those dreams you had of me, well, they left me hot and bothered. It kick started my elven maturation before the normal age of forty.'

Ake blushed. 'You weren't supposed to know of those private dreams.'

'I guess it was just punishment for scrying and then mind linking with you at night. You appeared restless, tossing and turning, so I mind linked with you via the bond you forged and, well, the shock at seeing what you wanted me to do to you left me aching.' Lan laughed. 'And yet in my innocence I still felt you may have wanted another despite those dreams. Imagine if I hadn't chewed the berries after that? I think I would have returned from my journeys earlier and it would have been passionate like this all the time before we could even marry.'

She pouted. 'No fair, this is exactly how it should have been. It's as heated as that time in the cave.' Ake put her hands to her mouth to stifle her cries as he continued loving her with relish. He grabbed her hands and pushed them away from her mouth.

'Oh no you don't. I missed you calling out my name.'

She glanced away from him, her cheeks flushed. Lan turned her head to meet his gaze, his mouth inches from hers.

'For over a thousand years I couldn't hold you in my arms. I want to f—'

Ake placed a finger to his lips. 'People might hear you.'

He smiled as he continued. 'You until the walls shake as you cry out, my name on your lips as you let everyone know you belong to me.'

He lowered her back on to the bed. She arched her back as he pulled her hips closer and changed his pace. Her hips bucked against his and he smiled languidly as she whimpered. Her eyes widened and went hazy from her release. 'Lan!'

His mouth took possession of hers and she sighed against him. His lips slid along her jaw and he nibbled on her earlobe. She shivered as his breath caressed her neck.

'*Ea jaen leven. Eu natas que.* Those words are true. My beautiful beloved, I will never have enough of you.'

Her eyes fixed on his, bright pools of devotion. *I feel the same, my darling. You are the reason I dream and the air that I breathe, and I will not let anyone take you from me again.*

'I can't believe that you are mine again.' His hand cupped a breast and his mouth followed. Glancing up, their gazes collided. 'I would shatter the world for you if it took away all the pain you have suffered waiting for me,' he said softly.

Tears brimmed in Ake's eyes and she blinked them away. 'Damn.'

'I mean it.' He brushed the tears out of her eyes and pulled her closer, groaning as waves of pleasure washed over him. Ake's face was flushed with the heat from their love. 'My loquacious bride is lost for words.'

Someone banged on the wall next to them. 'Shut up you two.'

'To hell with you!'

'Don't stir up trouble.' Ake glanced towards the door.

They heard the creaking of wood and a door slam open. Lan pulled away from her and began to dress. He had managed to put on his trousers and boots before someone pounded on their door. In a fury, Lan pulled open the door as Ake scrambled under the covers.

Arlys stared at him, his mouth wide open. 'I thought I recognised that voice. Trust me to find you half-dressed in this less than holy place.'

Lan walked back into the room and threw on his shirt and began to button it up. Arlys went to follow him but Lan glared at him. 'Give us some privacy.'

Arlys stepped back. 'Where is my son?'

'I don't think I should give out that information. I know how you treated your wife and child,' said Lan.

'You know nothing. How would you like it if I kept information on your child's whereabouts from you?' asked Arlys.

I would be devastated. I hope I am doing the right thing. 'He is downstairs with Het. They share a room on the bottom floor.' Lan glared at Arlys. 'That is if he wants to see you after you disowned him.'

Arlys roared. 'Disowned him! We argued, I said I didn't want to see him for a while. When I got home from work he was gone. You think I would ever come to Velterra unless I was searching for him?'

'Room seven.' Lan closed the door in Arlys's face.

Ake scrambled up and began to dress, her face bright red. Lan grinned at her. She poked her tongue out at him then turned away. He began to tie the laces on the gown for her, noticing the subtle gaps in the cloth between the shoulder blades for her wings to spread out without ripping the garment.

'You were amazing,' said Ake.

'*We* were.'

'Do you think Alwin lied to us?'

'I'm not sure. But we need to get downstairs and protect the boy either way,' said Lan. He blinked as the early morning sun streamed in through the window, waiting for Ake to lace up the boots Nuo had lent her before grabbing the key to the room and opening the door. He walked out into the hallway and Ake followed then he locked the door.

They hurried after their unwanted guest and stood back as Arlys reached the lower levels and began pounding on a door.

'Who is it?'

'It's your father.'

Alwin slowly opened the door to see his burly father staring at him. The man's green eyes were filled with concern. The younger man pushed open the door wider and gestured for them to enter the room. As he closed the door, Ake and Lan stepped away from father and son.

'Should we leave?' asked Lan.

Alwin shook his head. 'Why are you here, Father, and how did you find me?'

Het snored in one of the two single beds; his big feet hung off the end.

'I contacted a lawmaker who did some research and found your name as part of an employment contract as crew on the *Carnay*. I am here to bring you home. Velterra is no place for you, Alwin.'

'You disowned me,'

'I believe you misinterpreted my words, son.'

'You said "begone from my house until I am ready to forgive you",' cried Alwin.

'And you thought that meant permanently?'

'There were times when you wouldn't forgive me for weeks.'

'Silly boy, that isn't forever. I never mentioned disowning you. I assumed you would understand until I had calmed down. I would never indulge my anger in front of you. It's not done in Cirichad.'

'I may have misconstrued your meaning in my grief for grandfather.'

'Yes, that seems the gist of it.' Arlys held out his hand and Alwin shook it.

Het had woken and sat silently, taking in the awkward reunion. He grumbled and pushed himself to his feet, grabbing both men and ushering them towards each other. 'Hug it out you two. You are father and son for goodness sake.'

'Cut it out, Tylluan.' Arlys pushed the man's hands away, knocking his hat from his head.

Arlys sighed, straightened his blond ponytail and replaced the grey cap.

'My name is Het, Arlys, you stubborn ass.'

Arlys ignored him. 'There is something I would show you, my son.'

'Is it important? I have work in a few hours,' said Alwin.

'It is.' Arlys turned and gave Ake and Lan a cold smile. 'And you may want to see this too. It concerns your granddaughter.'

'I am staying here and getting more sleep.' Het yawned before lying back down on the bed and closing his eyes.

Alwin sighed. 'He isn't great in the mornings.'

'Never was,' said Ake.

Het opened one eye. 'Says the former lazy girl.'

Arlys cleared his throat and glared at Lan. 'Enough, you are a bunch of children.'

'Why are you implying that I am the least mature here?' asked Lan.

'Father, he is an intelligent and considerate individual. He may be partial to emotional outbursts but he isn't too childish.' Alwin gave his father a gentle smile. 'Luma on the other hand, let's just say she is cheeky, sensitive and spontaneous.'

'Really? She was always reserved around us,' said Arlys.

'Yes, I was surprised too,' said Alwin.

Everyone jumped when Het broke out in hearty laughter. 'Ask her about the bodies in the well.'

'No, I would rather not. There has been enough violence on this trip so far,' said Alwin.

Ake rolled her eyes. 'Thanks Het, now they think I killed people and shoved their bodies in a well.'

'The teachers thought it was real,' said Het.

'Intriguing. I shall get that story from you later, Het,' said Lan.

Het rose and as he threw on his shirt and shoes Alwin glanced at the wounds Lan had bandaged on the road, scavenging herbs to make a poultice to prevent infection, and Het was healing nicely.

'I'll tell you on the way,' said Het.

Ake poked her tongue out at the warrior.

Arlys grumbled. 'I see what you mean, Alwin.' He turned and opened the door. The others followed and Alwin closed the door behind him.

They exited the inn and walked past a yawning guard. Arlys strode ahead, his face a mask of determination. The sun had just risen and their breath steamed in the cold, wintry air. They walked past a steaming pile of ash and smouldering embers.

'I wonder if anyone died? How is it Velterrans seem to care so little for the lives of their brethren? That is the building I entered yesterday to gather information,' said Arlys.

Alwin knelt near the pile and chanted a Cirichad blessing. 'Blessed of the lord and his prophet Mandami. May all who passed be worthy of paradise.'

As Alwin rose, Arlys turned down a small alley and drew a small throwing axe from beneath his shirt.

'Are you expecting trouble?' asked Lan.

'This is Velterra. Being from here, I thought you would have been aware of the dangers that lurk in this city,' said Arlys.

'Shall we shiv them and take 'em for all they be worth?' said an unknown voice.

'Nah, look at that big brute with the sword,' said another.

'No need to fret, Arlys. You will be fine with Het here.' Lan grinned.

Arlys grumbled and glared briefly at Lan. 'Typical gloating Velterran.'

'I am not a Velterran, Arlys. I came from the island of Man'hannon.'

They passed two dishevelled men armed with makeshift knives. The men stared at Het warily. Arlys turned another corner before the path descended into what looked like a more sinister part of town.

'Welcome to the poorest district in Velterra, commonly known as Revengez, the elvish word for revenge.'

The air was thick with the smell of unwashed bodies, vomit and open sewerage. Giant rats ran freely through the streets, gnawing on refuse between the tightly pressed buildings. Ake squealed as one ran past her and Alwin shivered.

The paths between the buildings were cramped, barely fitting two people abreast. The roofs tilted forwards precariously, over-hanging the path on either side and blocking the view of the sky. Black smoke poured from chimneys and was carried up into the air between the limited gaps. The sun was mostly blocked out and the smoke was inhaled into their lungs. Ake coughed and covered her mouth. Lan sneezed and looked around in distaste.

Children sat on corners begging for scraps. A man stumbled past them, liquor in one hand, yelling at a woman he pulled along with his other. Het and Lan glared at the man, their eyes snapping to the yellowing bruises on her bare arms. They passed six older men in rags huddled in the corner of a small alley that strayed from the main path. Lan heard Ake scream and he was jolted out of his thoughts.

Ake knelt sobbing near a large crack. Dirty water had filled the crevice; a bare-chested man lay face down, his arms outstretched protectively over an infant wrapped in his shirt. Icicles still stuck to the child's fragile eyelashes as he stared up at the sky, the sun's rays unobtainable on the innocent face.

Arlys strode over to Ake and pulled her away. 'This is a common thing here. Do not let it make you ill with grief.'

Lan walked up to his wife and took her hand before smiling at Arlys. 'That was kind of you.'

'She is of the nurturing sex. Cirichad morals state that a little more care should be given to women, for their tender natures build home and community. Without these tenets our faith thus falls,' said Arlys.

'Are you okay, honey?'

'That poor man and baby.' Ake's eyes filled with pain and she took heaving breaths as she sobbed.

Lan pulled her away and they continued their journey. When they were further away, he held her to him.

'I know that was confronting. But you are very emotional in your response.' Arlys turned and gave them a cursory glance.

Lan spoke through gritted teeth. 'She's the Goddess of Mercy and Life. Any loss of life that is brutal will impact her more than most.'

'I don't believe in that stuff. Anyway, we are nearly there.' Arlys turned another corner, Het and Alwin taking up the rear.

'Just when I thought you had some empathy,' Lan muttered under his breath a few steps behind the determined blacksmith.

They came to a small house with a rusty wrought iron fence. The front gate hung at an angle. Arlys pushed it open and it creaked in retaliation before he took a key from his pocket and put it in the lock of a wooden door that was a faded white. The front garden was covered in dying vines and flowers, weeds strangled the desperate plants and encroached on the red brick well in the centre of a once pretty garden. Arlys jiggled the lock and turned the key and the door swung open. The dust made him sneeze as he went inside.

'Does no one else find it strange my father has a key to a house in Velterra?' asked Alwin.

'Well, come on in you lot,' said Arlys.

They entered the small abode. White, dusty sheets covered the sparse furniture and cobwebs fluttered in the odorous breeze that blew in through the open door. Gloomy light filtered from a small skylight. A tiny hearth stood to the back of the room.

'I would open the window but the stench is palpable,' said Arlys. He pulled a sheet off a double bed and a cradle. 'The other furniture is of little consequence. But these two items are part of your story, Alwin.'

He ran his hands over the cradle and sighed. 'A little over twenty years ago. I was part of a group that rescued Velterran refugees. We had safe houses in Velterra and would escort the refugees to Cirichad. I had supplied money, medicine and tools, but had never been on any of the missions. The members of the order complained that I needed to attend at least one mission so I did.'

'That's around the time Anwyn was studying in Velterra.' Ake frowned.

'Oh, by our great lord, have mercy on me. Do I want to hear this, Father?' Alwin looked concerned.

'Yes, Alwin. Your mother's past is a big reason why I hate Velterrans. They are prone to violence,' said Arlys.

Alwin sighed. 'Please continue.'

'I arrived in Velterra and spent several nights in Revengez escorting willing refugees to various safe houses. On the last night I ventured out into one of the drinking establishments. Against better judgement I had a beer.'

'One beer. Wow, you really are high strung,' mumbled Het. Ake gave him a stern look. The warrior grinned at her and made a motion of buttoning up his lips.

Arlys's eyes narrowed on Het. 'I was sitting minding my own business when I saw the most beautiful woman enter the bar.'

'That's sweet, Father, for you to refer to mother that way.'

Arlys gave his son a restrained smile. 'Well, it was true. Anyway, she looked frightened. On closer inspection she was shivering and she had a blackened eye.'

Lan growled and swore. 'Who hit my granddaughter?'

'I am coming to that, Trebrelan.' Arlys turned away from them; his breath trembled before he continued. 'The woman came up to the bar and asked if anyone would help her. She was belittled and hassled as if she were a woman of the night. As she was accosted, a man came into the bar, striding towards her with anger in his eyes. He was clearly intoxicated. I was not to have the woman bothered further as he began to scream at her with spittle on his lips. The gist was she had returned on the pretence to study, but in reality she was here to see her adult daughter, the product of a hasty marriage that lasted a few weeks. She had fled with the child many years before when she realised her husband, Wrin, was a despot, prone to spending all their money and too ready to use his fists on her.'

'Ake, did you know of this?' asked Lan quietly.

Arlys interrupted them. 'No, she wouldn't. I was to find out Anwyn delivered her newborn child to an orphanage on the out-skirts of Velterra. When the child was grown she returned to her father and established a relationship. The daughter, Vera, sent a letter to Anwyn to meet with her in the hopes they could get to know each other ... Anwyn had returned to Velterra the day before I arrived. Her husband had divorced her and remarried. When Anwyn arrived in his bar, his new wife had fought bitterly with the gentle Anwyn and hit her. She fled. He followed her hop-ing to get her to stay. It is not unusual for Velterrans to have more than one spouse. He was angry at her for deserting him and steal-ing his child, and demanded she make up for it by becoming his second wife.

Ake began to cry. 'I would have helped her if I had known.'

Lan squeezed her hand.

'Like Amities, she was prone to keeping her life from others. To summarise, Alwin, I beat up her husband and I escorted her to this safehouse. Caught up in the thrill of drinking and sav-ing a beautiful woman, I was not in control of my emotions and when she kissed me, well, let's just say I dallied with her and we conceived you that night. I was all for taking her back with me to Cirichad as my wife, but the next day she had fled. I stayed in Velterra for just over nine months waiting for her return. Cirite men take their duty as providers seriously and I would not leave until I knew she was without child. Lucky I did, she returned one cold, blustery night with you in her arms. She had managed to divorce her husband; Amities had paid her former husband enough to establish his bar and put some money aside for their adult daughter to enter the mage school. We spent a few weeks getting to know each other and it was the most joyous experience of my life. When you were a few months old, Hau heard word of a Velterran-born child of the fourth line. We fled to Anwyn's father who had arrived in Cirichad to learn more about the new sciences that were being studied there. We married and the rest is history.' Arlys's eyes locked on his son's.

Alwin stared at his father, his brow furrowed. 'You lay with someone who wasn't married to you and fleeing her former husband. How could you sin like that, Father?'

'We were both willing, Alwin. I loved your mother the moment I laid eyes on her. As for the sins, it only happened that night. I repented for years after, giving to charities, praying and controlling my emotions. I did not touch her again.'

Alwin sighed. 'That was cruel, Father. Even Cirites show affection to their spouse. Chaste kisses in a private household, gentle smiles and kind words are all acceptable. Why did you withhold them from Mother?'

Arlys gave a shuddering breath and composed himself. 'Because that would have led to improper affections, my son. It is time you knew. My father was a former Velterran. My mother lost many children to his inflamed passions and died having me. After that, my father blamed himself and followed Cirite ways almost to the point of fanaticism. Now you know I am a sinner like all men. I vowed I would never let my passions kill a woman I loved.

In the end that got to your sweet and loving mother. We argued for months and she swore that if I loved her I would show it. She threatened to leave and …' Arlys looked suddenly haggard; his shoulders slumped and his eyes filled with a bitter sadness.

Lan spoke solemnly. 'You accused her of being a disgusting Velterran that would abandon another child. That she wasn't worthy of being Alwin's mother.'

'And I will always regret those words that caused my beautiful Anwyn to feel the need to take her life,' said Arlys sadly.

Ake marched over to Arlys and went to slap him, but he caught her hand. 'We do not hit family.'

'Your cruel words caused our sweet Anwyn to take her life. How dare you mention family!' cried Ake.

Het cleared his throat. 'Ake, I think this time you are out of place. Alwin has just heard distressing news given to him by his remorseful father. Don't you think we should act according to Alwin's wishes?'

Ake took a step back. 'How inconsiderate of me. I am sorry, Alwin.'

Arlys put his hand on his son's shoulder. 'Did you inherit my lack of self-control?'

Alwin shook his head. 'Like all Cirites, I am capable of gentle affection and probably have the physical ability to reproduce. It is not a need for me though. My wife would have had that from me, but like most Cirites, it is taboo if used for romantic purposes, so I denied her. I looked up to you, Father. Mirroring your almost godly self-control and absences of vice, and because of that I let her go. I have somewhere I need to be. If my calculations are correct she would have told Hau Luma and Lufar are here, and after completing her task, will destroy herself one way or another.' Alwin turned to Lan and Ake. 'Best you be aware, Hartur is Hau's descendant some ten generations past. Blaze was her former fiancé. He stalked her and forced her into dangerous situations where she took life to defend herself. You were her first quest after entering the assassin's guild. She thought if she was forced to be a killer why not for the Velterran cause. I pushed her away, worried she would blight my soul. The truth is she enriched it. If I had let her in I probably could have prevented her from going to Hau. I am going to find my wife.'

'Wait, I will come with you,' said Het.

'We would like to help too,' said Lan.

Alwin gave them a gentle smile. 'I appreciate the genuine empathy and will to fight for me. But this is something I must do on my own.' He held out his hand to his father.

Arlys clasped his hand and shook it. 'Alwin, let me help.'

'No, Father, this is farewell. I forgive you and bless you, as is the Cirite way. Thank you for your honest words. There will come a time when we can speak freely again as father and son, but I am hurting. I will see you again, but not soon.' Alwin turned and sprinted from the little house.

Ake flinched as Arlys broke out in heart wrenching sobs. Her eyes were damp with tears and she wrapped her arms around the blacksmith. 'You helped raise a fine man. He said he will see you again, there is hope there, Arlys. Cling to that.'

He gently pushed her arms off him. 'Well, yes, he said that. Anwyn had your nurturing ways. I thank you for consoling me.'

Ake took a step back and Arlys's face became impassive. 'Well, I am heading back to Cirichad. Alwin has made his decision.' He walked over to Lan and handed him a key. 'I bought this house off the underground for my son. Please see he gets the key.'

Lan held out his hand and Arlys shook it, before he took the key and pocketed it. 'Take care and realise we have all made mistakes. Try to find comfort in Ake's wise words.'

Arlys stepped towards the door.

'Hang on a minute,' said Lan.

'What is it? I am bereaved at the moment; I would leave,' said Arlys.

'Did you give away a tome that was meant for me?' asked Lan.

Arlys sighed. 'Yes, I did. The book is full of sinful content. I didn't want it in my house. I can tell you where to find it.'

'No, it's fine, I have retrieved it.' Lan gave the man a forced smile. 'I forgive you for taking my father's book and handing it to someone else.' He gritted his teeth. 'It's best if I say it now because I doubt we will meet again. The way you treated Alwin, his mother and my son was awful. But you are forgiven for your son's sake.'

'I appreciate that.' Arlys strode to the door and turned to look at them. 'I may not believe your wife is a goddess and you a former God of Death, but I was part of the cause to resettle vulnerable and abused persons in places they could thrive. If you are a part of that cause, bless you all.' He then rushed from the little house.

'Well, that was surprising. The old fellow has feelings, limited, but he has them.' Het rubbed the back of his head.

'That was awfully sad.' Lan gave the departing figure a sad smile. 'So, we have lost our charge and we are out of money. What is our next course of action?'

Ake turned and stared at him, her arms crossed. 'How come you are not more upset?'

'I am still in shock and learning new stuff about grandchildren I only met in death.' Tears welled in his eyes. 'I am trying to keep my mind off it by concentrating on our concerning circumstances.'

Ake gave him an apologetic smile. 'I am sorry.'

'It's okay. But what of that brute over there, he showed no emotions.' Lan grinned, trying to change the distressing subject.

'Don't bring me into your lover's tiff.' Het laughed.

'We should head back to the inn and get our gear before they put it on the street,' said Ake.

'Yes, let's go,' said Het.

The three friends left the little house and locked the door. Lan broke out in raucous laughter as Het told him about the greatest prank of the era while they walked back to the inn. They avoided potential disasters with Lan's hearing and Het's intimidating size. Ake stuck her nose in the air as they made comments about her rebellious youth.

'My dear Anwyn, I am so sorry,' Ake muttered.

Lan grabbed her hand and squeezed it as he neared her. She gave him a grateful smile. 'I am sorry I couldn't be here for her and you.' Ake snuggled into the curve of his arms as they made the journey back.

—⁓—

Pennants fluttered in the breeze; the crowd mingled in the alleyways, barely leaving enough of the main streets clear for the riders to mount up. Mages used magic to vanish the piles of manure amongst the bizarre menagerie of creatures assembled, their riders eager to snag the purse of gold bars if they won. Thunder boomed overhead as grey clouds added a sombre, overcast sky to the early morning festivities; fat droplets promising a deluge landed on Lan's head and he held out a palm.

The festivities master stood on a wooden stool, dipped his head to the crowd and riders before he held his arms wide. 'I welcome all to this auspicious yearly event where the brave gather and test their prowess against each other for the enjoyment of our great lord.' The orator smiled and turned his head to where a hooded figure in red robes sat upon a chair of velvet encased wood.

A cold smile spread across the lord's mouth and he wrapped his ring-covered fingers on the armrest. 'Proceed.'

'The first to cross the finish line wins. Now, on to the rules. You must stay mounted until the end, that is all.' The orator stepped down from his perch.

Lan paced, scratching the top of his head. 'Het said he would be here early.'

He glanced about, his eyes settling on Het pulling a cumbersome, yet magnificent beast towards him. 'Come on, you stubborn thing.'

Lan scanned his opponent's mounts: a griffin with a humanoid rider, a goblin on a giant rat, a unicorn and its halfling owner, and their most worrying competition—a large ogre on a wyvern.

Het dragged the restless draught horse towards Lan. About seventeen hands high, its black coat was in need of a good brushing, and the white feathering was snagged with burrs. 'This troublesome beast was bought from a fish stall owner.'

Lan reached for the woven lead. He glided his hand gently down the crest of the animal, along the shoulder and lowered the horse's head to rest his forehead against the horse's own. The horse snorted and their breaths mingled as if testing one another's spirit. Lan drew away and leant down, running a hand down the left front leg to the knee and following down to the pastern to unpick the burrs. His new friend chewed the top of the cowl he wore. 'You need a good currying too, my good boy.' He rose and turned to face Het. 'How did you acquire him? We are short on funds.'

Het rubbed his chin. 'Ahh ... hmm. Your wife can be quite charming.'

Lan cocked his head as someone brushed against him, a cloak covering their face, that familiar scent causing him to brush her shoulder as she tossed him a curry comb. 'For after. I know you love your horses. The old owner is happy to stable him for us as well for a small fee.'

Lan hoisted himself up on to the horse's back. 'And just how charming were you?'

His wife pouted and drew her cloak aside to flutter her eyelids at him; he felt his cheeks burn. 'Well, that would do it.'

Het laughed. 'So easily overcome by her, aren't you?' Het patted the animal's flank. 'No saddle I'm afraid, and I was kidding, I gave the man the last of my arm wrestling winnings. He was glad to get rid of the animal, says he's stubborn and doesn't listen.'

Lan raised a brow. 'Shall I call him Ake then?'

Ake poked her tongue out. 'Don't you dare.'

'It would be accurate.' Het ruffled Ake's hair and she playfully swatted him.

'Ready yourselves,' said the orator.

Lan drew his hood over his head as Het and Ake merged with the crowd as the orator waved a green flag. Without warning, the competitors leapt forward. The wyvern screeched and took flight, the griffin on its tail. The rat hissed and bolted down the road while the unicorn pranced delicately before launching into a trot. Lan clicked his tongue and applied pressure with his knees. His mount huffed and hooved the ground with its right leg. Amongst the applause of the crowd and excited chatter, laughter swelled around Lan.

'The clowns come out today.'

'Very entertaining.'

Lan gritted his teeth and leant over his mount. 'Can you go, please?'

The horse's ears twitched.

'Go.' The horse shook its mane. 'Oh magnificent equine, I bid you make haste.' The horse's ears swivelled. 'Please.'

The animal lifted his head, whinnied loudly and broke into a trot before launching into a gallop.

Lan swore and took hold of the guide rope; his stomach plummeted before he let out a delighted whoop.

Lightening cracked, the tips of his hair stood on end, his skin prickled as the surge of power flowed through his body like seduction itself.

A screech rang out overhead as the wyvern turned and raked at the griffin, swooping under a raised wing. The griffin bellowed as it dived towards Lan. It shrieked as its rider clung to its back. Lan's mount bolted, and he pressed himself down as the griffin's claws grazed the withers of his horse before it circled back. The unicorn in front slowed and turned, Lan leant to the right, his mount fluidly shifting with his control and avoiding his competitors as the unicorn brandished its horn at the wyvern whose jaws latched on to rider and beast. Blood spurted against the crowd who cheered. Lan felt the bile rise in his throat. Out of the corner of his eye, someone tossed a cat in the path of the giant rat who jarred to the left and charged down an alleyway, almost dismounting its rider.

A bellow above and Lan veered to the right, the griffin's beak snapping around his head. The rider leant over and drove a knife into Lan's shoulder. Pain washed over him and he withdrew the pressure on his mount as the other rider aimed his dagger towards the horse's eyes. As they slowed down, the griffin shrieked and caught an updraft, sweeping it high into the air and in pursuit of the wyvern.

Lan squeezed his knees into the sides of his mount who bolted, lessening their distance from a large arch shimmering in multiple hues. The griffin crashed into a weather vane; it flapped its wings, feathers raining down onto the crowd below.

Lan bit his lip as the wyvern dived in front of them, his horse sweeping to the side and almost dislodging him as it halted. The beast stalked forward, hissing and snapping its jaws. As he drew on his magic, it made his blood sing. Lightening formed at the tips of his fingers and he gestured to the wyvern, merely a conduit to the ethereal power of storms as a bolt ripped through the monster in front of him. Its shrill cry tore through him, his breath wavering as it beat its wings in an attempt to block them as Lan spurred his mount forward; the horse's hooves thundering down the road. From the left, the giant rat trotted into view, crossing the finish line to cheers and applause, its rider still mounted but sporting a few scratches.

Lan smiled and dismounted as the orator handed him a single gold bar. 'Second place.'

'Wait.' The figure situated on the throne hurried towards those gathered, and gestured to the spectators. 'I sense kin.'

Lan drew his hood lower as the red-robed noble pointed to people. 'Remove your hood.'

A woman shivered, her head cowed. 'Yes, my lord.' She removed her hood.

'Alas, I must be mistaken.' The mage frowned and peered around, before shifting restlessly and dragging a blonde woman towards him. 'Ake?'

The woman squealed before the noble pushed her aside and hurried away with two richly dressed people falling in behind them. 'I will find her.'

Lan released the breath he was holding, then, taking his horse's guide rope, Lan led it away from the crowd and down a dark alleyway. He began to curry the horse, delivering gentle pats and kind words. 'Great job. I shall call you the elvish word *Uldare* because you are a shoulder to lean on, my friend.'

The horse snorted as gentle footsteps caused Lan to lift his head. Ake drew her hood and reached his side. 'Well done both of you.'

Lan smiled. 'We can eat today and I got a new horse. It's a good day.'

'You are so happy. You should ride more often.'

Ake's eyes widened as he pushed her against a brick wall, his knee parting her thighs as his mouth locked on hers. His rough beard tickled her ear as he then mouthed her earlobe and whispered, 'Oh, I intend to. Is tonight okay?'

As he drew away, he reached for Uldare's rope with one hand and Ake's hand with the other. As they proceeded away from the secluded spot, Ake's cheeks were a vibrant red. Lan tried to hide a satisfied smile. He grunted as he limped on his right leg.

'What's wrong?'

Lan sighed. 'Well, I did sort of age rapidly after that rite. I think past injuries are taking a toll on my body and my right leg was the worst injured.'

Ake shuddered. 'I am so sorry you got hurt because of my raw power. That is why I am scared to wield it.'

He smiled. 'It's okay. This old man will have to take better care of himself.'

She fell in step beside him as they entered the market quadrant; people scowled as the beast snorted and danced anxiously amongst the milling crowd.

'We have to get this guy to the stables,' Lan cried over the vendors.

Ake looked up at him with a quizzical expression. 'Have you gotten taller?'

He grinned. 'Yep, the final growth spurt for elves is from eighty to one hundred. I'm now five foot ten.'

Lan patted the horse who snorted his discontent but walked on at Lan's urging as the crowd parted.

'You measured yourself?' Ake gave him a sidelong glance. She halted outside a rickety lean-to, wrinkling her noise as the smell of not-so-fresh fish lingered. 'He is stabled here. He used to pull the fish from the docks to the markets.'

'Yes, I measured myself. I'm not ashamed to admit I'm a proud and vain elf.' Lan led the horse into the manger, corralled with a lattice of woven sticks known as a hurdle. 'I will get you better lodgings when we leave here.' Lan grabbed a rusty rake and loosened hay from a stack before checking the stone water trough. 'You should be good for a bit.'

He removed the rope from Uldare, patted him gently before pushing open the makeshift gate and retying it. 'Hungry?'

Ake's eyes filled with joy and she hurried past him in to the throng of people, he jogged to catch up with her as she stopped in front of a vendor selling breaded delicacies. Taking a pair of tongs, the vender lifted a fried round of dough, with the middle missing, and rolled in a tray of what smelt like sugar and cinnamon.

'Oooh.' Ake's eyes were wide.

'How much?' Lan asked the vendor.

'Two for a small gold bar.'

'Alright.' Lan handed over the money and the vendor gave him a miniscule bar in return before handing over the food.

Ake reminded him of Uldare as she almost bounced on the spot as he'd handed her a share. She bit into it before breathing through her teeth. 'Hot hot hot.'

'Wait until it cools.'

Ake grinned at him and he rolled his eyes as she bit into the food. 'Worth it,' she said between bites and deep exhales.

He began to eat his own, and her silly displays that made her his very own Ake warmed his heart. He couldn't help himself and brushed the tip of her nose with his sugar-coated hands.

She wrinkled the offended body part and stared him down. 'I hate my nose being touched.'

He laughed. 'I know. But your reaction is so cute.'

She murmured to herself about not being cute before she snatched his hand and led him amongst the market stalls.

CHAPTER FORTY-THREE

Hau glanced down at the young woman lying prone at his feet. She had demanded to be seen rather than going to the head of her guild to hand over her information. He rose from his throne and stalked towards her, fighting the urge to consume her soul for her audacity. She lifted her gaze; her large violet eyes made him take a sharp breath. *So like my mother's. Violet eyes are usually the sign of an enchantress.* While unusual eye colours were more common in Velterrans, violet eyes were reserved for royal elven women. *My mother and my beloved bride Atius were the last with violet eyes.*

'Stand up woman and give me your name and line.'

The woman trembled as she stood, her head lowered, refusing to meet his gaze. 'Hartur Halfey, tenth generation.' The woman trembled before composing herself.

He gave a low menacing laugh that made her jump. 'What are your parents' names?'

Hartur bowed her head and took a shaky breath. 'I am an orphan, my lord. I do not know their names; I was abandoned at three days old, or so I was told.'

Hau gestured and she was flung towards him. He hissed menacingly. Hartur shook with fear as he grabbed her by the back of the head, forcing her to peer into the depths of his soulless eyes.

'Please let me go!' Her internal screams rang in his mind.

Hau blinked rapidly before he laughed. 'Ah, an enchantress. You have my mother's gifts, descendant of Atius. You are a wonderful reminder of my former bride. Before I add you to my harem, what is the information you would tell me?'

'My lord, Trebrelan and Telewanake have entered the city. I failed in my duty to capture them and kill the crew of the *Carnay*. I am not worthy of your harem. Please release me from this world, I hear it is painless.' Her tear-filled eyes pleaded with him.

'I am aware when close kin have crossed my city boundaries.' *Except when Anwyn lived here. Amities gave her an amulet to protect her from me. He did the elves a great injustice by keeping a half-elf like that from me. With her divine blood we could have restored elves to the world after several generations.* 'You have won my favour for your honesty and your bravery in telling me. Why would you want a quick death?'

Hartur looked away and he turned her head to meet his scrutinising gaze. 'So, you are desperately in love. You are so easy to read. Well, we shall have to rectify the matter.' He released her and she stumbled back.

Hau sauntered over to his scrying bowl and began to chant in a sinister voice; the words were a mixture of growls, grunts and hisses. The blood began to churn in the bowl; steam evaporated in the air. Hartur wrinkled her nose as the metallic smell became overwhelming.

Hau breathed it in deeply and licked his lips. 'Blood is life and power.'

He turned and stared at Hartur for a while, like he was pondering his options, before he summoned her back to him. She exhaled suddenly as she was lifted off her feet and dragged towards him. 'You will bear me an elven child.'

'No, my lord, please no.' Hartur began to sob.

'Not with me, you stupid woman. You will seduce your husband and bear the child. It has been centuries since I have been able to sire a child,' Hau growled.

'But you have a harem!'

Hau laughed softly. 'I enjoy the company of beautiful elven women, or at least those that have some legacy to them. But I am working on siring an heir. My harem isn't just for sleeping with women. I train and educate them too. Never would I lie with someone descended directly from my loins. Even *I* have scraps of morality. And when they annoy me they have other uses.' Hau grinned eerily.

Hartur shuddered. 'Please my lord, do not harm Alwin.'

Glaring at her, he flung the scrying bowl off the stand in a fit of rage; it rang out as it hit the ground and Hartur covered her ears. Blood splattered to the floor and turned black. The ground began to crack as the tainted blood burned through the floor as he strode towards her.

'I would never kill a grandchild of my beloved cousin Amities. He was a beautiful soul. He was the epitome of elvenhood, family orientated, kind, loving, intelligent and elegant.' He reached towards her; black mist seeped from his hands. Hau composed himself and smirked. 'I forget myself. Go do this deed. When the child is born, you and your husband will be free of me as long as you promise to keep him from Velterra. He is looking for you in the market quadrant. You will find him near an apple stand. If you fail I will add you to my harem and see to it that your husband is my eternal guest.'

Hartur bowed, turned and ran; huge doors creaked open as Hau muttered some dark words and she hurried through them.

Their child's soul, if elven, shall return me to my mortal self. Then I will have my legacy with Alwin's sister. I have no need of Lan; I shall just have to kill him for abandoning me. But I cannot bring myself to kill Ake, my mother's dearest friend.

Alwin stared at the apples. He blushed slightly as he remembered Hartur's trick to gain a stolen kiss. *She is a thief so the market seems a place she would frequent, and it is close to Hau's palace.* Alwin looked up as the gates to the palace screeched open. With his exceptional sight, he saw a guard prod Hartur through with the end of his spear. *What an example of providence. Thank you for blessing me, lord.*

Alwin handed over a tiny gold bar to the vendor and grabbed the bag of apples he held out. He watched Hartur shiver and wipe her eyes with her hands. *Her lord better not have laid a hand on her.* He strode over to her and she looked up, surprised. Her eyes filled with tears. *Why is she crying? Does she not want to see me?*

He opened the bag of apples, picked one up, took a bite and held it out to her. She laughed and grabbed at it. He used his other hand to pull her towards him and kissed her, his tongue tentatively exploring her mouth.

She broke the kiss and pushed him away. 'No, Alwin, you must leave Velterra and return to Cirichad and forget me.'

He continued to eat the apple and threw away the core. 'No, I can't leave here without you. Apparently I was born here, this is my home. I also have a sister I must find.'

Hartur stared at him in shock. 'Did you know of her before you arrived?'

'Nope, just found out today.' Alwin gave her a sad smile and told her Arlys's tale.

'Are you okay?'

'I will be. Maybe we should head away from this palace and you can tell me what happened inside.'

They walked through the marketplace, casually glancing at the odd wares, from magic items to everyday foodstuffs and tools. Alwin grabbed her hand but she shrugged it off.

'Do you hate me, Hartur?'

'You said it yourself; we are incompatible.' She gave him a sad smile.

'What happened in there?'

'I cannot say. But you must leave Velterra.'

'Well, that's not happening. I have a job. Speaking of which, I am headed there now. Will you walk with me?'

'This is not a date, Alwin. But for future reference that apple thing was romantic. Handing a partner a reminder of an intimate thing is thoughtful. Just a pointer for any future partners you have.' Hartur stopped and stared at him. 'I guess I'll see you around.'

Alwin grabbed her hand and she tried to pull away from him. 'Not until you tell me what happened in there.'

'He wants to use us, Alwin. Your heritage and mine. Now let me go.' She struggled.

'And will he punish us both if we fail?'

'Alwin, please stop asking questions and let me go.'

'I will wait.' He pulled her over to a bench and sat down.

'Ah, you stubborn boy!' She sat down next to him, scowling.

He waited patiently. 'Aren't you willing to serve your lord faithfully?'

'Not at your expense,' she cried and balled up her other fist.

'I see.' Alwin stood up and exited the market district, dragging her by her hand. She stumbled and he stopped, waiting for her to gain her feet before he continued, setting a quick pace and entering the industrial district.

'Let me go now!' She pounded on his hand with her small fist.

They came to a small, rustic blacksmith amidst wealthier looking workplaces. Alwin smiled contently at the familiar sound of hammer pounding on metal and was hit by a blast of hot air as he dragged the grumbling Hartur with him through a set of open double doors. A large man hammered a metal sword over an anvil, tools hung from large chains in the steel ceiling, and a small furnace gave off intense heat and light. Alwin walked past a foot-powered grinding wheel to a set of shelves holding blunt, newly forged weapons and tools. He released Hartur, placed his bow down and took a leather apron from the shelf and put it on.

The blacksmith turned and stared at them. 'You're late, Alwin. What's with the broad?'

'Just my wife. She puts herself in danger and needs to be watched.' Alwin pulled up a stool and sat. He began to sharpen the tool.

'Okay, lad, it's odd, mind you. I don't need you on the bellows today. I will close the doors and take my lunch break. Mind yourselves, we don't want to draw Hau's attention,' said the blacksmith.

Alwin heard the doors close and the building was left in the soft glow of the forge. It began to heat the room quickly. Alwin took off his apron, removed his shirt and returned to his labours. Hartur tried to shove past him, but he put out a hand and eased her back. 'The Caelestis resistance is strong amongst the peoples of the industrial district. You will not mention this to Hau.'

Hartur sighed. 'I'm not interested in having random citizens killed.'

Alwin smiled. 'Good. And you can leave when you answer my question.'

'If it means I can get away from you, fine. He wants me to seduce you and give him a child we may conceive, for some odd reason.' She glared at him and stomped her foot.

'And the consequences if you don't?'

'I enter the harem and you are his permanent guest.'

'See, that wasn't too hard.' Alwin stood up and pushed open the doors. Cool air streamed in and he let out a contented sigh and wiped the sweat from his face with the apron. 'You can go, Hartur. I will see you tonight.'

'What do you mean by that?' She walked towards the entrance.

'We will pretend to make that baby. It will give us some time until the others figure out how to defeat Hau. You will not join his harem. I am staying at the Guggly Inn.' Alwin gave her a gentle smile.

'That is not happening, Alwin.' She stared him down.

'What choice do we have? We flee; he chases us, or starts a war with Cirichad.' Alwin gave her hand a squeeze.

'There's always another choice.' Hartur bolted out the doorway.

He grimaced as her fear flooded him; her need to relieve herself of her life in order for him not to suffer spurred him to action. *I won't allow that to happen.* Alwin stood up, grabbed his bow and hurried after her. *She's very quick.*

Hartur turned down an alley and he followed. She turned a sharp corner and leapt over a barrel; he knocked it out the way with a swift kick. Hartur squeezed past some women carrying sacks and entered a door. He followed and assessed the bakery where men and women were busy kneading flour and shaping bread. He coughed as he slammed into a baker carrying a sack of flour. In a cloud of flour dust and yelled obscenities, he shoved the baker aside as Hartur raced through another door and out of sight.

'Dage, you keep track of things, does that include directions?' asked Alwin.

'*Yes master,*' said Dage.

'Where is Hartur headed?'

'*That alley leads to the Revengez district. A dangerous place. You can cut her off ... If you turn back and take a left, if it pleases you,*' stammered the nervous bow.

Alwin grinned, turned and raced back the way he came. He made several turns at Dage's advice and saw Hartur sneaking through a small gap in a fence to enter the next quadrant. Through the gap, Alwin saw her huge sigh of relief before she covered her face with her hands and began to weep.

He attempted to enter the gap in the fence, but was too large. He took a few steps back, sprinted and leapt over the large fence; with Hartur's small stature she would have been hard pressed to climb it. He jogged over to her and picked her up; she began to scream.

'Put me down!'

Some of the poorest citizens gave her a cursory glance before concentrating on their own troubles.

'Quiet, Hartur. You could draw danger.'

He headed back to the forge with Dage's guidance and dropped her unceremoniously on the floor. Then proceeded to go back to his work.

'How can you be so cold about this, Alwin?' Hartur shivered.

'What can I do about it? Have my wife put in a harem with an evil being and be detained myself, attempt to kill the evil being, or sleep with my wife and hope my betters can defeat him before a potential child is born? Hau only needs to think you're trying. From what I know of scrying, sound cannot be heard or has that changed?'

'No one has been able to fix the sound issue.'

'Seems a logical choice. We can pretend, or take measures to prevent a child.'

Alwin stood up and reached for another tool. 'I won't force the issue, Hartur.' He sat back down and sharpened the tool.

Hartur sat down to think about her options.

'What were you going to achieve by running from me?'

'That is none of your business,' she muttered.

'It's very much my business. I would rather not be Hau's guest.' Alwin stood up as the blacksmith came back in.

'You're done for the day, lad. See you at dawn.' The blacksmith handed him two tiny gold bars.

Alwin nodded and reached for Hartur and pulled her up; she resisted and dragged her feet as they left the blacksmith. 'Were you intending to forfeit your life to circumvent this whole issue?'

'Yes.'

'I thought as much. That is why I insisted you stay in my line of sight.'

They entered the hospitality district and Alwin took her to the inn he had changed to while trying to avoid the others. It was small and cheap. They entered through the saloon-style doors into a room littered with straw. Men chewed tobacco and spat it into brass chamber pots at the base of the barrels that served as tables. A large, wooden bar lined with stools took up most of the floor. A staircase wound downwards near the door. Alwin turned and proceeded down the stairs. Hartur was crying and her sobs wracked her small frame, no good Samaritan stepped in to aid her despite her obvious distress.

'See, they do not care in Velterra. What does that tell you about your lord?'

'My lord is good, they are not.'

Alwin shook his head. 'You delude yourself.' He inserted a key into a lock, turned a handle before pocketing the key and pushing the door open to reveal a small, dank, windowless room with a single bed and a dresser. He lit a candle on the dresser with a set of matches before closing the door and bolting it. He sat down on the grimy wooden floor, his back against the door.

'Take the bed, Hartur, and rest. It's the closest thing to clean in here, and you may feel less inclined to harm yourself after rest.'

'Why are you so considerate, Alwin?' She began to sob and lay down on the bed.

'I told you; I love you. I will keep watch.'

Hartur stared at him before rolling over and closing her eyes.

Alwin jolted awake as Dage announced it was evening. He

stood up, stretched and went over and shook Hartur gently. She yawned and opened her eyes and turned towards him.

'Move over, Hartur, I have a plan.'

Hartur sat up as Alwin slipped under the tattered and worn, grey woollen blanket.

'Dage, can you use your danger sense to tell when someone is scrying on us?' asked Alwin.

Hartur stared at him as if he had gone mad. 'Who are you talking to?'

Alwin pointed to the bow on the hook near the door. It glowed suddenly.

'Yes master.'

Hartur turned as the bow hummed.

'Are you are having a conversation with a magic weapon?'

Alwin nodded. 'I can hear all of them and reply.'

'You are full of surprises, Alwin.' Hartur grinned.

'My plan is to make it look like you are seducing me when that pervert Hau checks in on you.'

'Please don't refer to my lord that way.' Hartur scowled.

'Is he still your lord after threatening you and me to get what he wants?'

'Lord Hau does what he does to restore the great elven kingdom. His actions are necessary for the cause.' Hartur's eyes filled with pride.

'So, threatening women and forcing them to bear children, allowing his city to be overrun with cutthroats, poverty and illness is vital to the elven cause?'

Hartur made a noise of annoyance. 'We will never agree on this, Alwin. If my lord thinks it is, then it must be.'

'Then why did you refuse to seduce me?'

Hartur's eyes flitted about. 'I asked myself that same question. I am torn. It is my duty to further my country's legacy, but I can't seem to do it at your expense. If it was anybody else I wouldn't hesitate.'

Alwin smiled. 'So, you do love me. I am not just some dalliance.'

'I already told you that,' mumbled Hartur.

'Master ... he searches for her,' stammered Dage.

Alwin reached up and grabbed Hartur. She struggled as he dragged her under the covers with him. He lay on top her and pulled off his shirt.

'Undo your blouse.'

Hartur blushed, her fingers trembling on the buttons. 'This is ridiculous, he won't believe it.'

Alwin rolled onto his back and pulled her on top of him. 'Well, make him believe you have seduced me.'

'He has found her, master,' said Dage.

'He's watching.'

Hartur sighed and her eyes glowed violet. *'Lay with me, Alwin.'*

Alwin made his expression blank for a few minutes before he tried a lecherous look. He saw her struggling not to laugh at his ridiculous expression. She began to falter and he pulled her face towards him, kissing her sweetly.

'Come on, Hartur, be believable. This way he will leave us alone for a little while.' Alwin pulled her against him and she blushed.

'I can't do this, Alwin. Forcing myself to pretend I am coercing you is abhorrent.' She shivered.

'You really are a good girl. I'll sort it.' Alwin pushed her off him.

She scrambled away from him but he dragged her towards him and lay on her, making sure the sheets covered them.

'Alwin, you of all people won't be able to convince him.'

'Is that a challenge?'

'I suppose it's worth a try.' She sighed.

He made a pretence of pulling down their pants. He began to go through the motions of loving her without doing so. Hartur lay back and closed her eyes trying not to laugh at the silliness of it.

'*He has gone, master,*' stammered Dage.

Hartur let out a breath and began to laugh. 'That was ridiculous.'

'I would not have someone watch the real thing.'

She gasped as he splayed her legs with his own. 'I don't think that is a good idea.'

'I think it is. I will show you I love you, our souls will bond, then you will stay with me no matter what he asks of you. You are too good to follow an evil man.' Alwin's mouth took hers in a semi-passionate kiss.

'Okay, but I doubt this will make me change my mind about my lord.' She caressed his face. 'I want this, but do you?'

Alwin shimmied out of his pants as she removed hers. 'I wouldn't offer if I wasn't willing. I am as curious to explore what's between us as you are.'

He moved her legs apart and fumbled around until he entered her. They both blushed.

'So different in a bed with candlelight. I can see all our embarrassing expressions and lack of skill,' whispered Hartur.

'You didn't do it in a bed?'

Tears appeared in her eyes. 'No, on a shag on the floor and it hurt.'

'Was it by force?'

'No, but it was rough, painful and without tenderness.'

'Then why did you want to try it with me in that forest?' He gave her a tender smile.

She growled through gritted teeth. 'Because I love you.'

'I guess it's the same for me.' He put his hands on her hips and began to set a steady pace. Her gaze met his. 'Your eyes are magnificent.'

She blushed and looked away.

'Hartur, please look at me. It's important we do this together, no matter how awkward.'

She trained her eyes on him and they filled with building desire. He reached deep within himself and forced his love for her to the surface; he saw her expression widen as he reached for feelings. Using his ability as an empath to draw on other's emotions and change them, Alwin wove their mutual fondness into an intangible web of love and loyalty to each other. He tested the strength of the bonds by thinking of Hau and his dedication to Velterra, including using him and Hartur to get his way. Hartur shivered and her mood changed, a rage against Hau washed over her.

Her eyes widened and she began to cry. 'How could you, Alwin? I will never be able to turn on the others now because doing so would hurt you.'

'I will not have you beholden to a cruel man when you are such an innocent thing.' He leant down and gave her a tender kiss. 'This magic is far older than blood magic.'

'You tricked me.' She glared at him through her tears.

'How?' He frowned.

'Sleeping with me and making me loyal to you,' she whispered.

'I told you I would bond our souls. I was upfront about it. If you didn't want to be bonded to me I couldn't force it, especially not in this vulnerable act. I just took away the anxiety of you having to make a decision between him and me.' He felt her need for him building and altered his pace.

'Why didn't you tell me you were an empath?' She gasped as he shifted his weight, her desire flooded him and spurred him to a faster pace and she locked her legs around his back.

'It seemed of little importance.'

'You should have sought training for it, Alwin. The ability to manipulate others is a dangerous thing.'

Alwin's eyes darkened. 'It's not like that, I tentatively connect with souls, offer reprieve or, if willing, allow them to forge a connection with me. Never do I force. Your soul cleaved to me like we are one.'

She cried out and he used that time to match her, experiencing a moment's relief as their bodies climaxed.

'I can't have so easily given up my lord's cause for someone I just met.'

'You did and willingly. Our bond is unbreakable now, Hartur.' Alwin clambered off her and began to dress.

'That's it? How can you be so cold after that? After that kind of connection?' She went to turn away from him.

'I'm not done, Hartur. I was just dressing.' He finished and got down on one knee.

Her eyes filled with shock; she smiled and sat up.

'Hartur Halfey, I vow to be a just and kind husband for you. I will treat you with respect and strive to protect your soul. Do you accept?'

'We are kind of already married.' Hartur laughed.

Alwin pulled a plain brass ring from his pocket and took her hand. 'Will you wear my ring? I know it's only brass, but over-adornment isn't done in my culture.'

She nodded and he slipped it on her finger.

'I love you, Alwin.' She leant in to press a brief kiss to his mouth.

He smiled, pulled her off the bed and into a firm embrace. 'I love you as well. Please don't hate me for the bond between us.'

She began to dress. 'I don't think I could if I tried.'

'I'm hungry after that. Let's go get some food.'

'I know the best street food. You have to try it!' Hartur smiled and grabbed his hand, she opened the door and he followed.

—◠◡◠—

Lan ran the long knife gently down his face and winced as it cut the skin. Blood welled up and dripped into the bowl. Ake had managed to find her way to the richer parts of the city and had lined her pockets with stolen gold. *I should be able to provide for her without her resorting to crime.* He threw the knife into the basin and grabbed the hand mirror. His face was an utter mess. After nearly a month of growth the facial hair was poorly manicured and extremely itchy. He scratched at his face.

'Stop that, Lan. Go ask Het to teach you how to shave or go to a barber.'

Lan turned to look at her. 'We can barely afford this filthy place. How can we afford a barber?'

Ake backed up on to the bed as a large rat poked its head out of the crack in the wall. 'I thought I had cleaned this place really well.'

Lan looked around the room that consisted of a double bed and a bedstand. When they had entered, it had been full of rat droppings. The smell of rodent urine had assaulted their nostrils but it was all they could afford. The room now shone after Ake's administrations.

'You did a great job, honey. Unfortunately, the other inhabitants of the inn are less likely to be as fastidious as you.'

A rat gave a loud squeak and Ake shivered.

Lan laughed. 'An all powerful goddess scared of a rat.'

Ake glared at him. 'Don't you remember those horrible rats on the ship? And besides, who knows what diseases these creatures spread.'

'I'll defend you, my lady.' Lan pushed the bedstand in front of the hole. The rat squeaked and scratched against the assault but gave up quickly.' Lan held out his hand to Ake and grinned. 'You are safe, my lady.'

Ake took his hand and slid down off the bed. She giggled and rolled her eyes at him. 'My hero.'

They had been in Velterra three weeks now and had begun to

understand the layout of the city. There was a loud banging on the door; Lan grabbed the knife and walked over to it.

'Who is it?'

A familiar laugh was the reply. Lan opened the door and ushered Het in before bolting it.

'Good morning you two.' Het waved.

Ake squealed as the rat managed to break through the gap between the wall and bedstand. She jumped on to the bed as the rat began to run around the room erratically, its mouth foaming. Lan threw the knife at the rodent, Het caught the blade in the air, knelt down and stared at the ill animal.

'Come here, little one.' The rat, as if almost hypnotised, crawled on to his outstretched palm. He ran his hands over the rat and green light flooded its little body.

'You can heal?' asked Lan.

'Only small creatures. Never got to learn the big druid magic.' Het smiled.

'Ake and I have lost any healing magic.'

Het shrugged. 'The gods are strange.'

The rat squeaked and Het approached Ake. She yelped and crawled backwards on the bed. 'She won't hurt you, Ake.'

'Don't push her, Het. She hates that,' muttered Lan.

Ake squealed as Het grabbed her hand and let the rat leap on to it. She shivered then smiled as the rat sat quietly and dozed on her open palm. 'Sometimes you have to push this one to try new things despite her stubbornness.'

'I am well aware, Het. I prefer not to if I can help it.' Lan smiled.

'One thing I love about you.' Ake blew a kiss at Lan.

Lan pretended to capture it and put it in his pocket.

Het turned, looked at Lan's face and laughed. 'I'll be back.' Het unbolted the door and threw it open and his large feet thudded across the landing.

Lan watched Ake feed the rat some scraps of stale bread before she went outside the room and placed the rodent down.

'You are kind of cute,' whispered Ake.

Het wandered past her back into the room and showed Lan the wooden-handled razor with a straight blade that could be opened and closed, and a leather strap.

'Right, you sharpen the razor by running the edge across the leather strap. Lather up your face and shave close to the face like this.' Het demonstrated how to shave, grabbing a rag and blotting any small nicks. 'Be prepared for the bloody terrors of shaving. You will either have to grow out a beard and maintain it to prevent itchiness and a terrible look, or shave regularly.'

'It's all got to go. I have a potential job lead in a workshop today. Can you escort Ake as usual?' Lan took the razor, wiped it on a towel and began to shave, lathering up the soap as Het had shown him.

'I can look after myself.' Ake glared at them and ran down the stairs.

Lan sighed. 'Can you handle her antics?'

Het laughed. 'Ake will be fine. She managed all this time.'

Lan frowned. 'Monsters are predictable. Evil people, including Hau, are not.'

Het rubbed his jaw. 'You are correct.' He grinned. 'Hey, I am supposed to be the wise druid.'

Lan put the razor down and washed his face and towelled it dry. 'Maybe I shouldn't take this position.' He moved towards the stairwell.

Het placed a hand on his shoulder. 'I will watch her. You two are very loud.' Het blushed. 'Don't you think you should be more careful? Hau will stop at nothing to get to an elven child.'

'I didn't think of that.'

'I know it's not my place to say, but maybe you should find a safe place for Ake to stay, she's been through enough. I am sure you and I can take on Hau with Alwin and Alena's help.'

'Yes, I shall look into that but I will not leave my wife's side.' He smiled. 'If only Flo was here. She would have known the most effective ways to prevent children.'

Het laughed. 'Like Amazon priestesses, female druids are also taught that knowledge. I once snuck into the class. I can write down the potion for you if you like. I am not sure how efficient it will be as I was booted out of the class very quickly.'

'I am the one to blame if anything happens. Ake couldn't bear any more children then I healed her.' Lan blushed. 'Yes, that may be handy. Feel free to jot it down.'

Het wandered over to Lan's collection of pencils, writing pads and charcoal and jotted down the concoction. 'Don't dwell on it, Lan. You are a family man whether or not you knew it back then. Good luck to you both if it does happen.' Then he exited the room.

Lan followed him out, locking the door and the two men shook hands before they both hurried down the stairs.

CHAPTER FORTY-FOUR

Lan grabbed the small saw and began to cut along the forty-five degree angle he had pencilled on the piece of wood. When he had finished, he took the piece and butted it up against another piece of wood cut at an opposing forty-five degree angle and marked the place it would be joined. Putting the pieces down, he watched the other apprentices applying glue and joining the pieces for the picture frame each were making. Lan had already produced thirty frames today. *Everything is so expensive in Velterra.* He had managed to find work as an apprentice carpenter and had been ridiculed for joining a bunch of youngsters until they realised he was a quick learner with deft hands.

Het and Ake had been tasked with finding Alwin. It was now August the tenth by the Cirite calendar and they had been in Velterra for a month. Alwin and Hartur were avoiding them. They had tracked down the forge Alwin had been working at, but the blacksmith had refused to give them any information.

The whistle blew, signalling the end of the Velterran five-day work week.

His boss walked over to him with his week's pay—the standard one centimetre gold bar for every fifteen frames he finished; the equivalent of ten Cirite credits. 'We need to talk.'

Lan brows knitted with worry.

The man smiled. 'It's okay. I want to promote you. Do you feel you are ready to move on to the furniture section? I'll pay you one small gold bar per piece. It's just kitchen chairs, but it beats frames.'

Lan held out his hand and the man shook it. 'I would be honoured.'

'Here's your pay packet and a small bonus for your hard work.' The man handed it to him. 'Have a good day off tomorrow.'

'You too.'

Lan turned and followed the other apprentices out of the industrial warehouse that seemed to be more popular as of late. It was dark already despite it being summer. He tilted his head, listening cautiously as he entered an alley leading to the Revengez district. Someone grabbed him and slammed him up against the wall.

Lan grabbed the hand and twisted it and was able to stumble back from the large, masked figure. He turned and dived out of the way as he caught movement nearby. Lan slid his mystic knives from within his sleeves. A breeze whipped his shoulder-length hair that he had grown back to cover his elven ears. The hot air of the Revengez quadrant was stifling, making it almost unbearable in the cramped confines of the suffocatingly close buildings.

'Get out of here before I am forced to defend myself.'

Another figure stepped from the shadows and laughed softly; his soulless hazel eyes devoid of any expression. 'Hello great uncle.'

Lan blinked and stared at the aged, familiar face. The man's patchy chestnut hair fluttered in the breeze. His face looked like an ivory porcelain mask that had begun to crack. Lan glanced up at the starless night sky. He closed his eyes and concentrated. He heard a crack of thunder and a gentle rain began to fall, cooling his sweaty face. Lightning streaked in the sky. He opened his eyes as he heard the faint humming that signified magic and leapt over Hau as red strands of blood oozed from his hands. The strands began to weave and spread in the water-filled air.

Hau hissed and the blood began to take on the form of a bizarre creature. The Swork was huge ball of rolling flesh that encapsulated corrosive digestive juices, and was warm and sweaty to touch. Its gaping maw was used to pull in a victim as it rolled over them. It was covered in suckers used to sense the vibrations of potential prey. Lan shuddered and stepped back cautiously; he had heard they could reproduce two every five minutes and grow to twenty metres when not summoned by a mage. Fortunately, the circumference of this particular creature was much smaller as it had to fit in the five foot wide alleyways. No one had lived long enough to discover their weakness and that's what frightened Lan.

'You have served your purpose, Lan. I will take another's elven soul and become a full elf. Full elven blood was wasted on you and Amities. You and your elven son could have taken a harem and restored the elven race. Your wife was the last female royal of Relequis and you could have made her bear you hundreds in the centuries you assumed I was dead. Amities could have aided you in that endeavour by choosing an elven bride over a human one. You failed your people, your wife's relatives and your son's legacy.' Hau gestured at Lan, directing his next words to the creature. 'Kill him.'

The Swork looked grotesque as it heaved in and out as if it was breathing. The suckers waved in excitement for its next feed. Lan called down lightning on the flesh-coloured creature. The creature glowed blue and yellow, and made a loud popping noise. When the noise dissipated, the creature appeared unharmed. The rain stopped as Hau held his hand to the sky. His hideous laughter echoed in the small, foul alleyway as the creature rolled towards Lan.

Lan slipped by a house and glanced up before sprinting at the wall and using the momentum from landing with his left foot to leverage himself on to the gutter and haul himself on to the roof. His wife's scream made him shudder and he bolted towards the noise, running diagonally across the roof. His eyes scanned the network of the Revengez district. From this vantage point it resembled a grid-like structure of filthy alleyways and large and small courtyards. Lan blinked in surprise as Het entered an alleyway carrying a struggling figure wrapped in a quilt tied with belts.

Lan swore. 'Hey Het, what the hell are you doing?'

The warrior moved slowly as if he was dazed, and turned left into the connecting alleyway coming to a stop beside Hau as the Swork rumbled back down the passage, to halt near its creator. Lan called down hail on the Swork, it didn't even flinch. Swearing, he glanced at Hau's grinning face before his eyes alighted on the blanket. *Hell is Ake in there? Do I go for her or Hau?* His stomach plummeted and he leapt off the building and landed near the monster. Hau winked at Lan before clicking his fingers; his creation rolled over the ground towards Lan, the suckers making squelching noises as they stuck then retracted from the rough surface. It tumbled towards him at an incredible speed. *Mystic Fire* burst from Lan's hands; the creature veered to the right as if the heat messed with its senses. Lan ran left and conjured more flames as the beast followed him, attracted to the heat and vibration. It cornered him between a reeking pile of debris and the exit to the large courtyard. He turned and ran, using his left leg to gain purchase on a barrel and jumping clear of the monster. The Swork began to puff itself up and shake. It opened its maw and spat out two more creatures in different flesh-coloured tones.

'As amusing as it is to see your talent as a fighter, I grow weary of waiting for your demise.' Hau cast a paralysis spell at Lan. He managed to dodge it and rushed towards Hau, his knives ready. His face contorted with anger.

'Remove the bedding,' said Hau coldly.

Het set the bundle on the ground and removed the bedding from the struggling figure. Lan stopped in his tracks as Ake gasped for breath, and scrambled to her feet, trying to get away from the father and son. The side of her face was swollen and red like she had been hit by the end of a blunt object. 'I would rather my father had captured her without injuring her delightful face. Hello, my dear cousin.' Hau caressed her face.

'You b——. Let her go and I will come with you freely.' Lan's eyes blazed with repressed rage as he slowly stepped towards them.

Hau cast the paralysis spell again and Lan leapt out of the way. He landed gracefully and felt warm flesh against him. Lan turned and slashed at the Swork before using his last mystic fire to distract the creature and get away. Hau shoved Ake into Het's arms and teleported behind Lan, whispering the paralysis spell in his ear, 'Hylt.'

Lan stiffened before slamming into the ground.

'Bring her over here, Father,' Hau sneered.

Het walked over, carrying Ake; her pupils were dilated and of unequal size.

'Het hit ... me while I ... I think ... was napping.' She appeared groggy, her words muddled.

Lan scowled. 'Let her go. Face me, you coward.'

Hau smirked. '*I'm* a coward? Who left a child on a battlefield to die?'

'I thought you were dead. I was also overcome by the Lord of Death and left to protect everyone. Is it because of that you have become a cruel and unjust thing?' asked Lan.

Hau broke out in maniacal laughter. 'To begin with. Then, as the loss of my parents and my people pressed in on me, the darkness took over. I vowed to restore my people no matter the cost to my own soul. Drianna showed me ways to increase my power before she was destroyed. The only problem is it made me an undead being.'

'Ake? Wh-y am I hol-ding you?' stammered Het, his eyes clearing.

Hau pulled back a crack in his skin and snatched up a fat worm that was gorging on his necrotic flesh. He waved his hand and the creature was flung towards Het as the big man gently lowered Ake to the ground.

'Het!' yelled Lan.

Het looked up and blinked back tears, wincing as he did so. When he opened his eye, the worm swam just under the sclera before it was absorbed. Ake gagged and wobbled to her feet. She cast a jet of water at Hau who waved his hand, countering the spell and drenching her instead.

Ake tried to gain control of her senses, her pupils focusing on Het. Hau laughed and gestured to Lan. 'I will take the legacy you don't use to aid the elves.' Strands of green light were drawn from Lan; his chest tightened as fatigue washed over him and his breath quickened. 'You are her counterpart. By drawing on your soul I can prevent her from taking her divine form.' Hau scoffed. 'You were never good enough for her. Your past makes you as bad as the man she feared the most.'

Ake cast *Mystic Fire* at Hau who swatted the flames away as if they were pests. She wobbled on her feet, trying to focus on her husband. 'Let him go.'

Hau tutted. 'Still concussed, my dear cousin?'

Lan tried to ball his hand into a fist; Hau turned and stomped his foot down on it with a sickening crunch.

'*Hylt.* That should stop you for a moment.' Hau leant forward, slid a pin from his pocket and pricked his finger. Lan's eyes widened as two drops of blood pattered on to his mouth. The blood-mage grinned and kicked him between the legs. Lan grunted.

Hau pressed his hand against Lan's mouth, forcing him to swallow his blood. *I will have my revenge on Lan for abandoning me and not doing anything to restore the elves to their rightful place in this world. Powerful blood magic will slowly strip away Lan's layers so that he reveals his sins to others and flees, a mere shadow of his former self. My parents never got to be happy. Why should Lan and Ake be allowed to? And Ake shall pay for weakening me. What is the extent of her power I wonder?*

Ake leapt forward and went to punch Hau in the back of the skull. She screamed and ran as the bloodmage lifted his bleeding hand in gesture to the Sworks who began to roll after her.

Hau laughed. 'What a family reunion. Let's liven this party up.'

The possessed Het turned and grabbed Ake as Hau waved his arm and the monsters rolled to a halt.

'No family reunion is complete without a little family drama. My dear father, you won't ever be able to face my beloved mother again when you pass again into the underworld.' Hau smirked. 'I should have had a father, but you died defending Lan's school instead of fleeing with my mother. Children of the righteous always suffer. Father, kiss Ake, you are young again and have never met Flo. Lan will steal her from you if you don't.'

Ake screamed and her voice was cut off as Het kissed her with a fierce passion. He pulled her against him in a crushing embrace.

Hau laughed cruelly.

Lan's voice was laced with rage. 'She is your cousin. You know what she went through and you would have her oldest and most trustworthy friend do that?'

'You will have to kill Het to stop him believing Ake to be his,' said Hau menacingly.

Het turned and glared at Lan. 'You think I would give her to you? You are vain, proud and moody,' he mumbled, as if drunk.

Ake struggled, reached up and slapped Het. She hissed through her teeth, the slap still ringing in her ears. 'Snap out of it, Het, you love Flo.'

Het glanced back to her and gave her a warm smile. 'Flo. Where have I heard that name before?'

Lan unclenched his stiff muscles, freeing himself from the paralysis spell. With a sigh, he leapt to his feet and rushed towards Hau. Het grabbed Ake by the scruff of her neck and she kicked him in the groin. The now smitten warrior grinned at her and pulled her towards him. She cloaked herself in a bubble of water and Hau dissolved it just as Lan grabbed the bloodmage's arm and threw him. Hau almost hit the ground until, at the last second, he levitated up into the air, hovering some twenty feet from the ground.

Het leaned in to kiss Ake again, then his eyes cleared for a moment as he fought against Hau's will. 'What have I done?' he whispered.

Ake raised her trembling handy ready to strike, but Het's huge arms encircled her.

'Ake, I am sor—' Het's eyes glazed over.

'Get away from her!' Lan brandished a long knife at the warrior.

Hau laughed and teleported Ake to him; she struggled in his arms, unleashing a kick to his leg when he grabbed her by her hair. 'Stop fussing.'

Lan turned and unveiled his wings, taking to the air to rush towards his wife and enemy. Ake screamed as Hau's eyes turned red and tendrils of golden light began to be drawn from her body.

The sky flashed with bright light and Hau grunted as Ake summoned bolts of sunlight that slammed into her captor. He muttered a spell to shield against her magic and the darkness returned.

Hail and lightning pummelled into Hau as Lan's rage overcame his limitations and he reacted in desperation. He dived at Hau who hissed, his serpentine tongue flicking in and out of his mouth before he teleported further away with Ake. Lan continued aiming strikes to Hau's more vulnerable parts.

'I thank you for the gift, dear, sweet Ake. Such power and this offering is but a little drop.' Hau licked his lips. 'I'll come for the rest soon.' He dropped Ake as his appearance began to change.

Lan caught her before landing on the roof. Hau smirked as his porcelain skin cracked, the necrotic flesh beneath peeled away, new muscle formed before fresh skin grew on the more diseased parts of his body. His half-elven ears became sharply pointed and his hazel eyes became more pronounced and flickered with merriment.

'You have saved your husband's life by giving me your elven essence freely. I leave you to witness my father die at the hands of the Sworks.' Hau's cruel laughter floated on the air.

Lan took the preloaded pistol from his hip and aimed it at Hau. It was an awkward shot with Ake in his arms but he fired anyway.

Hau cried out as blood streamed from a wound in his shoulder. He placed his hand over the wound and glared at Lan as he faded away into the darkness.

Lan placed Ake down and leapt off the roof, landing softly. The Sworks replicated again and the new ones sped towards him. Het was using his sword to hit at the monsters; it glowed black, his emotions confused. Lan flew up and over a Swork, landing near Het.

Het saw him and rushed at him. The sword came down between Lan's knives. Lan stumbled and was pushed backwards by Het's enormous strength. Lan gasped as his knives slipped and clattered to the floor. The sword gashed his hand open as it made contact.

'Het, snap out of it. This isn't you!' Lan scrambled to his feet as the warrior rushed at him again. He turned his head, his eyes widening as a Swork rolled towards him and he was dragged underneath it.

'Get off me!' He struggled to keep his head free of the wobbling mass.

'That's enough, Imeall. You are being used for evil,' yelled Alwin as he and Hartur ran towards them.

The sword flared then burst into flame. Het dropped it in pain; the fireproof hilt scorching him in protest against being used as a tool for evil.

'Luma, cover Lufar in water, even under the Swork,' yelled Alwin.

Ake suddenly cried out in pain. Tears ran down her face as she fluttered down off the roof, but she did as she was asked. Lan took a deep breath as the creature began to swallow his legs, the water shield sizzled as the corrosive juices fought against it.

Hartur stared at Het, catching the strange movement in the corner of his eye. She leapt onto his back, jabbing the big man in the eye with a finger. Het stumbled back, wincing, covering his eye with his hand.

Hartur jumped off him and landed, taking out her hammer. 'Nietra, show their weakness.' The hammer glowed and tendrils of black smoke wound their way around the monsters. 'Flaming oil or alcohol!' Hartur yelled.

Het blinked and the worm fell out of his eye and dropped to the ground. Returned to his senses, he turned and ran. 'I'll get it. Hold them off.'

Ake continued to maintain the water shield as Lan slashed at the creature while it drew him further inside.

Het soon ran back with several bottles of booze and some matches.

'Light them and throw them into the maws,' said Hartur.

Het ripped his shirt, uncorked the nine bottles and stuffed the hastily made wicks in. He struck a match and the light flared in the oppressive dark. As he lit each wick, he handed the bottles to the others, keeping some himself. Het, Alwin and Hartur lay down and waited for the creatures to roll towards them, stuffing the bottles into the mouths as the creatures attempted to swallow them. They rolled out of the way, scrambled to their feet and pelted towards the alleyway. There was a large collective gurgling noise that hit a crescendo before loud belches could be heard as the creatures imploded, acid splattering the nearby building and burning away the veneer of the aged brickwork.

When the scene cleared, Lan lay on the ground curled up into a ball as the water shimmered over him. They heard Ake sob as she removed the water shield.

Alwin approached Lan and knelt beside him. He formed a fist and began thumping Lan's chest.

Het glanced at Ake. 'I am so sorry for kissing you.'

'I can't look at you right now, Het. I am so ashamed,' said Ake.

There was a cough and splutter. Lan sat up, turned his head and brought up the water he had swallowed. He sat for a while getting his breathing back to normal.

Alwin offered Lan a hand up. He took it and rose wearily to his feet before rushing at Het. The warrior turned and grabbed him in a bear hug. 'I am so sorry, Lan.'

'I see you are yourself again.' Lan dropped his arms to his side. 'She may not want to see you for a bit.'

Het nodded.

Lan reached out with his other arm and drew Ake against him. He ran his hand over her head injury and peered into her eyes. 'Your pupils look normal again. We start Alwin's training in the morning. Hau will pay for this.'

'I guess it's time.' Alwin frowned. 'I doubt I am strong enough to defeat a bloodmage.'

Het patted Alwin on the back. 'We have faith in you.'

'You're the only ones.' Alwin sighed.

CHAPTER FORTY-FIVE

Alena stared at the missive in her hands. It had been drafted with care and even had an official seal.

Dear Alena,

We are sorry for the loss off your beloved Miss Nuo Cao; her gentle and caring presence will be sorely missed. You may not have been aware that Miss Cao was part of a rebel underground cause in Velterra, dedicated to rid the country of the evil Lord Hau Halfey.

We are known as the Caelestian Cause. We are dedicated to seeing the divine couple united to train their descendants in the hopes of removing Lord Hau from his throne and ridding Velterra of poverty, slavery and cruelty.

Lord Amities of Eriu founded us when his mother fled Caelestis after a hundred years of trying to maintain the school. Amities invited his sister to help; she agreed and the Caelestian Cause was created. The siblings believed one day their father would return, keeping his vow to his beloved bride.

When Mandami fell, Amities was rich due to Caoimhe's fairy luck and the right investments. When the emerging Cirites needed a place to flee he gave them a safe haven on the island of Man'hannon. They built their home within the fortress. As their belief system grew so did their population and Cirichad was born.

There was one condition, if the divine couple returned they would always have a home in Cirichad. Being the parents of the great Mandami, their innate skills were always used for good, so its use would never be seen as a sin. To benefit from this they would need to make themselves known to the king. This rule would apply to their descendants as well.

I am writing to you with a purpose. Lord Hau has attacked the divine couple; they failed to defeat him and he drained some of Ake's elven essence in the process. We do not know what the side effects will be from this. Lord Hau has been reborn as an elf and intends to take those showing the most magical aptitude and those of elven ancestry to his bed; even wives and mothers that would not have him.

Miss Cao made it her life purpose to help refugees and over-throw the abomination. She was tasked with finding the descendants and bring them to the Lord and Lady of Caelestis for training. The divine couple have begun to train Alwin Smith, but he will fail alone. I beg you to reach out to them and help defeat the abomination.

Kind regards,

Derel Werolf
24th of August 1700 CE

Alena analysed the seal; a rearing stallion with flames surrounding the animal. It was dated a week ago. She wiped the
tears from her eyes at the mention of her deceased love and stood
up from the desk, pushing back the chair. It scraped against the
slate floor. *That is Lufar's noble crest. I should pay my respects to
Luma and Lufar, and I am sure Caoimhe would love to visit them.*

Alena had kept her word. The buildings of the village were
restored and everyone had enough to eat. Alena had ordered a
proper bridge built and all the roads repaired. The farmers had
been supplied with the latest tools and agricultural information
and their thriving fields were filled with the bronze and gold of
wheat and rye.

Hurley and Caoimhe had opened a little bed and breakfast—
Alena supplying the funds, a reward for their loyalty to their employment contract. She had encouraged trade between her village now
known as Eriu and the village of Naofa on The Jagged Isle. Those
seeking to travel across Velterran lands could rest safely in Eriu.

Alena opened the door of her closet and took out some clothes
and a satchel. She filled the bag with things she might need for the
two day trek to Velterra. She left her room and headed towards
the kitchen to fill her pack with food, picking Din the staff up on
the way out of the stately home she had renamed Nuo Manor.

Hurley was outside washing windows when Alena walked
towards him down the cobblestone road. He smiled and waved
excitedly and ran inside. Alena reached the small bed and breakfast and waited outside as she heard excited whistles within.

The freshly erected building was two storeys and made of red-
wood. A large ranch style veranda, made of corrugated iron, ran
along the entire front of the building. The roof was covered in red
shingles and a large chimney rose from the establishment. The
couple had named their business *The Frolicking Fairy.*

Caoimhe came rushing outside; her translucent wings

shimmered in the midday sun. Alena held out her arms and the fairy rushed into them. The two women had become close friends. Alena had learnt some sign language but it was an ongoing process and she often made hilarious mistakes.

'Hello Caoimhe. How have you eaten?' asked Alena.

Caoimhe laughed. 'I always eat well with Hurley around.'

Alena smiled. 'I am sorry, Caoimhe.'

'It is fine. I appreciate you trying rather than Hurley always translating. Your understanding of my signing is almost flawless. Your replies just need more practice,' signed Caoimhe.

Hurley came outside with a tray of freshly squeezed apple juice and some small sandwiches. He placed them on a small wooden table and pushed up three small stools.

'Come eat with us, Mistress Alena.' Hurley grinned.

'I would love to.' Alena stepped up onto the veranda, walked over and sat down.

Hurley handed her a plate of sandwiches and a wooden cup full of juice. She nibbled on the sandwiches and drained the cup, before placing them on the table.

'Delicious as always, Hurley.' Alena sighed. 'I come with sad news, my friends.'

'Please tell us,' said Caoimhe.

'Hau attacked your parents, Caoimhe. They were defeated and Hau was transformed back into a living being using your mother's essence. Lan has begun to distance himself from your mother.'

'Mother was nearly ruined when Father left before. We need to fix this.'

Alena waited for a few minutes as Hurley consoled his grieving mate. Caoimhe wiped her tears.

'I am going to visit them. I received a letter from the Caelestian Cause, Caoimhe; your name was mentioned. Would you please elaborate on what they do?' asked Alena.

Caoimhe nodded and whistled her response as Hurley translated. 'Amities contacted me stating that Hau had been found. This was about two centuries after Father left. We discussed telling Mother but by then he had become an abomination and we had only just learnt of his true identity. Amities felt it would destroy Mother to know what gentle Hau had become, especially after all she had lost.'

Hurley stood up and stretched before he finished his drink and waited for Caoimhe to continue.

'At first, Hau took small amounts of blood from those who gave it freely, never killing, to improve his power. He researched everything on magic, and rescued tomes and elven relics, storing them in a safe place. Then the war happened and so many lost their lives, including Hau's unborn daughter. Hau fled with his bride Atius. After her death, he left his homeland with three sons and two daughters, raising them in lands filled with dangerous monsters.' Hurley paused. 'His children survived at their father's expense. Drawing on the blood of the monsters he killed defending his children, he contracted a disease that would eventually rot him from the inside out. A few hundred half-elves survived the war and sought refuge with their new lord. Hau built his harem, siring many more children with elven legacy before he went out into the now chaotic world to find mages who had a hint of elven legacy and brought them back as spouses for his children. He built Velterra up from the ruins of Regis, and the rest is history.'

Alena rolled her shoulders to loosen her muscles. 'And what of your involvement with the cause?'

Caoimhe signed the rest. *Before Hau fled into the land of monsters, Amities interpreted a reoccurring dream he remembered that Mother had from childhood involving an elderly slave man. Amities believed this to be a premonition. With the last six mystics of Caelestis and the money we had come by'*—Caoimhe winked—'we began to *train them in the arts of espionage, healing and diplomacy. Others joined us over the centuries. Hau's cruelty spread as he worked towards his goal of creating an elven city. Apart from the ongoing need for money, I played little part.'* Caoimhe reached for another morsel of food, she began to chew as she continued signing.

'About a year ago, Het joined the cause. His druid research revealed a sacrifice could bring back my father earlier. Amities could have lived another five or more centuries, but he noticed Mother was no longer chasing Orilan, the death warden, to send messages to Father. She became withdrawn and stopped interacting with us more and more, hiding in the worst places around the world hoping death would claim her. She even got into scraps, but Mother could never give in totally and would fight in the end; even taking a poisonous dragon down on her own that was ravaging a village near Velterra. Amities felt it was time to bring Father home and offered his life to become the God of Death. Father woke up on this plane moments after Amities's death. That is why I was not surprised about Amities's death or when Father returned.'

Hurley, having left halfway during the conversation as Caoimhe had already told him this story before, came out with two backpacks filled with food and clothing, a tinderbox, his chefs' knives and a cast iron pot and lid. They watched him take a key from a chain around his neck and lock the door.

'Your parents need your hope and joy, Caoimhe. Seeing their daughter may bolster their spirits. We should make haste.' Hurley turned to Alena. 'How long as Lan been ill?'

'I have no idea; I only just received the letter.'

'Let us go,' said Caoimhe.

Caoimhe stood up and Hurley handed her a pack. He took her hand as Alena turned and led the way.

—⁓—

Alwin yelped as he barely dodged the unarmed strike. He pivoted on his heel attempting a kick towards his opponent's stomach, wobbled and landed on his rear. Grumbling, he rose and rubbed his posterior which hurt less than his wounded ego.

'Your stance is wrong.' Lan shifted his feet. 'Try a wider one.' His voice was muffled by the cloth he had wrapped around his nose and mouth to ward off the atrocious stink of the section of city they had hidden themselves in.

Alwin spread his feet, his brows furrowed. 'I can't do this.'

'Yes you can.' Lan strode closer and helped adjust the boy's stance. 'See, now concentrate on your breathing.'

'Maybe he's a druid and not a mystic.'

Lan glanced towards Het who entered the small area they had cleared in the dumping grounds in the Revengez district. Littered with fetid garbage, rusty nails, and broken furniture, it was a vile place, even crevices in the ground pooled with sewerage and industrial run off. They had chosen here to train, hoping Hau would avoid such places as most of the residents did except when dumping waste.

Taking turns over the last few weeks, Het, Ake and Lan had begun to train Alwin who was not making much progress in the use of magic, unarmed combat or advanced sword manoeuvres.

Lan removed the cloth and wiped his brow. 'I am going now Het's here; this place is wretched.'

'Bet he's off to canoodle with his wife.' Het grinned.

Lan waved and hurried out of sight.

'Now, where were we two days ago?' Het dropped the wooden training swords he had brought on the ground.

Alwin rubbed at a bruise on his left arm. 'You were hitting me with training swords.'

'Ah.' Het chuckled. 'Not quite. I was striking and you failed to defend.'

'Why me?' Alwin gestured to Het. 'Why am I supposed to take down this bloodmage when the great Goddess of Mercy who defeated Drianna is here?'

Het leant down, picked up a training sword and tossed it to his companion who caught it. 'Lan's power is waning. The gods are stripping this world of great magic, disgusted by the mortals who abuse it.' Het stepped towards Alwin and charged; the boy stepped to the side, pivoted and slapped the warrior's leg with the wooden sword.

Het turned on his heel and clapped his hands together. 'Finally, a hit.'

'You are a scary man when you charge.' Alwin steadied himself, raised the sword and pointed it at his friend. 'Scary indeed.'

'Those with lesser magics or skills are more likely to keep them in a tense battle. Your great-grandparents' magic could fizzle out when needed most, and in the heat of battle we may have to rely on our young folk. Now come here, I want to show you something.' Het leant down and picked up a rock.

Alwin stepped towards the larger man. 'Please don't tell me you want me to fling rocks at Hau.'

Het laughed. 'You have a dry sense of humour for sure.' He shook his head and held out the rock.' Place your hand on top and draw deep within yourself and tell me what you feel.'

Alwin sighed, placed his hands on the rock and closed his eyes. 'The surface of the rock is jagged and cold.'

Het tutted. 'Feel for any energies within.'

Alwin reached within, searching for any sentient energies. The rock gave off a neutral hum, but something nearby latched on to him and an urge surged through him; *kill, kill.*

'A druid can sense the energies of any living or earthen thing and manipulate its composition. Try to urge the rock to bend to your will.'

Alwin's eyes snapped open as Het waffled on.

'Urge it to crack or expand.'

Alwins eyes widened. 'Behind you.'

The large warrior turned as something slithered out of the cesspool, heading towards them, sucking up debris and rot as it surged forth, taking the form of a large canine made of fetid waste the height of eight tall men.

The maw opened wide and it coughed, clearing its jaws of paper. Hau's voice roared out. 'You thought you could hide the boy from me, Father. Oh you did well for a while; I had my mages check all the luxurious places, but it seems Ake and Lan have fallen from their luxurious perch and train their descendants in a filthy, disease ridden spot.'

Het stepped towards the beast and urged Alwin behind him. 'What could you possibly want with a powerless boy?'

The beast growled; brown liquid pooled in its mouth, coating its makeshift fangs of rusted knives and spikes. It spat at the warrior before it, the rank moisture spattering on to him.

'Arrgh, that's foul.' Het wiped it off with the sleeve of his green shirt.

'Unarmed, Father?' The fetid wolf loosed a howl, worthy of shattering eardrums. A cracked mirror exploded and shards were flung towards Alwin. The boy gasped as one lodged in his thigh.

Het glanced about, reaching for anything he could use as a weapon. He sighed and picked up the leg of a broken chair. He sprinted towards Hau's creation. '*Moldis spear.*' The shattered wood lengthened and sharpened as the gallant warrior hurled it towards the beast. It flew majestically and hit a pile of refuse behind the wolf as the monster cocked its leg. Slicken, rank liquid pooled at its feet causing Het to slip and crash into the pile behind him, groaning as he was covered in chunks of metal and cracked stone.

Alwin pulled the jagged shard out of his leg and tossed it aside.

Ripping the hem of his shirt, he bound his leg before holding up the wooden sword as the beast padded towards him, maw lowering. Alwin thrust the sword at the creature; his breath caught in his lungs as its jaws snapped shut. His eyes widened as it transformed into Hau. The lord's mouth pressed against his, forced it open, and he gagged as he swallowed warm blood. Hau snickered as he pulled away. '*Falite Cuzen.*'

Hau turned and strolled towards his father. The pile of refuse exploded; debris flew towards the bloodmage who gestured and it was flung aside as Het pulled himself from the rubble. The warrior's skin was now grey; his muscles appeared denser, but his eyes were cold and a mustard yellow. As his spoke, his voice boomed as if the very stones rumbled. 'What have you done to him?'

'Hush, giant kin.' Hau faded away.

The giant's wild eyes locked on Alwin's and his big feet left cracks in the earth as he thudded over to him.

Het opened his mouth and roared, he picked up a large piece of stone and tossed it at his friend. Alwin dodged it and it crashed into a barrel behind him, splattering him with rancid water that soaked the linen covering his wound.

Alwin reached within; the urge to destroy and desperation to save his people washed over him and he urged the feelings to subside, filling the desperate void with warmth and friendship. As the giant's huge fist nearly made contact with Alwin's jaw Het halted, the grey washing away from the warrior like it was absorbed.

Alwin gagged and fatigue washed over him; he swayed on his feet as he closed his eyes. The strange feeling of being carried jolted him awake from the hideous nightmare.

'No.'

'It's okay.' Hartur bathed his head with a cool linen.

His frail body was wracked with pain and his lungs heaved as he coughed violently.

'He's awake,' she yelled.

The door flew open and a gathering of familiar faces peered through the gaping entryway.

'What happened?' Alwin's throat burned as he spoke.

Lan stepped through the door. 'Het said you were attacked by Hau. The wound became infected and, while I could treat some of it, I couldn't get the worst of it. It's like your blood was infected beyond disease.'

Alwin glanced at his friends. 'Where's Het?'

'He was devastated his druid magic couldn't heal you and said something about losing control,' Ake answered.

Alwin stared up at his wife. 'You look terrible.'

She frowned. 'Well that's a nice thing to say.' She rubbed at her red-rimmed eyes.

'She's barely left your side these last few days.' Alena stepped into the room. 'We almost lost you twice.'

Alwin groaned as he tried to sit up, his leg ached with stiffness. 'If Hau wears us down individually we are done for.'

'You need to rest.' Hartur brushed his hair out of his eyes.

'No, I need to train.' Alwin pulled himself into a sitting position.

'There is no rush.' Alena smiled kindly.

'With Hau's more frequent and brazen attacks. I think we are running out of time.' Alwin frowned and his stomach clenched.

———

Het slumped over the bar, his head in his hands. The cacophony of drunken people swearing, toasting or inciting fights allowed him to wallow unnoticed in the dank bar. The beer was weak swill but cheap and allowed him to imbue copious amounts on his way to sleepy inebriation.

A stool screeched nearby. 'Two wines, please.'

'We don't sell wine here; it's beer or nothing,' the barkeep roared over the din.

Alwin handed over a small gold bar. 'Two please.'

Het craned his head. Blinking his eyes, bleary from lack of sleep, they focused on the newcomer. 'You're alive.' He shot up on the stool and it almost slid out from under him.

Alwin's sunken eyes locked on his and he gave the warrior a weak smile. 'Barely, but I'm here. I wanted to thank you for defending me and carrying me out of there.'

The barkeep placed two iron mugs down on the bar in front of them.

Het reached for his drink and smacked his lips before taking a gulp. 'Do you remember anything else?'

'Oh, a rampaging giant, but you stopped him.' Alwin sipped on his drink.

Het's brows rose. 'Oh, is that what happened?'

'Have you ever used the stone form before?' Alwin brushed his mouth with the back of his hand and placed his mug down with a gentle clunk.

The warrior shook his head. 'No, I only remembered it after I died.' His brow furrowed. 'I lost control of it. You must keep this from the others; they are already going through so much.'

'It stays between us.' Alwin smiled before he coughed; his body shook.

'You okay, mate?'

'No, I better get on home. Hau has really set us back. I will need weeks to recover before I start training again.' Alwin held on to the bar as he hopped off the stool. 'I'm broke now since I can't go into work.'

Het reached into his pocket and grabbed Alwin's palm, pressing a large gold bar into his hand. 'Sorry, lad, but I doubt you will have days if Hau has his way. But pay for your room and eat well, and we will have you better in no time.'

'Thank you.' Alwin pocketed the money and shambled towards the entrance.

Chapter Forty-Six

Water pattered down on the flowers from the tin bucket. Ake sighed, basking in the sunlight. A horrid sound made her jump and drew her gaze; she placed the bucket on the ground. Ake tilted her head to the little shed in their yard as a low groan made her take a step towards the structure. Padding softly towards the building, she peered in the window. Her stomach plummeted and she hauled open the door.

'What are you doing?'

Lan glanced up from his seat at a desk, his face sunken, his eyes void of their normal lustre. 'This is my space. You know that.' He pushed away the vials labelled datura, nightshade and hemlock, and closed the book titled *Toxic plants and their uses*.

'When do we have separate spaces?' Ake frowned and reached for the book as her husband grabbed her arm.

'Don't.'

'I know you aren't sleeping well, but poisonous plants? What were you thinking?'

'It's the only way I get any sleep.' He released her hand. She reached out to caress his cheek and he hissed through his teeth. 'Please don't.'

Ake pulled back and took a deep breath. 'What's going on. Do you want to talk about it?'

He shook his head and covered his face with his hands. 'Ever since Hau fought us a week ago I haven't been sleeping ... I've been seeing things I'd sooner forget.' He glanced up and his eyes narrowed. 'Get out of here, you shouldn't be near me. I'm broken.' He stood up, his chair screeching in protest, and walked over to a water barrel. He scooped up a tin cup and water tinkled as he dipped it in. Hurrying over to the desk, he unstoppered the datura then reached for the other ingredients on the desk.

Ake snatched up the vial of hemlock before Lan could reach it and tossed it to the floor; it crunched under her boot as she ground it with her foot.

Lan scowled. 'Why did you do that?'

'You need a doctor, not to imbibe Velterran potions.'

'We can't afford that.'

Ake shrugged. 'You will see one.'

He shook his head. 'I've got work. I'll see you later.'

He leant down to kiss her; his brow furrowed and he pulled away. 'I'm sorry, how can you stand my touch?'

'I'll get the doctor to come at dusk.' She brushed her hand across his cheek. 'I welcome your touch.'

'I'm working late.' Lan hurried towards the door.

'How convenient.'

Lan looked over his shoulder. 'Quite. Money's on the table for dinner.'

'Lan, we need to talk.'

He sighed. 'I promise I will. I'm not the same since the fight with Hau. When I'm better we will talk then.'

As he pulled open the door and hurried through, she called out. 'Bloody stubborn elf.'

'I'm your bloody stubborn elf though,' he hollered back.

Oh dear, I'm late to take Alwin through his next lesson. Ake left the small shed and hurried away.

Alwin held out his palm and concentrated on conjuring a small flame. *I have been at this for days. I can't even summon the simplest of spells.* Hartur had even managed the spell. In Velterra, even small children had some innate magic; it didn't mean every child would grow up to be a mage. Mages had mastery in a single element such as fire or water. They could cast and manipulate their ability in any way they chose and were only limited by their creativity and stamina. The rare few that conquered more than one magical field were known as magen.

'Take a break.'

Alwin looked up at Ake and his shoulders drooped. He had been up since dawn working at the forge and then finishing late and skipping dinner to train with her.

'This is useless, Luma. We have been at this for days. I have not been able to conjure a thing.' Alwin sighed.

'I agree, Alwin. You are neither mage, mystic nor magen. When Het tried to teach you the faerie orb spell you failed, so you are not a druid either.' She gave him a wicked smile.

'I did my best,' grumbled Alwin.

'So did your grandfather Amities. He tried magic and failed and ended up becoming the greatest magical engineer in history. Go home and rest. Look within yourself and don't give up; you will find your talents.'

'Are you attending tonight's festivities?'

'Yes, it's about time Lan and I caught up. He has been engrossed in his work and alchemy since the fight with Hau.'

'That was certainly an odd affair. Have you recovered?'

'I'm fine. Lan, on the other hand, is not doing so well.' Ake's eyes filled with concern.

'Will you be okay, Luma, if I go now? I have to grab Hartur's gift; I left it at the forge.' Alwin gave her a kind smile.

'Yes, go, Alwin, I will be fine.'

Alwin smiled and turned, heading in the direction of the forge.

———

Lan placed his hammer down on the bench and picked up the carved wooden heart, formed of oak representing truth, courage and wisdom. He had engraved the names of his friends on the surface and added an edging made of ash; it represented strength and healing. The piece had been placed atop a hawthorn base representing love and protection. *This will be a nice gift for the festival of Sionreley to embrace affection for our loved ones.*

Lan was broken from his thoughts and looked up at the clock. Realising it was late, he picked up the plaque. Like most elves, when caught up in their projects they often forgot those around them, their minds focused on their work. He knew that Ake was aware he was limiting their contact. *I need to get through this deepening sadness. It seems every time we are together something happens to hurt her more. I will find us a safe place to live.* Het had confronted him yesterday and Lan had thought about his suggestion to take a few days to get away and clear his head while finding them a safe haven. *I hope Het knows I'd never leave her again and she won't remain in Velterra without me. Hopefully, Hau will think we have left for good.*

He slipped a resignation note from his pocket and placed it on the bench. His boss was aware that he was quitting and he had accumulated a reasonable amount of gold. He intended to pay Alena back for the damage to her ship before asking to stay with Caoimhe and Hurley until he decided what his next steps were. Lan intended to hand some funds over to Alwin for Ake's keep. Het would have been a reasonable choice, but even though he knew Het hadn't meant to kiss Ake, he couldn't get it out of his mind.

They had rented a little house in the Revengez quadrant and he had taken to sleeping in the tiny shed. His shoulders slumped and he pulled open the workshop door and trudged towards home. Lan took a shuddering breath as he passed the dreaded alleyway.

—∿∿∿—

Alwin sprinted towards the forge. Pulling open the door, he approached a bench and snatched up the dagger he had made for Hartur. His feelings of love rose to the surface as his hands made contact with the hilt.

Waves of dizziness suddenly overwhelmed him and he clung on to the nearby shelf to stop himself falling as the room began to spin. The feeling passed and, as his vision cleared, a childish voice entered his mind.

'Hello,' it reached out tentatively.

'Umm hello,' whispered Alwin.

'Oh umm, I recognise you as my lord. Master of the Forge,' said the unknown voice.

Alwin looked around. 'Show yourself and tell me of your intention.'

'I am the dagger in your hand, newly awoken. You must name me and with your empathic powers give me a personality and release the powers that lie dormant.'

Alwin shivered. I wonder if grandfather was an empath and channelled the emotions of sentient beings. That would explain why he always knew what I needed.

'That would be correct.'

'You can read my thoughts?'

'Only for a few moments when you talk to us directly. But you can always hear ours, Master.'

'What else can I do?'

'*You know of our innate abilities. Any command you give, we act on your orders before others. You can weave any emotion into us, good or evil, and we will develop accordingly as long as you forge the item yourself,*' explained the dagger.

'Do all the things I forge become sentient?' asked Alwin.

'*No, only when you work with emotion. In this case love.*'

'What if I choose not to invoke the innate abilities or give you a personality?' Alwin turned the dagger over in his hand.

'*Then I stay a child you will always hear, but I would never develop to my full potential.*'

'Oh, by the gods, a perpetual child complaining in my mind; no thanks. How do I awaken you?'

'*Concentrate. Weave the feelings that represent the traits you would have me develop and then visualise something that represents life beginning anew. It can be anything; a flower bud opening, a chick hatching, but it must be something that is important to you. Then you must name me.*'

Alwin closed his eyes and began to think of Hartur. Feelings of adoration floated on the surface along with joy and contentment. He wove them into the web, concentrating on the personality he would assign the dagger.

'Trust and loyalty will be your personality. You are called Tarven.'

The dagger began to hum and glow a bright yellow; it vibrated in his hand. The plain wooden hilt wrapped in leather began to change. The wood cracked, revealing shining steel. Golden leather strips appeared out of nowhere and bound themselves around the hilt as three ruby hearts emerged from the leather, shining a bright red as they formed a triangle. The dagger felt lighter as the blade shattered, revealing blue sapphire underneath.

Alwin stared at the ornate piece in shock. He took a cloth and rubbed it vigorously over the blade; the last shreds of steel chipped away and fell onto the bench.

'*I am Tarven. I will always be found when you need me no matter where you are. Like my name, I embody trust, duty and loyalty. I thank you for my life, Alwin, Master of the Forge.*'

'Happy birthday Tarven.' Alwin held the dagger up. 'What is with the hearts?'

'*They are your imprint. All of your work will have this and those who behold your creations will know it as your work.*'

'This is all very overwhelming.'

'*I assume it would be.*'

'*We are late, Master. It is ten minutes past the designated meeting time,*' stammered Dage and the bow glowed a brilliant emerald green. Alwin attached the bow to the strap on his back before pocketing the dagger and sprinting from the forge. *I hope she isn't too annoyed.*

Hartur looked at the tiny red box in her hands, wrapped with red ribbon. *I hope Alwin likes this gift.* Hartur had been looking forward to the elvish festival of Sionreley.

Held on the first of September on the Regian calendar, Sionreley is a day of passionate love and a celebration of the beginning of spring. It is when husbands and wives attend dances and give each other gifts. New lovers would try to win the hand of a potential lover by completing ridiculous feats at their lover's request. The requests could not be dangerous, but would often be comical in nature. As elves had traditionally liked to retain their composure and elegance, it was a real test of love.

Some examples included hopping on one foot all the way home, or donning strange garments and frolicking in the street for all to see. This showed that even humiliation would not keep you from your lover and that your love was not based on pride.

There was a dramatic increase in births in the nine months following the day.

Hartur tapped her feet in annoyance as she waited outside the hall where the dance would be held. She heard the sound of boots pounding on the road and turned to see Alwin approaching. He slowed down as he reached her.

Alwin grinned. 'Sorry, Hartur. I had to pick up your gift after training.'

Hartur smiled and handed him the box. 'Open it, quickly. I know it's corny.'

Alwin's eyes widened and a grin spread across his face. 'Toffee apples. That's perfect.' He leant down and captured Hartur's mouth with his own. As they pulled apart, their fingers entwined and they hurried into the hall.

Hurley prodded Caoimhe awake. The fairy rolled onto her back and stared at him.

'What do you want, Hurley? I was sleeping.' Caoimhe yawned.

The conversation sounded unusual as they both whistled in different tones to each other.

'It's the elven day of love. I want to get married.' Hurley giggled.

'Now?' asked Caoimhe.

'No, when we see your parents again.'

Caoimhe smiled. 'I would like that.'

Hurley leant in and kissed her. He drew back and blushed. 'I also want to try that passionate thing couples do.'

'Okay, Hurley.' Caoimhe kissed him back.

Lan opened the door to the cottage they were staying in and lit the candles with a thought. He placed the plaque on the picni-clike table and looked around, hoping to memorise the place before he left. The brick cottage had two rooms. The main room had wooden floorboards made of mahogany and the walls were exposed brick. A hearth took up the back wall and two rock-ing chairs were placed in front of it. *We have spent many a night talking there or keeping each other company or discussing the latest news and books we read to each other. I wish people would just leave us alone.*

The fire was banked low, making the small room almost suf-focating. He padded over to the kitchen bench and stared out the window. The stars in the night sky twinkled merrily. He grabbed a wooden cup and turned a small brass tap. They'd had cold water plumbed to the house. He filled the cup and drained it before turning to face the door that led to their bedroom. His nose caught the faint smell of roses and he wandered over to the fireplace. Ake had rose incense burning and Eriu stew bubbled gently in the cast iron pot that hung from a hook over the fire.

'Is that you, Lan?' asked Ake from the other room.

'Yes,' said Lan quietly.

'Come in here.' Her voice was full of longing.

'No, Ake, you come here; I have something to discuss.'

'Can't it wait?'

'I don't think so.' Lan sighed.

The bed squeaked gently. Lan heard the flutter of fabric and Ake left the room wrapped in the blue silk dressing gown he had bought for her that morning as a Sionreley gift. He had left it on the bed with a hastily scribbled note.

To my leven,
Happy Sionreley. We need to talk when I get home.
Lan.

She tied the ribbons at the front and their eyes met. Her long hair was braided and she had woven flowers into it.

'Suits you.'

His breath caught in his throat as she ran her hands down the gown enticingly.

'And ready to be unwrapped.' She smiled.

Lan turned away to compose himself and gestured to the item on the table. Curious, Ake went over and looked at it. She ran her hand over the engravings and read them out aloud.

'It is beautiful. Where should we put it?' Ake turned towards him and her eyes filled with adoration.

'Come here, please.' Lan's voice was laced with sadness.

Ake strolled over to him and ran her hands up his muscular arms. She glanced at his shoulders and her eyes settled on his now broader chest. While not as muscular as a human fighter, since his coming-of-age ceremony Lan was less lean and more muscled than the average elf due to his Anwyl heritage. She grabbed his hand and tried to draw him towards their bedroom, while giving him an enticing smile.

'No, Ake, I am leaving Velterra in the morning. 'I will find us a safe—'

Ake stared at him in shock, her mouth agape. Then her eyes filled with anger.

'Oh no you aren't. I knew you were keeping your distance from me, but I thought that was because you needed to work through what Hau had done to you. You haven't been the same since.' Ake glared at him. 'You are not breaking your promise again. You come back after all this time, profess you will find me no matter what, and now you say you are leaving. When did you become a coward?'

Lan stared at her, his mouth open in shock, before he gritted his teeth. 'I am far from a coward, Ake, and you know that.'

'Then why are you so distant?' She stared him down, hands on her hips.

'Every time I am with you, somehow you get hurt.' He looked away. She walked towards him, grabbed his face and kissed him. He pulled away and took a step backwards.

'You silly elf. That is hardly your fault, my leven.' She grabbed his hand. 'Evil comes for me no matter what. I am more powerful than you, and if *I* couldn't stop Hau what do you think your absence will achieve? We are stronger together.' Ake kissed his hand.

Lan pulled it back and she released it. 'He came after me and you got hurt.'

'He came for both of us, Lan. He would have hunted me even if you were not here. I would have stood less of a chance without you by my side. Next time, I won't give him another chance to do the right thing.' Ake began to unlace her gown. 'Enough of this distance, Lan. I will leave with you in the morning.' Ake removed the gown. 'Happy Sionreley.'

Lan's eyes skimmed her outfit. She was dressed in a lacy garment that barely came to her upper thigh. The frilly, red lace skirt was attached to a low-cut red brassiere. He let out a long breath of appreciation and she giggled before he composed himself.

'No, Ake. I will never sleep with you again. Not after my past.' Lan walked over to the rocking chair and sat down. 'Hau broke something in me. He dredged up things I never really forgave myself for.'

Ake took a seat in the chair next to him. 'That is fine as long as I can accompany you.'

Lan stared into the flames.

'So, that's it? After all we've been through?' Ake stood and walked over to retrieve her gown. She dressed herself and opened the front door. 'Thank you for so easily giving up on us.'

Lan stared at her. 'I am not giving up on us, let me finish telling you the plan.'

Ake slipped her feet into her shoes and turned to stare at him. 'I can't do this anymore. Every time we reach the hardest moments you leave, always believing somehow it was your fault. I am going to go talk to Het. You are never willing to tell me everything. Always leaving out the most important parts that could help us.'

Lan swore. 'Wait.'

Ake slammed the door on her way out.

Het trudged down the street, avoiding the lurkers making-out in the alleyways and the drunks ambling across the road, and stopped outside a wine vendor. *I'll drink away my loneliness tonight.* He handed over a few coins pulled from his pocket, uncorked the wine and gulped it down. The cheap, bitter brew flooded his half-empty stomach. His eyes watered as he took another swig and hurried towards his shack. The wooden door was cracked and the smell of cooking wafted through it. He pulled a dagger from his boot and pushed the door ajar.

The room was lit by a fire in the hearth and had been recently swept. A slender figure leant over a bubbling cauldron and she reached for a handful of herbs in the basket nearby.

'I hope you don't mind; I plucked them from the window garden you keep.'

Het closed the door behind him and bolted it before placing the dagger on the table. 'Not at all.'

She stood and glided towards him and reached for his belt.

Het took off his boots and tossed them aside. 'How?'

Standing on tippy toes, she pulled his head towards her and pressed a kiss near his ear. 'I'll explain later. Now take your clothes off.'

'Yes, mam.' Het shimmied out of his pants and top, and crashed his mouth down on hers. A gentle rapping came from outside. 'Who is it?'

Ake's voice wafted from outside. 'Can we talk?'

'Go talk to her, we have all night; and you are sworn to secrecy.' His lover fluttered her eyelashes.

'Give me a moment, Ake. I'll meet you at yours.' Het began dressing.

'Okay.' Ake's footsteps hurried away.

—⁓—

She has never asked me to leave her before. His eyes filled with tears and his breath came in ragged waves as he fought back the tears. *Is this how she feels when I left to protect her and all the times we were separated? It is cruel.* Lan rushed to his feet. *Why do I always believe every time Ake is hurt, somehow I am the cause? I will have to work through that.* Lan began to pace the room until his hearing picked up a familiar sound. He rushed to the front door and opened it. Ake sat on the stone bench in their small herb garden, sobbing uncontrollably. Het sat next to her. The big fellow had gotten a job unloading goods from the ships at the docks and lived a few doors down in a single-roomed shack.

'He blames himself every time someone or something hurts me. Does he not realise life has its ups and downs? Pain is part of life. It's almost as if he doesn't want to be with me anymore.' Ake blew her nose as Het handed her a handkerchief.

Lan felt his heart skip a beat. *How could she ever believe I don't want her?* His heart began to fill with an unfathomable rage for all the demands put on their relationship from prophecies to evil goddesses and mages, to corrupt men, women and their greed.

'You both have been through hell. Sometimes it takes one last thing to break us. He loves you, Ake, like no one else could. You know that. Maybe he needs help to express his misgivings and deal with them.' Het glanced up and gave Lan a meaningful look. 'I am going to go.' Het stood and strode over to Lan and patted him on the shoulder. 'Don't be foolish. Don't let your misplaced blame ruin your marriage. You get to be with your partner. Be grateful and get some help for the emotional stress you are under.'

'Hey, it was your suggestion we leave.' *Misplaced blame. What does he mean by that?* Lan sighed.

Het waved to Ake and pushed open the little gate; it squeaked as he hurried through it.

'I feel sad for the guy; he misses Flo dreadfully.'

Ake looked up, crossed her arms and glared at Lan.

He strode over to her and sat down, reaching for her hand. 'I am sorry. I am sick of all the demands on us. It broke up our family. Caoimhe wasn't even grown when I was forced to leave.'

Ake just stared at him, her face impassive, and withdrew her hand.

'Please talk to me, I am hurting so much,' he begged.

She sighed. 'I offered to talk for days, and as usual you retreated. I have had my fill of gods and evil beings as well; in fact, over a thousand years of them. I have had it with you emotionally detaching yourself when it suits you. I won't back down ever again and that includes anything to do with you. You don't get to just sleep with me and enjoy the happy times. It includes the dreadful ones too. Do better.'

Lan ground his teeth. 'Do better? I am doing the best I can. I have always been in it for the long haul, good and bad,' he growled.

Ake made a noise of frustration and swore. Lan's eyes widened with shock. *She rarely ever swears.*

'No, you ran.'

'You are mistaken, Ake; or you are just trying to goad me?' Lan glared at her.

'We were separated after we got together.' She crossed her arms.

'And you blame me for that?' Lan's heart skipped a beat as he was filled with astonishment. 'Flo took you while unconscious, Cephas kidnapped you, and the fourth time I kept my vow, becoming the God of Death. How are any of those my fault?'

'You ran the third time.' Her eyes filled with resentment.

'To protect you! I thought you were terrified of me. I tried to come home on several occasions; you are aware of that.' Lan clenched his fists. 'How dare you accuse me of cowardice? I have always tried to protect you. When did I say I was leaving you?'

'I am sor—' Ake went to apologise but pushed him off the bench instead. Lan fell back into the flowers. He laughed suddenly, all the emotional pressure too much. She threw off her robe and straddled him. Her touch ignited him as it always had and his body responded.

He reached into his pocket and withdrew a small vial. Unstoppering it, he downed the contents and threw it into a bush. 'Proceed.'

Her eyes were filled with possessiveness and he gulped. *I have never seen that look from her.*

The week of him distancing himself from her and the lack of touch hit them both. Ake unbuttoned his trousers and he pulled her on to him. *I broke my vow never to sleep with her again. I was lying to myself when I said that.* Ake threw her head back as she set an urgent pace. *Thank goodness I have taken that contraception potion; I can't keep her safe, let alone any of my blood Hau may come for.*

'You are mine, Lan. You will not leave me again, regardless of your intentions!'

'Slow down, I won't be able to match you.' Lan cried out and blushed. He had never lost control before satisfying her first. She didn't yield and he realised she had rekindled his passion. Her eyes glistened with tears and her mouth trembled.

This must be her way of coping with my supposed absence. Why don't I stop myself before saying such awful things? She is right, I must do better.

He reached up and touched her face, but she swatted him away and began to sob. Her eyes filled with pain. *She is trying to possess me; afraid I will run.*

'I am sorry for what I said.' He reached out his hand again, but she refused to accept it. 'Our lovemaking isn't what keeps me with you. Surely you know that.'

She glanced down at him. 'It's a big part of it. You used to barely keep your hands off me. When you stopped touching me, you retreated.' She began to sob and climbed off him. 'I am sorry, I should have heard you out.'

'We were separated for far too long and I almost died again.'

'Every turn something tries to take you from me.' She covered her face with her hands.

'I hate the world for that. I detest almost everyone, including the gods who put us through that. Most of all, I despise myself for having you for my own when I know I am unworthy. That guilt made me stop touching you. I love you more than anything and that will never cease,' said Lan through gritted teeth.

'What do you mean *unworthy*?' Her eyes softened. 'Open up to me.'

'When we were younger, men did not admit they were struggling mentally. I know it often made me appear harsh and detached, and I said terrible things to you. You should have run from me, but I am grateful you didn't.'

She caressed his face. 'You must promise to get help.'

'I will. Now, I must make you mine again.' His body was filled with a soul-shattering need for her.

He heard Ake's heart beat rapidly with anticipation and caught sight of her expression as her eyes filled with shock when they met his intense gaze.

She nodded.

He drew her against his chest and rolled her on to her back. She gasped as he took her urgently. His mouth found hers and she met him with equal desolation, their hands desperately exploring each other, caught up in the all-consuming need to feel something other than anger and despair. Like a dam opening, the release was mind-blowing and they stared at each other, lost for words. 'Bloody Hell!'

'I know, right.' Lan grinned and drew her down into his arms. 'He can't help you at the moment.' He glanced down before his eyes flitted back to settle on hers. 'But I have a mouth.'

Ake's turned a shade of vivid scarlet. She squealed with delight as he pulled her hips towards him and lowered his head.

———

Alwin wiped away the beads of nervous sweat on his brow as he walked on to the dance floor with Hartur on his arm. He watched the other couples dancing extremely close. The music was fast-paced unlike the waltzes of Cirichad. He watched one couple kissing as they swayed to the music. Another couple were given to fits of giggles as the lead lifted her partner into the air by her derriere. Alwin breathed a sigh of relief as the set finished and the couples moved apart.

'Now for a riveting one, the elvish dance *Fotrot* or swift foot,' called the conductor on the stage. Alwin looked around the hall. Every wall was mirrored. The wooden floor was polished until it shone and multicoloured orbs floated from the wooden roof. The conductor stood behind a podium dressed in a blue waist-coat with long tails; he wore a white wig with a long ponytail. He tapped a blue wand on the podium and Alwin watched in awe as sound echoed from the orbs in riveting refrains. The orbs changed colours in timing to the music. People began to clap along; one single clap, two swift half claps and ending in a double clap.

The dancers separated into groups of two couples. Hartur and Alwin were joined by another young couple.

'Alwin, we must hold hands. Then we move forward, taking a little leap forward onto the ball of our foot then land on our heel. We do this twice. Then the partners turn towards each other. The man pulls the woman towards him with his hands and she pulls back and dances a step to the right, then to the left as he releases her hands. He steps up behind her while she stands still and he dances a step to the left and the right before lifting her in the air. The couples then repeat the process three more times.'

The music reached a dazzling, lively note and the couple next to them went through the motions with great skill, laughing with enjoyment. Alwin tried to replicate Hartur and caught on fast; by the end of the first two sets he had mastered the dance. Hartur looked at him, her face beaming with pride, and he gave her a fetching smile. She blushed.

After they had finished the dance he got them some drinks. They sat and watched the other dancers while catching their breath. Alwin pulled the dagger from his pocket and handed it to her.

'Alwin, this is magnificent. Did you make this?' She ran her hands down the incredible dagger.

'I crafted it then something unusual happened. The weapon spoke as if it was a child, asking me to give it a personality and a purpose. It guided me and it became a blade named Tarven; a testament to trust and loyalty. It also changed its appearance from one of leather, wood and steel.' Alwin leant in and kissed her cheek. 'Happy Velterran romance day.'

Hartur laughed. 'It's Sionreley.'

'I couldn't pronounce that.'

Alwin began to hop on one foot towards the bar, several patrons jeered at him, then laughed with encouragement. 'See, Hartur, I can embrace your culture. Does this prove my love?' Alwin's cheeks were a vivid shade of crimson.

Hartur stood up and drew him into her arms. 'More than enough.'

CHAPTER FORTY-SEVEN

The gate squeaked open and Lan and Ake opened their eyes. They blinked in the morning sunlight to see Alena staring down at them.

'Fancy seeing you two outside clearly caught in a moment of passion.'

Ake blushed and scrambled up trying to cover her chest with her hands. 'Give me a moment, please.' Ake ran inside.

Lan stood and brushed the dirt off his shirt before covering his lower extremities with his hands and sprinted after his wife. Alena trailed into the doorway. 'Where are my other set of trousers, Ake? Didn't you wash them?' Lan called out from the bedroom.

'On the line,' said Ake.

Lan swore.

'Language,' reprimanded Ake.

'Like you can talk after last night.' Lan laughed.

'I learnt from the master.'

Alena walked over to the line and grabbed the pair of pants pegged to it. She went to the door and cleared her throat. Ake rushed over, dressed in red leather breeches and a long-sleeved white shirt. Alena handed her the pants.

'Come in.' Ake went over to the bedroom and threw the pants at Lan before closing the door.

'Have a seat; I'll put on some tea.' Ake washed her hands at the sink and filled an iron kettle.

Alena's gaze followed her as she walked over to the hearth and removed the pot and replaced it with the kettle. Ake swept up the ash with a metal pan and tiny brush before placing firewood in the hearth. Then she conjured a flame and lit the stack of wood; the fire burned brightly, consuming the wood in an ever increasing need to feed its ravenous appetite.

Lan exited the bedroom fully dressed as the excited whistles of Caoimhe greeted him. The fairy ran over the threshold into her father's arms.

Hurley yawned and knocked lightly on the open door. 'It is far too early for this halfling. Can I come in, sir?'

Ake stood up from where she had lit the fire and held open her arms. Caoimhe began to sob and ran into her mother's arms, both women weeping tears of joy.

'Of course you can, Hurley,' said Lan.

Mother and daughter separated as Ake turned and took some tea down off the mantle. She took a cloth as the kettle began to whistle and brought it over to the table. Lan grabbed a jar of sugar and five cups. They all sat down at the table and Ake put the tea leaves in each cup and poured the boiling water over them. Lan gave everyone a cup and pushed the sugar jar towards Caoimhe and Hurley who began to pour a large amount of sugar into their drinks. After the couple had finished Ake grinned and did the same.

Alena stared at Ake as she added more sugar to her drink. 'I received a letter from an underground cause. Caoimhe says that she helped fund it.'

'Why did you have to tell them that?' signed Caoimhe.

Alena turned back to Lan and Ake. 'They told me that all the descendants may be needed to dethrone Hau. I have come to help.'

'Father I am so sorry you are unwell and that Alwin got hurt,' said Caoimhe.

Alena cleared her throat and faced Lan. 'Are you and Luma okay?'

Lan shook his head. 'No, we are not. I need to leave Velterra and start fresh. I don't want to be involved in this Hau business. I want to settle down with Ake.' Lan blew on his tea and took a sip. He turned to look at Ake. 'If you will have me even after all the stuff I said last night.'

Ake gave him a gentle smile. 'We will work it out together.'

Lan stood up. 'Give me a moment, please.' He walked back into their bedroom and came back with a letter and handed it to Alena.

Alena felt the weight of it and ripped open the letter, shredding the envelope. She counted out four larger gold bars, the equivalent of two hundred credits. 'This is too much, Lufar.'

'No, it's adequate after all the trouble we put you through,' said Lan.

'I will read the note later.' Alena stood up. 'I must find the others.'

Ake drained the warm, sweet tea. 'Lan, I want to help Het. He defended me when I was young and he lost his life for Caelestis. I owe him that much.'

'But haven't we done enough?' Lan frowned and began to pace before he stopped suddenly. 'I'm sorry, I wasn't thinking straight. I don't know why I am acting so cowardly lately. It is like some unusual force is affecting me. Of course we must find some way to help Het even if Ake and I are not involved in direct combat.'

'Shall I call a meeting?' asked Alena.

'Please do. I will give you their addresses.' Ake began moving things around looking for a pencil; snatching up one, she began scribbling on a piece of paper.

'Did you write down the new address for Alwin and Hartur?' asked Lan.

'Oh right, you gave them Arlys's key to their new place.' Ake crossed out the address on the scrap of paper and wrote the new address down and handed the note to Alena.

'Mother, can we go get something to eat. I would discuss something with you as Hurley would with Father.' Caoimhe's face was a picture of delight; her eyes shone with joy.

'Of course. It is good you wear your necklace here, Caoimhe. I saw dried fairy wings for sale in the black market.' Ake shuddered.

'Black markets are real?' asked Lan.

'Of course they are.' Ake frowned. 'They can be both a riveting and scary place.'

'Of course you would find them. Let me guess, you and Het went together,' said Lan.

Ake laughed. 'Yep.'

'Stop leaving me out of the fun, Ake. Take me along next time.' Lan pouted.

'We will see,' teased Ake.

Ake stood up and walked to the door; Caoimhe followed, signing rapidly. *'I need you to help me plan my wedding.'*

Ake squealed with delight.

'Caoimhe and I are getting married, sir. Would you be my best man?' Hurley held out is hand to Lan.

Lan shook it and grinned. 'Of course, Hurley. I would be honoured. But it's Lan, not sir.'

'Okay, Lan, sir,' said Hurley.

Lan laughed. Alena waved as she left.

Alena stood outside the tiny, dilapidated building. *How is this the base of a secret underground movement?* The small, rundown building was little more than a wooden shack, with grimy windows and a fading number on the poorly painted timber door.

Where have I seen this before? Alena took out the letter she had received from Derel Werolf and read the address printed at the bottom of the page. Pulling out Ake's note, she compared the two. *What is going on here? The address of Het's is the same as this Derel's.* A muted conversation drifted towards her and she stepped closer.

'Flo, it is cruel to hide your presence from them,' said a man.

That's Het. But he sounds so sophisticated compared to his normal self. Flo ... I know that name from somewhere.

'You know the gods only brought me back to help find the descendants to defeat Hau. The condition was that no one must know a goddess, whose mortal life was cut short, can come back as long as they have a willing sacrifice. How could I tell my dear Ake that Mandami was that sacrifice? He could have easily defeated his attackers. Mandami had hoped to bring back Lan, but his father had already made his promise to take his place as the God of Death, which could only be broken by a full elf taking up his position. I could only come back if you went first. The gods needed to see you were committed to stopping Hau in atonement for past deeds.'

'How long have you been back?'

'A few days before Amities's death; he gave me Nuo's information. I took over Amities's position as head of the cause just before he struck a deal to bring Lan back by taking his place.'

'And you have only sought me out yesterday?'

'It would have been selfish of me to put my needs first before all the slaves and vulnerables caused by our son's cruelty. Believe me, I wanted to throw it to the wind to be with you.'

'So, who owns the shack?' asked Het.

'The Caelestis Cause.'

'So, how was I able to rent it?'

'Well, when you applied last week I was in a small village aiding the injured. I approved the rental and knew I would see you when I returned.'

'Ouch. Why did you prod me?'

'You made it messy real quick.'

Het made a long drawn out groan. 'You killed me.'

'You are silly.'

'Did I ever compliment you for always being the dedicated priestess?' asked Het.

'Most often.'

'Ah, you need a fine reward then. Now for some lovey dovey time.'

The woman laughed.

Het growled. 'Show me those wonderful bosoms my luscious ...'

Nope, I am not hearing any more of that. I must let Luma and Lufar know. But first to confront these two.

Alena knocked on the door.

'We should get that.'

'Must you?' asked Het.

'Hang on, please.' The door opened and a set of luminescent violet eyes peered through the crack. 'Can I help you?'

'Hello Elder Flower. Or is it Derel Werolf? I am sure Ake will be bursting with joy when she finds out you are back.' Alena glared at the elven woman.

'Hello Alena, call me Flo. I see you have finally made contact with us. I think it's time I met all the descendants and discussed the plan of action I have come up with to dethrone Hau. What do you think?' Flo opened the door and began tying up her messy chestnut hair with a ribbon she pulled from her pocket.

'Well, I am heading back to Ake and Lan to tell them of this incident. Het, you should be ashamed for keeping this information about Elder Flower's return from your best friends.' Alena turned and began to walk away.

'I was sworn to secrecy.' Het smirked. 'And it's not like I only found out last night.'

Barefoot, Flo followed her. Alena turned, and it appeared as if Flo's pale feet barely touched the ground as she moved with an unearthly grace. *Last I heard she was dead. I wonder if she is an unclean spirit trying to trick Het?*

Flo reached her before she took another step and grabbed her wrist. The hand was warm and very much alive. 'I will tell them everything. I just didn't want Hau finding out. But I am sure he knows now after you announced it for all to hear.' Flo gave her a sad smile.

Alena shook her wrist free of Flo's. 'That is fine, as long as I am present. Lufar isn't doing well mentally and Luma is very worried.'

Het scratched his head and his face became serious; his eyes were full of startling intelligence. Alena blinked in surprise. *Well, that is interesting. I wonder if he covers his cleverness with humour and pranks.*

'In my research I have found some information on empaths and their links to mastering magic weapons. I believe Alwin is an empath. He may be able to help Lan heal if he is struggling emotionally. I believe Hau had a hand in it. But I can't say for sure. This isn't the first time though. Lan always blames himself when something hurts Ake and I believe it is linked to some trauma. Somehow, I don't believe he wants to run,' Het said thoughtfully. They reached the little cottage and he pushed open the gate.

The group heard laughter and the voices of women crossing the road. They turned to see Ake and Caoimhe holding packages. Ake stared at Flo and dropped her parcels, Caoimhe picked them up.

'My dearest friend.' Flo held out her arms.

Ake sprinted towards Flo and into her arms; the women's eyes swam with tears.

It was midday and everyone had gathered in the little cottage. Lan, who enjoyed cooking, was preparing lunch over the hearth, while Ake placed a pot of tea and cups on the table.

'How I miss the pot belly stove we had at Caelestis. When we settle somewhere else that is the first thing I am getting installed.' He took the frying pan off the metal grill and walked over to the kitchen bench and placed the pan of spicy chicken down.

Ake began cutting bread with a knife and Caoimhe buttered the pieces. Het handed out plates. In the centre of the table were an assortment of condiments and shredded herbs and lettuces. Everyone began helping themselves.

Flo had just finished telling everyone her journey over the last year and how she had awoken in the stone circle near Velterra, alone and confused. She had journeyed to the city where Amities had found her and given her the bracelet that shielded her from Hau.

Alwin dragged the rocking chairs over so he and Hartur could be seated. He sat down and placed a plate piled with sandwiches on his knees and began eating with gusto. Hartur laughed and nibbled at her food with more decorum. Het wolfed down his serving before going for seconds. Lan pushed his plate away and reached for the cup of elven wine Flo had poured him.

'So, you were able to return due to Mandami's sacrifice?' Ake's eyes shone with tears.

Flo sighed. 'Yes, my dear friend. As you know, he was trying to save his father. He joined us in the underworld, saw his father still in the position of God of Death and thought his death wasted. He did not know it would take an elf willing to fulfil Lan's duties in the underworld for Lan to return. When Het returned to this plane, Mandami offered his sacrifice to me, hoping I could return and comfort his mother. I accepted and here I am.'

'Are you okay, Lan?' asked Ake.

Lan trembled and stood, hurrying towards the door. 'I need to get some air.'

'Keep him here, Luma, he is on the brink again.' Alwin stood up, walked over and stood by the entrance.

Flo began to hum. Everyone began to relax as her enchantress skills turned her words into magic, casting a spell to sooth weary souls.

Dee ea torreley ples,
ea syl crono.
Gifu ea hep.
Moldid ea torreley,
Dlen ples.

Lan's shoulders slumped wearily. He muttered the elvish translation to himself as he sat back down. 'Dee their hearts are weary, their souls are shattered. Gift them joy. Open their hearts and fill them with peace.'

'He's okay for now, but he needs real help.' Alwin returned to his seat.

'I'll talk to you about that after, Alwin.' Het turned to face his friend. 'You sure you are well enough to join this fight.'

'I am strong enough.' Alwin coughed and Hartur patted his back.

'I am fine.' Alwin shrugged off her hand as bright spots of scarlet appeared on his cheek. 'Not in front of Het.'

'I am just trying to help.' Hartur frowned.

Flo continued discussing her plans. 'I think we will have to deal with Hau soon. His attack on Alwin showed how unprepared we are, and the way Lan's been affected is very worrying.' Flo glanced at Alena. 'I need you to gather information around the dock; Het, you in the pubs. Alwin, I know you're still recovering but you will have to continue your training in case we need you; that is, if Hau starts a fight. I hope to prevent that and save the soul of my son.'

Alena scoffed. 'Hau is not Mandami or Amities; sons who built a religion in honour of their mother, sacrificed themselves to bring back their father and built a cause to save the world from your son.'

Flo gave her a gentle smile. 'And without my son there would have been no need of that. That is the balance in the world; darkness and light. One does not exist without the other.'

'I would destroy all darkness in the world,' said Alena.

'So, darkness gives you a purpose to do better, to be a decent person as it shows you what you would become had you embraced it,' said Het wisely.

'Hau wasn't always evil, Alena. He was a kind and gentle boy. It is how we handle the challenges thrown at us that can determine whether we take a path of evil or good.' Ake stood up and walked behind Lan. She wrapped her arms around his shoulders and he leant back against her chest. 'Your father Blaze chose evil after the fall of the Regian empire. You embraced the light.'

'So, I am not allowed to hate Hau?' Alena stood up and walked towards the window and stared out. 'How can you offer forgiveness to him, Luma?'

'I am the Goddess of Mercy. I will try to forgive, but that doesn't mean the pain and memory of what happened disappears. I am curious to see why people choose a path of darkness. Hau's was obvious; the genocide of his people, the death of his parents, and he believed Lan and I had abandoned him. Then Drianna latched on to those feelings of anguish and corrupted him. Yes, Hau had a choice, but he gave in to the darkness.' Ake sighed. 'But he has taken so many lives and must be stopped.'

'His people? Ake, they are your people too. You are half-elven,' Het announced. Lan gave him a grateful smile.

'No, my mother was half-elven, my father ...' Ake blinked in surprise.

Lan stared at Ake. 'You are half-elven. Half-elves either produce human or half-elven children. You don't get quarter of a person.'

'Have you known that this whole time?' asked Ake, her eyes wide with surprise.

Lan nodded. 'Of course. I assumed you did too.'

'How does that even work?' Ake smiled as Lan pulled her into his arms.

Lan leant down to whisper in her ear. 'I'll show you later.' He drew away. 'When a half-elf born of an elven and human union mates with a human their child is half-elven, like you, Ake. But as you do not have a full elven parent the blood is diluted, and while you could produce a half-elven child with a human spouse your grandchildren's children could only be human . Now, if a half-elf such as yourself mates with a full elf like me it renews the elven blood and our children can only be half-elven or elven. It's like how Ori inherited Lord Byron's, my maternal grandfather's blue eyes. Ori's chances of receiving Lord Byron's genes were higher were because of how closely related ...' Lan frowned and glanced away.

Ake laughed. 'Poor Mandami wouldn't have been too happy knowing he was half-elven.'

Lan smiled. 'I mentioned he had elven tendencies when I first met him, if you remember. I'm sure when he grew into his ears he knew.'

Flo smiled at her friends. 'Ake, do you even realise you were a princess of Relequis and, as a female, my direct heir for I had only sons?'

'No, I hadn't thought of that.' Tears welled in Ake's eyes. 'All this time I thought I never really belonged.'

'You have always belonged to my people and Flo's as well. You were never without family.' Lan leant in and placed a chaste kiss on Ake's lips.

'Rabbits; you two are always locking lips.' Het made kissy face towards Lan who cocked a brow.

'At least my wife gets all the attention she wants.' Lan puffed out his chest. 'She doesn't complain.'

'I wield a sword. Flo is doing alright.' Het reached back and stroked the pommel of Imeall.

'Hey, leave off,' said the sword.

Alwin chuckled. 'The sword likes you even more now, Het.'

Lan brushed the tip of an ear with a finger. 'Mine are bigger.'

Alwin groaned. 'Lame.'

Het chuckled. 'Longer; mine are rounder. Girth is important.'

Hartur giggled and Flo and Ake rolled their eyes.

'Always in competition,' Flo muttered.

'Right?' Ake poked her tongue at Het who shrugged good naturedly.

Lan, not to be outdone, glanced at his wife. 'We will make use of that later.'

Ake bit her tongue and closed her mouth before she hid her face against her husband's chest.

Alwin coughed on the cup of tea he had poured and started sipping. 'Oh my goodness.'

Caoimhe and Hurley exchanged innocent glances. '*Why is Mother blushing and Lady Flo giving Het a look of reproach?*'

Lan signed back. '*Flirting.*'

'*In front of your great-grandchildren and daughter. Father is so crude.*'

Lan smiled at his daughter before replying. '*We are all adults here.*'

Flo stood up. 'I think everyone is feeling overwhelmed. I would like to enact my plan in a week, if you are all agreeable.'

'Wait.' Hurley scrambled around, giving everyone small notes of coloured paper. 'Our wedding is in two days. Held on the local green.' Hurley's eyes filled with sadness. 'And we got catering.'

'He's sad because he wanted to do the catering himself,' signed Caoimhe.

'We would be honoured to attend,' said Hartur.

'As will I.' Alena smiled.

'Alena can't marry you in Velterra. That's only applicable on the sea,' said Lan.

Hurley turned to Flo and Het. 'Miss Priestess and Mr Druid, will you marry us in the old ways in honour of Caoimhe's heritage?'

'Of course.' Het patted Hurley on the shoulder.

'So, we are agreed; we attend the wedding and meet at dusk in a week's time outside Hau's palace?' Flo smiled.

With a collective yes. Alena, Caoimhe and Hurley said their farewells and left.

Het and Alwin walked outside for a moment and talked in whispers while Ake watched them through the door.

'You're an empath. Alwin. You can weave emotion into whatever purpose you want.' Het ruffled Alwin's hair.

'I am aware of this.' Alwin tried to push Het's hands away but the big guy grabbed him around the neck with his arm and used a closed fist to rough his hair up more.

Het laughed and released the boy. 'I want you to try and help Lan. I don't know what you should weave, but please try.'

'Depending on what his affliction is he may fight or run. I will need you here to contain him.' Alwin shivered. 'I am not sure if I can do this. Wouldn't it be best for Flo to maintain his mental health with her enchanted singing?'

'That is not a long-term solution. Please don't let your fear stop you from trying and possibly succeeding.' Het patted Alwin on the back.

They turned as they heard Ake and Lan arguing in the doorway.

'Ake, this is ridiculous. I can heal myself eventually rather than allowing an untested boy to play with my feelings,' cried Lan.

'No, Lan, you will stay here.'

Het turned and strode to the house as Lan stepped through the doorway and sprinted to the left. Het grabbed him and dragged him inside towards his bedroom as Alwin followed. Lan's eyes filled with fear.

'Does Het know what I did?'

Het dumped Lan on the bed and stepped back as Alwin and Ake entered the room.

'I will sit with Hartur,' said Flo from the other room.

Ake closed the door as Lan sat up and glared at them, his eyes darting between them before his gaze settled on his wife's worried face.

Lan sighed and his head drooped. 'Fine, get on with it, I know it's necessary.'

Ake sat down on the other side of the bed and he reached for her hand; she held it.

'Close your eyes, Lufar. I want you to visualise the thing that upset you the most over the years and hold that thought. Try to tell us about it and why it makes you feel the way you do. I will attempt to make sure those feelings don't overwhelm you,' said Alwin.

'You will hate me afterwards,' mumbled Lan.

'I doubt that mate.' Het gave the elf an encouraging smile.

Lan closed his eyes and lay back.

'Listen to my voice. Feel the darkness as it overwhelms you.' Alwin stepped closer to the bed; he reached into Lan's mind. He was met by a gentle soul full of love and protectiveness, interrupted by hints of jealousy, vanity, stubbornness and self-loathing. He touched the self-loathing with his mind and began to sift through the darkness.

Lan cried out. 'During a fight with Bozzwanna I was kidnapped. I was helpless against the spell cast on me. I sired Orilan on my sister.' He opened his eyes and he attempted to roll to the left. Het held him down and Lan fought against him, almost managing to throw the big man with his unarmed combat skills. Lan turned, his eyes full of anguish, and yelled at his wife. 'I thought no one could love me after that, but you gave yourself to me fully without even attempting to despise me for my past. I clung to that!'

'How could I ever despise you?' whispered Ake.

Alwin reached deeper, searching for the fear that made Lan flee every time he felt he was responsible for his wife's pain.

Lan growled and tried to get up. 'Ake was attacked by Cephas multiple times. I know what that's like, to lose control of your body and have someone use it for their own purposes. I failed to protect Ake, and after what I did to Goriard, I was afraid I could be as evil as Cephas. I am not free of that sin. Yet, she still loved me and treated me as innocent of that kind of crime. I am afraid she will realise how evil I am and hate me.'

'So, there it is.' Alwin's power flowed along the webbing that a soul manifested. Slowly, the self-loathing Lan felt within himself unravelled. Sweat beaded on his brow as Alwin created new strands, weaving in Ake's overwhelming love and trust. 'Het, do you hate Lan after that admission?'

Het shook his head. 'It was a spell, old friend. I knew you had a child through no fault of your own. I didn't know it was with a sister. That would have been extra traumatising. You even tried to take responsibility for the child. You were, and still are, a good man.' Het smiled sadly. 'Do you hate me for kissing Ake not so long ago?'

Lan stared at Het. 'Of course not, you were under a curse. But it was just a kiss.'

'Yes, but Hau could have made me do worse.' Het released Lan.

Alwin's brow furrowed and his breath shuddered; he clung to Het's feelings of friendship and pity and wove them into Lan's emotional web. 'You see, Lufar, they may pity your past, but they love and respect you. Above all, Luma trusts you. You are blameless of your imagined crimes.' The pattern in Alwin's mind sparkled with luminosity; ragged patches still clung at the web's edges to shine even brighter when he wove in his respect and appreciation for all Lan had ever done, weaving in the stories of the great feats Amities had told of him.

Lan began to cough and rolled to the side of the bed; he retched and coughed up blood. Wiping his mouth with his sleeve, he sat up. 'What the hell was that?'

'Maybe Hau's blood leaving your body.' Ake rubbed her husband's back.

'Be bold, Lufar. You are kind, protective and are a good man.' Alwin turned and opened the door.

Het looked at Lan. 'Hope you are okay, mate.'

Lan sighed wearily. 'I feel lighter and strange.'

'I think we should leave them to it.' Alwin strode from the room.

'We should go too,' said Flo.

Alwin turned to Flo. 'I sensed your son warping Lan's feelings. It seems to have been there since the night of the attack.'

Tears started in Flo's eyes. 'Why is he so cruel?'

Het growled. 'He needs to be taken down.'

Alwin ducked his head in briefly to say goodbye. He watched Lan lay his head on Ake's lap; he appeared exhausted and closed his eyes.

'I would never try to deliberately hurt you or others,' said Lan.

'We are all aware of that.' Ake leant down and kissed him.

Alwin smiled and pulled the door shut.

CHAPTER FORTY-EIGHT

Hurley jumped up and down as Lan tied the little groom's cravat. 'Hurley, please settle for a few moments.'

Hurley gave him a cheesy grin. 'Can't do that, she will soon be here.'

Alwin was setting out chairs. Flo and Het had finished their decorations and stood back admiring the setup. They had woven an arch of young, supple green branches. Het's strength had come in handy when Flo's dainty hands could no longer weave the last few branches as the tight weave was hard to separate and add to. Flo began to hum and the little arch was soon covered in tiny, shimmering gold lights.

Het grinned and brushed his hand over the top of the arch and spoke softly in ancient Eriu. '*Blàthhanna tyfu.*'

Tiny hollyhock flowers, a delicacy for fairies, sprouted and grew over the top and sides of the arch.

Flo gave him an irresistible smile. 'I thought you never finished the apprenticeship.'

'I was a prodigy, a master of arms and a druid. I had already conquered flower magic, faerie orbs, some ceremonies and translations of ancient written texts.' Het laughed. 'I am not completely useless when it comes to secrets of Dee.'

'I never thought you were, Het. You are not an oaf.' Flo fluttered her eyelashes at him. Flo jumped when he leant over and squeezed her derriere. 'Not in public, Het.'

Het gave her a cheeky grin and pulled her to him. With a quick kiss, he drew away. 'Typical shy elf.'

'There is a time and place for such things.' Flo turned and watched Lan chasing Hurley to try and finish tying his cravat. The caterers had arrived and the halfling was attempting to try everything. Lan's cheeks were flushed and he frowned as he tried to keep the halfling from getting dirty.

Flo turned back to Het. He pulled out some papers from his pocket; they were slightly scrunched and had a food stain on them.

'What are those?' asked Flo.

'Velterran marriage certificate. I pre-registered them. September fourth.' He smiled and pointed to the date. 'At least Velterran society recognises halflings and fairies as adults after eighty. Cirichad society sees them as perpetual children.' Het's eyes widened. 'I have heard rumours of an institution on Cirichad soil where they lock up innocent fae and long-lived races.'

Flo laughed. 'They are just city legends, utter nonsense.'

Het shrugged. 'All stories have some form of truth to them.' Het licked his finger and tried to wipe off the smudge. 'I wish there was some safe place for the fae.'

Flo fidgeted and glanced away.

Het grinned. 'Is there a place like that?'

Flo nodded. 'On all the maps, the capital of Breteyne, Ludan, fell. The Academy of Ea spread the rumours after the war. The city suffered a lot of damage, but the buildings left became a refuge for the fae, protected by my order.'

Het hugged her. 'That is wonderful.'

'Did you eat while filling the forms out?' Flo laughed and covered her mouth daintily with her hand as she glanced at the forms.

'Changing the subject?' asked Het.

Flo nodded.

'Hell, it won't come off.' Het tried to straighten out the crumpled paper. 'I saw a jam tart at a bakery. It was beckoning me. I purchased it and sat down to enjoy it. I placed the form on the table and as I bit into the delicacy, flakes of tart landed on the paper.'

'That explains the stain. Why is it crumpled?'

'Well, I grabbed a napkin and wiped my mouth and crumpled it up before I realised I had two. I had placed the paper upside down on the napkin pile.'

'I am sure it will be fine.'

Het nodded. 'It's just their copy, the other one was fine and I registered that with the numbers board.'

'Numbers board?' asked Flo curiously.

'All births and marriages are registered at the numbers board. Those more closely related to Hau's original bloodline get higher benefits. It's like the Cririans' family registration board. It lets the city know how many citizens they have for planning and development, to build structures to the benefit of their people. Not that Velterrans care much for that. They are more interested in power; those with lower numbers have higher magical aptitude. Creating a magical legacy, means more power. Marriage partners are often based on number compatibility. Those of lower numbers don't often mix with those of higher numbers.'

They turned as Alena arrived and sat down on one of the chairs. Alwin had completed his task and joined her, leaving a space next to him for Hartur. Hurley ran over to the arch.

'Are we ready?' asked Hurley.

'We sure are, little fellow.' Het ruffled Hurley's hair.

Hartur wandered over from where she was helping the caterers. 'Shall I go get the bride?'

'That would be great,' said Flo.

Hartur smiled, turned and walked away.

—∽∾—

'Caoimhe, stand still.' Ake tried to place the wreath of flowers in her daughter's hair, but Caoimhe kept fidgeting.

Caoimhe picked at the lace on the top of the white gown that fell to her knees. *I can't believe I am finally getting married. I have dreamt of this for centuries, but no one was right for me. Hurley is the cutest man ever; I just want to squeeze his cheeks and hold his hand.*

Hartur knocked on the door. 'They are ready for the bride.'

Ake managed to pin the wreath to Caoimhe's blonde hair. 'I have something for you, my darling daughter.' Ake reached into the pocket of her new dress and drew out a small box; she handed it to Caoimhe.

'Thank you, Mother.' Caoimhe opened the box and drew out the small, silver fairy brooch. Its wings were inlaid with blue sapphires.

'Something blue for a beautiful bride to wear on her special day.' Ake smiled.

Caoimhe whistled with excitement and hugged her. 'Thank you.'

Ake sighed and tears shined in her eyes. 'You are welcome. I can't believe I get to see another one of my children marry.' She pinned the brooch to her daughter's dress.

'Let's go, Mother; Hurley awaits his bride.' Caoimhe smiled.

Hartur, Ake and Caoimhe exited the house and headed towards the green.

Lan stood next to Hurley by the arch as the little halfling leapt from one foot to the other in excitement. Flo and Het waited nearby. Everyone turned to stare at Caoimhe as she walked towards them followed by Ake and Hartur. Hartur took her seat next to Alwin and Ake followed Caoimhe whose eyes sparkled with joy. Hurley stood staring at his bride, mouth open in shock as she reached him. Ake fixed Caoimhe's train then went and stood next to Lan.

'You are the most beautiful woman in the world; more precious than dessert.' Hurley reached for Caoimhe's hand. She took it and responded in fairy and Hurley translated. 'You are more precious to me than those delicious-looking hollyhocks on our wedding arch.'

Het grinned and stepped forward. 'This couple has chosen to be married in the elven and halfling way. While we cannot provide them with the true elven rite of marriage, we have set them up a little test. Caoimhe and Hurley, you once agreed to be lovers. Would you be willing to be mates? This is not an easy path and is often fraught with situations beyond your control. Will you join each other on that path?'

Flo reached out her hand and pointed to the arch. 'These paths and the trials within will test your love and compatibility. If you agree, make your choice.'

Caoimhe and Hurley grinned at each other then turned and nodded.

'Step through the arch then,' said Het.

The little couple walked through the arch and encountered a table that only they could see. Everyone watched them curiously.

'They will encounter a hidden vice that they must overcome to be married in the elven way,' said Flo.

On the table were an array of desserts, cream, milk and rare flowers. Hurley and Caoimhe's eyes widened with delight and they grinned at each other and went to reach for the treats. They stopped and took a step back.

'It looks so delicious.' Hurley looked at Caoimhe in despair.

'You are better than cream ... And hollyhocks,' Caoimhe whistled in agitation, struggling with the very notion.

Hurley gave her a cheesy grin. 'Am I really?'

Caoimhe nodded. Hurley leant in to kiss his wife.

'I declare them wed by Dee and Sorendee,' said Flo.

Het began to clap and the others followed. 'Now marriage via the halfling way.'

The table materialised and everyone bore witness to the amazing desserts and rare flowers.

'How did you find those flowers, Het?' whispered Flo.

'Druid secrets.' Het smiled. 'The couple must agree to feed only each other and their weans with their own hands for the rest of their days. If the pair agree, link arms and feed each other your partner's favourite treat.'

Hurley and Caoimhe linked arms. Hurley picked up a petit four filled with cream and put it to Caoimhe's lips and she ate it with flair. Caoimhe picked up a hollyhock, her eyes filled with envy, and popped it in Hurley's mouth. Everyone cheered.

'They are now bride and groom in halfling culture and mates in the elven tongue. I present to you Mr and Mrs Graysby.' Het gestured to the couple.

Hurley and Caoimhe bowed with hands held, turned and grinned at each other and began helping themselves to the treats.

'So, I am Mrs Fish now?' whistled Caoimhe.

'Halflings usually live near the sea in caves. They hunt fish and forage shells and seafood. They take their clan names for their most common catch. As much as I hate fish, my family does not. Our clan is Graysby.' Hurley grinned at Caoimhe. 'Hello Mrs Fish.'

Caoimhe sighed. 'It is fine.'

Het gave Hurley the wedding certificate.

'Thank you, sir.' Hurley shook his hand.

Ake rushed over and swept Caoimhe up in her arms. 'Congratulations, my darling daughter.'

Lan shook Hurley's hand. 'Congratulations, I hope you are both happy.'

Caoimhe struggled and Ake put her down. Caoimhe straight-ened her dress. *'Mother, I am a woman grown. Please don't pick me up anymore.'*

'Okay, Caoimhe.' Ake wiped a tear from her eye.

'Don't cry, Mother. We are happy,' said Caoimhe.

'I am happy too.' Ake began to weep.

—⁓—

Lan smiled in amusement and held out his hand to Ake. 'They haven't disappeared, honey. Let them enjoy each other. We wanted to be alone for weeks after our marriage.' He winked at Ake who blushed.

Lan laughed and led her over to the caterers. Her eyes settled on the desserts, and she began helping herself as Lan went in search of more savoury fare.

Ake glanced at the caterer dressed in a robe covering most of his hazel eyes. *I know him.*

The man grinned, showing perfect teeth. 'Nice ceremony, wasn't it?'

Ake nodded. 'Hau?'

'Of course, cousin. Wouldn't miss a family affair.' Hau reached out and steadied her hand as it shook. 'Hush now, you don't want to ruin your daughter's big day, do you? I have no need to harm any of you now since you gave up part of your heritage for me. Maybe you will give me the same courtesy and leave Velterra.'

'We will stop you.' Ake put down the plate and went to back away. Hau grabbed her hand. 'I see my mother has returned and didn't think it was necessary to reach out to her son. I am not pleased.'

Hau turned his head to watch Flo caught up in his father's large arms. Flo was trying not to giggle as Het kissed her cheeks. He turned back to smirk at Ake. 'My father's body remains the same, reborn from the mass grave Lan constructed. Father isn't the mortal he claims to be and he now knows it. He was once as ruthless as I. Maybe you should kill him, Goddess of Mercy, and use his soul to bring back Mandami, whose life was short and full of suffering yet remained pure.'

Ake glared at him. 'Why would you want your father dead?'

Hau shrugged. 'He abandoned me and my mother.'

'Are you really so stupid, Hau? He died protecting those he loved, *including* your pregnant mother.' Ake pulled her hand away. 'You would have been dead too. I would never sacrifice a friend or loved one for another.'

Lan walked towards her, his plate filled with fish, fruit and vegetables. 'These caterers Hurley got are great.'

Ake glanced at him.

'You look worried. What is it?' Lan dropped his plate and drew his knives.

Hau laughed softly and disappeared.

Ake hurried over to Lan, leant down and retrieved the plate that now had very little on it, and handed it to him as he sheathed his knives.

'Hau was here.'

Lan face darkened with anger. 'How dare he!'

'Lan, keep this quiet for now. We can't ruin their day.'

Lan nodded and the pair turned as Hurley and Caoimhe were making their exit. Ake clapped along and Lan joined in the cheering as the newly wedded couple left.

Het and Flo wandered over.

'What do you two say to a double date?' Het grinned.

'I could do with a drink. Hau was here,' Lan blurted out.

'Are you both okay?' asked Flo.

Ake nodded. 'It's fine, he didn't do anything. Just mentioned sacrifices and such.'

'He really is a bad sort,' grumbled Het.

Flo sighed. 'Let's enjoy the rest of the day. Who knows when we will get another?'

Ake and Het grinned at each other.

'We know a place that may be daunting to two elegant elves,' said Het.

'Flo may be elegant, but I am nothing of the sort.' Lan laughed. 'Lead on.'

Het and Ake led their partners by the hand towards their destination.

CHAPTER FORTY-NINE

It was late afternoon; Lan had decided to shout his friends a late lunch while they waited for nightfall to enter the black markets. Glass chandeliers hung from the ceiling. The tables seated up to six and were covered in silver tablecloths.

Het shifted in his mahogany chair upholstered in sumptuous red velvet and lined with gold trim. *It matches the plush carpet.* Het reached out and ran his hands over the multiple forks and knives either side of his plate and smirked. *What do I do with all of these?*

Flo, seated next to him, leant in and whispered in his ear. 'Start from the outside and work your way in.'

The waiter came up to take their orders. 'What will it be?'

'I will have the grazing board.' Lan handed over his menu.

'I will have the collection of tiny desserts followed by the soup of the day.' Ake smiled.

Het grinned. 'I'll have the same as her, but add the steak to my order please.'

Flo and Lan stifled their laughs.

'They are like brother and sister,' said Flo.

'I mentioned that once,' said Lan.

'And you, miss?' asked the waiter, turning to Flo.

'I am sorry. I will have the fish and salad,' said Flo.

'Get the chips, they are fried potato sticks. They are amazing. Speaking of which, can I please add a serve? Actually make it two serves or Ake will steal mine.' Lan winked at his wife.

'Okay, please add chips,' said Flo.

The waiter bowed and took their order to the kitchen. Het began eating the breadsticks. He took a stale one, leant across the table and tapped Ake on the head. Ake poked out her tongue and grabbed another then they proceeded to have a breadstick fight, pretending the items in their hands were swords.

'They are like elflings.' Flo smiled.

'At least we aren't boring.' Ake's breadstick broke and she bowed her head, conceding victory to Het.

'I am not boring,' said Flo.

'I suggest you two teach her how to play.' Lan grinned.

'We intend to,' said Het.

The waiter came over and handed them their meals. 'Do you want any drinks, sirs and madams?'

'A bottle of elven wine and four glasses,' said Lan.

'A jug of sarsaparilla.' Ake smiled.

'A pint of beer,' said Het.

'Eww, beer,' said Ake.

'Mmm, that refreshing foamy bitterness.' Het smacked his lips.

'Will that be all?' asked the waiter.

'Flo, do you want anything to drink?' asked Ake.

'The wine is fine,' said Flo.

The waiter left and returned with their drinks as everyone began to enjoy their meal. Ake was eating her chips when Het reached over and grabbed some, wolfing them down and emptying most of the bowl. Het grinned at her. Ake sighed and rolled her eyes and started on the cakes.

In a quick movement, Lan had replaced her bowl with his and he finished off the last few chips in her former bowl. She turned and gave him a look of adoration.

'Those two are so sweet,' said Flo.

'I know, right,' said Het between mouthfuls of his steak. 'Is that a hint or an observation?'

'Interpret it how you will.' Flo took a sip of her wine the waiter had poured.

Het grinned. 'Well, if we are no longer sweet together, I have a backup.' Het battered his eyelashes at Lan and Ake laughed as Lan blushed.

Flo raised her eyebrows at Het.

Het shrugged. ' The funeral was a dreary affair and Amities was a happy chap. I gave Lan an innocent peck to lighten the mood. Amities would have appreciated that.'

Flo laughed, the sound sweet to all who were near. 'I have competition then.'

'I'll duel you for him.' Lan tried to remain serious, but failed and his laughter was added to the others', the banter flowed as easily as the wine.

'I must go use the facilities.' Flo stood and gestured for Ake to join her.

'Umm, yes, I must also use the facilities.' Ake scrambled to her feet.

The women headed towards the restrooms. Velterra had installed flushing toilets in the more prestigious private areas and this attracted many a curious customer.

'Lan, I may need some help with advancing my relationship. I believe you can now give a man advice?' Het ran his hands through his hair nervously.

'Remember to notice the small things like, when she is feeling down, cheer her with a favourite thing; Ake's is cakes. I am sure Flo has her own preferred treats. Be affectionate and try to listen. Don't get caught up in jealousy and anger.' Lan brushed a crumb from his robes. 'Put her needs first. I wasn't good to Ake in the beginning, caught up in my past traumas.'

'Why would I get jealous of Flo?' asked Het.

'I meant other men around her or admiring her. I have stopped that over the centuries.'

'Flo is a beautiful woman, if men and women admire her that is fine. I know she is loyal to me.'

'You were always a wiser man than me.' Lan sighed.

'We all have things to learn. I am flawed too.'

'How?'

'I am playful and sometimes a little too much. It's often my way of coping in serious situations.'

'Fair enough. What are you going to do next?'

'I want to marry her before we face Hau. I want to do it at dawn. Will you help me arrange it?'

'Of course, I love a good romance as much as the next person.' Lan smiled.

<hr />

Ake dipped her finger into a small metal canister and applied the blood red substance to her lips in front of the full length mirror.

'What is that?' asked Flo.

'It's called lipstick. When I went shopping with Caoimhe. We entered a toiletry store and the woman showed us this stuff called makeup and how to apply the lipstick. What do you think?'

'It makes your mouth appear more luscious. May I try some? Then maybe Het will ask me.'

'Ask what?'

'To marry him. I know elven empresses don't marry their lovers and usually wed a distant royal cousin, but I only ever wanted Het.' Flo's eyes softened and she smiled. 'He is my everything.'

'When did you feel that way?'

'When I first set eyes on him. I knew he was meant for me.'

Ake smiled. 'That is so cute. Mine and Lan's relationship was complicated due to age.'

Flo laughed. 'Think about what you just said.'

Ake blushed. 'I am sorry Flo; I meant no offence to you.'

'It's not offensive. In our last life I was around forty years older than Het. This time a little over twenty or something like that as he is in his forties. You and Lan are only fourteen years apart.'

'Hau told me something.'

'What is it?'

'Het wasn't born again. The gods returned Het to the same body using the skeleton that Lan buried and caused his body to age when they brought him back to life. Amities found him about two years ago and helped him remember who he is. Het is in his fifties. His body is also imbued with blood of giants. Marry him and you will have at least four centuries with him. Giant longevity follows the male line unless the females are at least full or half-giants. Het's mother Kathy had a mortal lifespan.' Ake smiled sadly.

'How do you know this?'

Ake shrugged. 'I can sense his lifeforce, being the Goddess of Life and Mercy after all.'

'So, you know when we will die?' Flo asked.

'Not the exact day or time, but the year.'

Flo shivered. 'That is awful. Must be a burden.'

Ake nodded. 'I hate it, but I have learnt to live with it.' Ake blinked and her eyes widened as she focused on her dearest friend. 'You don't look completely the same; there is a glow to your hidden aura. Almost as if your previous mortal shell was a cover.'

Flo felt her cheeks burn and tried to redirect the conversation. 'Have you always had this ability?'

Ake shook her head. 'No, it came on after Drianna was defeated. It is also useless on the unborn. But I know the souls of all who are reborn. I can sense the divine too.' Ake's eyes locked on Flo's.

'Did you know some divine can cloak their divinity?' Flo's eyes flitted towards the mirror and she began to apply the lipstick. 'What else did you buy?'

'Something called mascara.' Ake frowned. 'Oh no you don't. Don't change the conversation. Is it true?'

Flo nodded. 'I didn't know when I was born into a mortal vessel last time. I realised who I was when I passed away. Most immortals who choose to do a mortal journey forget our past when we are born into this plane.'

Ake tried to apply the mascara and failed. She tried wiping it off with a paper towel and was left with black marks under her eyes. Flo laughed.

'I see. Well, if you didn't know then I guess it's not a secret you kept from me then.' Ake smiled.

There was a flush and a woman came out from one of the stalls and began to wash her hands. She watched Flo and Ake attempting to reapply the mascara.

'Would you like some help?' asked the woman.

'Yes please,' said Ake.

The woman pulled out some concealer and applied it under the women's eyes and then showed them how to apply the mascara.

'Thank you,' said Ake.

The woman left. Ake turned to Flo.

'Tell Het how you feel and ask him to marry you. He adores you.'

Flo blushed. 'I am aware of his strong feelings for me. You don't need to be divine to know that. I am the goddess—'

'We don't know whose listening.' Ake placed a finger to her lips.

'So, about Het.' Flo glanced at Ake.

Ake laughed. 'You two suit each other. Het was always like a brother to me and I would love to see him happy with you, my dear friend. You deserve it more than most.'

Flo smiled. 'What do you mean by that?'

'I have always harboured guilt for your deaths. Het died defending Caelestis and you died trying to find me.' Ake's eyes filled with tears and her mascara began to run. 'You got injured, and even though I rescued you, I should have done more. Because of my grief and fear of Cephas I did nothing. If I had known Dane was aboard I would have had him remove that bracelet and try to heal you myself.' Ake's body shook with her sobs. 'I am glad I can tell you this now.'

Flo, her eyes wet with tears, embraced Ake.

'You both haven't shown any anger towards Lan and I for that.' Ake stepped back.

Flo gave Ake a gentle smile. 'They kept your memorial garden in Cirichad. People tour it. I visited it and saw the love and dedication you put into it, Ake. For someone who is so outspoken you have a hard time divulging complex feelings and I understand this. I know you care for Het and me.'

Ake began to wash the mascara off. 'It doesn't suit me.' Ake turned and held out her hands to Flo. 'I am truly sorry for the past; I love you, dear friend. Please forgive me.'

'Done.' Flo smiled. 'Het wasn't without anger, Ake. When we were reunited in the underworld he harboured great anger towards Lan and his treatment of you. He lost to someone who was immature and prone to darkness. He didn't understand why you chose Lan over him. He was never worried about losing his life for you.'

Ake backed away. 'I never saw Het that way. I made that clear. He is like a brother to me.'

Flo smiled. 'I am not jealous, Ake. He still cared for you for years after we got together. We had one night together on this plane. Our love grew over the years in the underworld and now it's unshakeable.'

They moved away from the sinks as more women washed their hands.

'You are a very kind woman. I wouldn't have been so patient.' Ake smiled at Flo.

Flo chuckled. 'Rubbish. How many centuries did you wait for Lan?'

Ake grinned. 'True.'

'Het is an innocent man. I believe he never understood elven culture. Elven children, particularly boys, must be protected from pain. They cannot process it well into their forties. You could see past Lan's pain, resentment and confusion to the sweet, passionate and protective elf underneath. Not everyone has that ability. Most women would not have forgiven him for his early words to you. Het didn't get that.'

Ake shrugged. 'He had been through a lot. I can't help who I fell for.'

Flo laughed. 'I am not picking on your relationship, Ake. It is unique. It would have to be between a goddess of life and god of death and one of the Fiadhri. Het doesn't dislike Lan now. He sees the change in him and considers him a friend.'

Ake smiled. 'Lan isn't a god of death anymore.'

Flo looked away.

Ake frowned. 'What is it?'

'Just because Lan outsourced the job to his son doesn't mean he isn't still a divine being. He is still Lord Bás, an immortal. Unlike other gods who must take new forms to enter different mortal planes, you and Lan do not need to.'

Ake gasped. 'Why? It doesn't make sense.'

Flo tapped the side of her nose. 'Who knows why?' Flo glanced away from Ake as a woman pushed past them. *One day, my dear friend, this plane will hold the last few remnants of magic and fantastical creatures, a refuge for the unbelievable. As Dee and Sorendee withhold their light from their creations, our world will drift away, alone in the universe. Two adorable gods who have experienced all the trials of mortality will become our caretakers. I will not retire with my divine parents but stay by my dear friends' sides. Dee and Sorendee never experienced mortal suffering and cannot understand humanity because of it. You two know what it means to hate, love and forgive. My darling Ake, think kindly of us when the time comes.*

Ake laughed and sighed, drawing Flo from her thoughts. 'Again, I am sorry for the past.'

Flo hugged her. 'We were all young and made mistakes. Hopefully, this time round we can approach problems with maturity.' Flo sighed. 'Mandami's sacrifice wasn't the full amount needed for an elven goddess to return. I too have made a mistake by leaving out the full truth.'

Ake sighed. 'I gathered. I'm guessing your parents interfered?'

Flo nodded.

'So be it,' said Ake.

'We should really get back to the men. They will wonder what is going on. Plus, I have a beloved to marry.'

Ake smiled. 'At least another happy moment to enjoy.'

They left the bathroom, arms interlinked, and chattered briefly as they returned to their table. They grinned at each other as they watched their menfolk. Lan and Het clanged the glasses of beer together and began to chug them down, trying to outdo each other. Several onlookers cheered as Het crashed his glass down on the table.

'Five.' Het laughed.

Lan finished and grinned. 'Also five, but who is more drunk?'

Het stood up. 'I don't care about that.' He turned to stare at the women. 'Ah, here they are. I thought they may have realised we were crazy and ran off.' Het belched and blushed. 'Sorry about that, ladies.'

Lan proceeded to pay the bill. Ake hurried over to join him.

'What's with the facepaint?' asked Het.

Flo looked shocked. 'I though it made me look nicer.'

'It accentuates what is already there.' Het picked her up and Flo gasped, trying to get down. Het turned to Ake. 'Off to the destination then.'

Ake grinned and turned to stare at Lan.

'Oh no you don't.' Lan laughed as Ake attempted to carry him. He ran past Het and Flo and out the door, followed by his wife.

Flo resigned herself to being carried. 'Ake and I had an intense conversation. That is why we took so long.'

Het smiled down at her. 'Are you both okay?'

Flo sighed. 'Ake blames herself for our deaths.'

Het's eyes became serious. 'Glad to see she did care.'

Flo stared at him. 'Of course she did, Het. What makes you think she didn't?'

'She hasn't brought it up.' Het hoisted Flo up.

'I guess we really should have you confront them. Put me down, Het.'

'Not tonight, Flo. I would marry you.' Het leant down and went to kiss her.

Flo turned her head. 'Het, you are drunk.'

Het placed her down. 'No, I am not. But Lan certainly is.'

They watched Ake walk slowly towards an almost invisible gap in a wall as Lan stumbled across the path staring intently at Ake's behind. 'Mine.'

Flo smiled up at Het. 'You want to marry me?'

Het nodded. 'Elder Flower, will you make our union official?'

'Of course. When?'

'When the office opens tomorrow. I don't want any fanfare and just want it to be the two of us.' He kissed the top of her head.

'Sounds perfect. We don't know if we will survive Hau.'

Het sighed. 'Then I best have it out with them before I spend the next few days alone with you. I must get it off my chest. The black market isn't the place for an empress anyway.'

'Shouldn't I be the judge of that?' asked Flo.

'Fine. But will you wait while I talk to Ake?'

Flo nodded and Het strode towards Ake, his eyes filled with determination. Lan approached Het. 'I would have it out with you, Het. Confront me, it needs to be done.'

Het stared at him. 'Okay then. Ake was a good, kind and joyous girl and you said some awful things to her and didn't show her the depth of your feelings. Things would have been very different if you didn't let your pride get in the way.' Het glared at Lan. 'You could have teleported away from Caelestis with Ake and returned when Cephas left.'

Lan shifted his feet. 'I regret my pride the night Cephas took her.' He frowned. 'And to believe I didn't show her the depth of my feelings. The night Drianna destroyed Caelestis I nearly made love to Ake.'

Flo covered her ears. 'I don't want to hear that.'

Lan's eyes filled with intense emotion as he remembered that night. 'I was held back by my past and my intense feelings. I believed I was soiled. With that in mind, I couldn't unleash a wave of all-consuming desire on an innocent young woman. How could I tell the gentle Ake that I would die for her, kill for her and keep her in my bed night after night?'

Het cleared his throat. 'I didn't think an elf had that kind of desire.'

'I am Arakaen, we are notorious for not leaving our lover alone. I didn't know that at the time though, but by the gods, I was going to have her. The night we were married she believed I was holding back due to my past. While that was part of it, it was more the fact I could have easily been reckless with her.' Lan grinned. 'How do you know I held back for years? You had died.'

Flo hummed to herself.

'The dead can witness the living.' Het smirked.

Lan blushed. 'By the gods, no.'

Het gave him a bitter smile. 'I did not witness your intimacies, but rather saw your reservation within your words and behaviour. It was dreadful to hear your rash words and see others destroy her. I refused to watch after the battle with Orilan and your harsh words that night. Flo filled me in on the events on the *Syl* after you became the Lord of Death.' Het grinned. 'I thought that was befitting for you. I was kind of pleased you were separated from her and couldn't even mingle with us. She didn't even fight when the *Syl* sank. That wasn't like my Ake.' Het sighed. 'But she is happy now, and you have certainly matured and redeemed yourself. You have become a good husband to her.'

Lan sighed and his shoulders slumped. 'Finally, some honesty. You don't think that crossed my mind in the years that followed? I hated myself; even at one stage thinking Cephas was a better man for her than I. Who thinks like that?'

'You must have been in an awful place.'

Lan nodded. 'I was literally burnt to a crisp, with no magic, and couldn't speak. My sight was limited too. But that is no excuse for such a thought. I won't justify it.'

Het turned to stare briefly at Flo. She uncovered her ears. 'You said he had sustained injuries. You didn't tell me the extent of them.' Het turned back to Lan. 'That explains why you didn't fight for Flo and Ake.'

'I didn't know the bracelet she wore trapped her powers. Orilan knew and should have removed it earlier. Ake probably could have saved Flo and maybe even the rest of the ship. At that time, my son cared little for the souls on that boat other than Ake and his own kin.'

While they were speaking Ake had slipped into the crack and now gave a low whistle.

'That's the signal that the area is safe of snitches.' Het held out his palm to Lan; they shook hands. 'I believe that is all of it. I must confront Ake now.'

'Do you still want me to help you look out for wedding items in the market?' asked Lan.

'Sure.' Het smiled.

'I will stay with Flo for a moment.'

Flo wouldn't look at Lan, her cheeks tinged with red. 'You are very open about your intimate moments.' Lan shrugged and they walked slowly towards the crack in the wall.

Het walked quickly away, hoping to catch Ake.

—∽∾∽—

Ake popped her head through the gap in the alleyway for a few minutes and watched as people finished pitching the black tents that served as stores. She wrinkled her nose as the smell assaulted her nostrils; a mixture of incense, greasy cooking and unknown pungent odours. A goblin child ran past with a giant rat on a leash; it hissed at her and she stepped back into the alleyway. She looked up at the sky; the stars twinkled merrily. She jumped as someone stood close to her. Thinking it was Lan, she smiled up at Het, eyes full of love.

Het laughed. 'I can see how you turned a vain, immature elf into a good man.'

Ake blushed and backed away. 'I am sorry, Het. I thought you were Lan.'

'I have missed our games and long conversations. We had many a good one, did we not?'

Ake smiled. 'Yes, we did.'

'Now we must have a hard one, Ake.'

'Shouldn't you be concentrating on Flo?' Ake looked away.

'You run too, Ake.'

Ake put her hands on her hips and faced him. 'No, I do not.'

'You try to distract others when the hardest conversations must be had. Sure, you are physically here, no one denies that, but you aren't confronting me directly, Ake. Talk to me like you used to. Let it all out.'

'Here?'

Het sighed. 'We don't have time for this. I have already said my piece to Lan. Now, I will confront you. I was angry you chose him. He never pursued you with the confidence of someone in love. To me, it looked like he wanted to protect you, but wasn't in love with you.'

'Hey—'

Het gave her a look of reproach. 'I bore witness to it when I was dead. I heard all the cruel things he said to you and you still forgave him. I was distressed that you could love a man like that when I never treated you like that. And on the night you chose Lan, I gave my life willingly for you, Ake. I never expected you to return my feelings.'

'What did you see?' Ake placed a hand to her mouth..

'I had intended to propose to you. I saw him sing to you and lean in to kiss you. The look in your eyes said it all. It was easy to lay with Flo after that. I still have the guilt of imagining it was you.'

Ake felt her stomach drop. 'That's awful.'

'Don't get me wrong, I fell in love with Flo that night too. But it wasn't easy to let you go.'

'I couldn't imagine that of you, Het. Pretending Flo was some-one else is cruel. Does she know?'

Het nodded. 'We discussed it at length. Flo is the kindest woman I know. Gentle, wise and understanding. She knew I was in love with you and told me to let you go as you only wanted Lan. She was aware that she would need to give me time to process my feelings.'

'I am sorry, Het. You knew I wasn't in love with you when we kissed. I did not have to return your feelings. In fact, you with-drew from me.'

'I never said you did. I withdrew to give you a chance to pro-cess your emotions. I wasn't angry you loved someone else. I was angry that you chose someone who was so different to you. Where was the brave Ake that should have confronted Lan for his faults?'

Ake gave him a look that made him back off. 'How dare you, Het. If you had continued to watch and not only take parts to com-plain about, you would have seen the whole picture. He changed, became loving, kind and protective. He sacrificed himself for me and Caoimhe. Mystics prefer quiet lives of learning and he was thrust in front of me and expected to protect me against the wrath of a goddess until I was strong enough to defend myself. Are you aware that he was a god in a previous life? He made a pact to serve me, but in the next life he was unaware of that until much later.' Ake paused, her eyes locked on his, waiting for some form of con-firmation. 'I also understand him. Being an orphan of a down-trodden mother, I resonated with an abandoned child. Regona was kind, but put him in a school too young, where responsibility was thrust upon his elfling shoulders. Do you understand elves, Het?'

His eyes riveted on hers.

'You will need to learn for Flo's sake. While you were a man of twenty-four, Lan's body was thirty-three, his intellect around twenty, but his emotional maturity was closer to eighteen. He was a boy. Those of us with elven blood mature differently to giant kin who mature rapidly.'

Het's eyes trained on hers. 'What do you know of that?'

She shrugged. 'Your mother was said to be descended from giant kin.'

'It wasn't a rumour. She was descended from the adopted son of Demund, the last giant king.' Het let out a deep breath. 'I now know why you didn't fight on board the ship.'

Ake looked down at her feet and began to sob. 'I had just left Cephas. Five years of abuse. I saved Flo, but in my grief and fear it didn't register Dane might be aboard and could remove that infernal bracelet. I assumed Serenade would have had the greatest healers on board and she would be okay. Then the ship began to sink.'

Ake glared at him. 'I did try to go back for her. I even asked why Dane couldn't heal her. Why didn't they put her in the boat with us? I never understood that. I could have tried to heal her when we made shore.' She looked up at him through bitter tears. 'Drianna sent those monsters after you, and also sunk that ship. Did we not avenge you both? We took on seventeen hives of Drianna's then defeated the evil goddess herself. I understand if it isn't enough. How can I atone?'

Het pulled her into his arms. 'I understand now. That more than settles it.' He ruffled her hair as she stepped back.

'I must know something?'

He clucked his tongue before clearing his throat. 'It was very painful.'

'How did you know I'd ask that?'

He placed his hand on her shoulder. 'I know you well enough. You sure you want to hear this?'

Ake nodded. 'Please.'

'Flo and I were discussing how one of us could get back to deal with Hau. She said she could ask the parents of her soul.'

Ake's brow furrowed. 'What does that mean?'

'Don't know if I should say.'

'Out with it.'

Het sighed. 'Beldivin, Destiny, Manhannon and Gepatok are her brothers.'

With a tiny gasp, Ake took a step back. 'She's the Morning Star; only daughter of Dee and Sorendee? And my aunt? And cousin in this mortal realm?' Her eyes blazed with fury. 'She should have told me.'

'Yep.' Het shifted on his feet. 'Please don't go off at her. You two women are scary when you are furious.'

'Then why did she need a sacrifice to get back here if she is divine?'

'You should ask your husband about that and the restrictions on the gods. Drianna prevented their mortal forms returning and only a great sacrifice allows them a mortal shell once their first one is destroyed. Or better yet, read that book of his father's he carries with him. It's great reading.'

Ake tapped her foot before crossing her arms. 'Changing the subject, are we?'

'Damn, I thought I could get out of it.' Het grinned but it faded rapidly. 'There were no feelings in the afterworld; no painful ones anyway. Something whispered "Demund, time to return". All at once, I was numb and freezing at the same time is how I would describe it. Screams tore out of me as Flo held me to her, my spirit slowly fading in that place as I could hear bone crunching, before a heartbeat pounded in my ears. Visions of the battle of Caelestis swam before me and my body dumped in a pit with the fallen as a slab of cement slowly blocked out the light.' Het shivered. 'I saw my literal grave. As a human I can return multiple times, but the gods wanted me in this form and made me suffer through that as a reward for their daughter so that she might recognise me when she came back. They are kind and cruel.' A tear rolled down his cheek. 'The pain can only be described as hot; glancing needles in every vein, every pore like a million stings building to some greater agony but never quite reaching it as my body was made flesh again.' Het reached out a hand and touched Ake's shoulder. 'You are very pale now. You shouldn't have asked.'

'I am fine.' She smiled sadly. 'You were always brave no matter the pain you had to endure for those you love.'

'Are you still up to looking around?'

'Yes, but I would prefer to accompany Lan for a bit. This has been taxing. I am sorry I hurt you, Het. How could I have known that in the afterlife you would experience pain? I couldn't talk to a dead man.' Her eyes brimmed with tears and she brushed them away. Het took her hand and kissed it. He gazed down at her; his expression was full of yearning.

Ake stared at him, her mouth agape before she spoke. 'What does that look mean?'

'It means what it means. I will always have a fondness for you.'

Ake backed away from him. 'What about Flo?'

Het reached forward, lifting his hands to cup her face. 'It's time you knew the truth. I've always been able to tell you anything. I died willingly centuries ago, giving up my immortality, my strength, all to seek the voice of a goddess. One who beckoned to me to cross over into the mortal realm to love her when she was reborn. I was once a god too, Ake, and a brother and rival of your husband. When I saw you that day at the village school when we were children there was a feeling of déja vu, and for all those years I thought you were her. I clung to those great feelings of love.' He pressed his forehead to Ake's, his hot breath mingling with hers. 'That stupid prophecy meant the God of Death and Demund,

Lord of Giants, vying for the hands of a goddess bride only for the younger divine twin to be reborn and follow his betrothed to defeat Drianna and sire a saviour.' Het sighed. 'Funny how we only learn of these things when we leave the mortal plane.' He gritted his teeth. 'I thought I had dealt with it all, but when you are returned to your former body your last thoughts and feelings plague you once more.'

'I am sorry for that.' Ake shivered. 'Don't make me remember the bloodshed you caused. I was a golden canary made to sing for the gods. When I was lonely, waiting for my freedom in that gilded birdcage and, as the gods slept, a magnificent fruit bat would settle on top of my enclosure, his unusual dragon wings sparked with lightening and had clawed tips. He spoke with the voice of my betrothed.' Ake paused as her thoughts turned to eons ago when in a past life she had belonged to the Velterran pantheon.

'Lan regaled me with your exploits and how, even though he was blamed for the massacre you created, he still loved and forgave you. He said he was going to become mortal to free me and get away from the responsibility of godhood and right the wrongs by destroying Drianna. That we were not to be married the next day as Drianna had won his title and he'd need to make a great sacrifice in the mortal realm to earn it back.'

'Were you born with memories of Lan?'

'There were whispers of a great love when I reached eighteen, but when Flo told me of my betrothed, I had dreams, visions almost, of a previous life from time to time and Lan's voice reminded me of that great love.'

'So, you were plagued with despair too.' Het gritted his teeth. 'Have you told Lan any of this?'

She tried to draw back, but Het prevented the movement, his hand placed on her hip.

'Not as yet. Please finish what you need to say.' Ake's eyes widened. 'We are both hurting from the pain of the past now. I don't want that for you Het.'

'Ake's gentle mercy continues.' Het smiled. 'Lan kept his word. Our parents followed their favoured child to see he was given justice and that Drianna was defeated. I was too raw, too primitive, being the firstborn during the primordial stirrings of this plane. At least our sisters were born during softer times.' Het pressed a kiss to her forehead and dropped his hands. 'It hurt to realise that even after my confession of love, my protection, you chose my rival, the God of Death, the one responsible for stopping my designated people from killing more of the abhorrent, primitive humans who hunted my kin in my previous life. That it wasn't you who was calling to me, but Flo. But ... you and I had grown up together, and Kathy, my mortal mother, showed me I was worthy, that humans could love giant kin and in turn I loved you as one mortal to another. Do you know what that feels like? To have your heart torn asunder?' Het pulled away, his eyes filling with tenderness. 'To love two women so immensely and the guilt that comes with that?'

'You can't look at me like that? I only ever saw you as a brother.'

He chuckled softly. 'Your heart was his before you were even earthside. I was never a match for that. I won't ever look at you like that again.'

'Make sure you don't.' Ake sighed. 'I will never see you as a rampaging giant king. You are far too gentle this lifetime, and long were you forgiven because of your pure actions this time round. I understood your need for revenge, but it was not the most merciful of choices. Are you okay?'

'All is well between Lan and me, and also you.' Het grinned. 'Don't dwell on it. I bet you feel better now you have let it all out?'

Ake nodded. 'You will inform Lan of your kinship?'

'I can do that.'

'Good. Now, why did you look like a human and Lan an elf?'

Het loosed a long breath. 'Gods have a divine form. Mine is the owl, yours a canary and Flo's a silver rabbit and so forth. The greater gods—Dee, Sorendee, Drianna—and my divine parents can change their forms at will. But their children are lesser gods, born with a singular animal spirit and a mortal form based on the physique when their parents had them. Before the creation of the elves, there were prototypes of people: giants and strange hominids. My people were not the twenty foot tall creatures of fairy tales; humans gave the term giant to anything above six feet tall during those times. We vied for resources in our primeval world. We prefer the name Galroon in ancient Divine, or tall folk. We weren't ridiculous in size—ranging from six foot five to eight feet—but to the tiny humans, we were deemed a threat on resources and their lives so they hastened to kill us.

'My parents conceived me when Regona was favouring the form of giants during the primordial upheaval when the land was one mass with great volcanoes and savage denizens and Dee was beginning to create patches of forests. Our father tried out a new form and that became his favourite and Sorendee's inspiration to create the elves. My parents preferred elvish and half-elvish forms ever since, and then had my sisters. I inherited Regona's giant abilities and Lan Dane's elvish traits. I had to be reborn into a mortal family with giant blood or the infant wouldn't survive the birth.'

'I see. I am glad we had this discussion.'

'We both needed to let the past out, Ake.' Het's eyes filled with fierce intellect. 'As much as you were the bookworm, Ake, I may have appeared to not be as well read as you. But you need to remember, I was the apprentice of an elven druid. I am well aware of elven maturity, despite what you and Lan think. But even I had feelings, Ake, that couldn't be helped. I think I can be forgiven for having emotions.'

'And your feelings for Flo?'

Het blinked in surprise. 'You aren't surprised by my intelligence?'

Ake shook her head. 'You were always cleverer than me.'

'That is not true, Ake. Yours was a lack of application; you were clearly daydreaming. Especially in your last year. I can guess who you were thinking of.'

Ake blushed. 'Well, that's irrelevant now. What of Flo?'

Het smiled and she saw his expression soften. 'The Morning Star shines in the darkest night when all other stars would be dull. My love for her burns like that.'

Ake smiled. 'Never thought I would see the day when you quoted poetry.'

Het guffawed. 'So, I pass your test in regards to my feelings for Flo.'

'Yep.' She rolled her eyes. 'Great, Flo and I must deal with poets, and brothers at that.'

Ake turned as Lan and Flo entered the alley. Her husband held out his arms to her and she ran into them. Lan glanced up at Het. 'I hope you weren't too harsh on her.'

Flo gave Het a gentle smile. 'I doubt it. They needed to vent so we can all move forward.'

Lan turned to Ake. 'I have been reading my father's biography. Dane's druid information is helpful, but I am disturbed by my father's wanton past. I can't believe elves were like that.'

'That is not the norm. Arakaen are very amorous after adulthood with their mates. Unfortunately, Dane met his mate late. You had the luxury of meeting yours early. Usually, Arakaen elflings are betrothed to their mates before their hundredth birthday, beginning around forty human years,' said Flo.

Lan paled. 'I would never have played around.'

'I never said you would have.' Flo smiled. 'Most Arakaen never act too much on these feelings and throw themselves into their vocation, taking an occasional lover until they meet their mate. Your father—'

Lan blushed. 'Like I said, he was a cad before he married my mother.'

Het laughed. 'Should have got him to give us some pointers.'

Ake grinned. 'Nah, he's fine.' She gestured to Lan. 'Tell him now.'

'Not yet.' Het patted Lan on the back. 'Well, it's in the blood.'

'Het,' Flo admonished.

Het gave them all a cheesy grin. 'No, it's really fine. Dane was loyal when he remembered who he truly was. He loved to rile Regona up about it and she returned the favour. It was their thing. He also had a tendency to exaggerate everything.'

Lan cocked his head. 'How would you know that?'

Flo smiled. 'Het. Did you get any pointers?'

Lan and Ake laughed.

'Hey, you are supposed to be on my side.' Het grinned.

Het and Flo began to walk ahead of Ake and Lan. Flo took the big man's hand as he smiled down at his lover and Ake could see the genuine love they had for each other. She turned her head. Her husband watched her, his eyes reflected his all-consuming love and passion for her and she shivered with delight.

Het turned and grinned at her. 'Only you are bold enough to endure love from one of the Fiadhri.'

CHAPTER FIFTY

Lan and Ake wandered through the market. Lan made several purchases for Het that included elven wine and food. Hau encouraged Velterrans to practice elven craft and that included wine making and food preparation, and it saturated Velterra in abundance. They passed various black tents as beings of every kind plied their wares. Lan leant over a tent that was selling various herbs, and breathed in the familiar scents of rosemary, lavender, fennel and many more.

A being with feline ears and tail hissed as he reached out to touch some of the dried herbs. 'Pay first.'

Lan handed over some coins. The cat lady began to purr as she passed over a small pouch of mixed herbs. He moved on to the next stall where a green goblin with blue hair styled in a mohawk grinned, showing serrated teeth.

'Lan.' Ake squeezed his hand.

'Yes honey.' Lan was distracted by some blue flames that wove themselves around the string of a yoyo. He reached out his hand and the flames were cold to the touch. 'I like yoyos.'

Ake gave him a bemused smile as he handed over the gold to the goblin and put the toy in the pocket of his robes.

'Het admitted he cared for me for years after his death. He was angry I chose you. He may not be in love with me anymore, but he still harbours some fondness towards me in looks and touch. I feel guilty telling you this … like I have told on him.'

Ake's gaze dropped and her hand trembled in his.

'I am your husband, Ake. Het would expect you to tell me. We had a discussion of our own. He had already told me that he has a soft spot for you. Don't worry about it. I doubt he kissed you passionately, and I have no doubt of your loyalty. I am not a jealous fool anymore.'

Ake sighed and lifted her eyes to his, her brows knitting in concern. He glanced at a stall selling red roses with burning hearts hovering over them. Grabbing one, he handed it to her then paid the reptilian vendor. She gasped and leapt at him, wrapping her arms around him.

He reached out, guiding her head against his shoulder. 'You have my love, Ake, remember that. Het is not some unscrupulous lecher. I can't think poorly of a man who was so honest with you and me.'

Ake smiled and he pulled away from her, grasping her hand.

Lan's ears picked up the cries of some strange birds. *She adores birds.* He grinned at Ake and led her over to a tent. He could hear a mixture of unusual bird song, including squawks and shrieks.

They entered the tent and were greeted with a multitude of strange birds in every conceivable colour. Some had sharp beaks, others had hollow tubes with tongues that flicked in and out as they made hornlike noises. Others had scales as well as feathers. They fluttered from perch to perch that had been hung from the roof of the tent.

Ake stared at the birds in shock. 'In all my adventures I haven't seen anything like these. Some appear to be a hybrid of several monsters.'

A woman approached them, throwing sawdust on the floor from a bucket to cover any messes. She put the container down. 'Hello my dears. How can I be of assistance?'

Ake pointed to the bird with the strange serpent tongue. 'What is that?'

'That my pet, is a horpent. A mixture of a hornbill and a vicious Regian serpent.' The woman grinned eerily. 'It looks harmless enough and the sounds it makes are delightful, almost comical. It is loyal to its master and can spit toxic poison five feet. The poison doesn't have an odour and burns the skin on contact. The victim falls into a deep slumber before passing away. Beautiful, isn't he?'

Ake shivered. 'No thanks. What is that small one over there?'

'Unlike all these other delightful birds, it is not made at the hands of Lord Hau, may he be eternally blessed.' The woman picked up the bird and brought it over.

Ake held out her hands. Lan went to stop her then put his hands down. 'Not my place to always intervene,' Lan said quietly to himself.

'This is a dragier.'

The little scaled bird leapt about in the woman's hand. Its green scales reflected in the light of a torch nearby. The little bird leapt on to Ake's hands and walked up her arm, nestling itself on her shoulder under her hair. It nibbled gently at her neck.

The woman cackled. 'It has claimed you. Sixteen gold bars, no refunds.'

'Ake, I am happy to buy you anything else.'

Ake smiled at him. 'It's so cute.'

Lan sighed. 'At least be honest about what it does.'

The woman grinned. 'She is a baby now. A harmless baby.'

'Please tell me, Lan,' said Ake.

'That thing is a pest for elves. She will grow to be huge, Ake. She enjoys the flesh of elflings. She will have some kind of toxic breath from fire to poison and the like.'

'Hand over the gold. It has imprinted on her and cannot be resold.'

'No.' Lan glared at the woman.

'There are no elflings anymore. Why would you be concerned?'

Ake tried to remove the little bird and it crawled down her dress, cheeping pitifully.

'It has imprinted on her. Hand over the gold.' The woman reached out and put a firm hand on Ake's shoulder. Ake pushed it away. The woman stumbled back, swore, then smirked at them.

There was a loud growl and a muscled troll came out of a large pile of hay in the corner. At ten feet tall its large bulbous head scraped the roof. It snarled and saliva dripped from rotting fangs as it scratched at the filthy fur that covered most of its grey skin.

'Come and deal with these thieves,' cried the woman.

Lan sighed. 'I can kill that in a few minutes. I will strike a deal with you. I give you five gold bars and you keep the bird.'

The woman began to screech. Her long, grey hair began to writhe and she opened her mouth. A reeking yellow miasma streamed from it. Lan coughed and rubbed his stinging eyes. There was a sudden thud and he jumped out of the way. He swore. *Damn it, I must protect her.*

Ake blinked her bloodshot eyes and stormed towards the vendor who scratched at her arm, causing Ake to wince. The hag screeched and bit her as Ake flung her away. The bird climbed out of her dress and onto her head, cheeping angrily before diving into a pocket. She grabbed her opponent by the hair and dragged her outside.

With the room clear, Lan leapt onto the troll's back and the creature grabbed him by his arm with its huge fist. Lan grinned, pushed himself off the troll and began to swing back and forth, trying to get enough motion to deliver a kick. The troll looked confused before drawing him up to its snarling lips and drool dripped down on to Lan.

'Urrgh.'

The troll replied. 'Urrgh'

Lan made a ridiculous growl.

The creature's lips curled back in an angry snarl as it roared in Lan's face; spittle and decaying food was flung over him.

Enough with these games. Lan used his other foot to gain purchase on the troll's arm. He landed one way then rotated off the same foot and delivered a sharp kick to the monster's nose. The troll dropped him and grabbed its nose. He ran towards the monster as it tried to bring its huge fists down on him. Running up its arm, he delivered an open-hand strike to its neck. It roared and stumbled back.

Lan was about to release his hidden blade to deliver a killing blow when he saw the spiked control collar around the creature's neck, hidden in its fur. *I would have delivered that blow centuries ago.* Instead, Lan concentrated his *Mystic Fire* on the latch. The latch absorbed the fire. There was a large click and the collar fell to the floor.

The troll reached for him and Lan rolled out of the way. 'You are free!'

'Grrrrroowl.' The beast picked up one of the rare birds and popped it in its mouth. There was a terrible crunching noise.

'Ah, okay then.'

As the beast began to eat more of the rare birds, Lan captured some of the less dangerous ones and thrust them out of the tent. While he was distracted, the monster grabbed him.

'I don't want to kill you.'

The monster looked confused.

I wonder. Lan swore. The beast blinked in recognition. 'Oh gods, she named you that?'

The troll opened its hideous mouth. It thrust its tongue towards Lan. He struggled against its grip, searching around for something to help him. His eyes fell on the torch, too far out of his reach. Instead, he picked up a nearby pitcher of water with his telekinesis and doused the flames, throwing the tent into darkness. The monster began a hideous whine, a mix between a large dog and a gorilla. *A troll frightened of the dark, how absurd.* He heard it pant.

'Ah, good boy S——.'

The beast made a smacking noise with its lips and Lan felt its rough, moist tongue lick him.

'Damn it. Down, S——.'

The troll dropped him and Lan lit the torch with *Mystic Fire*. He stood staring at the troll. The troll grimaced at him and whined.

—~~—

Meanwhile outside, the hag leapt at Ake, jabbering like a fool. Ake felt the hairs on the back of her neck stand up. Her enemy cackled and Ake turned towards the tent. Fear washed over her, distorting her reality. The tent's opening appeared like a cavernous mouth. Her eyes glazed over as it leant towards her, its fangs dripping ...

Ake shook her head, resisting the curse. She pivoted on her heel to face her enemy, shooting a jet of water at her, sending the crazy hag stumbling into another tent.

With her enemy down, she returned her attention to the tent, wanting to help Lan. A flood of birds erupted from the doorway as she reached it, pushing her backwards. In her distraction, the hag leapt on to her back, tearing at her hair and pulling out clumps. Ake cried out, then held her breath and engulfed them in water. She stepped out of the bubble and watched as the hag began to swim around searching for an exit. Ake reached into the bubble and grabbed the woman by the hair and proceeded into the tent. As she did so she released the spell.

—~~—

Lan turned to see Ake dragging the hag back into the tent. Ake's arms were bleeding from bites and scratches and parts of her hair was patchy. Lan glared at the hag.

'We will leave you five gold bars; we are not thieves. We will take that damn bird of yours and try to set it free, away from cities.'

The hag got up and ran, screeching, towards Lan. The troll grabbed the mad thing.

'Put it down, S——!'

Ake stared at him. 'She named it that?'

'I think so.'

The troll shook its head and threw back its head. The hag bellowed. Ake cast *Mystic Fire* at the troll's hand. 'Please put it down.'

The troll whined, and Lan saw Ake's eyes fill with pity. 'No, Ake, we can't keep it.'

Ake inched towards the troll. It snarled at her and sucked on its thumb and the hag's hair, getting a taste, and then the troll shoved the hag in its mouth. Ake gagged as a nasty crunching noise filled the tent. Lan rushed over, grabbed Ake's hand and ran from the tent. The troll howled and thundered after them.

Lan wove down alleyways and screams echoed after them as the troll flung people out of the way.

———

Het's arms were loaded with purchases. He stared at her as she added more parcels. 'Umm, Flo, isn't this enough?'

'I can't find these elven delicacies in the rest of the city. Did I ever tell you I am an outrageous shopper?' Flo gave him a wicked smile.

'The great empress has a weakness.'

She turned her violet eyes to him and he became lost in the depths of them. 'Is that okay?'

'It's fine.' Het blushed and looked away.

Something bellowed and came thundering between the tents. Het tossed the parcels, picked up Flo and captured most of the parcels in his other hand as Ake and Lan ran past, a troll in hot pursuit.

'Do you need any help?' asked Het.

'We've got this!' yelled Lan.

The troll rushed past and Het leant Flo against the wall with his large muscly body pressing into her tiny frame. Flo blushed.

'Danger gets a man's blood up.' Het dropped the parcels and kissed her. He saw an opportunity and took her down an alleyway. Caught up in his need for her, he didn't have the grace or charm to take her somewhere posh and befitting of an empress. He kicked open the door of a warehouse he knew was empty, dropping her gently on a stack of cardboard. Flo giggled as he ran out the door. He returned shortly, his arms loaded with some of their parcels, which he tossed in a corner. 'I left the heavier ones near the door.'

Flo shyly began to undress as Het slammed the door shut and threw off his clothing before kneeling down beside her. She lifted her head and kissed him with gentle need.

'You should know, I expressed my fondness to Ake and hugged her closely.' Het's hand trembled. 'It was wrong of me. But when I came back into this body, I was just so angry; it was suddenly raw again.' He shuddered. 'I needed to make sure she knew how I'd felt for her, to make her understand.'

Flo smiled gently. 'Thank you for your honesty.' She caressed his face. 'And, does it feel like what is between us? Would you have kissed her?'

He shook his head. 'No; it is a memory of a shared past. Those feelings were never my future. My heart was never meant to be hers.'

'So, it is all mine?'

'It has always been, I just didn't know it.'

She leant into him. 'I knew as much. There is nothing to forgive then.'

'How can you be so understanding?' He pressed a soft kiss to her mouth. 'So gentle and kind.' He leant in to whisper against her neck. 'I know I lack finesse.' He growled and pulled her hips to his.

'I love your wildness, my primordial, gentle giant. Show me. I can handle it; as I always do.'

Het's expression darkened. 'As long as I'm giant in the areas that matter.'

Her sweet giggles were muffled as he kissed her fiercely. Her nails dug into his back as he took her; his need deep and wild. She responded with such skill it drove him to complete abandonment. Flo's body trembled with delight as her petite frame was cradled against his muscular one. Het's hazel eyes were feral with need as they rode the frenzied waves of pleasure together. He loosed her hair from their fastenings and his hand coiled among the silken locks. Grabbing her small chin in his other large hand, he savaged her lips with his own. When he pulled away, her delicate mouth felt swollen from his intensity. As their bodies reached their climax, their breathing came in ragged waves before Het collapsed on top of her.

When their hearts began to beat within their normal rhythm, he rolled off her. Flo sighed and he turned towards her; their eyes met, his loving gaze made her heart flutter, and when he kissed her gently, she melted against him.

———

As they reached the outer parts of the city, Lan turned and slowed down. 'No hurting, S——.'

The troll howled then tried to be more considerate of others by not slapping the citizens out of the way as he followed Lan.

'This is absurd, Ake. Do things like this happen often in black markets?'

Ake grinned. 'Not unheard of.'

They reached a wall that was beginning to crumble.

'Climb, S——, there's a good boy.'

The troll began to clamber over the wall. It turned and picked a large glob of earwax and offered it to Lan.

'No thanks.'

The troll whimpered.

'You won't come back if I take it?'

The troll growled.

Lan reached out a finger and touched the quivering jelly substance; mites wriggled in the muck. He felt the bile rise in his throat.

The monster grimaced, climbed over the wall and ran on all fours away from Velterra.

'You didn't kill it, Lan. Thank you.' Ake went to hug him and stepped back as the smell hit her.

'Public baths?'

'Yes.'

'But first, let's find Het and deliver his goods.'

'Where did you put them?'

Lan swore; he heard a very distant growl and smiled.

'I am sure they will make do without us.'

He reached out and untied her hair and winced in sympathy. 'I will have to tend those wounds.'

Ake shrugged and kissed him. 'Ick, I shouldn't have done that.'

Lan laughed. 'Probably not.'

As the morning sunlight streaked in through the dirty window, Flo rose and dressed. She took a little pouch from her dress, wadded up a ball of herbs and chewed the bitter concoction. She pulled a face. *I shouldn't ever bear another child after what our Hau has become. Maybe I should teach Ake and Hartur this secret too.*

Het yawned, rolled over and stared at her. 'I am sorry it was done here.'

Flo smiled. 'It's fine.'

Het eased himself up. 'I am going to marry you and I couldn't be happier. I am sorry I am not some royal elf worthy of such a magnificent empress.'

'Thank goodness you are not. I never went in for that cousin-marrying nonsense.'

'Can I ask you something?'

'Of course.'

'Ake and Lan, what are their bloodlines?'

Flo's eyes filled with guilt and her forehead wrinkled in concern.

'Sorry I asked. Please forgive me.' Het reached out and stroked her face.

'Serenade would have had them related by blood. As an empress I had a say. When he asked my opinion on the impending births of the children of prophecy he asked how close their blood should be. Disgusted at the thought, I suggested Dane and Teja as sires. Lan and Ake would only be related by marriage and not blood, because they were destined to be gods that walked the earth and not the heavens, and their bodies would remain the same. I knew that would be important to them. I should never even have suggested marriage bonds.'

'Serenade dared to ask a young elfling maiden that?'

'I was in my twenties, Het. As an empress, there was no time for the luxury of elflinghood.'

'Does Lan know you are related to him by blood? Heck, I kinda let Ake know that not only are you her cousin in the mortal realm, but in the Velterran pantheon you are her aunt.'

'Oh dear. I'll deal with that backlash later.' Flo sighed. 'Lan believes we are related by marriage only. I would prefer him not to know. He would be devastated to know how close he came to being related by blood to his wife.'

'I will not tell as it is done. But they should have known.'

'Ake is aware of the marriage links.'

'She may have informed him.'

'No. Ake and Lan had a simple conversation. Lan said he knew he was my uncle, but he never mentioned blood. I witnessed Dane bring up a simple conversation with Lan once, stating that Serenade's daughter was related by marriage. I assume poor Ake believed Lan already knew.'

'Children of prophecy.' Het grinned. 'Did you know I originally thought the prophecy was only about Ake? Before I died and knew better.'

Flo shook her head. 'It was as much Lan's prophecy as it was Ake's and yours.'

'Explains a lot. Those two are very odd.' Het grinned. 'Adorable but odd.'

Flo laughed. 'Don't be mean.' She pushed him away playfully and threw his pants at him. 'Let's go. I would marry if you still want me after that lengthy omission.' She gave him a tender smile.

'Thank goodness you did intervene. I would love nothing more than to marry you, Flo.' Het rushed to put on his clothes. 'Please wait a moment.'

He walked over to a stack of newspaper where he had hidden the more valuable item he had purchased. He picked up the item wrapped in brown paper and tied with string and held it out to her. She opened it daintily, unwrapping the gift and pulling out the garment within; a beautiful red and gold brocade gown. The sleeves were long and there were magnificent silk petticoats underneath.

'You can't afford this, Het.'

'I will be able to over time. Lan lent me the money. But I chose it myself. Do you hate it?'

Flo undressed and donned the gown. 'It's perfect.'

She began to tie up her hair. He pulled a silk ribbon from his pocket. 'Let me do it, please.'

She let him; his big hands were gentle as they tied her hair up in a simple ponytail.

Het took her hand and led Flo from the building, picking up the parcels along the way that were strewn outside. Several were missing. The tents were gone; the market moved to a different area each night. It was home to scoundrels, cutthroats and outcasts, selling stolen and dangerous goods as well as rare luxuries.

They took the ten-minute walk down a weaving alleyway and entered the hospitality quadrant. Het smiled lovingly down at her as they entered a four-storey, red brick building. There were many people coming and going. People turned to stare at Flo and bowed.

'It's a real elf maiden.'

'I've seen a male elf hanging around the industrial district.'

'By Hau's grace, he is restoring the elves to their glory.'

Het pulled her into his side and pushed past the people; they scattered. Several began to follow them inside the building. They entered a beige room with multiple stairwells leading to the upper floors. Men and women in robes sat at desks with signs on them, their faces impassive as they laboured at their tedious tasks. Het's boots made a dull thud as he walked over the grey floorboards.

They lined up at the union registration line where the clerk would look at the number on their arms and then ask them a few questions before signing off on the paperwork as a witness. The process was bland and efficient.

'You sure you don't want a fancy wedding?' asked Het.

'No, I just want to be officially yours.'

'Next,' said a clerk.

They walked up to the clerk who thrust a paper and quill towards them, barely glancing at their arms as he said in a bored tone, 'Write your names. Read the terms and sign them, and I will give you a copy.'

Het read the form. 'Do you agree to this union? This union will confer benefits to the married couple in accordance with their birth rank. These details are found on the back of this form. Each party enters into this equally and all assets shall be split evenly in case of separation.'

Flo reached out and took up the quill and began filling out the form. Under birth rank she wrote zero and signed her name.

Het did the same with his details. The clerk stamped the form and gave them a copy. 'May you be blessed with elflings that will see your legacy grow. Next.'

Flo and Het stepped to the side. Het kissed her. 'Are you happy, my beautiful bride?'

Flo smiled. 'Yes. I get to be with you.'

As they were walking through the door Flo heard the clerk call out. 'Get this copy over to Lord Hau.'

CHAPTER FIFTY-ONE

As Ake left the wooden building, she was greeted with the hum of city life. Children played in the dirty streets, their faces streaked with dust, their clothes stained with breakfast and mud. Rider and horse clattered by, the skirts of her yellow dress wafted upwards and a drunk man lurking in an alleyway leered at her legs.

'Can I blow up your skirts for a gold bar, missy?'

She hurried past clutching her woven basket closer and crossed the street. *I hope this counsellor can help Lan. He has much improved since Alwin helped but I think talking to someone will help long term. Too bad we have to lie a little as no one would believe we are gods.* She smiled to herself as she drew out a list of Lan's favourite foods. *Hopefully a nice dinner will cheer him somewhat.* She turned down an alley and exited into a small courtyard. She stared down at the address the counsellor's assistant had given her. *This can't be right.*

Surrounded on three sides by large stone buildings, with only one exit, the structures appeared to lean in, their long roofs sheltering the area from direct sunlight. Ake rolled her eyes as she heard footsteps behind her.

'I'm not interested in your gold.'

'Oh really? I am a very rich elf.'

Ake stiffened and turned to face the newcomer.

'Fancy meeting you here.' Hau stood there, dressed in white

velvet robes embroidered with golden leaves surrounding a white leopard. 'Oh I am dressed for the occasion it seems. Join me for lunch.'

Ake scoffed. 'Why would I do that?'

Hau snickered. 'Well, that lovely assistant who gave you that list is in my service.'

Ake's nails dug into her palms. 'What have you done to Lan?'

Hau's eyes narrowed. 'Join me for lunch and I will give you the antidote. Don't and he will die. I've had enough of your little ragtag band of misfits interfering with what I've built.'

Ake laughed and strode towards him. 'Built. You are proud of this den of sin and cruelty?'

Hau glared down at her. 'At least I have a legacy. Lan has a forgotten school and you are lost to some ancient story that is often mistaken for myth.'

Ake's eyes softened. 'All names are eventually lost to the passage of time. When a loved one is long forgotten something enduring remains. A seed once planted and nurtured from acts of kindness and lessons of compassion handed down through the eons, that is a legacy that blooms and never dies.'

Hau sighed. 'You always were extremely soppy.' He closed the gap between them and held up his arm. 'Luncheon or your husband dies.'

Ake hooked her arm in his; he turned and led her towards the exit then stopped suddenly. Releasing her arm, he reached into the pocket of his robes and withdrew a dagger. Her eyes widened and his arm lashed out and grabbed her throat. 'Sweet, gullible Ake.'

He raised the dagger and slid it along her neck, nicking the skin and bringing it to rest under her ear. He reached into his pocket and lifted a vial to the small nick. Pressing his fingers to the wound, blood dripped into the vial and he stoppered it as Ake scratched his face. Hau gasped as her knee came up to deliver a blow to his abdomen. He stumbled out of the way as she summoned flame and hurled it at him.

'Is that all you've got? Childish spells?' He made a v with his index and middle finger, bringing them to his lips he blew through them like he was trying to inflate a wineskin. There was a horrid roar as a green wave of viscous fluid splattered Ake from head to toe. Hau stalked towards her. 'Don't gasp, dear cousin, one breath and you would die a horrid death.' Hau tutted. 'Basilisk poison; the pain is described as having your stomach rot from acid, then you are filled with horrid thoughts and visions before you fall into a coma and your emaciated body succumbs from starvation, craving only more of the venom. There are no known survivors without a ready supply of the diluted toxin.'

Ake's cheeks bulged as she held her breath and her eyes flitted about. Hau lunged towards her and her fist connected with his nose before she torched her dress, leaving her in only her shift. Her face contorted in pain until she covered herself in a water shield, taking a hug gasp of air as her enemy caused the sky to darken in the small space. All light suddenly failed to exist.

She shivered and held up her hand. A large gash appeared in the suffocating dark; a hint of sunlight in the depths of the void began to spread outwards, chunks of darkness fractured and vanished

Her water shield exploded, spraying her shift and she glanced to the now visible exit. She gasped as a hand grabbed her by the hair and wrenched her head back, a dagger slipping under her chin before, with a swift movement, he cut a lock of her hair and stepped away.

'This has been fun.' He winked at her. 'Powerful, aren't you?'

'Give me the antidote.' She held out her hand. 'You know you could sit down and talk to us and we could help you stop your wicked ways.'

He chuckled. 'You really thought I would bow before you, dear cousin. What, should I start weeping with remorse? Shall we hug it out?' He held up a middle finger. 'Oh, better yet, I will just hand my crown to my mother, step down and beg her for forgiveness.'

Ake rolled her eyes. 'Whatever.'

'Do not roll your eyes at me. I am your king.'

Ake snubbed her nose at him. 'Uncrowned prince. Just a lord.'

He scowled, reached into his pocket and retrieved a vial. He wove it between his fingers before he tossed it in the air. 'Very rare cure.'

Ake bolted and caught the object; her lip trembled when his dagger drove into her side.

'Best try and heal up before taking me on again.' He held up the dagger; her warm blood coated the blade and ran down his fingers. He put the knife to his mouth. 'Divine.'

Ake clutched at her side and winced as the blood gushed over her hands. 'You are sick.'

'Oh Goddess of Mercy, what do you suggest for a cure?' Hau turned on his heel. 'Say hi to Lan for us.'

Hau stopped suddenly; the ground beneath him cracked. He craned his head over his shoulder to watch a slow grin spread across Ake's lips before she muttered to herself. The ground at his feet fell away and his chilling scream echoed as a stalagmite loomed upwards and stabbed into his right arm. He groaned as he pulled his arm off the spike. Leveraging himself with his left, he pulled himself out of the man-sized hole. He lay a few minutes, breathing heavy as Ake stumbled past him and out of the courtyard.

—∿∿—

Lan turned his head as the door crashed open. He sat up on the sofa; the look of the man seated opposite to him writing with ink

was one of fear as Ake stood in the doorway, her hair dishevelled and dressed only in her shift. It would almost be comical if
it wasn't for the blood running down her side.

Her eyes flitted to the half-drunk cups of tea now cold on the
tray, before she hurried past the flustered counsellor, unstoppered
a vial and held it to Lan's lips. He gulped when the look she gave
him could wither a hag, before he bolted upright and removed his
shirt to press it to her wound.

'Go get help.' Lan stared at the poor therapist whose mouth
looked almost unhinged.

As the counsellor scurried away Lan positioned his wife on
the sofa.

'We need to get the others together to discuss how we are
going to deal with Hau.' Ake scowled. 'The sooner the better.' She
smirked. 'But he's wounded too.'

Ake winced as Lan shifted his hands, there was a kerfuffle outside and Het filled the doorway.

'Was in the pub. Someone was shouting about blood and dead
women.' Het pushed himself into the even more cramped space
and knelt before Ake. She closed her eyes and unleashed a long
sigh as green light flooded from his hands. 'I need more practice.'

Lan cleared his throat and Het turned his head away as Lan
ripped Ake's shift and lifted away his shirt. ' Not bad. It will hold
until we get her to Flo.'

'Het turned back as Lan covered his wife with the soiled shirt.
'Why did you take on Hau.'

Ake frowned. 'I thought I could reason with him then he said
he'd poisoned Lan with basilisk venom. I got the antidote though.'

Lan's gaze softened. 'Honey, I'm immune to most toxins. You
got yourself injured for me.'

'Always foolhardy for those she loves.' Het stood and strode
towards the door.

'Like you can talk.' Ake winced as she sat up.

Het turned and grinned. 'Of course. Now, we have to look for the others and deal with this lost kid of mine.'

Ake's brow wrinkled. 'Het, you don't have to be cheery all the time.'

The warrior's eyes locked on hers. 'It's that or fall into a pit of despair. We meet at mine at in an hour. Flo will patch you up, and the drinks are on me.'

Their friend strode from the room, Lan lifted his wife into his arms and followed.

—∾—

Pleasure tingled down Hau's spine as he dropped the dagger, holding his bleeding hand over the lock of hair, allowing his life forces to be absorbed before adding the hair to the vial of Ake's blood which he drew from inside his robes. Then he wrapped his hand in a cloth. His right arm still ached despite the administrations from his healers and it was stiff when he moved it.

Vera walked into the room accompanied by a guard. She approached him and lay prone on the ground in total obedience to her lord.

'You can leave us.' Hau approached Vera and offered her a hand. He pulled her up and dragged her over to his throne.

Vera sat down, her body shaking and her face paler than usual.

'You are right to be afraid.' Hau unstoppered the vial and pressed it to her lips. 'Drink.'

Vera gulped the contents down. 'Urgh, it tastes foul.'

Hau's gaze softened. 'I know, but it must be done.' He placed his hands on her abdomen.

She screamed as her face contorted in pain; tendrils of blood seeped from his hands and entered her writhing body. 'It hurts.'

Hau sighed. 'Birth always hurts; it's a dangerous affair.' *And my blood and Ake's has made it worse.* He scowled. *My link to Lan has somehow been severed so I cannot see what they are up to. Alas, I need an heir in case I die, Velterra must go on, with or without me.*

Hau smiled as Vera grunted. 'Why, my lord? I have done everything you asked of me.'

'Your brother will come for me soon. That is why this child needs to come early, having his nephew on the throne may deter him and the others from harming me. That is why I accelerated the child's growth. Your great-grandmother was born months too early and survived. I hope, by using my blood and your divine heritage, our child will be able to survive the quickening process.' *If this works out I can replace the elven population quickly.*

'Was I nothing more than a brood mare?' Vera bit her lip.

Hau patted her on the shoulder. 'No, you were amusing. I am fond of you, but the elven legacy is more important. More important than even my fondness for your grandfather.'

A baby wailed. Hau reached down and looked over his son.

'You have failed me, Vera. I needed a girl.' Hau picked up the child and cut the cord with a dagger. 'He is half-elven as well.'

The baby had pointed ears, but his face was broader, and the hazel eyes did not have the luminosity that was common with elves. Hau felt the child's downy chestnut curls.

'He is a reasonable child, I guess.' He went to hand the baby to his mother, but she had slumped down in the chair. Pressing a finger into the hollow of her neck, he sighed. 'Well, death is an unfortunate side effect. I will have to work on that.' He quelled the urge to weep, clicked his fingers and a servant came and dragged Vera's body away while another proceeded to clean the throne. 'Bury her with the honours befitting an elven consort.'

The baby began to wail and Hau cradled him against his chest. 'Your name is Vero in honour of your mother. She was a docile and willing mate. You are my heir. It is unfortunate you are not female and not fully elven, that would have made me happier, but you will have to do. My father brings danger to my doorstop.' The child snuggled into him and he brushed a tear away with the back of his hand. 'I have lost many wives and children and did not weep. Why so now?' Hau walked over to a desk and sat down. He placed the baby over his shoulder and the newborn lifted his head and sucked on his father's cheek. Hau laughed and glanced at a servant, expecting them to flinch. They gave him a nervous smile.

'It seems my laughter is a sound no longer feared.'

'It is almost joyous, Lord Hau.' The servant lay prone at his feet.

'You must fear me or how else will you respect me?' Hau picked up a book and raised it above his head. Vero cooed and Hau smiled. 'Oh, just get out of here.' Hau waved the servant away. They scrambled to their feet and sprinted out of the room.

'Hau is at his weakest after our last encounter.' Ake squeezed Flo's hand and the friends smiled at each other.

Flo took a sip of wine and turned to the others. 'We cannot assault the palace directly. This is where Hartur and Ake will come in. They will sneak into the palace and secure the where-abouts of Hau.'

'Yay, my wife is directly in danger again,' mumbled Lan, as he edged closer to Ake who was seated on the floor next to him in Het's shack. A few bottles of ale and wine sat between them all.

'Why are we meeting without the whole group?' Hartur frowned.

Het smiled. 'Do we really want to involve a newlywed pair? Besides they are on their honeymoon for at least another week.'

Flo shifted and placed her glass beside her then leant forward with her hands on her crossed knees. 'I say we strike within a day or two. Ake says there is no reasoning with my son, and with all of Amities's weapons gathered in one spot we may have a chance.'

'What does Hartur's hammer actually do?' asked Alena.

Hartur unhooked the hammer from her belt. 'I can show you.'

'Try it on me.' Alwin glanced at his wife.

'That may humiliate you, master. Are you sure?' asked Nietra.

'It is fine,' said Alwin.

'I obey.' The head of Nietra began to glow; whisps of smoke seeped out of the weapon and wove themselves around Alwin.

'Still can't get used to pictures forming in my head against my will. You refuse to open yourself to your full potential, Alwin.' Hartur giggled. 'And you are deathly afraid of cockroaches.'

Het broke out into jovial laughter. 'Cockroaches. What a strange thing for a man to be frightened of.'

Flo and Ake grinned at each other. 'They are more eerie looking than moths.'

Lan smiled briefly. 'Are you afraid of moths, Het?'

Het shrugged and smiled. 'Have you seen those large, hairy moths? They are the big buggers with four hairy tails they wave around. Hideous things, and when they land on your face it makes your skin crawl.'

Nietra, attracted to the fear, reached out its smoky tendrils towards the group. The waves shot out towards Lan.

Lan shivered and his eyes filled with pain.

'Poor guy.' Hartur shivered.

'Enough, Nietra.' Alwin handed the hammer back to Hartur. 'I can wield the hammer so there is no need for my wife to join us. She is not a god, a mage or even a warrior.'

'You don't get to decide that.' Hartur brushed her husband's shoulder with her hand. 'I will stay in the shadows and out of the main fight.'

Alwin nodded. 'Alright then.'

'Do you think we can do this?' Lan picked up a glass of beer and took a swill.

Ake shoulders slumped. 'He is very powerful.'

Flo sighed. 'That could be a problem. But I have crafted some items that could aid us.'

Alwin shivered as fear, dejection and hopelessness flooded his senses. He pointed above the large warrior leaning against the mantle of the hearth. 'Look a moth.'

'Where?' Het jumped before he grinned. 'Wow, you finally managed a joke.'

Hartur waved her hand and Het's smile faded as a large pencil moth flew towards him, its tail almost mocking him as it swayed back and forth.

Flo and Ake giggled as the big warrior stumbled then composed himself as the creature disappeared with a resounding pop.

Het tutted. 'Always the butt of jokes.'

'So, a week from now at the palace?' Lan stood and stretched.

'Correct.' Flo smiled and her eyes softened. 'I believe we will get through to him.'

Ake's eyes darted to her husband's and they exchanged a worried glance. 'Let's hope so,' she muttered.

CHAPTER FIFTY-TWO

There was an embellishment of trumpets as nobly dressed musicians marched through the street. People clapped and cheered as magen and mages cast illusions of a young prince Hau riding a unicorn stallion. Hau was dressed in richly adorned robes and borne on a litter hoisted by an ogre. People gasped as he stood and raised a tiny infant with pointed ears to the crowd. The feisty baby wailed and waved his fists and kicked his legs from under his white, silk gown lined with lace.

'This is your crown prince. Vero, son of Lord Hau and consort Vera, born this morning, the twenty-first of September. His mother was a daughter of Anwyn, the granddaughter of Telewanake and Trebrelan, Lord and Lady of Caelestis. Royal elven blood runs through his veins.' Hau smiled. 'Do you accept him?'

The crowd cheered. 'By Lord Hau's grace we accept him.' The citizens of Velterra knelt down.

'His mother was a willing mate and met her demise heroically giving life to him. May she rest in peace.' Hau gestured to the musicians and they began to sing the Velterran dirge.

Alwin dropped the bag of groceries he was carrying and stared at Hau as he mentioned a dead daughter of Anwyn. He shuddered. *I never got to meet her and now she is dead because he took her to bed and she bore his child.* Picking up the groceries, Alwin sprinted home.

The procession continued as he ran, and Hau held out his hand in greeting to his assembled citizens.

Alwin thrust the key into the lock and pushed open the door. Hartur had swept the floor and cleared the room of spiderwebs. She was busy applying paint to the inside of the tiny house. She coughed as the fumes of the red lead paint reached her nostrils. She turned as Alwin flung a bag of groceries on the table, drew a ragged breath and pulled her into his arms.

'Alwin, what is it?'

'My sister is dead. She died giving birth to Hau's new heir.'

'That seems improbable. He hasn't been mortal long enough for a child to be born. He has probably adopted some infant to pass off as his own.'

Alwin shivered. 'His emotions suggest the truth. He also knew her name.'

Hartur made a noise of disgust. 'There is only one way he could have done that. Blood magic.'

'We can open that window now I am back.'

Hartur bopped him on the nose with the tip of the paintbrush, leaving a tiny bit of paint and laughed. Alwin grinned at her and walked over to the window.

Alwin glanced at his bow leaning against the wall. 'Dage, is the wind right to not let a dreadful stench in?'

The bow hummed and glowed. '*Yes, m-ast-er.*'

Alwin pulled the window ajar and a warm breeze rustled his hair. He turned to stare at her as she began sorting the groceries: bread, eggs, butter, tea, flour and bottles of clean water. *No one dares to drink the water in the Revengez quadrant.*

'I couldn't afford meat or vegetables, Hartur.'

'We will make do. We get our benefits tomorrow.'

'We never went without in Cirichad. What are benefits?'

'I reregistered our marriage at the union office. It gives us benefits depending on our birth rank. You are a four due to Amities's bloodline.'

Alwin puffed out his chest. 'I can look after us.'

'Don't be proud, Alwin.'

'I am not being proud. Cirichad responsibility dictates if a man cannot provide for his household he is frowned upon.'

'And what of the woman's responsibility?'

'Cirites are not opposed to women being providers, Hartur.'

'Don't Cirites also provide for those without?'

Alwin pondered for a moment. 'That is correct.' He sighed. 'I suppose it's no different. What are they giving us?'

Hartur took out the marriage certificate from a cupboard and handed it to Alwin who gave it a cursory glance.

'That's a lot for free.'

'It will be useful.' Hartur smiled. 'They will deliver it in the morning. I've already chosen the items.'

'Okay. What should we make for dinner?'

'Eggs on toast it is.' Hartur took out a frying pan and proceeded to the hearth. Alwin smiled as she conjured a flame and fed the fire with kindling before lowering the pan on to it. The pan sizzled as she cracked the eggs into the pan and threw the shells upon the fire. Alwin tore up hunks of bread before placing them on a knife and holding them over the flames as they toasted.

As they ate their meal, seated near the hearth, Alwin became lost in thought.

'What is it?'

'Lufar wants me to alter his pistol for him.' Alwin sighed. 'I'm not sure I am capable of it.'

Hartur squeezed his hand. 'Amities believed in you. I do as well.'

Alwin gave her a chaste kiss before he rose from the floor. He held out a hand; she took it and he pulled her up.

'I guess I can try.'

Hartur yawned and they strode over to the bed. Alwin pulled back the covers and she climbed in.

'I need to distract myself from thoughts of Hau and my sister. Do you mind if I go work on this now? I'll only be gone a few hours.'

Hartur nodded and closed her eyes. He covered her with the blankets and grabbed his bow as he exited the cabin, pulled the door shut and locked it with the key. He jogged towards the forge. His master came out and began sweeping the surrounding area.

'Wait.'

The man turned and smiled at him. 'What is it?'

'Are the fires out yet?'

'No, not for another hour.'

'I'll close. I want to finish a project I've been working on.'

The man handed over a set of keys. 'Make sure you put it out properly.'

Alwin entered the forge and strode over to a cabinet. He unlocked it with a key and pulled out Lan's pistol.

Alwin stared at the pistol; feelings of frustration welled up as he had already attempted the task earlier that day. He had talked to it calmly, yelled at it, prodded it and even pulled it apart and put it back together. He needed to get to a sealed chamber only accessible with a password. He had tried many including Anwyn, his name and Carolina's.

'Why won't you talk to me?' he asked gently.

Lan had asked him to add an option to fire small canisters of oil and his bullets as necessary in case Hau called on his Sworks. Alwin dropped the pistol on the bench and went outside for some fresh air. He breathed in deeply. *I am looking at this the wrong way. This is Lufar's gun not my grandfather's.*

Alwin strode back inside and sat down, staring at the weapon.

He began to concentrate and closed his eyes. Reaching out with his emotions, he sent a wave of love to the gun. The weapon began to hum. Alwin stood up quickly and walked over it.

'Ake.'

The humming rose to a crescendo. Alwin watched in fascination as words, that had once been hidden, began to glow on the barrel. He ran his hands over the barrel and translated the elvish runes. 'In the silence of death your name brings me peace, my beloved Ake.' *Grandfather really was overly romantic.*

'*I greet you, Lord of the Forge. I am Hushin. How may I be of assistance?*' asked the pistol.

'I need to alter you, get to your heart.'

'*You will need the mistress for that.*'

Alwin sighed and picked up the gun. 'By that I assume you mean Ake.'

'*Yes,*' said Hushin.

Alwin jogged out of the forge, taking the twenty minute short-cut to Ake and Lan's house. He hammered on the door with his fist. His heart pounded in earnest as he was caught up in the joy of his craftmanship. The door was pulled open and Lan smiled at him.

'Hello Alwin.'

'Hello. Where is Luma?'

Lan opened the door. Ake was asleep in one of the rocking chairs. 'Come in.'

Alwin strode past Lan and gently shook Ake awake. She looked up at him. 'Hello Alwin, are you okay?'

'Yes, Luma, just touch the pistol.'

'Okay.' Ake reached her hand out and placed it on the gun.

It glowed gold then silver. '*Hello mistress. You unlock the heart of me.*'

Alwin smiled and began taking the gun apart. He reached the

centre of the gun and it opened without any resistance. 'Okay, I have to go. I will have this back to you in a few hours.'

As Alwin ran out the door, he heard his great-grandparents' conversation as Lan began to close the door.

'That was strange,' said Ake.

'Not really. Amities was like that.'

'True.' Ake giggled.

Alwin ran back into the forge and grabbed the new sliding mechanism that would be fitted to the top of the pistol's barrel so Lan could load the metal canisters full of oil into the weapon. The opening was small and he hoped it would work. *Lufar came up with a clever idea.*

He altered the weapon and smiled at the result, sliding a canister into the compartment.

'How do you feel, Hushin?'

'*All is well.*' The weapon hummed and went silent.

'Hushin?' He was greeted with silence and shrugged. *Lives up to its name.*

Alwin grabbed a coal rake and separated the burning coals from any unburnt materials. He waited until the coal burnt out completely before taking a coal scuttle and removing the used-up coal. *I better get this to Lufar.* He locked the forge doors and proceeded to Ake and Lan's.

Alena sat drinking in a bar in the hospitality district. She sobbed and her angry tears splashed into her drink. *My darling Nuo, it's been so hard without you. How is it everyone else gets to be with their partners, even being resurrected, but you cannot?* 'You hear that gods? I hate you. You lazy good-for-nothings. Why have you forsaken our world?'

'Hey there, darling. You look like you could use some company.' Alena looked up to see a waitress dressed in a skimpy uniform.

'I am not looking for that kind of company.'

'Well, excuse me. I see a crying woman and thought I would offer an ear. Who are you to assume I am some wench?' The woman slammed Alena's drink down and turned away.

'Wait. I am sorry. I just lost my girlfriend. I am bitter and meant you no distress.'

'That is terribly sad. Tell me about her.'

Tears filled Alena's eyes and blurred her vision before she brushed them away. 'She was loyal, sweet and she knew me so well. She died protecting me.'

'Oh darl, survivor's guilt is a terrible thing, and on top of that you are grieving a lover. Take care, and I suggest you seek out a way to honour her memory. The next drink is on me.'

'Thank you.'

'Remember, one day you will be reunited with her as we all will with past loved ones.' The woman smiled. 'I'm Geraldine.'

'Alena.'

I need to be strong enough to take Hau down. In Vera's memory and for the sake of my new nephew. Alwin began to jog up and down on the spot. He counted and got to two hundred before he became breathless. *Still not great but it's better than a count of fifty from a few days ago.* He reached for the training sword at his feet and lunged forward, brandishing the blade as if his sworn enemy was before him. His cheeks burned as someone clapped behind him.

'Good show.' His employer had entered the forge where he

practiced on his break. 'Very dashing, Alwin, maybe you will make a swordsman one day.'

Alwin shook his head. 'I am terrible.'

'I can show you a few moves. I used to be quite the fighter back in the day.' The blacksmith removed an unsharpened sword from a shelf nearby and approached the boy. 'On your guard, lad.'

Alwin's hand shook as he hefted the blade, but he deflected several blows from the larger opponent and he smiled. *Maybe I will succeed.*

'You're finished for the day, lad, I am closing early.' The blacksmith tossed him dull blade. 'Keep it; you are past a wooden sword.'

'Thank you.'

'Think nothing of it; you are a good lad and a hard worker.'

Alwin placed the wooden training sword on a shelf and hurried from the forge with his new blade. The fresh breeze caressed his cheek and he sighed in relief. As he wandered homebound, he tested his new weapon; weeds and trash its latest victim as he swung the blade. 'I am the mighty Het. Legendary weapons master.'

His skin prickled as something screeched; he lifted his gaze to a shadow hovering above and changed his stance as the creature dived. *Ah, my training heck.* He attempted to conjure a path of smoke; the smell of sulphur then nothing. Claws raked his cheek. *Heck I can't even produce a puff of smoke to deter Luma's pet.*

The dragier turned and flapped its wings furiously. Alwin's eyes widened; the bird had doubled in size. It opened its beak and coughed. A cloud of green mist floated towards him and he ducked to the left, crashing into a pile of discarded crates. He nursed a grazed elbow and leapt to his feet as the refuse began to burn with green fire. Then he bolted past two girls carrying their shopping.

The dragier screeched and it swooped from above, pulling strands of hair out. He clutched at his sword. 'I don't want to hurt you, where is your master?'

The beast wheeled about and hastened after the girls. Alwin's heart hammered in his chest. 'No, leave them alone.'

He closed his eyes and stilled his ragged breathing, drawing in the feelings around him. *Grandfather warned me to never use this unless necessary.* Fear from the two girls, delight from the bird. He latched on to that delight and pulled it towards him, weaving in the trait of domination. His eyes snapped open as the bird changed direction in the air and dived towards him, its beak inches from his eyes. Its wings beat furiously before it nibbled gently at his hair and took off, landing several feet away near Ake who grinned at the boy.

'You are brave, Alwin, but a little too laid back. I knew, just like Amities, when tested, you would find your way.' The dragier screeched and took wing as she turned on her heel. 'You are ready.'

'There are nicer ways to go about teaching me,' shouted Alwin.

CHAPTER FIFTY-THREE

The sun was beginning to fade into an evening sky. A warm summer breeze caressed Ake's skin, suggesting gentle summer evenings and picnics by moonlight. While others might dare to arrange such activities, the small party gathered outside Hau's palace instead planned to rid Velterra of a great evil. Lan held Ake against him; his grip was like a vice.

She pried him gently off her. 'It will be okay.'

'Don't make any brash decisions; you're just a scout.'

Ake nodded.

Alena walked over to her. 'She isn't going in alone.'

'That is a good idea.' Het strode over and patted Ake on the head.

'I really wish you would stop that. I am not a child anymore, Het.' Ake pushed his hands away.

Alena pulled out her staff and gently poked Het in the stomach. The big guy did a dramatic attempt at pretending to die; stumbling around as if he was drunk, clutching his stomach.

'That isn't funny,' said Lan and Flo in unison.

'I agree,' said Alwin.

Alena, Ake, Hartur and Het laughed.

'Alright, I lied. It was funny.' Lan's laughter joined theirs.

Flo blinked in surprise. 'Lan, that's not very elvish of you.'

'Hill elf and Arakaen.' Lan grinned at Flo. 'Not a posh Relequis noble.'

'I am with Flo on this one. Stop acting like children. You could lose your lives.' Alwin sighed. 'I intend to survive, but this motley group's chances of survival are lessening by the minute each time you mess around.'

'Okay, Alena, let's go.' Ake trotted to the gate. They waited as a guard went past before Ake began prying open the large steel lock with her thieving tools. She ducked out of sight as the guard returned. The lock fell towards the ground but was caught before it made a noise.

'Thanks, Alena,' said Ake.

'You really are a bunch of buffoons, cousin.' Hau grabbed her throat through the gate.

Alena's staff glowed yellow and she crashed it down on Hau's hand. A shield erupted from the staff and Hau winced, pulling his hand back. Alena dragged Ake away from him.

Hau grinned. There was a click as he snapped the lock back in place. 'Try again, cousin. You really didn't think this through. I can sense kin. This should be amusing.' Hau's form faded away.

Ake stormed back over to the others.

'We really didn't think about this. Hau can sense kin.' Hartur sighed.

Het rolled his eyes. 'Flo, did you maybe forget something?'

Flo smiled apologetically and she pulled out several chains from the apron of her dress. 'Please don these, he will not be able to sense you.'

'What about scrying?' asked Alwin.

'Scry proof too. I say we make a pretence of leaving,' suggested Flo.

'No, I have had enough of this.' Ake grinned. There was a flash of light. Ake's golden eyes flashed with determination. Flapping her golden wings, she alighted on the decaying wall. 'Hau is strong and intelligent; he will be expecting us. So, let's pay him a visit.'

There was a holler from the guard and Ake leapt on to their back. The guard grunted and struggled briefly. Ake sprinted to the other side of the gate, hoping to unlock it.

Het grinned. 'Now that's more like it. Stand back, Ake.' He drew his sword as another guard gave up a cry. The sword flared into life and the fairy light made it look like a glittering beacon. A guard looked around, his bow furrowing as his gaze swept past the warrior sheltered by the sword's magic. Het kicked down the gate in one mighty blow.

'Hey you.' The guard rushed Ake and she blasted the guard's metal armour with *Mystic Fire*.

'Hot hot.' The guard swore, threw off the helmet and drew their sword, charging at Ake. Het leapt in the way and blocked the blow.

'Impressive.' Ake grinned and drew her own sword. 'I had it, Het.'

'Where did they go?' The guard backed off as the faerie orbs gave them cover.

Alwin, Flo and Alena trailed in behind them. The guard's eyes suddenly widened with surprise. They grunted and drooped to the ground.

Lan grinned. 'Let's get this done.' He drew his knives.

Ake's eyes darted towards the palace and recognition rushed through her. She closed her eyes as the first vision she'd ever experienced flooded through her. *Hell, it's happening now. Oh gods, they were all real.* Trembling, she felt bile rise in her throat.

Hau took his dagger and threw the elderly servant to the floor. The man cried out and began to sob. Hau grabbed the man's arm, held it over the basin and made a small cut. Blood began to pour into the bowl.

'Please, my lord. I have grandchildren; we are loyal to you.'

'Silence, slave.' Hau's nose wrinkled as he smelled a sickening odour as the wizened old man emptied his bladder in terror. Hau struck the man. 'Filthy beast.'

Hau breathed in the metallic smell of blood as the man spat out a rotten tooth. Hau let the man's arm fall as he bled out.

'I will always remember the shimmering lake and the wind caressing the leaves of the oak tree,' the man whispered as he faded away in death.

Ake took a sharp breath, realising she could briefly read Hau's thoughts.

Clever Mother. I cannot see you now, but I am not stupid enough to believe you have left. This is Ake's former residence. I believe I should have my cousin reacquaint herself with it.

'Cousin, you are home. Be prepared for Cephas's presence.'

Vero began to cry and he walked over and held the child.

'I better get you ready to meet your grandparents.'

Ake screamed at the memory of the palace and Cephas's cruelty. Fear threatened to overwhelm her as her connection to Hau was severed. She opened her eyes as Alena rushed over to her and embraced her.

'It's okay, Luma, he isn't here. It's just Hau playing games.'

Ake clung to her for a few moments then gently broke the embrace. 'Thank you, Alena. You really are a kind person.'

Ake turned and glared up at the walls of her ancient terror. 'No, I have dealt with that, Hau.'

Fifty guards rounded the corner, summoned by the noise. Het and Lan exchanged glances with each other.

'No deaths if it can be helped,' said Lan.

Het nodded.

'You okay, Ake?' asked Lan, his eyes riveted on the guards.

'Fine,' she yelled back.

'I get the robed ones, Het,' said Lan.

'Fine by me.'

There was a thunderous crack as one of the mages called down lightning. Bolts crashed down to the earth, cracking the cement paths. Lan dodged each bolt as the mage continued to unleash an unwavering magical onslaught directed at him. He swore as a fire mage stepped up and stood next to the other. 'Ake.' He dodged out of the range of the mages' spells, weaving between the attacks. 'Honey!'

Dead vegetation caught alight and wooden benches burst into flame. Beads of sweat ran down Lan's face and he brushed them out of the way as the heat from the fires caused him to sweat profusely. The smell of burning hair assaulted everyone's nostrils and Lan blinked as black, acrid smoke wafted past and his eyes began to water.

Ake ran forward and engulfed the fire mage in water. As she concentrated on maintaining the spell, Lan dived between the lightning mage's legs, turned and delivered a blow to the mage's neck. The combatant slumped down in a pile of rags and ashes.

'What the hell?' Lan booted the pile of ash, shrugged and turned his attention to the fire mage. 'I wonder if it is undead too.'

Het laughed as several guards ran at him spears and swords drawn. There was a clanging as Het deflected multiple blows. He changed his position and was given cover by the sword against his enemies.

'He has magic coverage,' cried one of the guards.

'Why hello, sergeant obvious.' Het laughed.

The guard grunted as Het belted him with the hilt of his sword and thrust him away with a boot to the derriere. Flo began to sing in elvish and several guards turned on their allies, engaging them in battle. Flo strode forward, surrounded by the guards who were now protecting her.

'That's how an empress does it.' Het grinned at Flo before turning back to his fight.

Alwin turned as guards and mages swarmed in behind them. He fired his bow at the limbs of their enemies, trying to maim rather than kill. Victims screamed; tears welled in his eyes.

'I will nullify your pain,' said Alwin. The guards' faces became a mask of bliss.

Hartur drew Taven and disappeared into the shadows. A guard gurgled, clutching at his throat, his eyes bulging before he slumped to the ground. As she dashed by a flaming bench, her dagger glinted in the light of the flames as she plunged it into a guard charging Alwin. 'I can't take Lord Hau's life, but I can protect yours.' She smiled sadly and twirled around. Unhooking her hammer from her belt, she swung into the belly of another enemy who doubled over gasping for breath.

Alena rushed to Alwin's side. Her staff flared to life, deterring a barrage of arrows and spells slung at them. Fire, ice and lightning bounced off the shield, injuring people in the process.

Ake retracted her water shield. She stared in fascination, her mouth agape as the skin fell away from the fire mage, showing a skeleton in various stages of decay. It gnashed its teeth at her and flame burst from its now bony hands. Ake countered with jets of water as Lan's knives arced down and were driven through the mage's side. As it disintegrated, a wave of ash was released into Lan's face. He coughed and drew back, shivering.

A large general in a golden helmet exited from a hidden door to the group's left and turned to speak to the guards that filed in behind. 'Hau wants the golden- and red-haired women as brides for his favoured advisors. Do not damage them; any blemish will have you punished. Subdue the big fellow, other woman and the boy. You can kill the dark-haired elf,' cried the general.

Het growled as he was surrounded by many guards. 'I have to kill them now,' he shouted to Lan, 'if you are to survive.'

'Don't worry about me. No one will lay a hand on my Ake and the other women.' Lan's eyes filled with a fierce determination. 'Or you, my friend.'

Alwin fired his bow and guards screamed as their lives were

taken. 'Just do it, Het. They have chosen their fate.'

Alena's staff glowed black and she delivered blow after blow to the heads of the guards. They grunted as they fell to the ground, their helmets caved in with Alena's deadly blows.

'*I will defend,*' cried Din.

Alena was rushed from behind; Din deflected the blow from the weapon that would have taken her life. Alena swivelled and marched forward, opening up a path, Alwin's bow defending from the rear.

'We can't hold this forever,' yelled Alwin.

'I agree,' cried Alena.

Guards leapt on Het but he threw them off. His sword became a blur of deadly swings. Blood glinted off the blade as it swung again, clearing his path. Bodies lay at his feet and blood pooled on the ground.

'Cover your ears,' cried Flo.

'A little hard,' grumbled Het.

Flo closed her eyes and began to sing. Ake covered her ears and flew towards Alwin and Alena.

'*Dee moldis,*' Ake yelled. The air was rent with the sound of screams and cracking stone.

The earth shatters and bends to the will of the earthbound goddess, thought Alwin. He and Alena now stood on an island of stone, surrounded by guards who couldn't reach them.

'Din, shield,' yelled Alena.

'*I obey.*'

A barrage of arrows was fired at them as Alwin covered his ears.

—⁓—

Lan flew over to Het; his knives joined the deadly array, splattering himself and Het with the blood of the fallen. Clearing his way to Het, he used his wings to cover his friend. Blows rained down on Lan's unprotected body, making him wince, unable to defend himself as he used his hands to cover his ears.

Het unleashed a held breath as the faint restrains of an elvish melody disappeared. A chilling wind passed through him, clenching its icy breath around his heart. He took a sharp breath as his blood began to circulate again and warmth returned to his extremities. He saw Lan shudder and take a deep breath. 'You felt it too?'

Lan nodded and lowered his shredded wings. Blood ran in rivulets, pooling at his friend's feet, from the multiple lacerations on the back of his arms and legs. Lan swooned and Het steadied him.

'You'll be okay, mate.' Het reached out and green light passed from his hands and into Lan.

Lan smiled with relief. 'When did you learn to heal at such an advanced level?'

Het grinned. 'Flo taught me this spell a few days ago.'

'Thank the gods.' Lan shook his wings. 'They appear to have been repaired.'

'That was very brave of you. Thank you.' Het patted him on the back.

'It was long overdue. I got to protect *you* for once.'

They turned to see the ground covered in blood and mangled remains. The cuts were clean, as if a giant axe had cleaved their opponents in half.

Lan's eyes widened in shock. 'Well done.'

Flo nodded wearily. 'I had to do my bit.'

Het sheathed his sword and ran over to his wife as she slumped to the ground. 'Are you okay?'

Flo smiled at him. 'I will be. But that took all I had.'

He helped her stand. 'You are incredible. Where did you learn that?'

Flo winked at him. 'A priestess of Ea never gives away her secrets.'

Lan swore as hundreds of guards exited the building. His eyes suddenly filled with anger and Het watched him stride towards Ake, muttering to himself.

Ake grabbed Alena and flew her across to the others, returning for Alwin just as more soldiers exited a hidden door in front of her.

'Get behind me,' Ake growled.

Alena and Alwin ran behind her.

'*Facstym mentys,*' growled Ake.

The guards screamed and began striking at their own helmets with their weapons. They collapsed, their eyes open to the sky, devoid of any signs of life. Their tongues lolled in their mouths as all remnants of vitality left.

Het glanced at Lan as he caught up to him. 'Our wives are deadly.'

Lan nodded. 'True.'

———∿∿∿———

'Through here.' Ake pointed to the cleverly designed hidden entrance. She watched the others' backs as Alwin and Alena rushed inside, followed by Het with Flo in his arms. Anger surged through Lan and he growled softly as he coughed up some dust.

'Let's follow them.' Ake stepped towards her husband.

He raised his hand to slap her. 'How dare you put yourself in danger again.' As he went to strike he snatched at the offending appendage with his other hand, gritting his teeth as his limbs vied for control. His offending hand won as Ake slipped from his grasp; Hau's words driving him to anger.

'*This is your wife, Lan; you let her put herself in danger yet again. What kind of husband are you?*' Hau laughed. '*An elven lord would never allow a woman with royal elven blood to put herself in danger. They are rare and far too valuable.*'

There was a loud thud as the door closed behind their friends locking Ake and Lan outside.

The distraction was enough to give Lan a chance to compose himself and he pushed her away. 'Run!'

Ake turned and flew up onto the roof of the palace. He fluttered his wings and followed her. As he landed, he rushed towards her, the need to possess her surged through him and he scowled.

'Lan, fight him.' Ake backed off against the battlement.

She realised her mistake too late. As she tried to turn and run, he paused in front of her, his hands trembling before he shoved her against the battlement. 'You're not going anywhere.' He crushed her to him, shivering, his skin hot with fever.

'You're burning up.' Ake touched his forehead gently. 'It's okay, we will stay here,' she soothed.

He relaxed against her and she tried to slip out of his grasp.

'Liar.' He grabbed her and pushed her back. 'You will not put yourself in danger for some noble cause.'

He gritted his teeth and groaned. Turning, he began slashing at himself with his own knives. Bellowing with pain, he coughed up the dust. 'Get out, you foul fiend!'

Lan turned to her, tears in his eyes. 'I can't believe Hau would force me to hit a woman.'

Ake scoffed. 'Of course he would. Look around, Lan. Do you think he cares for any of these people?'

'I am sorry. I would never willingly raise a hand to you.'

Ake put her hand to his forehead. 'The fever has relented.' She smiled at him. 'I know you wouldn't.'

She ripped the sleeves off her dress and bound the wounds on his forearms. She kissed him and he leant her into the wall. He broke away and glanced around.

'We should try and find a way in.'

Ake nodded and they flew down, looking for windows and

hidden doors. Ake pounded on the walls and yelled out of frustration. She turned to Lan. 'What should we do?'

'You used to know this palace, Ake. Is there another entrance?'

Ake shuddered. 'I was confined to one room. The window was often my only source of access to the outside world.'

'I see no windows.' Lan squeezed her hand. 'Are you okay?'

Ake nodded. 'I am fine now that you are with me.'

Lan drew her against him and wrapped his wings about them both, sheltering her with his body in a physical attempt to protect her from her internal fears.

'Sir,' whispered a small voice nearby.

Lan unfurled his wings and glanced down. Hurley smiled up at him. 'Hartur found me. Caoimhe doesn't know I am here; I saw her sneak in.'

'You two shouldn't be here. You just got back from your honeymoon,' cried Ake.

'We needed to know you are all are okay,' said Hurley.

Ake frowned. 'And where is Caoimhe now?'

'I am sure she is fine, honey. Our daughter can hold her own.' Lan smiled and pointed to the palace. 'Hurley, do you see any windows and doors?'

The halfling jogged over to the wall, thrusting a hand forward and twisting his wrist as if he was turning an invisible handle.

'Step back.' Hurley pulled his hand back and a doorway appeared. 'I didn't want to hit you with it.' A blast of stale air whooshed past them and they were met with the sound of unnerving silence.

'Go through before Hau finds you. I will find Caoimhe and let her know you are safe so far.' Hurley turned and sprinted through the outer gate.

Ake and Lan held hands as they entered the palace.

—⁓—

Alwin, Alena and Het with Flo in his arms rushed down a corridor lit with magical lanterns.

'Welcome, Mother and Father.' The walls vibrated with Hau's voice. 'Hello Alwin, grandchild of my dear cousin.'

The walls suddenly began to ooze with a clear liquid. As it began to evaporate into a mist, everyone held their breath and ran down the forever receding corridor. The noxious gas swirled around them and their eyelids began to droop as they were overcome with fatigue.

I am Din, protector of the descendants. Hoist me to the heavens and bask in my protection,' cried Din.

'Alena, hold up the staff,' yelled Alwin.

Alena nodded and hoisted the staff in the air. A huge transparent globe engulfed her and the others. They took huge breaths, filling their lungs with the clean air.

'Dan-ger, Ma-ster.'

Alwin turned and saw a huge set of yellow eyes staring at him in the dark; the globes had gone out behind him. 'We should run,' said Alwin.

The others turned as the pair of eyes rushed towards them. The remaining globes went out one by one as if snuffed out by an invisible wind and they were suddenly engulfed in darkness. Alwin heard Het draw his sword. It shone brilliantly in the dark and Het placed Flo on her feet. The set of eyes stopped just beyond the edge of the shield. A large spider leg reached out and touched the forcefield. Something hissed as Din flared and celestial light struck the creature.

'What is that?' asked Flo.

'Giant spider or something worse,' said Alena.

There was another hissing noise and a serpent's face peered

at them, its yellow eyes intently watching its prey. It opened its mouth, showing two large fangs; poison dripped down and hit the shield.

'Guggly,' said Alwin.

Flo looked confused.

'A monster that has the body of a giant spider with a serpent's head. It is both carnivorous and venomous and hunts in packs.' Alena shivered.

Alwin glanced around as more sets of eyes peered at them.

'It is you three that need to get to Hau. Run.' Alena lowered her shield. She turned to face the mass of gathering eyes and ran towards the gugglies.

'Help her, Het,' yelled Flo.

'Go save our boy.' Het put Flo's hand to his lips and kissed it.

'I can't face Hau.' Hartur materialised out of the shadows, raising her hammer; grey glittery strands swirled around her. 'They are frightened of cats.' Hartur tossed Nietra to her husband. 'Take care; you will need this.'

Het's brow furrowed. 'How did she get in here?'

Hartur grinned. 'Skulking in the shadows and following unwary travellers.'

Het glanced at the door behind them. 'Alwin, you need to get my wife to our son. We will deal with these beasts.'

Alwin waved to Hartur before he grabbed Flo's hand and ran. They came to a door and Alwin flung it open, dragging a weeping Flo with him, then he slammed the door shut.

Back in the passage, the gugglies rushed at them. Alena valiantly held up Din, her brows etched in concentration. She held her stance as long as she could. Waves of monsters slammed themselves into her shield; the room filled with a cacophony of hissing. Alena's shoulders slumped and she was swept under a mass of hissing, fuzzy bodies.

Hartur closed her eyes and reached into her pocket, withdrawing a small purple ball. She tossed it at the gugglies. With a loud crack, followed by a terrible yowling, a large cat appeared, padding towards the large swarm of monsters who shrank in fear

Het smiled. 'Did you make that?'

Hartur nodded. 'Minor illusions are handy sometimes.'

'As swift as night descends,' yelled Het. He leapt into the pile, slashing his way through until he dragged a nearly unconscious Alena from the pile. She had bite marks all over her. He pushed her behind him and slaughtered wave after wave of the gugglies.

Alena mumbled and stood. Green poison oozed from the bite wounds. Din flared and she and Het charged forward.

The gugglies hissed and Alena closed her eyes. 'Hungry, famished, kill,' she translated what appeared to be the language of the monsters.

Tears rolled down her cheeks as she began to squeak. Het stared at her as if she had gone mad. An overwhelming sound of squeaking filled the space and tiny paws scurried on stone. The gugglies turned at the sound, releasing a loud, collective hiss, and the wave of monsters reared up. They rushed after thousands of tiny grey mice who now occupied the passageway.

Alena opened her eyes and they suddenly glowed a vibrant green.

'Why did you disturb us, lady of the woods? We were feasting on the discarded corpses of slaves in the basement,' muttered Alena in a tiny, almost inaudible voice, broken up by the occasional squeak.

'I am sorry, my little friends,' said Alena in her normal voice as her eyes returned to normal.

Het grinned. 'What a useful skill.'

Alena coughed up blood whilst Het attempted to heal her wounds.

Hartur smiled and disappeared into the shadows. 'I will clear the path outside.'

CHAPTER FIFTY-FOUR

Alwin and Flo stopped in their tracks when they saw Hau sitting upon his throne. He laughed and the sound echoed eerily in the silent hall.

'Welcome my beloved mother and my dear cousin Alwin.'

Undead magen surrounded them. Hau stood up and walked over to his mother, Vero asleep in his arms.

Hau stroked his son's head. 'This is your grandson. I have had other children over the centuries that you have missed because you decided to try and find cousin Ake. Would she have done the same for you?'

Flo wept as Hau approached her and held out her arms. He handed her the infant and approached Alwin.

'Most women are so easily overcome by mere babies and baubles. My mother is no exception. What would make you realise I mean you no harm, cousin?'

Alwin stepped back, clipping the hammer to his belt as Hau placed a hand on his shoulder.

'Your grandfather was a sweet boy. I was fond of him.' Hau gave Alwin a charming smile. 'I would love the company of someone who can tell me of his exploits. Sit,' commanded Hau.

Alwin gasped as he was lifted off his feet and thrown into a chair. He sat up and stared at a huge feast on a magnificent table decorated with a red satin tablecloth and adorned with golden dinnerware. The door was thrust open and Alena and Het ran through, slamming it shut. Het was thrown against the wall by some unseen force. Flo screamed.

Hau marched over to Alena. 'How dare you enter my home, descendant of Mandami, son of Cephas. I find it hard to believe Mandami is Lan's, despite Orilan's assertions.'

One of the undead mages bellowed and a wave of sound rushed towards Alena. Din glistened and the blow was deflected.

'So, it's true then, Mandami *was* Lan's.' Hau smiled. 'Only those bonded to Amities by blood or friendship could wield his weapons, and I doubt *you* ever met him.'

Het struggled against the force. Flo handed the baby to Alwin and rushed at Hau. He turned, clicking his fingers and she was catapulted towards him. Hau raised his arms to belt her but dropped them to his side. 'I don't hit females, except in self-defence. And even then, most aren't a challenge.' His eyes narrowed. 'Most.'

Flo's pupils glowed and Hau's eyes became expressionless. Het dropped to the ground and Flo sprinted over to him.

Hau shook himself and his undead mages thrust their arms towards his father. Dark light streamed forth from their hands. Alena leapt in front, holding out her staff. With a fizzle, blue light surged around them as Din held the onslaught at bay.

Het drew his sword and stalked forward. 'You dare lay a hand on a woman, especially your own mother? What kind of man are you?' Het glared at his son. 'Face me, you coward.'

Hau's laughter echoed in the room. 'You are being protected by women. You seem to think they are incapable of defending themselves. Your noble ramblings are outdated. You belong to the past.'

The wall slid away behind Alwin and he turned as Ake and Lan crept into the room. Vero wailed and Hau turned to stare at Alwin before his gaze fixated on Ake and Lan.

'The coward lives.' Hau pointed at Lan. 'You left me to die. Your despicable wife never even looked for my remains. I was a child, alone and injured.' Hau scowled. His break in concentration caused his undead duplicates to halt their attack on the others.

Hau disappeared and reappeared sitting on his throne, he clicked his fingers and Vero floated out of Alwin's grasp and into that of his father's. 'Now, be seated. I have prepared a great feast for you and you rudely attack me in my own home.'

Lan and Het rushed at Hau, weapons drawn. Alena swayed with exhaustion, Alwin tried to stand up only to realise he was held in place.

'I said sit!' yelled Hau casting a command spell.

Het and Lan struggled against the spell, scowling and clutching on to objects as their bodies disobeyed; their feet marched them towards the seated area against their will. Ake sat, smiling benignly. Alena sprinted towards Hau, her eyes fierce. Hau gestured and she reappeared in a seat. 'Predictable; tiresome woman.'

'As Arakaen, I am well aware of which children are mine. I knew I had sired Mandami the moment I met him.' Lan scowled at Hau.

Hau smirked. 'Well, he also failed the elven people, never taking a bride. It seems all your children failed you and your heritage.'

'*Alwin, can you manipulate Hau's emotions?*' a voice asked in the boy's mind.

Alwin turned and stared at Ake. She smiled. '*Yes, it is me.*'

He gave her a brief nod.

'*Play on his fears. I will try to distract him so he releases his hold on the others.*'

Hau gave them a fake grin. 'Isn't this charming? All reunited and enjoying a delicious meal.' He waved his hand; the undead mages came over and filled the glasses with wine from decanters and began serving the meal. 'Please eat.' He began to sip the wine before stabbing a strawberry with a fork and placing it in his mouth and swallowing. 'It has been many years since I could taste such food. You will appreciate it though.'

Alena shuddered as she glanced at an undead mage. 'What a foul use of the dead.'

'Be quiet, cousin.' Hau pointed at each guest and they were forced to consume the repast.

Lan tried to resist as his hand reached for the cup of wine and held it to his lips. He coughed as he tried to spit out the drink. His eyes blazed with determination. Ake grabbed a cake and ate it without complaint.

'Why do you fight me, Lan? Look at your delightful wife, so willing to indulge me.' Hau smiled at Ake who gave him a blank expression.

Alwin shut his eyes; his heart swelled with pressure and a deluge of emotions rushed in. *Hau's emotions are hard to find among the others gathered here. Alena is tired, Lan is disgruntled, sadness swells in Flo like a raging river, and the urge to protect others surges through Het.* Two emotions were left other than his own. Sadness and feelings of revenge washed over him and he shivered. He reached out to the sadness; an image of a wounded child alone on a battlefield calling for Ake. Alwin sniffled back his tears. *Such anguish burns in Hau's heart.* He choked on his saliva. Hau scowled and bloodlust, hate and Hau's unwavering self-righteousness surged through Alwin as he began to play on Hau's feelings of abandonment.

'Time to punish her, Lan.' Hau smiled cruelly. 'Sweet cousin Ake, come here.'

Hau stood and placed his son in a cradle nearby. Dropping a small, coloured stone in the crib, a forcefield erupted from it and surrounded the sleeping infant.

Ake walked towards him, smiling innocently.

'Kneel, cousin,' said Hau.

Ake knelt.

'Why did you never come back for me? That doesn't seem like you.' Hau pointed at her.

Ake was lifted off the ground by an unseen force and dragged towards him. She didn't struggle. Hau's eyes burned with malice as his gaze fixated on hers. 'Let me glean a little from your memories, dear cousin.' His eyes widened before he placed her down gently and turned away. 'So, you did try looking for me.' Hau turned back towards the table; his eyes suddenly filled with rage. 'It matters little. Did your husband do anything to restore the elves? Our people gave everything to find you, and you, holed up in that little fortress, not once did you reach out to them.' Hau turned to glance at his child.

'Whenever time didn't leap forward and he was in control of himself, Lan rescued many and sent them to our door. You didn't reach out to us, Hau. Instead, you let Drianna's malice consume you. I would have come for you if I had known you were alive.' Ake smiled sadly.

'Enough. You lie,' Hau roared.

Ake drew her sword and walloped him on the back of the head.

Their host cried out and turned on her. 'You will pay.'

Black magic blazed from his hands. Ake smiled as golden light flared; his magic ricocheted off her in a thunderous crack. He lashed out; his left hand clutching her throat. With his right hand, he dug his nails into his left palm before smearing his blood down her neck. 'So soft.'

'Let her go, you evil b——.' Lan squirmed in his seat; it rocked and almost toppled over.

Ake aimed a kick at Hau before he leant down and whispered in her ear. Her eyes glazed over as he lifted his head to gloat at her husband. 'How delicious and so dramatic. Father admitted his fondness for your wife.' Hau's eyes snapped to Lan's. 'A family affair it seems. Do you remember the symbol for brother no one could translate? That was the champion made mortal on earth to aid the goddess. He was brother to the shadow in the drawing, the Lord of Death, her counterpart who would one day sire the gods of war and crafting. Yes, Mandami was the chosen, but without Amities's sword he would not have been.' Hau smirked. 'Her intended believed he could trust his brother not to cross a boundary, but the older had other designs, for his hate for his prior situation nearly overwhelmed him.'

Lan's eyes narrowed on their host. 'You are trying to cause trouble amongst us again. This doesn't make any sense.'

Ake took a deep breath. As her eyes cleared, her gaze turned to Het, who stared off into the distance, lost in thought.

'Het?' Ake's voice wobbled. 'Explain to Lan.'

Het sighed. 'Now is not the time.'

Flo's lip trembled. 'Do you still love her?'

Het attempted to slam his fist down on the table. 'Not like I do you. You are my everything; he is trying to tear us apart and you are falling for it.'

Hau's eyes shone with mirth. 'Ever the wise one, Father. Mother has never doubted you until now.'

Lan shook with anger. 'Stop reaching into their souls and adding hate and fear like you did with me.'

Alwin cleared his throat. 'There is love, almost a kinship between Het and Luma, but not the raging romantic love Het feels for your mother, Hau. You are so callous.'

Hau guffawed. 'So like Amities, so careful with the emotions he weaved to his bidding.'

'He would never,' Ake yelled.

Hau caressed her cheek. 'So sweet, so trusting.'

She punched him in the face; his nose cracked and blood spurted from his face. He dropped her to her feet and she rubbed her neck that was beginning to bruise while her husband glared daggers at their host. Ake raised her hands and sent a wave of steam towards her opponent.

Hau winked at her. There was a cacophony of hideous bellows, shrieks and growls. Ake was forced backwards as the room began to fill with nightmarish creatures. Her shield faltered as monsters rushed towards her friends while their host waved away the steam as if it was nothing. 'You hold back, little goddess. It will be their deaths.'

As the bonds broke, Lan aimed his gun. There was a horrible gurgling noise as he fired into a Swork as it rolled towards Ake, its suckers quivering with undeniable anticipation. The cannister of oil lodged just inside the maw, the bullet flared to life. Ake gasped as Lan sprinted and slammed her into the ground, shielding her with his body. Acid sprayed everywhere as the creature imploded.

'You have ruined my family reunion,' hissed Hau.

Het rose, rage contorting his usual kindly expression. He drew his sword and advanced on his son. 'You are despicable. We all go through horrid things, yet you gave in to evil. I will put down what I helped create.'

'No, Het, he's our son.' Flo held out her arms to her son. 'Hau, stop this.'

'It matters not who he is. He has killed and tortured thousands for his cause. I am sorry, Flo.' Het charged at Hau; the sword burst into green druid fire and sliced down towards his enemy.

Hau laughed. 'Ah, a fitting tribute to my sire, a massacre to rival his.' He became a blur before appearing next to his mother as the monsters charged the group, thrusting her out of the way as a random giant's fist crashed down on the centre of the table. Alena and Alwin were thrown backwards.

Alwin stood and brushed himself off. Everyone's fear, anguish and hate crowded in on him and he shuddered, his heart aching with despair. He drew back his bow as the giant charged at him.

Alena leapt in front, delivering blow after blow. Alwin's arrows pierced the giant's tough hide and it soon became bloodied. It bellowed and crashed down on to the table, renting it in two.

Het's sword slashed at his son's shield, the blood magic swelling and shrinking. As the sword blazed green, weak spots formed gaps in their enemy's shield. 'Fancy calling upon your father's people to slaughter your kin.'

'You are protective it seems.' Sweat beaded on Hau's brow. '*Horb, morte, devala*.' A portal appeared behind him; red eyes glinted in the fiery depths. A large troll leant forwards, its huge muscular hand grabbed the gallant warrior. Het's eyes flashed with rage. His mouth was set with a fierce frown as green *Druid Fire* burst through the sword, burning off the fingers of the troll. The troll bellowed and took a step backwards and dropped him as more monsters surged out of the portal.

'You are dead inside. Consumed by malice and a warped sense of honour and duty. No *real* elven king would destroy others to benefit their people. They were the sworn people of Dee, dedicated to peace, love, magic and the ways of nature. You have befouled their memory.' Het advanced on Hau. 'You are no prince of the elves. Your mother is the true sovereign, embodying all the virtues that made your people great!' The warrior's strong and heartening voice bolstered everyone as feelings of strength and resolve flowed through Alwin.

Hau glared at him then began to laugh maniacally. 'She allowed the downfall of her people. She let her heart guide her actions trying to find some useless goddess who could not take down one emperor, and my people were destroyed because of it.'

'That so-called useless goddess was stalked throughout childhood by Drianna. She never gave up and helped defeat her in the end. You gave in easily to Drianna, fuelled by misinformation and misguided hate,' cried Het.

'See how he admires her too much, Mother?' Blood began to seep from Hau's pores and drip on to the floor, pooling at his feet. Het crashed his sword down onto Hau and green, heatless fire surged through his enemy. His screams echoed in the cavernous space as his father's earth magic rushed through him. Lacerations appeared along his arms and he stumbled backwards, grabbing at the wounds, trying to stem the bleeding.

Het struck him again. Hau screamed and teleported behind him, blasting his father with dark light. The fighter fell to one knee groaning for a moment before he rose, his back singed and beginning to blister through the burnt cloth. 'Oh no, this is for your mother. This is a husband correcting their son when he couldn't be there for him. This pain isn't enough to prevent me from killing you.'

The blood on the floor in front of Hau frothed and grew in size and his double appeared, their expressions and movements coordinated and exact. Alena leapt in front of Het, Din shielding them in a clear wall of light as Hau and his double blasted them with magic, Alena's unwavering loyalty shielding them from probable death.

'The bracelet that quelled Ake's powers was forged in the underworld by Drianna's own hand and gifted to Cephas by a follower of her blood cult. I found this out later during my research on the divine couple,' yelled Alena.

'That explains it. A goddess should have been able to overcome a normal anti-magic bracelet.' Hau laughed. 'It doesn't matter now.'

Alena began to struggle and Din's light wavered and flickered out. Het shoved Alena out of the way and took the full blast of dark magic. With a grunt, he slumped to the floor.

Alwin gritted his teeth and pushed Hau's dark emotions to the surface. Hau's expression was frightening, a mix of malice and merriment as he glanced at Alena. 'So like Mandami. Giving his life for others so they could live and thrive.'

Show us your real form corrupted by centuries of evil deeds. Alwin tensed; fatigue washed over him until he sensed the shift in the air. Hau's eyes widened in surprise as his form began to change, his gaze sweeping the room.

Flo dashed towards Het and Alena, her hands glowed green as she began to heal them. Lan rose and held out his hand to Ake, pulling her to her feet.

'I am done with the greater gods and their lack of help. We dedicate our lives to them for what? Our prayers and wishes fall on deaf ears.' Ake smiled and closed her eyes. 'They allow this heinous person to live.'

Alwin felt her reach deep within herself where her immense power lay dormant; fear brushed his senses, a worry that she'd hurt the innocent if she couldn't control it. There was the sound of ethereal music: a huge gust of flower-scented air rushed through the room. Ake opened her eyes and her golden eyes blazed with an unnatural, fiery light.

The room was filled with golden sunlight; beautiful droplets of light rained down. Beads of sweat began to form on everyone's brows as the room became sweltering.

A cacophony of growls, shrieks and howls assaulted the air as monsters swarmed through the open portal. Hau was the most frightening. His head was a mixture of shadow and flesh. His arms and legs began to mutate as he strode towards Ake. Two ogres grabbed Ake and Lan from behind.

Lan summoned lightning and hail down onto the ogres and they growled as they pulled away before he turned and leapt onto the shoulders of one and fired his pistol into its mouth. As its head exploded, Lan leapt on to the other. His long knife plunged through its eye, embedding in its skull. The elf applied his boot to its face and grunted with the effort of retrieving the blade before gracefully landing on the floor.

Ake turned and her eyes scanned the room. The golden rain swirled around all the remaining monsters. Golden fire burst through them. As they imploded, divine light danced amongst their ashes like celestial golden embers.

Hau stared at Ake in awe. 'Impressive, my sweet cousin. Where was this in the battle against Cephas?'

'My powers were contained. Even if Dane had released me from that bracelet I could not have controlled that kind of power with so little experience. I could have killed hundreds of innocents.'

'But you would have survived, and Lan would never have become the Lord of Death.' Hau laughed evilly.

'It was his destiny. Dormant since birth.' She gave Hau a look of pity.

Hau's left arm became a huge black claw, his right a tentacle. He cried out as his face split down the centre; new flesh erupted from beneath, a hybrid of both elf and demon—red eyes, leathery flesh and sharp fangs. He roared, pain contorting the elven side of his face as serrated spines emerged from his back, leaving his robe in tatters.

Hau stumbled as his legs became crooked, scaly and twisted. Doubling in size, he opened his mouth; his serpent tongue flicked in and out before he hissed his words. 'What have you done to me, wench?'

Ake smiled sadly. 'This is not of my doing. Only an empath can force your body to reflect your soul.'

Hau screamed and everyone covered their ears as the room shook and began to crack. Vero wailed and Hau's eyes darted briefly towards him before Ake and Lan were blasted with black fire. Ake clicked her fingers and the dark rays disappeared.

Ake gave her enemy a gentle smile. 'I forgive you. Please surrender peacefully or you shall perish.'

Hau smiled. 'Never. He rushed towards her, his tentacle wrapping itself around her middle. 'Ake, so-called perfection. But you didn't even recognise your son Sia when that priest stopped to offer you a drink in Mandami's war.'

Ake's eyes narrowed on the elven lord. 'You lie. We all know you manipulate information to suit yourself.'

'I was there that day, fleeing Regis with my bride Atius. You sat upon a rock, your golden hair dishevelled, your face streaked with dirt and blood. A middle-aged man in green robes approached you and lifted a ladle from his pot of water to your lips.' Hau's mouth curled in a callous smirk. 'You thanked him and as he hurried on to the next person he whispered, "Goodbye Mother".'

Ake's eyes swam with tears. 'You lie. You lie.'

'Your emotional response proves it to be true. Mandami was never the true heir, but Sia never wanted the throne with its den of Regian serpents coiled around its base, ready to strike.' Hau's eyes narrowed. 'Oh how I almost chuckle with glee knowing I searched him out and befriended him. Your son was desperate for parental affection; he was raised by a cold Regian priestess whose hatred for her brother Cephas made her treat Sia harshly in revenge. I encouraged him to leave his faith and we became close, him becoming a staunch supporter of my cause. And when I needed divine blood to grow my power, he gave up his godly blood—a gift from his mother—freely, and so did his kin through the centuries. How else could I manipulate a goddess all these years to wallow in sadness and wither away to a former husk of herself? His descendants still fuel my power. Your visions were a warning of things to come but you did not heed them.'

Ake sobbed, her shoulders slumped.

'Your guilt shines through those immortal eyes,' Hau crooned.

'I am sorry, Sia. You deserved better than the parents who made you—a cruel emperor and a despondent mother who hated your sire.' Ake sniffed, trying to dislodge the barrage of tears, her arms pinioned in her opponent's grasp. 'So be it. I was never a perfect person or parent, but at least I can admit that. You on the other hand think you are without fault.'

Hau was engulfed with brilliant light. Flo screamed. Ake risked a glance at her friend. Multiple lacerations began appearing in Flo's skin as the blood dripped on to the floor. The droplets were snatched up into the air and began swirling around Hau, forming a new shield. Flo's eyes pleaded with her son's. 'Let this rage go and we can rebuild together. They don't want to kill you.'

'Speak for yourself,' cried Alena.

'A mother's instinct. It's about time you protected me, Mother.' Hau laughed. 'This is what you deserve when you chose Ake over me and your people. You didn't even teach your pupil well, disregarding the visions that could have lessened her heartache.' Hau turned his attention back to Ake. 'You are my real threat. Just imagine, Sia's cold and lonely grave is overgrown with weeds and discarded trash. He too is discarded; a nobody, long forgotten.'

Ake covered her ears. 'Stop it.'

Rage worthy of a higher goddess surged through Alwin, his heart skipped and he almost swooned. *Luma would never forgive herself for taking Hau's life without giving him a chance to surrender and be punished lawfully, despite his cruel words.* He reached for Nietra, unlooping the hammer from his belt.

Hau's gaze snapped to Alwin and he spat on the ground. 'Contain the boy so he can't harm me or himself.' An orange smoke began to form from the saliva, it hissed and Alwin's eyes began to droop. 'In honour of your grand-sire.'

A blur surged past Alwin; he glanced wide-eyed at his empty hand.

'Nietra, show me Hau's weakness.' Hartur almost appeared to come from nowhere as she held up the hammer. 'For Alwin.'

'*Yes, mistress. This is so depressing, Lord Hau is such a powerful foe, worthy of my respect.*' A wave of bitterness swept through Alwin as Nietra's dark mist seeped towards Hau. '*He is afraid of being left behind and forgotten. Having heirs ensures he lives on.*'

Hartur turned and bolted towards the baby. 'His legacy is all that matters.'

Hau's monstrous cries raged behind Alwin as the boy sprinted towards Vero and past his wife. Alwin reached out to the child with thoughts of safety. When the baby felt safe, the forcefield sparked and went out and he scooped the boy up, snatching his wife's hand.

They jogged towards the door they had entered through, opened it and ran down the hallway. They stopped to listen, waiting in the oppressive darkness.

'Thank you, Hartur.'

She kissed his cheek; he felt her hot tears on her face. 'Only for you.'

As he cradled the fussing infant to his chest, Alwin pulled his wife towards him and kissed her. 'It will be okay.'

'Noooooo!' Hau's tortured cries hounded them. 'Not my son. Please, cousin, let me say goodbye to my child before you relieve me of the burden of life.'

'No. How many parents were killed by your hands leaving orphans in your wake? How many families were wiped out for your hate?' Ake's voice rose, demanding respect.

Alwin waited. Hartur, hidden in the shadows, whispered, 'I can't destroy my lord.'

'I understand.' Alwin passed her the child and squeezed her shoulder before sprinting back into the dystopian battle scene filled with divine light, hideous apparitions, torn upholstery and shattered furniture. He stumbled over some broken crockery; the smell of death, blood and butchered flesh made him gag.

Hau laughed and the insidious noise made Ake shudder. 'Thousands of *human* men and women.'

'How many innocents did you slaughter?' Ake began to weep; her tears floated as golden specks of light in front of her.

'Too many humans to count. I especially enjoyed killing Regians. They slaughtered my people.' Hau grinned.

Ake screamed. 'You b——.' She pointed and the golden specks shot towards Hau as barbs of light. They pierced the shield, which exploded. Ake wiped blood out of her eyes as she was splattered with viscous fluid. Hau's tentacle had been cut in half; blood decorated the floor like spilled wine and she wiped her mouth as the metallic taste lingered on her lips.

Het groaned and hoisted himself up as Flo stumbled towards Ake, her dress stained with red. 'My darling friend, you are not Hau. Let him surrender and we will administer justice properly.'

Ake turned to meet Flo's fear-filled eyes. 'His death *is* justice. He is a monster. How would you administer justice? A regular person would be powerless against him.'

'We strip him of his powers and hand him over to his slaves once we have read his crimes out to his citizens,' said Flo.

'Then we remove any trace of his name and likeness from Velterra. We install Vero as king and never tell him of his heritage.' Alwin sniffed.

Hau roared with grief and he charged at Ake. Lan jumped in front of her. His knives slashed towards Hau and captured the light as Ake imbued them with divine power. Hau bellowed as Lan's knives glowed and slashed at his skin, scorching his hideous form, and he stumbled back.

'You took the lives of others, including children. Your baby has now been taken from you,' said Lan.

'I lost countless children,' bellowed Hau.

'This is your last and you are about to perish.' Ake's eyes were filled with rage.

Alwin reached within and tried to calm Ake's anger, but he could not break through her celestial wrath.

'Agree to surrender and I will bring your child to safety. He is surrounded by gugglies, his only defence a shield that is controlled by his emotions. I am sure the hisses from those monsters will eventually overwhelm him and the shield will falter,' Alwin said.

Ake gasped. 'He is just an innocent baby.' Her eyes brimmed with tears as she glanced at Alwin.

Hau's claw reached out and grabbed her, before he manipulated his tattered tentacle into a dagger and drove it into her side. Ake screamed as she bled; a new blood shield erupted around them both. Ake burst into golden fire and the light crackled against her enemy's forcefield.

'Now, Alwin, bring my baby here or she dies.'

Lan was suddenly surrounded by a barrage of new monsters. His face paled and he took a step back. Trolls roared and beat the ground with their clubs, hyena hybrids cackled as a surge of goblins charged at Het, Flo and Alena who turned to fight their new combatants.

Several goblin heads flew past as Het lopped them off. Flo whispered something and a troll was split in half. Alena jabbed a hyena hybrid in the ribs and it grunted as she delivered a blow to its side with Din.

Lan dived into Hau's shield and groaned as scorch marks appeared along his arms. Fighting against the pain, the shield bent to his will and he crossed the barrier to deliver a blow to the side of Hau's face with one knife then the other. Ake drew on her power and shattered Hau's shield, and all three were flung to the floor by the explosion. Lan grabbed Ake to cushion her fall. His right ankle gave way and he fell, cracking his skull on the floor. His pupils dilated as he mumbled incoherently to himself.

Ake began to weep and Flo rushed towards them, falling to her knees beside Lan. Her hands gently brushed his forehead as green light engulfed him. Groaning, Lan sat up and winced, putting a hand to his head as he cursed.

Hau turned on Alwin. 'Give me my child or they will all die!' Hau waved his hand and Alena, Flo and Het were held against the wall as monsters charged towards them, weapons aimed to kill.

Hartur rushed into the room, with the infant cradled in one arm, the other outstretched towards their foe. 'My lord, take the child but let Alwin and his family go.'

'Never; they must die,' roared Hau.

Hartur stared at their foe, her eyes filled with tears. 'I believed in you.' As she rushed towards her husband, she handed him the infant.

'You are incapable of killing them.' Alwin smiled gently and reached into Hau's feelings. 'You came to respect Ake and Lan as substitute parents, and Amities was like a little brother to you.'

'What would you know?' Hau growled. Weapons clattered to the ground and the loud outburst made Alwin jump.

'You thought they betrayed you and that was the final thing that broke you, allowing Drianna access to your soul. I forgive you, Hau.' Alwin smiled sadly, his eyes awash with tears. 'But your life is forfeit.'

Hau roared and charged; a huge wave of blood swept towards Alwin. In the foul depths were distorted faces, hellish monsters and twisted forms. They began to claw their way out, scrambling to consume their victims, their screams and bellows distorting all pleasant sound.

'Defend us,' yelled Alwin, his eyes wide as he backed away. 'Hurry.'

'I shall defend,' yelled Din.

'For honour,' cried Imeall.

'I shall master their weakness,' said Nietra.

'Of cou-rse,' stammered Dage.

'In the silence of death, even the godless will answer to me,' stated Hushin as the monsters rushed towards Alwin.

The smell of rotting flesh made Alwin gag and terrible screams rent the air. His body shook with Hau's feelings of hate and revenge. Vero wailed and he held the infant to him. 'I am sorry, little one, your sire's beliefs are more important than his love for you. I understand.'

Forgive me, Hartur. Alwin placed a hand to his heart. *You made my heart complete.*

Nietra almost splintered Alwin's consciousness as it screamed in his mind. *'I refuse to be destroyed. You must make use of the weapons, master. Strip Hau of his powers.'*

'And you only tell me this now.' Alwin bent down as the monsters left the wave of blood. A claw raked his back as the hideous maelstrom of crimson swirled around them. Metallic droplets settled on his tongue and he spat them out. 'Aid me now.'

'Well, his power is entrancing. But my self-preservation is more urgent.' The hammer vibrated.

Alwin blinked in surprise, Alena let out a gasp as Din flew out of her arms and straight towards the Master of the Forge. Din floated in front of him, its blue forcefield holding off the onslaught. Dage fired and a wave of vibrant arrows shot across the room. Hau bellowed as they struck. Hushin shook in Lan's hand and he aimed the weapon at Hau, ducking as the weapon unleashed a catastrophic explosion forcing him to drop his weapon before scarlet ribbons spurted from Hau's face.

Alwin's eyes snapped to his companions, Lan, Ake and Het, using their magic to defeat the other monsters. Waves of druid fire, bolts of lightning, and jets of water lashed out at the hideous apparitions as more swarmed across the field of battle.

Alena summoned some rats from within the walls to cover Hau, who growled as the beasts nipped and scratched before he shook them off.

'I am no warrior.' Alwin swallowed hard.

'There comes a time when the meek must rise up to defend them-selves and those they love,' said Hushin as it lay fallen on the ground amongst flesh, pooling blood and the corpses of fallen foes.

'Your voice sounds very familiar. Grandfather?'

'When an empath and a Master of the Forge creates a sentient weapon and imbues it with thought and emotion a little part of them is left behind, including their wisdom,' explained Hushin.

'Thank you, Grandfather.' Alwin blinked back tears. 'Din, come here.'

'Yes, master.' Din floated backwards, keeping him and the baby shielded.

'Protect this child at all costs, he is the future of Velterra.' Alwin turned and placed the baby down under a large pot that had fallen off the table. 'Hopefully it will give you some protection.'

'And you, master?' asked Din.

'I am insignificant. Just a lowly blacksmith's son. My duty is to our lord father and he has deemed I should fight. Do not falter in your protection of the child.'

As blue light radiated in a sphere above him, Alwin turned to face Hau. Het hefted his sword at Alwin, the sword clattered to the floor at the younger man's feet.

'Remember our lessons, Alwin. Become one with the weapon.'

Alwin snatched up the sword, his muscles heaving with the effort. Imeall flared with iridescent light as the empath chan-nelled all his emotions into the sword and charged.

Hau laughed as he easily dodged the blows. Alwin closed his

eyes, his heart twinging with pain as he latched onto his opponent's need for a legacy, and it bubbled to the surface between them like a festering wound, bonding them.

'You stole my child,' roared Hau. His damaged arm changed back into a tentacle and it reached out and grabbed Alwin who thrust the sword at his enemy as a crab claw clamped down on his arm. 'I do not wish to kill you, boy.'

'I will kill you and your son will be raised with no knowledge of you.'

'Die then.' Hau squeezed Alwin, whose chest heaved as dizziness made his vision blur.

While Alwin blinked to relieve his distress, golden light pummelled into the claw, snapping it off. Thick dark blood gushed from the wound and Hau turned to face Ake as Alwin dropped to his knees, the sword still gripped in his injured arm.

Het and Lan had leapt to Ake's defence; long knives glinted as they struck. Monsters retreated as the large warrior smashed his fists into the face of a huge, unrecognisable beast. Alena was flinging whatever she could find at their enemies from rocks and chairs to knives, and delivering her share of kicks and strikes. Flo sang in a near whisper; beasts and demons dropped to the ground, cradling their heads with claws and appendages, their snarls and grunts near inaudible as they gave in to sleep. A shadow flitted past; a glimpse of red hair and purple eyes as blood spurted from the retreating enemies.

'*She is safe*,' muttered Tarven as he sparkled briefly before dissolving into the minute shadows.

'You don't give up, do you, cousin?'

'Never.' Ake glared at Hau.

His cruel eyes settled on his sire. 'Dearest Father. A newborn who grew too quickly and too strong to be human. One who had to be born into a family descended from the hated giant. His rage for humans fuelling his decisions. One who convinced others he was human yet he should have died at the hands of the Shadow Masters. One who could harden his skin to deflect deadly blows.'

Het's eyes burned with anger. 'I never told anyone that.'

'Lucky for you, your little brother may forgive you for not telling him all this.' Hau grinned.

The warrior's hands clenched into fists. 'I never told them because I only knew after death.'

Hau chuckled coldly. 'Convenient lie.'

Lan gripped his long knives, his knuckles white as sweat beaded on his brow. 'How did Dane not know of Het's rebirth?'

Ake's power blinked out and Hau smirked, his eyes pools of glee. 'Dane knew something was missing. He had been stricter with his eldest when the earth was new, trying to impart his wisdom to his temperamental eldest and felt such guilt for it. Why do you think he felt the need to train a replacement? Some instinct to right a wrong. When he failed to keep Het alive, he tried with Ori and failed again.'

'A giant's natural stonelike skin; Het should have died when the Shadow Master struck and poisoned him. Heck, even I wasn't immune to their poison.' Ake paled and whispered to herself. 'Yuck, kissed by two brothers.'

'Maybe this is a discussion for later.' Flo glanced to her friend. 'You probably shouldn't have spoken that last part aloud.'

Hartur's voice floated from the shadows. 'Some people are into that.'

'We aren't blood brothers in this mortal form, Ake.' Het sighed. 'I favour the giants; my form couldn't change earthside.'

Lan shook his head. 'This is ridiculous.'

Hau's right brow rose as he focused on Ake. 'Distracted again when it matters most.'

Alwin stood up as Hau's magic streamed towards Ake, divine

light and dark power vying for control. It sparked and hissed as Ake's own inner light flooded forth. Alwin's power prickled beneath his skin. He unleashed it, his body almost buckling under the enormity of it. He shook as he reached for the deepest, most primal part of Hau's soul, drawing all the essence into himself. He bolstered himself, snatched the sword with both hands and bolted towards his enemy, dodging the bodies of dead monsters before he plunged the sword into Hau's side.

Black blood spurted into Alwin's face and he wiped it away as Hau roared and slumped to the ground moaning. Their enemy's magic suddenly went out like a lone candle blown out in an otherwise dark room.

Hau turned, his eyes locked on a corpse. Droplets of blood shot towards the blood mage and Hau grunted with effort as Alwin was lifted from his feet and flung across the room. Lan's powerful wings beat the air and he shot up and caught the boy before landing and placing him on his feet. Lan winced, stumbling as his right leg jarred.

'Thanks, Lufar.'

Lan shrugged. 'No problem, I'll always be there for you.'

'Middle age hitting you hard?' Het laughed.

'What about you, warrior?' Lan grinned.

Het thumped his chest. 'Giant blood, grrr.'

Ake's mouth set in a hard line, twitched at the corners. 'Always the prankster.'

'Got to lighten this grim affair.' The large warrior shifted his stance. 'If Hau makes us clutch at despair he wins.' He glanced to Lan. 'Your injuries sounded horrific. Your body has lost its youth so take it easy.'

Lan nodded. 'They were.'

Alwin jogged towards Vero. Din's shield dropped away and he tossed aside the pot, snatching up the infant. 'You're okay. Thank goodness.'

'No, Alwin, he doesn't deserve to say goodbye to the child,' Ake cried.

Alwin turned to Lan. As Hau's powers waned, the sealed doors screeched open and the windows shattered. As glass fell to the floor like frozen tears, early morning light filtered into the room, bouncing off the shards as if they were sparkling diamonds. 'Lufar, bring the slaves here.'

Lan nodded and sprinted through a door. Alwin stepped towards Ake. 'Have mercy before he is justly punished.'

Ake sighed. 'So be it.'

Alwin held out the baby to Hau.

'I can always make more, if I survive today. I am sorry my child, but you will be a worthy sacrifice for Velterra.' Hau's hideous laughter reverberated around the room. 'Give up your life-force.'

The baby began to wail. Ake's eyes narrowed on Hau and golden light streamed forth.

The urge to exist, to live and succeed at all costs flooded Alwin. 'Dage, fire and do so bravely.'

The bow glowed a startling emerald. *Yes, master.*

A huge arrow made of scintillating colours struck Hau in the chest. Alwin charged at him and pushed on the sword already stuck in his opponent's side. Hau gagged and blood oozed out of his mouth. He slumped to the ground and closed his eyes. 'It is over. No more.'

Lan ran into the room with slaves of various ages, all armed with makeshift weapons. Their eyes widened with fear and they began backing off as they saw the hideous creature on the ground. Alwin drew on Het's chivalry, flooding their hearts with the wrath of the righteous. They rushed towards Hau as cries of justice and suppressed agony spilled from their lips.

'For the just.'

'For the innocent.'

'My child. You took her from me.'

'So I can eat something other than bread.'

'I don't want to hurt anymore.'

Flo screamed and Het grabbed her as Hau's victims ran towards their son. The abomination bellowed in pain as his former slaves drove their weapons into his flesh, peeling off the outer shell of the monster to the person below. The sword in his side clattered to the ground at Alwin's feet. Ake wept as pain filled Hau's eyes and she squeezed her own shut. Alwin felt her bittersweet emotions; pictures flittered across his consciousness as she remembered Hau as a gentle child and teenager.

'Enough,' Ake yelled and the slaves backed off, their heads hung in reverence as Ake spread her shimmering wings, her golden eyes softening as several cowered before her. 'Go, be free and try to have mercy despite what you've been through.' The crowd departed through the doors.

Hau grinned and Vero began to thrash about. The infant's cheeks reddened.

'Stop, Hau.' Ake's eyes snapped to Hau's. 'He is your child. Be a father and give him to me to keep safe.'

'Never,' Hau screamed. 'I need his power to live, to defeat those who abandoned me. The child will live but have no magic.'

Het rushed at his son. Alwin threw him the sword and filled the sword with all the love Hau's family had ever felt for him, Lan's respect and pride at his endurance when he was a teenager, Ake and Flo's love for him as family.

Het swung the sword and plunged it into Hau's heart. Hau clutched at it, his jaw agape as he locked eyes with his sire who dropped to his knees in front of his son, his eyes wet with tears. 'I had no choice. You left me no choice.' Het's eyes softened. 'You tried to hurt your own son and made me kill mine.' Het gripped

Imeall and pulled. Blood pooled on his shaking hand and he thrust the weapon aside before he snatched his son to him as Hau gagged. 'My heart is broken.'

Hau spat on the ground. 'There was always a choice, Father. Just leave me to die on my own. You abandoned Mother and me to save Ake and Lan.' Hau groaned and tried to rise.

Het lifted his haunted eyes to his son. As a gentle gust of wind like the wings of a butterfly caressed him, Caoimhe appeared, her beautiful wings shimmering, and she began to sway as if dancing to a horrid tune in the aftermath of powerful magic and bloodshed. Hau's eyes filled with joy as she began to whistle in tune to some ancient song. *Fairies bring joy and open even the hardest hearts,* she signed before, in an instant, she was gone.

'I am sorry. Forgive me.' Hau began to weep; his eyes shone with remorse. His now mortal hands clutched at his father's shirt. 'Stay with me.'

There was a hellish scream as an ominous shadow squeezed out of Hau and rushed towards Ake. Her eyes blazed and it was surrounded by brilliant light.

Alwin felt excruciating pain as Hau clutched at his heart. He nullified his former enemy's pain as Ake obliterated the shadow then knelt before Hau, picking up a discarded knife.

'For the pain Drianna caused and still causes. And the fact you accepted her.'

Shadows seeped from Nietra and swept around Ake. *Feed me, sweet goddess. That's it, yum yum.*

'Nietra is feeding on her and forcing her fears to the surface,' shouted Alwin.

Lan grabbed his wife's hand and she dropped the weapon before she rose and tried to take flight. He hauled her towards him. 'No you don't, my darling. You have dealt with Drianna before. Does Hau's soul deserve less mercy? Release him.'

'He slaughtered too many and embraced Drianna's hate.'

Lan took her face in both his hands and their eyes locked. He gave her a gentle smile. 'And how many children did Drianna kill?'

Ake nodded. 'I don't know what came over me. His life must be taken first.'

'Please take his pain, Alwin.' Flo went and sat down by Hau. 'I love you, my son. You are forgiven but you must pay for your sins. Do so bravely and you can join your beloved cousin and your twin brother in the underworld if Amities allows it.'

Hau reached out and clutched her hand. 'I did love you, Mother. My hate was borne of the loss of my people, and no matter what I did as their prince, I couldn't save them.'

'I know.' Flo caressed his face and began to sing an elven lullaby.

Sleep my dear one, you are safe and loved.
Dee and Sorendee watch from above.
Thank them for animals and the forest so green.
Their love can be found in a wholesome dream.

Dream of mother's and father's love.
Wrap yourself in sleep's sweet embrace,
Forever held in the gods' grace.

Hau's eyes began to close. Alwin dragged out the pain; it swirled around the empath in a grey haze.

Flo cradled her son's head in her lap before drawing a dagger from her dress, a beautiful piece of fine workmanship. Wolves baying at the moon were etched into the silver hilt while blue sapphire had been worked into the sharp steel blade, spelling out the elvish word for honour and duty, Osen. 'This is Mandami's dagger. Reserved for the righteous God of War, it offers the chance at redemption when a defiler clasps it in their hand in their last moments and admits their sins.'

'Is that what I will be remembered for? For my admissions on my death?' Hau reached up and kissed his mother's cheek, crimson streaking her face, before he took the offered dagger. 'I freely admit I was a sinner, a defiler. That I should have done better. Give me a chance to do better. Let me live.' He glanced at Ake. 'I return freely what I took.' A white haze surrounded Hau before drifting towards Ake and disappearing as if she had absorbed it.

Blood oozed from Hau's lips and he gagged. 'Death comes for me.' His eyes widened before he chuckled softly. 'Of all the people to greet me in the afterlife. Hello Orilan.'

Ake knelt beside Flo and pressed a kiss to Hau's brow as his eyes fixated on something beyond their realm. 'It takes great remorse for someone to admit their wrong doings and seek redemption before they pass.'

'Amities,' whispered Hau. The weapon clattered to the floor as Hau took his last breath.

Flo and Ake's wails rent the air as they lowered their charge to the floor and rose. Het crushed both women to him, his eyes liquid pools of despair. 'I could have gotten to know him, but he was defiled by Drianna's taint and now he is dead while I'm alive.'

'It had to be done. By our lord's grace, he had to answer for his crimes against Cirichad and for all the lives he took for his cause.' Alwin picked up Imeall, handing the sword to Het who released Ake. A terrible sadness swept through the empath and he took a shuddering breath. 'My own soul has been stained with murder in the process; no matter how just the cause.'

There was a tinkling noise and a small black flame arose from Hau's body and floated towards Ake who turned away and crossed her arms. There was a ringing of bells and Orilan appeared in his skeleton form. He removed his mask and gave Ake a sweet smile.

Alena gawked at the newcomer. 'I can see the dead now?'

'We've all been touched by it,' whispered Hartur.

'Delightful goddess, take that power for yourself in case Drianna returns someday.' Nietra's head glowed and a flash of crimson pooled in Ake's eyes.

Alwin patted Lan's shoulder. 'That hammer is not necessarily good. Look at Luma.'

'I see you ignoring that soul, Ake. You must decide whether its worthy of the underworld or must be destroyed. It is an elven soul now and cannot reincarnate without great sacrifice.' Orilan brushed her hand tenderly and she snatched it away.

Lan walked towards his wife and shot his oldest son a scathing look. 'Still trying to flirt with her, Ori?'

Ori shrugged. 'A guy gets lonely.'

Lan sighed and turned his attention to his wife. 'You are the Goddess of Mercy. It isn't like you to delay forgiveness.'

Alwin reached for Ake's soul, taking a breath as it swam behind his eyes—webs of sunlight interlaced with delicate silver stars, magic crackled along the weaves like banked embers, blotches of decay from trauma, fear, desertion, righteous anger and desolation. He began to bend it to his will, snatching at the core of her overwhelming mercy, kindness, loyalty and forgiveness. 'Such, such power,' Alwin gasped.

Ori grinned. 'Yep, and I tasted that power once. That's why Sorendee kept her caged.'

Ake's power bubbled to the surface; her lip trembled and her gaze flitted to Alwin's. 'You really want me to forgive him? He knew how evil Drianna was yet he sought out her knowledge. Thousands lost their lives to his whims, not just soldiers but elderly, children and whole families. How can I forgive that?' Tears welled in her eyes. 'Trust me, I have seen his remorse and want to, but I don't know if I can.'

Alwin gave her a gentle smile. 'Luma, you have forgiven worse souls than this.'

Het strode over to his friend. 'Ake, you stubborn, kind, merciful woman. Look at me.'

Ake raised her tear-filled eyes to his and the warrior gave her a sad smile. 'You will not destroy the soul of my son. He has been punished and I am willing to sacrifice my life so he can reincarnate as many times as necessary until he learns how to love and live without hate.' Het reached out and hugged her. 'I beg you take my soul for his.'

Flo began to weep. 'Please, Ake, there is no need for any of this. Let go of the pain.'

Het released Ake and knelt before her; she placed her hand on his shoulder. 'He will be destroyed. He readily embraced Drianna's evil taint which can swallow life itself.'

'Perfect. Delicious.' Nietra hummed with power.

Alwin snatched up the hammer and it radiated with iridescent light. 'Be good or you shall be recast as a different weapon.'

'I'll be good. Too bad I was originally forged for Hau and now he's dead.' The hammer shuddered and fell silent.

'Ake, please don't do it, you will regret it.' Lan gave her a gentle smile. 'I trust you to do the right thing.'

'Your faith is misplaced.' Ake held her hand out to Hau's soul, weeping softly as the soul fluttered in her hand like a moth.

'She's done. Along with Drianna's and Hau's betrayal, she feels she cannot risk their influence ever returning.' Alwin sighed. 'She has also pushed me out. I can't help.'

'My leven, you will leave me with no choice,' cried Lan.

'Do as you must,' said Ake.

'Get up, Het.' Lan turned and gave Ake a commanding look. 'I am sorry to do this, honey. You can berate me afterwards. I command you to commend Hau's soul to the underworld. His pain and Drianna's influence corrupted him. You will not destroy his soul because you would regret that decision and the suffering it would cause your dearest friends. Drianna's curse is broken, and please know that I am here for you. Don't let fear prevent you from doing the right thing.'

Ake glared at him. 'How dare you command me!'

'You chose me as your soul's counterpart.' Lightening streaked along Lan's wings as he unfurled them. 'The gods have allowed me to do so as the Lord of Justice. Everyone has a breaking point, and even a merciful goddess must have a failsafe in case the world falls from her power.'

Ake's eyes flashed with anger; she attempted to brush the soul aside. 'Seek redemption elsewhere, it's the best you will get.'

Lan strode forward and pulled his wife into his arms, dipping his head to whisper against her mouth. 'I command you to send him to my domain.'

Ake's head snapped back and a tear rolled down her cheek. 'You, of all people, forcing me to do something against my wishes.' She scooped up the soul hovering nearby. 'You are hereby trapped in the Lord of Death's domain, alone, without a friendly touch until you are filled with enough remorse and love that the good souls in that now sacred place may reach out to you when you are free of taint.'

Flo began to weep. 'Farewell, my son. Your soul will suffer in retribution, but if you learn to be free of hate you will be united with loved ones.'

The soul floated across to Orilan. He swung his serrated scimitar over Hau's body, separating the connection between flesh and soul. The soul landed on his hand. 'Be at peace.' The soul quivered before fading away. Orilan smiled and winked at Ake. 'I bet my father is going to get it later. If he gets too much you know where I am.'

'Goodbye son.' Lan gritted his teeth as Ori waved and disappeared.

The room fell silent as if all living things held their breath. Ake turned and ran through an open door and the others followed. As the dawn light washed over them, Alwin felt their hearts soar; Drianna's final taint had left their world.

CHAPTER FIFTY-FIVE

They had not spoken to each other as they all separated and returned to their homes, exhausted and overwhelmed with all that had happened. Ake put the key in the lock and pushed open the door. She stripped herself of her tattered and soiled clothing and threw it in the fireplace, conjuring fire to consume the garment.

Filling up the sink, she began to lather herself with soap, washing herself thoroughly before she pulled the plug. As the dirty water drained away, her shoulders slumped with sadness and exhaustion, and she grabbed a hand towel and patted herself dry. Ake turned to face her husband who was outside, stripped to his waist, washing himself at the cast iron water pump. He pushed the handle several times and the water filled the watering can. Lan poured it over himself and scrubbed himself with some rough bark.

He entered the house and stared at her, awaiting her wrath. She walked past him and crawled into the bed and closed her eyes. He climbed in next to her and wrapped his arms around her as she began to weep. She opened her eyes and turned in his arms.

'I am sorry I commanded you.'

Ake gave him a bitter smile. 'I am glad you did. Flo and Het would never have forgiven me. They may still not.'

Lan kissed her. 'I doubt it. Het drove a sword threw his heart as he had no other option.'

'But he didn't condemn his soul.' Ake began to shake with sobs.

'I am sure they understand.'

'I want to leave this horrid city tomorrow.'

'Give it a few days, so we can make arrangements.'

Ake snuggled into his arms and they both fell asleep.

The crowd was divided as Hau's body was readied for cremation. He was dressed in royal robes and lay on an ornate pyre covered in jewellery, valuable sketchy tomes and rare flowers.

'He doesn't deserve a royal burial,' muttered a barefooted, dishevelled woman.

'Chop him up for hog feed,' said a small child dressed in rags, his dirt-streaked face locked on the corpse. It was four days later and Flo's lineage had been established. She had even undergone a truth ordeal where a magen had flicked through her mind while repeating questions and seeing if her thoughts stayed the same. A sample of hers and Het's blood had been taken and sent to a blood magen and compared to a sample of Hau's, confirming the legitimacy of his parents.

The poorest citizens sided with Flo, hoping she would become regent until Vero came of age. The nobles of the fourth line and above argued and showed no compassion as they began to adorn the body in gold bars.

'Usurpers.'

A mage in blue robes muttered within hearing of Ake and Lan. 'I vow to rise against them if they dare to change Velterra in any way.'

Word had been sent to Cirichad via magic and had been received by the Caelestis Cause and relayed to the king. The king of Cirichad questioned how they received messages so quickly when the service was so advantageous for his people. He sent word that Cirichad would send five hundred troops by ship and they would aid Elder Flower as regent until she was able to rally enough followers to ensure her and Vero's safety.

Flo had sent King Cirus a note of gratitude and it was received warmly.

Some of the lower ranked magen had decided to side with Flo and stood by, awaiting her command to light the pyre.

'Hau has fallen and with him crumbles his society based on slavery and exploiting the poor and vulnerable for his cause. His actions started out noble and that is why I wish to give his body to the gods in the ancient way; in memory of the person he used to be before he allowed evil to corrupt him. The dark tomes that will burn with him gave him access to dreadful blood magic and will be consumed with him. I will weep no more tears of sorrow for they are lost on someone so cruel. Instead, I will turn my guidance to Vero and hope that he will be a better man than his father.' Flo gestured to the baby in Het's arms.

Flo turned to look at her friends gathered nearby. Hartur and Alwin stood, heads bowed. Alena's eyes were filled with wariness as she scanned the crowd looking for would-be assassins, Din clutched in her strong grip. Ake and Lan clasped hands and gave the new regent a sad smile.

Flo bowed her head and the magen conjured flame. Hau's body began to burn. No one shed a tear as flames consumed the body eagerly; the only sound was Hau's sizzling flesh.

Lan glanced up from Dane's tome and smiled. The sound of clacking needles was comforting as Ake practiced her newfound hobby of knitting. Several misshapen squares of wool had been discarded on the table, ready to unpick later. Lan turned to the last few pages of the tome and his heart threatened to stop in his chest. His breath came in quick waves as his eyes scanned the last few words before he tossed the tome on the table, tore open a letter and began reading. His hands shook and he stammered as he struggled to get the words out.

Ake put down the needles and grabbed the tome; her eyes roamed over the text before she gently closed the book.

'He tried to save my sisters.'

Ake stood and came around to where he sat and knelt down next to him.

'All this time I thought my father didn't care. He adored us and my mother. He protected me with the last of his strength, ensuring one day you and I would be together. Read the letter.' Lan began to weep, his head on her shoulder.

Ake picked up the letter and read.

To my son Trebrelan,

My name is Dane. I am a prince of Anwyl and married to your mother Regona whom I love dearly. Unfortunately, due to a cruel ward I cannot touch Regona or be anywhere near her until you are in your twenties. This has rent a hole in my soul. You may have heard that I abandoned you, your sisters and mother. By the time this letter reaches your hands I will have either saved them or been defeated by their captor Bozzwanna, your mother's sister.

My dear son, you will find out after your coming-of-age ceremony at one hundred that you are an Arakaen, a type of winged elven prince who can master a domain such as air and I believe, in your case, storms. It is around this time I beg of you to seek out your grandfather Swan Rider, King of Anwyl. He has information about your alter ego that I cannot mention in this letter for fear of Drianna's minions finding out.

When you hit your teenage years in your third decade, your Arakaen blood will burn with the need to find your mate. If I am correct, Hanton will betroth you to your mate after a year's courtship as per mystic customs. If you are anything like your glorious mother, you will try to defy the prophecy, but you are destined to be the spouse and champion of the Goddess of Mercy.

At first, it may seem as if your budding powers are weak in contrast to the tasks expected of you and your spouse. These powers will take decades to master and will grow once your union is official. Drianna will try to kill your mate and torture you in the hopes to separate you. Stay strong for each other. Your son is destined to bring about the downfall of Drianna and lessen her influence on our world.

I am so proud of you, my dear child, and I love you. Please be happy with your mate. By bringing her to Caelestis under Hanton's protection I hope you can avoid the misery of the long, lonely search I had for my wife Regona. This journal has resided with the head of my order and I assume has been delivered by a druid now that you are eighteen.

Your loving father,

Dane.

Ake wrapped her arms around him. 'He loved you all. Take comfort in that.'

Lan pulled away from her. 'This information brings me peace.'

Ake smiled and kissed him.

Lan blushed suddenly. 'I did skip the bits my father scribbled in as an afterthought, where he and my mother were intimate. Ma even made notes of her own.' Lan's cheeks reddened. 'Her additions were not about them fooling around.'

Ake laughed. 'Good call to skip those parts.'

'I am a lot like my mother it seems. I enjoy music, especially the harp and I like to think I can sing.'

'From what I remember of Regona she was sweet and kind, but had a terrible temper. You are much like her and you have a beautiful voice.'

Lan gave Ake a radiant smile and began unravelling the discarded squares of wool as she sat back down to continue her knitting. 'My mother wasn't always sweet and humble. It seems she learnt patience eventually and quarrelled mightily with my father in their early marriage. They were both stubborn. But they made their peace in the end. I remember having a conversation with my father a day after he encouraged me to write to you and profess my feelings. He, in his wisdom, advised me to never let an argument or misunderstanding stagnate or my relationship could sour. Dane's biggest regret was that they never truly settled into a peaceful life or curbed their misunderstandings.' He smiled. 'My father was wise.'

Ake nodded. 'True, and while we are on the talk of parents … My mother mentioned you brought a circus on two occasions while visiting my tribe.'

Lan looked up from his task and grinned. 'Did I ever tell you that I went through a phase of wanting to be a ring master? I hired the entertainers from nearby villages. I wasn't meant to be a ring master and failed terribly when I didn't realise I needed to travel with the circus and provide food and lodging. They stayed at Caelestis for a while until the teachers ordered them away. I was a terrible headmaster too.'

Ake laughed. 'You are so cute. You were a great headmaster when our sons attended Caelestis.'

'I wasn't fourteen by then. And, by the way, elflings and pets are cute, not full grown elven males.'

'Am I cute?' asked Ake.

'Yes, but that's different.'

Ake gave him a sultry smile. 'Well, if I'm not allowed to find you cute your bed can stay empty.'

'Fine, I'm cute.'

Ake laughed and Lan joined in.

Alena looked at her bandaged body in the mirror. She handed over some coins to the healer and stood up. The healer handed her a bitter potion.

'You will need to take this daily for six weeks to negate the poison from the gugglies. I am amazed at your resilience.'

Alena smiled. 'When my family and friends are in danger it's amazing how resolute I can be.'

'Are you going to the coronation?'

Alena nodded. 'Yes and thank you.'

She threw on her finely made shirt and brushed her hair as the healer left. Picking up Din and her backpack, she headed out of the inn towards the palace.

'Hartur, I am safe.' Alwin squeezed her hand as they walked towards the palace while his wife glanced about warily.

Hartur had clung to him ever since they had returned home a week ago and was warring within herself for betraying the lord she had once idolised. They were both dressed like royalty. Flo had sent over several garments, but they had declined a royal escort. Velterra needed to return to some form of stability so Flo had ascended the throne and was to be crowned today.

There was a whistle behind them and they turned and saw Alena striding towards them dressed regally herself.

'We are running late,' stammered Dage.

'Who cares,' muttered Nietra attached to Hartur's hip. 'All that power, wasted.'

Alena reached them. 'Mind if I walk with you two?'

'Of course not.' Alwin smiled.

Hartur's eyes alighted on Alena's backpack. 'Are you leaving?'

Alena nodded. 'After the ceremony. Luma and Lufar are coming with me. They are going to settle in the village.' Alena grinned. 'Luma wants to open a school and Lufar wants to be a carpenter. It's so quaint after they have been gods and royalty.'

Alwin smiled. 'My grandfather said all they ever dreamt of was a quiet life together surrounded by friends and family. Mystics are eternal students not cut out for the evil in the world.'

Hartur smiled. 'They did a fine job defending it. I think they were more than adequate for the task. I hope they find some peace.'

'I agree,' said Alena.

As they reached the palace they waited for the crowd to pass. The gate had been replaced with a portcullis and the decaying walls had been buttressed with stone. Flo had hired anyone who could wield a weapon from villages nearby and several stood dressed in comfortable attire armed with pitchforks or scythes, guarding the path. The pay was excessive and the meals nutritious and filling. As it nourished the soldiers' bodies, it nurtured feelings of loyalty towards their generous Regent who treated them as people rather than tools. Alena had given Flo some of her loyal soldiers as a gift to the new monarch and, as they crossed into the courtyard, they noted some of them on patrol.

A guard approached them and bowed. 'You are expected, please follow me.'

The three friends fell in line behind and entered the palace.

———∿∿∿———

Ake shouldered her pack and turned to watch her husband lock the door. The little dragier cheeped inside its cage atop her backpack. *All that we own is in these bags. A tome from Lan's father, our wedding rings, a pistol, Caoimhe's first drawing, Amities's first mechanical formula and Mandami's wolf dagger. This is all I have from centuries of life.* Ake sighed.

She was dressed in a purple dress with a well-fitted bodice which was attached to a four-tiered skirt. The gown had long, puffed sleeves. The dress was a gift from Flo; purple was the colour of nobility. Ake tightened the belt around her waist and slipped a few extra coins into the purse attached. She smiled down at the new, colourful, engraved buckle that bore their new family crest—a rearing rainbow unicorn on a royal blue backdrop encircled by mystic flames and wearing a blue crown as the sun blazed in a corner. She glanced at Lan who wore his mystic robes at Flo's insistence. He had altered the high collar so that it didn't rest around his throat. Black, fitted trousers were worn underneath, and slung over his shoulder was a sash with the same design as Ake's belt, but the blue centre patch extended into white cloth with multiple blazing suns instead of a singular one. This, coupled with the golden suede riding boots trimmed with silver that graced his feet, were a little ornate for his taste, but the boots were a gift from Het so he wore them without complaint.

Lan turned and frowned at her; his eyes filled with concern. 'Are you okay, honey?'

'We have accomplished what we set out to do. Every happy day after seems so surreal. We are adding to our family and will likely have a peaceful life now. Our sons never got that luxury. All we have are our memories and a few rare mementos kept from rotting by magic.'

'Did Mandami and Amities never experience peace and joy after Drianna's defeat?' Lan gave her a gentle smile.

Ake nodded. 'Yes, they did. I meant their formative years were chaotic. We often had to leave to defeat Drianna's hives just so that we could stay together.'

'I agree, the gods have tested us sorely. Dee told me they had given up on this world. Sorendee intended to destroy it as humans had continuously corrupted this plane with war and cruelty. After every apocalypse they crawled out from the earth and rebuilt their civilisations with the aid of the dwarves and elves. This time round the humans rewarded the elves' kindness with suspicion and genocide.' Lan pulled Ake into his arms. 'Dee created a gentle soul and pleaded with her husband to give the humans one last chance. But Sorendee felt she was too powerful and withheld her. Gepatok went to mingle with mankind under the pretence of gathering information and you were born.' Lan stroked her hair and gazed down at her; his eyes filled with love. 'As Drianna's powers grew, she drew on the magic in the world, closing the gods' access to this plane by installing demons to guard the gates to our world. Magic will slowly leave most planes of existence, and as humankind starts to rely on science they will forget the gods and their morals. When this world winds down for the last time, the gods will ask you whether it is worth saving the souls of humankind and let them enter heaven.' Lan kissed her. 'There are so many people worthy of saving, my leven. Het, Flo, Alena, Hartur, Alwin and so many more. I vow to spend my life making you happy and hopefully your heart will be filled with love once more.'

Ake's eyes filled with tears before she suddenly grinned. Lan stared at her, his brows furrowing. She drew a handkerchief from her sleeve and wiped his mouth. 'That shade of lipstick suits you.'

'Well, in that case, I'll add to it.' Lan laughed then began showering her cheeks with kisses, his eyes softening as Ake giggled. 'Best sound in the world.'

'How are you dealing with the fact Het may be your divine brother?'

Lan's eyes softened. 'I don't know how I feel yet. I need time to process it. But if it's true, I'd be honoured to name him brother.'

'You really are a good man.'

'How insulting.' Lan tickled her. 'I am an elf.'

Ake smiled and ran away from him. He hurried after her but she kept out of arms' reach on the twenty-minute journey to the palace. He followed, not even attempting to close the gap, his eyes trained on their surroundings before he halted and grabbed her hand and gestured for her to be quiet.

A hooded figure stepped out from the alley. '*Edal vedar ruin.*'

The ground began to crumble beneath their feet. Ake stumbled as Lan leapt and pulled her over the newly formed crevasse. He swore as his ankle creaked. 'I can't keep fighting all the time.'

The figure turned and pointed at them. 'For Lord Hau.'

Green gas sprayed from the assailant's hands, spattering Lan's robe, and they began to hiss, forming a hole. Ake's water shield flared around them and Lan delivered a hand strike to the attacker's throat who gasped and slumped against him. He hoisted the unconscious body over his shoulder and began walking. 'The sooner we leave, the better.'

Ake nodded and they made the rest of the journey in silence. As they approached the palace, a guard came to meet them.

'The mage attacked us on the way here. I am assuming they are one of Hau's followers,' said Lan.

He handed the guard the assailant and they entered the palace.

—◆◆◆—

The throne room had been updated. Hau's hideous throne had been replaced with two stately chairs atop a small, golden wood dais. A purple carpet led from the main entrance to the dais. The doors were wide open and every curtain was drawn allowing sunlight to fill the room with natural light. Het and Flo were seated on the chairs. Het rocked a cradle nearby where Vero lay cooing softly. Banners on the walls, depicting a white leopard in full sprint surrounded by elven runes, blew gently in the breeze.

Alwin smiled. *So, our world has made another revolution and the glorious past gently merges with the present. Grandfather is right, the end will come soon and we will all be reunited. It may be weeks or centuries, but I intend to live my life to the fullest.*

The trumpets sounded as they had for him, Alena and Hartur, and Ake and Lan entered and were introduced.

'Announcing Lord Trebrelan, Arakaen of Anwyl, Lord of Justice, and his wife Telewanake, Princess of Relequis and the Goddess of Mercy.'

Alwin watched Hartur hold in her laughter. He glanced at Ake's face covered in red kisses and Lan wore a bright shade of lipstick.

Lan bowed and Ake curtseyed.

Flo stood and smiled. 'Welcome, my dear friends. Please join the others on this special occasion.'

Ake and Lan strode over to their comrades.

Flo looked exquisite in a golden, long-sleeved dress. The sleeves were lined with purple lace as was the hem. The garment fit snugly against her slim figure. She wore a pair of dainty white slippers. Her long chestnut hair had been curled and the ringlets crowned her face. A silver head chain crowned her brow; a single ruby glistened between her angled eyebrows, just above her button nose.

There was a cacophony of voices as a horde of excited peasants and former slaves entered the room, chatting excitedly among themselves. As they approached the throne, the noise died down and they knelt.

Het's voice boomed out over the crowd. 'No, we serve the people, please stand.' And the group stood and stared at him in awe.

He rose and made a kingly figure dressed in white plate mail. Imeall was attached to his hip in a silver leather sheath with golden elven runes. His long chestnut hair shone. A purple cloak with white trim was draped across his shoulders.

The room fell into hushed whispers as Hurley entered the throne room followed by Caoimhe. The little couple made a striking pair. Caoimhe was dressed in a scarlet skirt and halter top; her gossamer wings shone with ethereal beauty. She wore a dainty ivory crown. A robust ruby fish studded with black diamonds representing the speckles on a gatsby adorned the front of the crown.

Hurley grinned as he translated her whistles. 'I am Mrs Fish.'

'Queen Fish.' Hurley turned and smiled at his queen.

Hurley was dressed in a black leather jerkin of exquisite make. Embroidered on the piece were red gatsby leaping out of a brilliant blue sea. He wore a green, woollen kilt and in his hand he held a ruby trident studded with diamonds.

The trumpets flared and they were formally introduced.

'Introducing Hurley, King of the Halflings, sired by Jorgan of clan Gatsby and his new queen, Princess Caoimhe of Caelestis, daughter of Trebrelan and Telewanake.'

Lan turned and grinned at Ake. 'So, our Caoimhe married a king.'

'Who would have thought that the kind and humble Hurley was a king.' Ake smiled at the pair as they approached the deck.

'King Hurley has agreed to sponsor us and recognise us as regents as only another established monarch can do so. He has agreed to vouch for our characters and our intent.' Het stepped down off the dais and bowed to Hurley.

Hurley tried to place his hand on Het's shoulder. Het glanced down and knelt, allowing Hurley to place his hand on his shoulder.

'I vouch for this man's strength and integrity, and know he will make a fine protector for Vero and consort to our future Regent,' said Hurley. The halfling turned and Caoime handed him a wreath of white gladiolus. 'My beautiful bride collected these flowers and wove the wreaths with her own hands. I crown you as consort to Velterra, may you continue to display the virtues these flowers represent; loyalty, generosity and honour.' Hurley placed the wreath on Het's head and Het stood to the cheers and adulation of everyone.

Het bowed and took his place on his seat. Flo descended and knelt before Hurley who took a wreath made of bluebells from Caoimhe. 'I am honoured to crown you Regent Elder Flower of Velterra. May you continue to display the virtues of kindness, love and friendship. Between you and your consort, Prince Vero will become a wonderful person. Rise, Regent of Velterra.'

Flo rose and hugged Hurley. He blushed and giggled. The crowd welcomed their new regent with loud exclamations. As the noise settled down, Flo gestured towards Ake, Lan and the descendants.

They approached her.

'These people battled long and hard to rid the world of a great evil. We would not be standing here today if it wasn't for them. Take a bow.' Alena, Hartur, Lan and Alwin bowed and the crowd cheered. 'They will be rewarded from Hau's own treasury,' said Flo.

'I was honoured to serve, but I will not be cheered for something anyone would have done if they were gifted my powers. In fact, I made many mistakes I regret,' said Ake quietly.

The citizens of Velterra suddenly knelt. Lan grabbed her hand. 'The honour was ours, Telewanake, Goddess of Life and Mercy, memory to the gods. Where other gods did not intervene you did.' He grabbed her chin and kissed her. She closed her eyes and he released her.

When she opened her eyes everyone had knelt with their heads bowed, including Lan, Het and Flo.

'Please don't honour me as a goddess. I am just Ake.' She smiled through her tears.

'Always watch over us, great Goddess of Life and Mercy,' Flo chanted.

The other's followed suit, their voices lifting in a beautiful harmony as they chanted several times.

Ake bowed back, her cheeks red with embarrassment. Lan rose and drew her into his arms, beaming with pride.

'Ake, I thank you for not destroying my son's soul and taking on the burden of deciding which souls return to learn new things or rest in the underworld.' Flo smiled gently at Ake.

'You are not forgotten, former God of Death. You dedicated your life to her.' Het clasped Lan firmly in a bear hug and the crowd cheered and called out Lan's full name: Trebrelan. Het released him. 'I understand you turned down being my advisor. I wish you happiness and peace in your new endeavours. Go with our blessing.'

Flo embraced Ake and Lan.

Het stopped when he came to Ake. He patted her on the head and laughed as she blew wisps of hair out of her mouth. 'I am proud of the woman you became. From a wild and lazy girl to a merciful and brave divine being. Go with my gratitude, my oldest friend. Be happy with that outrageous Fiadhri you call husband.'

Ake laughed and hugged Het who returned the embrace. Lan grabbed Ake's hand and Alena followed them out of the room to cheers and exclamations of her own.

'That's Alena, Lady of Eriu and wielder of Din.'

'I hear she can summon animals to do her bidding.'

'If it wasn't for her and her staff the others would have been mortally injured on many an occasion.'

Alwin and Hartur approached Het and Flo.

'We are staying for a bit to help you out. We will return to Cirichad to make peace with my father.' Alwin held out his hand to Het who grabbed it and pulled him into a brief hug.

'Old friends hug it out.' Het grinned.

Hartur curtseyed to Flo. 'You will make a wonderful regent. I take my leave now.'

Flo reached out and took Hartur's hand. 'I hope we can become friends.'

Hartur smiled and Flo released her hand. Alwin offered his arm and they began to leave the room to hushed whispers and bowed heads.

'That is Alwin the Great, a mage of emotions. I hear he can't be overwhelmed with the darkness of others, despite feeling their emotions.'

'There are whispers that he is also the Master of the Forge. Crafter of sentient weapons which he can command and bend to his will.'

'He helped stripped Hau of his power leaving him vulnerable to death.'

'I hear his wife is an enchantress and forsook Hau's favour and that of another powerful mage to give her heart to Alwin.'

'That is so romantic.' Several women made sounds of adoration.

Alwin blushed and strode towards the exit. He turned briefly and spoke to the crowd quietly. 'It wasn't like that at all. I am just a blacksmith's son from Cirichad. May you all be blessed with our lord's favour.' Alwin made a sign of the circle.

'Go in peace, grandson of Amities of Eriu.' Het's voice rose over the crowd as citizens began to cheer.

Hartur took Alwin's hand and they left the room

———

Uldare held his head high as he trotted out the gates of Velterra, his riders merely lightweights as he was given his head, charging across a bridge before flying across the fields.

'We finally can live our life for ourselves.' Lan kissed Ake's neck.

'Finally.' She sighed.

CHAPTER FIFTY-SIX

Ake checked her supplies of chalk and slate boards again before walking over to the blackboard to make sure it still had the alphabet written in cursive on it. She was dressed in black scholarly robes that Lan had made for her. It had been a month since they had arrived in the village of Eriu.

Alena had cleared out an old, one-roomed house. She had gifted Lan carpentry tools, paint and wood, and told him to get to work and make his wife happy. Lan had repaired the veranda and roof and had made twenty chairs with a small desk attached. He had installed shelving and Cirite lighting as well as the blackboard. A large walnut desk and comfortable chair sat left of the blackboard. His skill hadn't gone unnoticed and he had joined two master carpenters as an apprentice a week ago.

Ake had lovingly painted the walls with brightly coloured letters and numbers. She had been to every home in Eriu and introduced herself. Using her reward money from Het and Flo, she had ordered books on literacy, mathematics and basic sciences from Velterra and the books lined the shelves.

Ake began to pace and Lan grinned at her from the doorway as he swept the veranda. 'You will wear a hole in the floor.'

'Don't you have work soon?' Ake smiled at him.

'I have a few hours reprieve. I wouldn't miss your first day.' Lan leant the broom against a wall and strode into the schoolhouse. He opened the draw of the large desk and drew out a brass plaque. Engraved on it were the words *Mrs Marcóir*. They had come to accept their last name as it meant a fresh start away from the ballads of the Lord of Death and Goddess of Mercy. He stood it on her desk.

'Thank you.' Ake grabbed his hand, pulled him towards her and kissed him.

They pulled apart as they heard the voices and laughter of children. The children entered the room and began to take their seats. Lan took his leave and stood in the doorway, beaming with pride as the children's happy faces turned towards Ake.

'Good morning children. Welcome to school. I can't wait to get to know you and teach you. I am honoured to serve you.'

'Good morning Mrs Marcóir,' the children chanted.

'The reluctant student became the teacher,' said Lan in Ake's mind.

Ake handed out the slate boards and chalk to the students. 'These letters are from the alphabet; the sounds they make form words. When you learn them all you will be able to read books. Books can take you on great adventures, bolster your courage and teach the hidden secrets of our world. The first letter on our magnificent journey is A.' Ake drew the letter on the board. 'Please try to draw it. Take your time, children.'

Ake turned and smiled at Lan.

'And if it wasn't for an introverted elven master, that student would never have read all those books at eighteen in the hopes of impressing him so they would have something to talk about when he returned. As I read, I learnt to love the written word.'

Lan smiled and waved.

'Have a great day. I will be back here at dusk.'

Ake waved back. *'Have a great day as well.'*

She turned back to the board and began drawing pictures to represent the letters.

—⁓—

Lan leant over his scythe, breathing heavily. He wiped the sweat from his brow with a cloth he pulled from his pocket. 'At least it is clear of weeds and debris now.'

'True. While we don't know the exact coordinates, Het's research of the records gave a basic area where Hau laid his friend Sia to rest.' Alwin knelt on the earth, digging up the soil as Hartur stood by ready to plant the Glenda sapling that all elves traditionally planted when laying down roots. It would grow into a large tree with a silver trunk and soft scarlet leaves that almost resembled feathers and harboured renewal magic. The tree nurtured all plant life in the vicinity and was named after a fabled elven youth who stayed in the fairy world to save his brother.

'Yep, marked by an elven stone, and the only one in this area was a smooth piece of granite with the word Relequis in elvish scraped upon its surface like an afterthought, or possibly worn away by the centuries.' Het's hands shone green as he encouraged the flowers that had been gifted by Flo and planted by Hurley to flower at the base of a memorial stone supplied and engraved by Alena. The flowery scent made him take a deep breath. 'Love my flowers. Hey Flo, for my birthday I want a bouquet.'

Flo smiled. 'How about fifty?'

Het raised a brow. 'Excuse for shopping?'

She paused and released a sigh. 'Possibly.'

'What's up, bunny?' Het hurried towards her; the light dispersed.

Flo's cheeks turned scarlet. 'No nicknames in front of our kin, especially Lan and Ake. I'll tell you after.'

'*Quick, here she comes.*' Caoimhe fluttered her wings excitedly.

Ake chatted with Geraldine, Alena's new fiancée, and stopped suddenly, her eyes widening as they alighted on her family. 'What is this?'

Lan dropped the scythe and strode over to his wife as Geraldine hurried to Alena's side, who leant down and gave her a quick peck, before she snatched up her hand and led her over to the stone. Alena's words drew Ake's gaze, her eyes flittering over the surface as she read aloud.

'To all those that fell by a cruel hand;
To all those whose circumstances ripped their kin away from them.
To the orphans of the world who never felt a kind touch or word;
To the sons and daughters who felt they were never enough.
We lay you to rest under the watchful arms of Glenda,
Who in his sacrifice knew that family and friends are everything.
In memory of Sia and his descendants so he is never forgotten. For the sons of Trebrelan; Amities of Eriu and his beloved twin Mandami who was always enough. We must not forget the babes who never attained adulthood: Hamish, Julius and Cephsa; know that your mother Telewanake has wept for you and her love for you will dwell forever in her immortal heart. For Orilan, whom death followed, though he bravely defied it. For Falcon, whose sweetness will bring a smile to Heta Falcon and Elder Flower's souls, and his twin Hau, remembered so that his callous ways are a reminder for us to do better.'

Ake turned on her heel and raced out of the field pockmarked with holes from countless graves. *I can't face this yet.* She stopped, her breath heaving as a light step behind her made her crane her head over her shoulder.

'They meant well.' Flo stepped towards her friend as Ake turned and raced into her outstretched arms.

'I know. And I will thank them. It's magnificent, but just still so raw.'

Ake glanced down as her friend's warm tears splattered on to her bare shoulder.

'It is, isn't it? I said no more tears.'

'Oh, my dearest Flo.' Ake unlocked her arms and encircled her friend in a firm embrace. 'Grieve for him, for the goodness he displayed in his youth and the elf he would have become if it wasn't for Drianna.'

Flo wept, until her eyes were bleary, clutching at Ake's clothes, showing a side she had never willingly shared with anyone other than Het.

When the final tears were shed, and a look of mutual under-standing passed between them, the women hurried back to their family to mourn with their kin.

———

A glistening white unicorn peeked out from the tree; the moon was full, lighting the night sky, dwarfing the twinkling stars. A hearty laugh shattered the silence and the unicorn snorted, ready to flee if the need arose.

The tall warrior, clad in a green shirt and breeches, had strapped his long sword across his back. Some of his hair had been tied back in a ponytail, half hung loose. He sat on a picnic rug, the uncorked bottles of wine were half full, golden goblets had been dropped haphazardly on the blanket, the plates of grapes, bread and cheeses nearly empty as they had been enjoyed by the group of friends on a double date. Het rolled his eyes at the couple seated next to him. Lan sat and Ake lay with her head in her hus-band's lap, weaving bright light around herself and her husband, her golden wings on full display. Lan's cheeks were flushed as he leant in to kiss the cheek of his bride, whose eyes were shining with love. His stormy dragon wings were visible to those around them; lightening flashed across their span to the clawed tips and crackled when Ake pulled his head closer to hers.

A broad grin spread across his face as Het held up two fingers in a v shape behind Lan's head. 'Like rabbits how often those two make out.'

Flo laughed, and glanced up at Het, nestled into his chest, goblet of wine in hand. Her diaphanous gown shimmered in the moonlight, a shift beneath it to afford her modesty. 'They are so cute.'

'It's been a month since we have seen you two. This was a great suggestion, Flo,' said Ake.

'You know, I've lived on islands, but never swam in the ocean. That's what I want to do next.' Flo lifted the goblet to her lips and took a sip.

'We should make a promise to meet regularly.' Het leant down and grabbed a bottle and refilled Flo's goblet.

'That could be hard with a kingdom to run.' Flo sighed.

'At least twice a year.' Lan stroked Ake's hair.

'I think we can manage that.' Not to be outdone, Het leant down and kissed Flo.

'Even I didn't go that far.' Lan laughed and was caught off guard, blinking in surprise as Ake pulled his head down to kiss him.

Het laughed as he pulled away from his wife. 'The women are drunk.'

'I suppose we better get off home.' Lan stood and pulled Ake up with him.

Ake wobbled on her feet before she began putting their picnic things away. Flo was lifted in Het's arms; the goblet clunked as it dropped to the ground. Flo had closed her eyes, already asleep in his arms.

Ake grinned. 'I won. I out-drunk Flo. She owes me a trip to the dress shop at her expense.'

Het laughed. 'You are a bad influence, Ake. My reserved wife has started playing practical jokes that are kind of lame. But a betting gal? I wouldn't have thought it of her.'

Flo opened an eye. 'Who are you calling lame?' Her speech was slurred.

Ake shrugged, then a wicked grin spread across her face. 'I am the master.'

Het shook his head. 'You will never beat me.'

'Hmm, I did pretty good with that porridge in your shoe, Ake.' Lan leant down to grab the basket and rug.

Het slapped him on the back. 'True enough.'

The friends began to part ways; Flo in Het's arms and Lan gripping Ake's hand so she wouldn't fall over, the rug thrown over his shoulder and the picnic basket in his other hand.

'*Falite*, old friends,' said Het.

Lan dipped his head in acknowledgement, his hands full. 'Falite to you, my brother.'

'Ah shucks.' Het blinked back tears.

Ake giggled and wandered away to stoop down and pick a bunch of glowing flowers.

Het's eyes narrowed on his friend's. 'In what context do you name me brother?'

'I wasn't sure if it was true when I left this plane, as new memories emerged, but your words have confirmed our connection that we were in fact blood brothers in a life before this one. And we were close until you decided human life was worth taking.'

Het chuckled quietly. 'So, you care to remember that our divine souls share the same parents, but in this life you again were their favourite and I was so easily forgotten, and I was born into a different family because I received the accursed giant blood.'

'Do you resent me for it?' Lan frowned.

The larger man shook his head as his lips curled up into a warm smile. 'Never have I resented you. Though I have been unhappy with the pressures placed on us that made us rivals. You received the title of the Lord of Death, but any title I would have earned was discarded and I remained "The Dreaded" for the bloodshed I caused when humans were eager to slaughter anything different.'

'Is that what angers you the most?' Lan smiled and turned to watch Ake stumbling towards them.

'With your title you were given a queen—the Goddess of Mercy, your Ake.' Het shifted his feet as Lan turned back to face him. 'I wanted a wife too.'

'You once told me a goddess called to you and whispered of love.' Lan hoisted the blanket up as it slipped. 'I told you it wasn't my betrothed, then you went on that murderous rampage, increasing my workload and causing Sorendee to disfavour me and deny me my bride the night before our wedding. In the end it was Dee who allowed me to get Ake as a bride, but at the expense of forgetting my memories and having to endure mortal life. When I died, I regained them. I didn't bring up the subject when you returned because I wasn't sure if you remembered. My dear Ake is oblivious as she was caged before the mortal realm.' Lan emitted a happy sigh. 'I used to spend time with her, you know. Watching her play among the flowers in her cage in the heavens, when I was allowed a respite from my twilight throne. Others were leery of my bat form.' He gritted his teeth. 'It made me self-conscious, but she accepted me as I am.'

Het rubbed the back of his head with a hand. 'Yeah, I know now it was Flo who quieted my rages with her beautiful voice when I was Demund. And fruit bat suits you, with your love of berries and vegetables.'

Lan rolled his eyes. 'Thanks. You got a majestic dire owl.'

'Yep, all the better to chase a little bat brother around when he was bugging me.' Het grinned. There was a tingling of bells and the couples appeared in front of a house. Ake kissed Lan suddenly causing him to drop his burdens. 'That brother part was so beautiful.'

Lan rolled his eyes before breaking into laughter. 'My sweet, adorable Ake.'

'But you said Het was now your brother.'

'And he is not just as a brother that fights by my side, but in other meaningful ways too. I'll explain later. No need to get all teary-eyed over it.' Lan smiled and pressed a kiss to each eye. 'You can't help it and I never want that to change.'

Het sighed. 'I may have informed Ake in a moment of argumentative passion.'

'I see.' Lan smirked.

'Well, the past is truly done then.' Flo mumbled in her husband's arms and opened a sleepy eye.

Ake picked up the basket and rug and entered her home and Lan waved to Het and Flo as he followed.

CHAPTER FIFTY-SEVEN

Ake giggled as Lan carried her over the threshold of their new home.

'Put me down. I am too old for this.'

Lan smiled down at her. 'No, you aren't.'

He turned and kicked the door shut before placing her on her feet. They had stayed with Alena for six months while the house was built. Ake glanced around their cosy home. Lan had helped build it with his own hands, working along with two master carpenters.

Entering the living space and kitchen area, there was a large window overlooking a plumbed sink with large bench space. Towards the back of the house two bedrooms and a bathroom could be accessed by doorways. The floor was made of slate. Ake's eyes fixed on the high, naked beams; Lan had also had electric lights installed.

'I want to show you something.'

Ake smiled. 'Sure.'

He led her over to a large pot belly stove with various pipes mounted against the wall leading to various sections of the house. Hot air warmed her face as Lan opened the door to the oven and added more coal from a pail nearby.

'When the stove is in use it heats the house. We have hot running water in the bathroom because of it.'

'Incredible. Show me.'

Lan led her through the bathroom door. He went over and turned on the brass taps that sat over a large, brass clawfoot bathtub. Steam began to rise in the air and Lan stood up and opened the window.

'Why are you running a bath?'

'I thought you might like to relax.'

'That's thoughtful.'

'While that fills up, I want to show you something else.'

He left the bathroom and entered their bedroom; Ake followed him. A four-poster bed sat in the middle of the room. The green drapes were closed. Ake drew them apart to see the bed made up with a golden coverlet. 'This house really is wonderful.'

'I am happy you are happy.'

She leant in to kiss him.

'Hold that thought.' Lan raced out of the room.

Ake waited for a few moments and undressed herself. She heard the water stop running.

'Now, where were we?' Lan entered the room and smiled. 'Fair enough; your bath is ready now anyway. Do you want me to put some scented oils in?'

Ake laughed. 'After.'

'You don't want any oils until after you get in?'

Ake grabbed his hand and led him over to the bed.

—∿—

Hartur opened the envelope and pulled out a letter and tiny package. Alwin had returned with Hartur to Cirichad a few months ago and he was trying to establish a better relationship with his father. She opened the package and the bitter smell of acrid herbs hit her as her gaze settled on a bundle of dried leaves. Curious, she unfurled the letter.

Dear Hartur,

I hope this letter finds you well. Het, Vero and I are safe. Thank you for your concern in your last letter. It is taking time for the citizens to accept us and we have had to call on Lan and Alena to help us quell riots in the streets. We are glad you are all safe in Cirichad.

In regard to your question of preventative measures, the method Alwin suggests is quite effective. But I have also included these herbs. Take a pinch and wad them into a ball and take after intimacy. This practice has been a secret of my priesteshood for centuries and I would prefer it to remain so. I have forwarded this same information on to Ake.

You asked me if you should be honest about Arlys's quips towards you when Alwin is not around. I think you should raise the issue, but approach it in a tactful manner. Continue to stay well.

I would like to a arrange a reunion for the descendants of Velterra. I will be in touch with information regarding the times.

Friendly regards,
Flo.

Hartur placed the letter down as Alwin entered the room, his face covered in soot, his shoulders slumping as he lowered himself into a chair groaning. 'Father has got me working hard in the forge.'

There was a shout as Arlys entered their room unannounced. 'You worked hard today, son.'

Alwin rose and hurried over to a stand and began filling a bowl with water from a porcelain jug.

'Unlike you.' Arlys stared at Hartur.

Alwin tensed and turned, water dripping from his face, his mouth dropping open before snapping shut. 'Father, what did you say?'

Hartur grimaced. 'It's fine, Alwin.'

Alwin stepped towards the pair. 'Does he often talk to you like this when I'm out of earshot?'

Hartur's cheeks reddened. 'Don't worry about it.'

Alwin glared at his father. 'I see. I think we will make a journey. Leave our room, Father.'

Arlys smirked. 'Just like your mother.'

As Arlys sauntered from the room, Alwin closed the door. 'And proud of it.'

Het leant on his sword, breathing heavily. The men and women at his feet moaned and clutched at their non-lethal wounds. Het wiped the sweat from his brow, appearing exhausted from the fight.

'Twenty-six,' said Het.

'Fifteen,' said Alena.

Lan rolled his eyes. 'This is ridiculous, I will not count how many of Hau's followers I took down.'

A small gathering of citizens had begun to gather, murmuring to themselves. The sound of trudging boots met Lan's ears as several of Elder Flower's guards marched towards them.

'Greetings, my Lord Consort.' The head officer bowed.

Het bowed back. 'Put this lot in the dungeon so they can await trial.'

As the guards began to round up the convicted, Lan assessed Het. He had a few minor cuts and bruises but appeared to be okay. Another guard applied bandages to the minor lacerations on Lan's arms.

'How long are you staying?' asked Het.

'I intend to leave in a few hours. While Ake is getting better at short separations I would still rather ease her anxiety,' said Lan.

The guard bowed to Lan. 'My prince.'

Lan handed him a coin and the guard bowed again and wandered away to help round up the minions of Hau.

Alena smiled. 'Well, that's it for me, I have a date with Geraldine.'

'Enjoy,' said Lan as Alena waved and left.

'Need any healing?'

Lan shook his head. 'I like Ake's administrations when I have minor injuries.'

Het laughed heartily. 'No shame. Have a drink with me.'

'I can have one for the road.' Lan smiled.

'Follow me.'

Het strode towards a small, seedy alley, took a right turn, then a left before they stood in front of a set of steps leading into a cellar.

'Looks kind of unseemly.'

'You'll see.' Het winked and strode down the steps and threw open the doors. 'Caoimhe's new investment for the small fey. The more corrupt still hunt down fey creatures despite it being illegal, and Caoimhe wanted a haven for them.'

Lan entered the small, pleasant cellar; a wooden bar was off to the left with a few cushioned bar stalls and a tiny fairy serving coloured drinks that some rare creatures were ordering by writing them down. Lan watched an ardaverk sip a clear drink with termites floating in the glass, his long tongue lapping at the drink. His humanoid body was covered in soft brown fur and his claw like hands cupped the glass carefully. Lan glanced around; there was luxurious rainbow carpet on the floor and glowing orbs in pink floated around the room. In the corner, seated on a stool, sat a terrach, a terrier like humanoid with the head of a dog and body of a human. In his hands he held a stick sharpened to a fine point. He was creating tattoos on the arms of a client by pricking the surface of the skin with the pattern he had temporary drawn and then adding different coloured inks.

Het brought over a drink for Lan, and the men watched the process. 'Caoimhe has done well.'

'Certainly has.'

After two drinks Het took a seat and paid the vendor before pulling out a piece of paper with the design he wanted.

'Rings are great, but I want Flo's name on me forever.'

Lan wandered over to the bar where a goblin was serving. 'Can I get a paper and pencil for the artist over there?'

'Sure. But he's called a tattooist.'

Lan wandered over to Het, drawing his design on the paper as he did so. Colour drained from Het's face as the tattooist continued to ink the design on his bicep. Tiny white elder flowers on a green stem with the words *Flo and Het forever.*

Het stood and wobbled. 'Well, that is more painful than a sword to my gut.'

Lan laughed. 'Can't be too bad. He is very quick.'

The tattooist pointed to the chair. 'I aid the process with magic. Quicker, but more painful.'

Lan sat and handed over the design. The tattooist drew the extensive design on his chest near his heart, dousing the sharp end of the stick in alcohol before dipping it into the ink. Then he began to tap vigorously at the surface of Lan's skin. The first half of the tattoo made him slightly uncomfortable, but soon the tiny pinpricks became sharp jabs to his skin. His quick healing hadn't fully returned until now and it tried to fight the intrusion on his body like it was a parasite.

Lan clenched the armrest, his knuckles white.

'Well, his body is trying to heal. This will be extremely painful if I continue,' said the tattooist stopping.

'Finish it. I don't want an incomplete design.' Lan gritted his teeth as blood welled on the surface of his skin as he tried to settle his rapid breathing.

'Poor fellow,' said Het.

After twenty minutes of agony, the tattooist finished and Lan leapt up from the seat, handed over the fee and sprinted out into the street cursing loudly until he felt better. Someone patted him on the back and Lan turned to see Het grinning from ear to ear.

'That was disturbing to see you put yourself through that, but the final product looks great. Here.' Het handed him a warm wet cloth to wipe the blood and ink away.

'Thanks.' Lan dabbed away the worst of the damage and waved to Het as he did up his shirt.

'Goodbye, and thanks for the help,' said Het.

The men gave each other a brief handshake before there was a loud pop. *Can't get used to Het learning to teleport others.* Lan looked around his kitchen; his bedroom door was open. He strode to the doorway and watched Ake reading with packets of biscuits open around her. Ake's eyes glanced from the food to Lan and she uncrossed her legs and rose.

Then her eyes welled with tears. 'You are safe.'

She rushed into his arms and he cried out as she made contact with his chest. She pulled away and hastily undid his shirt. 'I was so worried you would get injured, or worse, kil—'

He put a finger to her lips. 'Don't say it.'

Ake gasped when she saw the addition to his body—an ornate purple scrying mirror; in its inky depths was a fallen star. Elvish runes were written in a circle around the tattoo, *eturn ea Ake, ley Lan.*

Ake traced the words with her finger, translating the runes. 'Forever yours Ake, love Lan.'

'It's permanent. Like us,' said Lan.

Ake traced the design with gentle kisses. Kneeling, she followed the trail lower, her mouth kissing and caressing. 'I love it.' Her gaze swept to his bandaged arms and she stood quickly. 'Let's treat those.'

'No, continue. I am fine up top, but as for below, you better check.' Lan grinned.

Ake laughed. 'Wounds first.'

Lan sighed. 'Okay.'

Lan winced as Ake undid the bandages and applied the iodine solution. 'I would have been fine.'

'Hmm, I remember centuries ago you saying infection can attack the smallest wounds. Sometimes people die from small cuts from dirty surfaces rather than wounds gained in battle.'

Lan smiled. 'Best continue then.'

Ake giggled as Lan squirmed while she applied the solution to his other cuts.

'Now to give some attention to other areas.' Ake knelt before him.

'I am down with that.' Lan grinned.

CHAPTER FIFTY-EIGHT

There was a flair of trumpets and Hartur and Alwin stepped to the side of the road. A richly adorned coach pulled by six large horses began to slow as it reached them. The driver pulled back on the reigns and the coach came to a halt. The door was flung open and Het leapt out.

Hartur began to laugh. 'Well, if it isn't the consort of the empress, dressed accordingly.'

Het was attired in a pair of puffy red shorts known as trunk hose. He wore a long-sleeved, red velvet doublet with huge silver buttons and embroidered with gold elvish runes. His large legs made his black tights bulge at the seams. Alwin glanced at Het's big feet fitted in black shoes with a silver buckle.

Het grinned, took off his dainty silver crown and gave a mock bow. 'Consort of the gracious Empress Elder Flower at your service.' He stood up. 'Do you want a lift?'

'Are you headed to the reunion?' asked Hartur.

'We wouldn't miss it.' Het opened the door.

Flo waved; Vero sat in her lap. Alwin helped Hartur up into the carriage. The carriage had two archers either side of the driver who had a large sword strapped across his back.

Can't be too careful, even along this main road, Alwin thought.

Brigands and monsters still roamed Velterra and evil mages, who had been stripped of their positions by Flo, sought revenge.

I am surprised they left the safety of Velterra.

Alwin was interrupted from his thoughts as Het ruffled his hair.

'Get in, lad,' said Het.

Alwin stepped up into the carriage and sat across from the women. Het jumped in next to him, closed the door and thumped on the roof. The carriage began to move.

'You two shouldn't be on the road by yourselves. There would be many a great dethroned mage willing to kill the great Alwin Smith.' Flo gave them a look of reproach.

'We didn't want to bother you,' said Alwin.

Het punched him playfully. 'Silly lad. How could you ever be a bother? Helping us save our son's soul and replacing the fallen lord of elves with its true empress.'

'How goes the process of removing slavery?' asked Hartur.

Flo sighed. 'It is a slow process. The nobles and citizens outside Velterra are reluctant to give up their free workforce.'

'At least you are trying.' Alwin smiled. Hartur shifted in her seat. 'Bumpy, isn't it?'

'Ouch, yeah, hit the old noggin.' Het rubbed the top of his head.

Flo laughed. 'Takes on evil denizens without worry; felled by an insidious carriage.'

'Ah, you are sweet to care, my little bunny.' Het pinched the tip of his wife's nose whose cheeks began to redden.

'How long until we arrive?' asked Alwin.

'An hour if nothing stops our travel.' Flo ignored her husband who leant in to kiss her cheek; her hand struck out and clasped his upper thigh, slowly moving upwards.

Het's eyes became wary then he shrugged as she stared at him with meaning. 'Going to strike me, oh gentle empress?'

Flo placed her hands back in her lap. 'Not in company.'

Het's sudden burst of loud laughter made Alwin nearly jump out of his seat. 'Oh dear.'

'She must be getting flirting tips from Ake.' Het winked at Hartur who covered her smile with a hand.

'I am hungry,' complained Vero.

Het reached into a pocket hung on the coach wall and withdrew some fruit and handed it to the boy.

'Are you getting along with Arlys?' asked Flo.

Hartur shook her head. 'It was okay for a while, but things got worse when we mentioned we weren't ready for children. Arlys kept trying to tell Alwin he is too soft and that a Cirite man produces a family and provides for it. We have left Cirichad. We are going to ask Alena if we can settle in Eriu.'

'My father is a hypocrite.' Alwin sighed.

Het clapped Alwin on the back. 'That's great. We have missed you lot.'

The carriage slowed down.

'We are nearly there, Empress and Lord Consort,' cried the driver.

Flo breathed a sigh of relief. 'We have made it safely.'

The carriage came to a gentle stop and the door was pulled open. 'Yay, they've arrived.' Hurley grinned at them.

Alena cleared her throat.

'Oh, sorry, mistress Alena.' Hurley bowed.

Everyone began to exit the carriage.

Alena was dressed in breeches and a tailored silk shirt. Lan and Ake stood next to her. Lan was dressed in his mystic robes, his long hair pulled back, and Ake wore her yellow gown. Alwin stepped from the carriage and glanced at the citizens dressed in their best attire.

'We welcome you, Lord Smith, Master of the Forge and mage of emotions,' said Alena.

Everyone bowed. Alwin blushed and stepped to the side as he helped Hartur down.

'Welcome, Lady Smith, Master of Nietra,' said Alena.

Hartur dipped her head in acknowledgement. 'I thank you for the gracious welcome.'

Alwin whispered in her ear. 'When did you learn such grace?'

'I've been taking Cirite deportment classes while you were at work. I wanted to surprise you.' Hartur grinned.

'I like you the way you are.' Alwin squeezed her hand.

Het descended.

'Welcome, Heta Falcon, Lord Consort of Empress Elder Flower,' announced Alena.

Het gave them a sweeping bow before turning to help Flo down. He took Vero in one hand and offered his other to her; she grabbed it and descended from the carriage.

'Announcing, Crown Prince Vero and the gracious and just, Regent Elder Flower.' Alena stepped towards Elder Flower and handed her a huge bouquet of flowers. 'Welcome to our humble village of Eriu.'

Flo smiled and accepted the bouquet. 'I am honoured to be here.'

The crowd cheered. Flo began to hand out flowers to the villagers as was the elven custom. 'Accept this gift of Ea,' she said as she placed them in the villagers' outstretched palms.

They were greeted with smiles, curtseys or bows while others took off their hats as they gratefully accepted their gifts. After the task was completed, the villagers began to disperse. A celebration had been provided for them at the newly expanded inn, they were not about to give up free food and drink.

Flo breathed a sigh of relief and ran towards Ake and embraced her. The women drew apart and held hands.

'I have missed you, my dear friend.' Flo smiled.

'As have I.' Ake beamed back.

Caoimhe fluttered down and began to sign, '*Falite, how are you all?*'

'What have you been up to, Caoimhe?' asked Het.

'I have been doing research on Anwyl. The place is somewhat intact despite being abandoned. I have checked it out and cleared it of the caveron who were residing there,' Hurley translated.

Alwin's eyes widened. 'Impressive. Truly.' Hurley puffed out his chest with pride. 'Yeah, Caoimhe is impressive.'

The fairy blushed.

'How sweet,' said Flo.

Alena approached them. 'If you follow me to Nuo Manor, we can have a rest before the evening celebrations begin.'

'That name is a beautiful gesture to Nuo,' said Flo.

'I thought so as well.' Alena smiled.

The group proceeded through the forest. They heard birds singing in the trees and sunlight shone through breaks in the canopy.

Alwin turned to Hartur. 'Her protective nature really has rid this area of Blaze's influence.'

Hartur smiled. 'Yes, his essence is gone. I hope we can settle near here.'

A bird fluttered down and landed on Alena's outstretched hand. She whistled to it and it chirped back. 'My friend here has informed us that the path ahead is blocked by a fallen tree. We will turn here and take an alternate route.'

'When did you learn to speak to birds?' asked Lan.

Alena petted the bird before it flew away. 'How do you think I have been able to navigate this forest. It's not just the birds but the trees and woodland creatures.'

'Why didn't you tell us you were a Malviðr or forest speaker?' asked Ake.

'It was unnecessary. I do not crave for others to know my inner secrets and actions,' said Alena.

'Mandami divulged very little too,' said Lan.

They reached Nuo Manor as servants hurried down the steps and took the guests' belongings.

'Feel free to lounge in the parlour or enter one of the guest bedrooms for a nap. You have several hours before the reunion dinner.' Alena smiled.

While the others proceeded into the building, Alwin and Hartur approached its owner.

'How was your journey?' asked Alena.

'Quite rough. The weather was terrible and we encountered monsters.' Alwin sighed.

'It is not a trip to take lightly. You should have written and I would have had you join one of my trading fleets. You would have been safer.'

'We will not make that trip again. Alena, may we settle in Eriu?' asked Hartur.

'Of course. Come inside and we will discuss the details.' Alena turned and strode into the building, the others followed. As they entered, they were greeted by Alena's wife Geraldine.

'Hello.' Geraldine placed down the portrait she was hanging of her standing next to Alena.

Hartur went over and hugged the friendly woman. 'Good to see you again. We haven't seen you since the wedding half a year ago.'

The two women chatted as Alwin and Alena struck up a conversation.

—᠊ᜂᜃ—

Ake sat upright, refusing to move a muscle. Tempted to scratch at her itchy nose, she kept her gaze trained on the man in front of her. The camera had only just come on the market and Alena had hired a photographer, insisting each family took a photo for posterity. Lan joined Ake standing behind the chair. There was a knock on the door and Caoimhe and Hurley entered.

'Hurry up you two.' Ake laughed.

They rushed over and sat at Ake's feet.

The photographer walked over to a wooden contraption. 'Hold,' cried the photographer. He removed the lens cap and held his hand in the air for about twenty seconds and no one moved. He released his hand and everyone breathed a sigh of relief. 'Please wait while I process this.' The photographer hurried into his portable dark room made of black cloth.

Lan slipped into the dark room to watch in fascination as the photographer worked. The man moved from one contraption to the next with practised ease. A small alcohol lamp burned under it. Lan's nose wrinkled as the photographer added chemicals, before completing a few more tasks. The image was beautiful. The photographer smiled as he washed the plate. 'I am so lucky to meet such famous people. No one would believe me if it wasn't for these pictures,' he muttered to himself.

He exited the dark room and didn't notice Lan follow him out.

The man jumped as Lan spoke. 'How did you make that appear?'

The photographer smiled and handed Lan the plate. 'A mixture of chemicals and exposure to light. You can help me prepare the next plate if you like. I would be honoured to teach the great Trebrelan.'

'We will meet you downstairs, Lan. Don't take too long,' said Ake as she trailed out the door scratching vigorously at her nose. Lan followed the photographer back into the darkroom.

—✦—

Alena lay back on the bed with her eyes closed, trying to nap. She heard Vero running through the hallways laughing and she smiled to herself.

'Your friends and family really are lovely people, Alena.'

Alena opened her eyes. Her wife was seated at the dressing table fixing her hair for the celebrations that were to come. Alena sat up.

'That hairstyle is really becoming of you.'

Geraldine blushed and looked away. 'Why thank you.'

Alena pushed herself off the bed, walked over, wrapping her arms around her shoulders.

'Elder Flower has asked us to become sponsors for Vero. We will be responsible in aiding his moral upbringing. What do you think?'

'I would be honoured.'

Alena leant down and kissed her. 'I thought you would say as much.'

The door crashed open and Vero ran into the room giggling before scrambling up on to the bed and jumping on it.

'Hello Geradin. Hello Lena.' Vero giggled.

'Growl.' Het poked his head around the door. 'Oops, sorry. This little terror has bothered you.'

'Yes, the little pirate has commandeered my ship.' Alena pointed to the bed. 'There it goes, out of my reach.'

The child giggled.

'You can leave him with us if you want to go spend some time with the others.'

'Thank you. See you later, kiddo.' Het strolled over and hugged his grandson before turning and leaving.

'Play with me, Lena,' said Vero.

'What do you want to play?'

'Hidey seek.'

'Okay, we will go hide and Geraldine will come find us.'

'Sure.' Geraldine smiled.

Alena lifted Vero into her arms and they hastened from the room as Geraldine began counting.

Half an hour after his family's likeness was captured, Lan rushed into the guest bedroom holding his first photograph. He glanced down at the blurry photo before he rushed over to Ake. 'Ake, I just learnt photography. I am not very good yet but I will improve.' He held up the image of a blurry vase.' His eyes were filled with wonder.

Ake gave him a smile. 'You are always quick to learn new things. Why don't we go get a cup of tea and you can tell me all about it?'

Lan nodded and began to explain the mechanics of photography as they descended a set of stairs and entered the parlour. They sat down at a table and a servant hurried over with a pot of tea and Lan placed the image down and poured them a cup each as he continued his explanation. When he had finished, Ake was on her third cup.

Lan smiled. 'I am sorry, I got so caught up in my new hobby I forgot to ask after you.'

'See you can be adorable too when caught up in a new interest.' Ake stuck out her tongue.

Lan laughed and pulled her on to his lap. He whispered in her ear. 'How are you, my darling?'

Ake shivered as the breath tickled her ear. Lan nuzzled her neck and lifted his head before taking her mouth with his own.

Alena cleared her throat and Lan broke the kiss, his eyes still hazy with desire. 'What is it?'

'We have rooms for that kind of display.' Alena laughed.

Ake turned her head; their friends filed into the room and took a seat at the large dining table. Ake blushed and hid her face in her hands.

Lan laughed and stood up, drawing Ake up with him. 'You

could have announced your arrival. Then you wouldn't have seen that wonderful display of romance between husband and wife.'

'That's making it worse,' cried Ake.

Alwin chose that time to carefully drop a glass of wine. A servant rushed over to tend the spill. 'Oops, I'm clumsy.' Heads turned towards him

Ake and Lan hurried towards their daughter and clutched at the drinks that Alena pressed into their hands.

'I would like to raise a toast.' Het stood and lifted his glass in the air. 'May we toast to family and friends' past, present and future.'

Everyone lifted their glasses and cried, 'Hear hear.'

Ake squeezed Lan's hand, grateful they were surrounded by their loved ones.

'I love you,' Lan mouthed.

'I love you too,' she whispered.

Ake looked at all the people she loved gathered in one place. *Life has certainly been an adventure. I look forward to many more with these wonderful people.*

Glossary

Ake is pronounced Ar-key.

Caelestis means celestial.

Caley pronounced Kay-lee. Means Forest's Heart and was once home to forest elves who were healers and hunters.

Caoimhe is pronounced Kee-va.

Hau is pronounced Hey-ooh. It means spiritual essence.

Telewanake (pronounced Tel-a-wa-nar-key) means Stars Fallen and is shortened to Ake.

Trebrelan (pronounced Treb-re-lan) means Star Scryer and is shortened to Lan.

Relequis means the remaining.

Star Stone very precious gem. It has a gold base and tiny slivers of silver crystal weaving its way to the heart of the stone.

Carnay pronounced Car-nay is the or the elvish word for cantankerous

Anam Imeall translates to Soul's Edge.

Nietra means darkness in elvish and suits the sentient magical hammer crafted by Amities.

Dage means danger in elvish. The sentient bow is named after a famous elven explorer.

Din means safety in elvish. This sentient staff crafted by Amities is named after a famous elven explorer.

Glamoire A spell that is used to cover the obvious.

Hushin means silence and stillness in elvish. This sentient flint-lock pistol was crafted by Amities.

Tarven is the elvish word for trust and loyalty. Alwin crafted a sentient dagger and named it Tarven.

Eiiro pronounced E-eye-row

Vero pronounced Veer-oh.

Mey Pronounced May-ay, is the elvish word for song.

Fiarn pronounced Fee-arn, is the elvish word for ember.

Rayu is pronounced Ray-ooh, has several meanings in elvish which are frost, ice and winter.

Seydarn pronounced see-darn and translates to gust or breath in elvish.

Appendix penned by Regent Elder Flower in the Velterran Book of Heraldry

At first, the descendants of Velterra were eager to catch up annually, but life soon got away and they began to drift apart. Hartur and Alwin welcomed a son Eiiro. After Arlys's accidental death in his forge in 1721, they settled back in Cirichad as Alwin took over the smithy. Hurley and Caoimhe returned to the Gatsby Clan and Caoimhe delivered her winged son Caley in 1723. Heta Falcon and Elder Flower welcomed an elven daughter Mey when Vero was seven. Alena and Geraldine remained in Eriu.

After fifteen years of being empty nesters and being rightfully wrapped up in each other, Trebrelan and Telewanake retired from their jobs and adventured to Anwyl. The journey was exciting and dangerous, but that is another story. They began to rebuild Anwyl, and in 1725, Ake bore Arakaen triplets.

Fiarn, Lord of the Hearth, Home and Summer, had ruby eyes and feathered dragon wings; one orange and one red. His skin was a light tan that flickered a reddish orange in contrast to his obsidian hair.

The second, a girl, Rayu, Lady of Ice and Winter, had green eyes, dark blonde hair and fair skin with a blue sheen and icy-blue feathered wings.

Seydarn, the youngest, Lady of Winds and Autum, had grey

eyes and wings, and fair skin with a silvery shimmer; her hair was a platinum blonde.

Regent Elder Flower sojourned on the once ancient island of Eriu for three moons after the birth of the triplets, engaging in diplomatic discussions with a once thought lost human clan Daingean, and the dwarves of Rock Fell. The humans welcomed Velterran technology and became the Velterran province of Kenshay, named after Dane's daughter and Flo's mother, and agreed to a boundary around Anwyl. The dwarves conceded to a peaceful truce and agreed on a student exchange program so each could learn from the other. Trebrelan, as the last prince of Anwyl, was crowned king, and Telewanake became his queen.

The reunion of the descendants of Velterra was shifted to once a decade, except for the four best friends. With Het's teleportation abilities, they caught up every few months and Flo finally got to swim in the ocean, while Lan took a copious number of photos.

Acknowledgements

Special mention to my editor Jenn Zabinskas of RedInk Creative. Jenn is a talented and dedicated editor who pays special attention to consistency and flow. Her comments are clear, and her suggestions are inspiring. I look forward to collaborating with her again.

Deborah Daken is a talented proofreader and editor. Her keen eyes pick up on subtle errors that are easily overlooked, and she makes excellent suggestions to any changes she has recommended. She is incredibly fast and thorough. I found her to be amicable, flexible and approachable.

To all my friends and family members, thank you for your support.

Nadine Abrahams

The Primal Heartbeat:
Book One in The Stars Fallen Series

Born into a world where humanity has been corrupted by evil, can one tribal girl fulfil a prophecy and defeat a dark goddess?

Ake's peace is fragile. Trying to carve out an existence in a land torn by strife and famine, her destiny has made her the target of terrible creatures. And as her divine nemesis's power grows ever stronger, the young mage knows she must awaken her own otherworldly heritage if she wants to survive.

Enduring endless hardships with aid from her soulmate, Ake bravely battles the forces attempting to tear them apart. But being fated to save the world and actually doing it are two very different things…

Ake's Ascent: Book Two in The Stars Fallen Series

'You must kill her, elf. Kings will rise and fall, and they will want a powerful queen. You will spend the next centuries giving your life for hers as they seek her out.'

Ake and her son are destined to defeat the evil goddess Drianna, who has hunted her since childhood. Now a powerful mage, Ake is tortured by her past. Her elven husband has vowed to protect them, but evil has a way of sinking its fangs in and refusing to let go.

As Drianna reaches the peak of her power Ake realises she must fight for those she loves if she is ever to defeat Drianna and find peace.

Trying to save the man you love while he is consumed by an inner darkness always comes at a cost…

Dane: Tales Of Velterra Series

Set decades before the events in The Primal Heartbeat, Dane enjoys his carefree days filled with countless beautiful women offering to warm his bed and luxurious hospitality offered from the noble houses he alternates between.

Dane's life is changed when he is ordered to either marry the bride chosen for him and return to his druid studies or be forever confined to his father's lands. At first Dane refuses to risk his life in the elven challenge of marriage, until a cruel man offers to take his place.

For all his faults and womanising reputation, Dane cannot allow the woman chosen for him to fall in to the hands of a cruel man. Dane accepts the challenge until he realises he may have taken on more than he can handle.

His tempestuous bride, known for her mean back hand and noble heart, appears impervious to his charms. Can the man with the heart of a bard seduce the fiery warrioress with a will of iron?

RPG Muintir Game

The inclusive RPG Muintir is set after a great catastrophe. The people must come together and battle mutagen in this shout out to home brew. The simplified six-sided dice system allows for quick and easy play. Those with diverse needs are celebrated, often having unique gifts that allow them to thrive in the world of Muintir.

MEET THE AUTHOR

Nadine has been an avid reader and writer since her early childhood, from publishing poems to creating her first novel at thirteen, *The Primal Heartbeat*, and publishing it in her early adulthood. *The Primal Heartbeat* has since been edited and updated.

Nadine is an avid gamer and role-player, as well as creator of fiction and fantasy novels. She also loves archery and nature.

After dealing with adversity and overcoming it, Nadine writes books that show even powerful characters are inherently flawed. That these weaknesses can often become our strengths as long as we remain true to ourselves. Nadine's writing reflects on the dark side of humanity as well as the good side and how, even though we think we are worthless, we can change our destiny, just as her memorable characters do.

Nadine's other books were written on a whim, designed for and dedicated to a special needs child who didn't relate to any of the books on the market. Seeing a representation of themself in the children's book encouraged them to improve their reading skills and develop a love of reading.

www.ingramcontent.com/pod-product-compliance
Lightning Source LLC
Chambersburg PA
CBHW070149120726
47909CB00001B/38